PAPA MARTEL

PAPA MARTEL

A NOVEL IN TEN PARTS

by Gérard Robichaud

with an introduction by Jim Bishop

UNIVERSITY OF MAINE PRESS
ORONO 2003

07 06 05 04 03   1 2 3 4 5

ISBN: 0-89101-108-0

The paper used in this publication meets the minimum requirements of the American National Standard for Information Sciences—Permanence of Paper for Printed Library Materials, ansi z39.48–1984. Printed and bound in the United States of America.

Front cover photograph: View of Auburn and Lewiston, Maine, *circa* 1900.
Reproduced with permission from the Androscoggin Historical Society, Auburn, Maine.
Cover design by Anita F. Poulin and Michael Alpert.

In memory of my wife, Elizabeth

Papa Martel, his family and his friends, have no counterpart in real life. All family names used here bear no relationship whatsoever with anyone now living, or dead. All cities, streets, institutions, churches, schools, organizations, locales, employed here, have nothing in common with those which, by chance or otherwise, might be found to have existed, or to exist now, in Maine, in Canada, or anywhere else. These tales are fiction.

They are told here, however, with affection and respect for those who have inspired them: French-Canadians, and others I have known and loved, and more specially for my beloved father, Michel Robichaud. May his soul rest in peace where the pipe tobacco is ever fresh and strong, the whisky flows wisely, the steaks come thick and juicy, and the poker cards, more often than not, fall right for him.

CONTENTS

Introduction

Far, far away is Acadee, a land of plenty and of more-to-come . . .
where all prayers are answered in full in time, and there again you
meet those you loved, and lost once, and there find again for good. . . .

Gerry Robichaud did not set out to be a cultural historian. He
began, as most fiction writers do, by wanting to tell a story. Or
rather, several stories, which had their common roots in his
own family history. Gerry had grown up in Maine, but was
born—you might say, "intentionally born"—in the Beauce
region of Québec, the family home of his mother, who
returned there during her pregnancy expressly to give birth to
Gerry on the advice of her family doctor, who counseled her
that in this way, the child could, "first breathe the air you
breathed." Gerry's father, a contract carpenter like Papa
Martel, travelled widely throughout the state to work on jobs
often quite far from their eventual family dwelling in
Lewiston. Gerry's mother died when he was ten years old, and
he and his brother were placed in an asylum for children run
by Catholic Sisters while his father continued to work as a carpenter to support the family. Like Emile Martel, Gerry left
home early (he was twelve) to study in a preparatory school
near Montréal with the intention of becoming a priest.
Eventually, drawn to other callings, Gerry left the seminary at
age nineteen. He worked in a bank in Connecticut for a short

time before moving to New York City and finding the life of 1930s Greenwich Village much in keeping with his youthful spirit and bouyant nature. In 1941 he enlisted in the army, serving in the Pacific until 1945. After his discharge, he arrived in New York City on VJ Day and met Elizabeth, his wife-to-be, that very evening—a great story in itself (she told her friend the next day, "I've met the man I'm going to marry."). In 1951 he enrolled in a special non-degree writing program at Columbia University, and, at the prompting of Elizabeth, began incorporating materials from the family stories he would share with her in his writing.

Papa Martel, published originally by Doubleday in 1961, represents the first full-scale expression of that strategic inclusion. Most prominently, the book elaborates the loosely autobiographical story of the Martel family, related episodically through the coming of age of their seven children, from 1919 to 1937, with flashbacks to the youthful premarital years of Louis and his future wife Cécile; on a second level—more significant as the passing years separate us from the story's time frame—the book draws out the social context of this distinct chapter in the four-hundred-year Francophone presence in North America. We are allowed to witness Maman Martel, who had once studied to become a nun, taking a hard stand against her Parish hierarchy, and Louis weighing in on everything from strong drink and the evils of Prohibition to the right relationship of God and man in the world, as enunciated in his own eleventh commandment, "Thou Shalt Not Fear"; we see the Martels inhabiting and testing the edges of their traditional gender roles, creating the family rituals and relationships that become the ground of self-discovery and allow them to find their intended places in the wider world. Reading *Papa Martel* forty years after its original publication, and a full lifetime's distance from the events chronicled by the story, one is struck by the power of that familial embrace, both nuclear and cultural. Here is a story told by a man who understands his life, and the life of his family, as part of the larger story of his tribe—a community of men and women, generations in the making, who share a common tongue, a common myth, a common window on the universe.

"Acadee!" he said, and sighed. "Sweet Acadee!"
"What's that?" asked Félix.
"Acadee," explained Louis, "is the land that no longer is, a second Garden of Eden . . ."

A land, Louis goes on to explain to his son Félix, that takes in what is now, "Nova Scotia, the Bay of Fundy, . . . New Brunswick, . . . north through the Province of Québec and the State of Maine to the St. Lawrence. . . ." But the soul has its own geography, where, for Louis, Acadie more truly resides at the spiritual intersection between his childhood home in St. John, New Brunswick, and the mistier homeland of his cultural ancestors in that shining moment before *le grand dérangement* of 1755 had exiled them from the sanctity of their Nova Scotia settlement and scattered them to the four winds. Both these realms, the recollected childhood and the mytho-historical Acadie, as operative touchstones for Papa Martel and his family, allow a survival of innocence, where the mystery of existence—with all its sorrows, its grief, even the deep and unhealed wound of exile—has not yet soured to estrangment. Here, the world still turns on a fixed axis; here we need not question our belonging—not, at least, within the secure perimeter of the larger "family" circle. It is this palpable sense of belonging that so strongly informs the narrative of *Papa Martel*. As if its author had himself become a kind of spiritual Papa to all descendants of this far-flung North American

French *famille*, living and to be, and would recount for us the iconic story of the Martels, in the moment of its unfolding, before the fractures already making themselves known in his time, and the later dislocations of our own, would render belief and belonging no less conditional than the provinces of Eden or of childhood.

Sadly, not all our our papas were able to navigate the terrain they inherited with quite the insouciance and sustained *joie de vivre* of Louis Martel. Certainly, many who grew up in working-class Franco-American homes will remember a darker side of Franco-American working-class life that is largely held at bay in *Papa Martel*. We will remember the factories and the men and women who spent half their waking hours inside them, coming home each evening, more emotionally than physically eroded from the drudgery and dead-end nature of the work. And the toll of the years, how the fathers often became far less available than Louis to their wives and children, turning too often to drink or receding inward to blur lifetimes of frustration and blunted hopes. The Martel family, while certainly tested and seriously so, is largely spared this darker affliction of the spirit. Whatever challenges posed to this sturdy Martel clan, they will keep alive the flame that allows, at the end of each week, "the bag of candy, and all that meant, and the little things that were the good life, where laughter more often than tears would abide, if Papa could make it so . . ." By Papa's inexhaustible good humor and worldly wisdom, by Maman's grace and clear-mindedness, and by their collective faith in Divine Providence—they *will* survive their tests of the spirit and emerge the stronger for it. Paradoxically, it is just this undiminished stream of grace in the book that may present a difficulty for the ever-wary contemporary reader, who can hardly hear the word "sentiment" without reflexively calling up the word "false." That *Papa*

Martel manages after all these years to home in under our highly developed radar and still touch us suggests a sustaining power beyond the surface appeal of the the family's winning ways.

Since its original publication this book has been field-tested by thousands of readers, Franco and non-Franco alike, and has aged remarkably well. Recently, the Baxter Society of Portland, Maine included *Papa Martel* on its list of "one hundred distinguished books that reveal the history of the State and the life of its people." I've personally taught the book in Franco-American studies classes with university students and led community discussions of it as part of a book reading series held in town libraries throughout the state. Always the book has been a favorite and has prompted spirited discussion (the points of departure here for cultural exploration are endless). Readers "buy" the Martel family and relate to them in that special way we come to know fictional characters once they've earned their way in, which they do, I think, because Gerry Robichaud has "remembered" from his heart. He cares for and respects each member of the Martel family, including Papa and Maman, in a way that allows them the space to emerge and realize themselves individually, with dignity and charm. Even at times with a little less than charm. As when, in telling his children of the drunken Indian, who taught him herbal medicine as a young man, and of his two lovely daughters, Louis reveals a part of himself quite capable, however innocently rendered, of social attitudes and ethnic stereotyping all too common in his time (and, in slyer renditions, in our own). Gerry's unflinching willingness to register such glimpses into the less-than-enlightened corners of Louis's universe speaks to his trust in Louis's essential humanity and reflects an authorial version of the discerning but unconditional love Louis himself expresses for his offspring when he assures Félix that he does not expect him to becomes heavyweight champion of the world: "I want you to be champion of yourself." And that includes the room to stumble along the way. If Gerry has chosen in *Papa Martel* to steer clear of the black holes of the spirit, he does not shy away from the shadow places, and in that, he earns our trust.

There is another thing though, a bit harder to get at, which I think further explains the staying power of the story, and argues compellingly for this reissue of *Papa Martel* after years out of print. Let me approach it indirectly by way of personal anecdote and invite the reader to supply his or her own translation. There are certain memories we harbor from childhood that have less to do with incident than with a particular quality or character of experience. Not too often, but on occasion, my aunts on my mother's side from New Brunswick and their husbands would visit. They would be in the living room, telling stories the way they did, their voices overlapping one another at times, throwing in bits and pieces, moving back and forth between French and English (the off-color parts mostly in French, I think), gathering a kind of rhythm and surge. And then, less to do with any punchline than with a kind of spill-over point, when the story itself couldn't seem to contain any longer what was welling up inside it, their words would give way and the laughter erupt and break over them. It is the quality of that laughter, not the stories themselves, that has imprinted itself on my memory with the power of dream. A kind of edge-of-tears laughter which I would hear later in the south, echoed among older black women, and be reminded. It had to do, I've come to understand, with a sense of connectedness that went far deeper than personal relationship. It had to do with generations of common history, on the farms and in the woods, embedded in the inflections, tapping the pool of shared sorrows beneath the words. A laughter that emanated in the truest sense from Acadie, their province of mutual belonging. In that collective dream—which manifests in inflection, in gesture, in a recognizable turn of phrase, in that which occasions laughter, in how we imagine a beginning and an end—resides the mythos of a people. And that mythos, like an underground river, which Gerry so tellingly dowses, resonates throughout the book as a kind of subtext in the story of the Martels; it is why their story gathers power beyond the margins of the text and speaks to us still, to a hunger for authentic connection, over forty years after its initial publication.

Sadly for me, I didn't discover *Papa Martel*, or Gerry himself, till the early '80s, when I was past forty. Had I known about the book in my early 20s, when it was originally published, I wonder what influence it might have had on my life. I had gone through high school in a heavily Franco-American mill town in Maine, a heavily Franco-American state, and earned a B.A. at the main branch of the state university, without once in sixteen years of school encountering any book written by a Franco-American (or anyone else for that matter) about the Franco-American experience. The invalidation of North American French in the public schools and the absence of any reflections of Franco-American experience in the world of the written word created over time an unbridgeable space between the world I negotiated daily and increasingly looked to for my points of reference and the Franco-American constellation of my home and my neighborhood. Slowly my home world lost touch completely with my public one, and was displaced, and became, for lack of a better word, history. But even then, a peculiarly submerged and separated kind of history, more the story of a twin brother who did not survive childhood than one I could meaningfully claim as my own. The impact of this divide on my life and on the lives of most

Franco-Americans of my generation and its reverberations in succeeding generations is incalculable. I don't think we have yet come to appreciate the spiritual cost of that kind of collectively administered amnesia. It is the rich legacy of a people's passionate engagement with life that is leached out in that process. And what is left is not whole.

Figuratively and literally we have entered a new millennium since the first edition of *Papa Martel* (Had we even been introduced to our first McDonald's in 1961?). The onrush of corporate "globalization", the "information revolution", and the emergence of a "virtual universe" have proceeded at cyclotronic speed. With our laptops and cell phones we are "connected" now with everything and everyone—just hit SEND—and yet too often strangely disconnected from the pulse of life itself. It's hard to know how the long, slow rhythms of cultural knowledge can merge with the trigger-quick impulses of this digital paradigm and emerge in a way that can still inform us. And similarly, how the DNA of vernacular culture can withstand the corporate leveling of all that is distinctive among us. What language will Papa Martel speak to his grandchildren and their children to be heard ? How will they translate what they are able to hear? And to what purpose? These are serious questions, not about the preservation of old folkways, but about access to the richness of our own beings. One important clue may be in listening to young people today at particular moments when "the power's off" and they are able to respond without the usual background hum. Then something of their suspendedness does sometimes peek through, a feeling of dislocation, a vague hunger for some unidentified, deeper sense of connection. That hunger, I think, is itself the open channel. It holds out the opportunity for genuine correspondence, continuity and renewal. I would place my hope there. We may not all be able, as was Gerry

Robichaud's good fortune, to draw breath from the air first breathed by our mothers and fathers, and perhaps it is as well that we have been offered a freedom from some of their constraining boundaries. But we can renew and reclaim our connection with them, and with *their* mothers and fathers and all they still have to teach us, through the words of our artists and our elders. And that is another kind of inspiration.

Years ago I was allowed access to a lost place of once-possible belonging through the echo of laughter from a distant room. The place was in myself, of course, but it had lost its reflection in the outside world, and so gone underground. I caught the echo here, in the pages of this book —a dimension of experience rescued from the ghost island of unrecorded memory into this public realm of words, and so, strangely confirmed and allowed residence again in the daylight world. No small thing. I am truly gratified and honored now to welcome back *la famille* Martel on the occasion of their long overdue return. I commend the University of Maine Press, and Michael Alpert, its Director, in particular, for making this family album available again to a whole new generation of readers, Franco and non-Franco alike. And to you, Gerry Robichaud—artist, and elder of our tribe—a fond and grateful Merci.

-Jim Bishop
Orono, Maine, February, 2003

PAPA MARTEL

1. The Great Adventure [1919]

It was a cold, windy January night in Groveton, Maine. It had snowed all day, and it was snowing now, a thick, wet snow that settled to stay as it steadily fell. From the kitchen window of his apartment, Louis Martel peered out on Oak Street into the floury, swirling world, pierced only by the new electric bulb on the corner of Pine Street. Surely, he thought, it must be snowing all over the world; surely it would snow all night, and probably would snow for seven more days. . . . *Bonguienne*, had not this happened before?

Certainly. Seventeen years ago, on his wedding day, when a thick snow had stacked up to one's eyebrows and the morning cold had frozen the spit on a man's whiskers. Not a day for honeymoon traveling, the old folks had said, but he'd taken Cécile, his new bride, for a bobsleigh ride. . . . Alone, and far away in the back country, he'd overturned the sleigh on purpose. . . . Thrust suddenly into the shifting snows, Cécile had found herself straddling him in a snowbank and gasping at her upturned skirts. . .

"Louis!" she had squealed. "*Mon méchant!*"

She had slipped a snowball in his warm neck. Around her warm knees he had pushed a handful of snow. How quickly both had forgotten where they were! How quickly the snowbank had become a warm haven for History to be made!

Seventeen years of marriage later, with seven children, six living, this night of cold and snow Cécile awaited the eighth. At supper, she had said to him, as if he could do anything about it, that the snow must surely stop soon. The doctor might have to come in a hurry. Yes, it must, agreed Louis Martel, but it won't, dear God. Louis knew about snow. Sometimes it had the odor of a fresh breeze and hinted at an early spring. This afternoon, at work, he had smelled this one, and it smelled of mountain ice and eternity.

He turned from the window and toward Cécile. She sat quietly near the wood-burning stove, her hands folded over the baby-to-be to give it warmth. On a cord line, near the other stove, a small kerosene burner, were drying his six children's assorted snowshoes, mufflers, coats, hats, and mittens. The clothes gave out a wet, woolly scent. Beneath the chime clock, the crucifix, a homemade blackboard, and a print of the Blessed Family on the wall stood the two stoves, and they huffed and crackled to send waves of warmth toward the children themselves as they huddled around the large dining-room table where they studied in silence or scribbled at their homework. All except little Marie. She was only two, and she sat in the little rocker and watched her Papa as he stood near the window, and waited for something to happen. She clapped her hands and looked at her Maman quickly, but Maman only smiled and put a finger over her lips.

Good thing, too, for Louis was about to say something, and now he did not. For this was the period of silence, given over to scholarly pursuits, that followed supper every day of the school year. Long ago, Cécile Martel had so ordered it, and even now, she sat quietly near the stove. She waited for the requests of assistance that might come from her children. She watched to intercept distractions that might come to them, especially from their Papa. Tonight, particularly.

But he too was silent, and everywhere the world was hushed, Louis concluded. For above the earth, where such miracles are performed, God quietly studied the blueprints of all the ages the better to fashion once again yet another soul, carefully now, a little bit of this, and a little bit of that, a little bit of boy, perhaps a little bit of girl, for the new Martel soul soon to be dispatched to Groveton, Maine, to enter the tiny bit of roundness residing for the moment within Cécile's body, near her heart, and grant it the likeness of God Himself. . . . What an intricate piece of work! Alike to all other souls, and yet a soul unique unto itself, unlike any other He'd ever fashioned before, or ever would again. . . . No wonder this always took such a long time. . . . Too long, he concluded.

"It's the kind of a night," he burst out finally, "to spend in bed with a good pipeful or a good woman . . ."

"Now, Louis . . ." Maman warned.

". . . if you can't find any tobacco," he finished off.

Little Marie smiled, and began to hum a song, and Maman smiled and again put a finger to her lips, and little Marie was quiet for a moment, and then turned toward her Papa.

"Maman," Louis suddenly announced, "it is not good that this house be as quiet as a convent. Not tonight."

At the table, all the children looked up.

"Homework is important," said Maman, "and we must act as if nothing was going to happen." She closed her eyes and rested a bit.

The children sighed and went back to their work, and Louis sighed, too. Maybe—just maybe—it would work. When he saw Laurent, age sixteen, and the oldest, put down his *Histoire Moderne* and look up, he thought it might work. He was sure, now, when he saw him wink at Maurice, who was fourteen, smaller but beefier. Maurice stopped in the middle of an algebra problem and turned to Thérèse and nodded.

She was twelve, and skinny, but her black hair tumbled gracefully down to her shoulders. With intent dark eyes and ink-stained fingers, she scribbled tirelessly on a *cahier*.

"Psst!" whispered Maurice.

Louis Martel turned back to the window. Yes, it was working. Now, Thérèse looked up quietly, nodded to Maurice, put down her pen, and posed her oval face into an attitude of piety. She frowned in warning toward Félix. He was eight and held a French grammar in his hands and gazed everywhere but at it.

"Papa?" Thérèse asked sweetly.

Quickly he turned from the window.

"Yes, my pretty one?"

"Papa," she continued, "did you really meet Maman in a convent?"

Now all the children looked up toward him.

"Why, yes," replied Louis, surprised.

"And she was a Sister?"

"Of course. With the Ursulines. But you know all that!"

Thérèse quickly turned toward Emile. He was six, his eyes were half closed in sleep, and his mouth was open. Maurice shook him with his elbow and he woke up.

"But I never heard it!" he squealed.

Maman sighed.

"It's all a little plot," she said gently.

"So," said Louis, "but it's not good that you should fret about anything tonight, lest the baby-to-be fret also for a year and a day after it is born."

Please, Papa," implored Thérèse, "tell it again. For Emile?"

Louis picked up Marie, who now fought hard to keep her eyes open, sat down with her in his lap, and kissed her nose.

"It is good to be inside, and all together, eh, Cécile?" he said.

"Yes, Louis, it is."

Maman clapped her hands twice. Quickly the children put away their books, pens, and pencils, and turned toward their Papa. He was over six feet tall and lean. His face had the perpetual hard tan of the outdoor workman, and he had long arms that spoke as much as did his deep voice.

"Your Maman and I knew," he began, "as soon as she saw me that I was the man in her life. . . ."

This opening was meant to draw Maman into the fray, and he waited, but tonight she sat quietly. She said again that she hoped the snow would stop soon, and that if Doctor Lafrance had to come tonight, that he would be able to make it.

"Nowadays," added Louis, "women have their babies in safety, with a good doctor in attendance. Not one of those *accoucheurs*, like my own Maman had, when babies did not always make it. . . . Nowadays, the doctor comes right to your house, and you hire a good woman to help around the house. Besides," he added with a chuckle, "your Papa can afford it."

The children settled themselves more comfortably, and Maman smiled a bit.

"Not bad," added Louis, "for a man who can't read and write."

He turned toward Maman to see what she would do, and say, and she did. She sat up in the chair and looked at him.

"Louis Martel," she snapped, "those whom the Lord has spared from the weight of knowledge should speak little and pray more!"

The children giggled, and he guffawed.

"Now I worry no more about you!" he said. "For you still have the scrapping spirit. . . ."

"Papa," said Thérèse, "the story. . . ."

It had been a long way from an impoverished farm, near St. John, New Brunswick, where Louis Martel was born thirty-seven years ago, to Groveton, Maine, and the apartment his family occupied, on the second floor of the Pelletier "block," as apartment houses are called in Maine. Two doors led up to it, the front or street door, up one flight, that opened on the front room, or *parloir*. This room, however, was seldom used except for funerals and visits from the curé. The second door, in the back, was reached from the street, past a back yard, up a stairway that crisscrossed each apartment's back porch, and opened into a hallway that led to the kitchen door, and into the large kitchen itself.

Besides the *parloir* and the kitchen, there were five bedrooms, and a large bathroom, which, to the embarrassment of Maman and Thérèse, Papa never failed to call the backhouse, or "becosse." The house was relatively new, and yet it was already old, but the apartment was serviceable for a large family. After the various houses, and in northern Maine the two shacks, Maman had known in the early years of their married life, this apartment was a little touch of that Heaven to come to all those who died in a state of grace.

On the right, two rooms faced the porch, one occupied by Laurent and Maurice, and the other, the front one with south and west exposures, by Thérèse. Louis and Cécile's room, on the left, was the largest, and nearest to the bathroom. Next, was a room for Marie, and the other lodged Emile and Félix.

Each bedroom had plain oak and pine furniture, large closets, a crucifix over the bed, holy images on the walls and family photos on the dressers, but only the *parloir* could boast of real expensive pieces, a large loveseat in red plush, and chairs to match. Every room was clean and spotless, the papered walls, the waxed floors, the Bates bedspreads in each room. . . . For Maman often told Thérèse: "A woman's virtue shines best in a neat house."

The focus of family life, however, was the large kitchen—

all doors led into it—and it was meant to and could welcome and sit ten adults and ten children in chairs that stood all around the wall. Louis's easy chair was near the armoire, where the whisky and the pipe tobacco were kept, and situated so that he could watch the old clock with the chimes on the wall above the stove, take an occasional look outside on Oak Street, or easily reach for the whisky or the tobacco.

He never sat for long, however; the pipe he held in his hand was never the one he wanted, and so he foraged forever in all parts of the house wherever he might have left the pipe he needed. He had several: the old ones, burnt out long ago, which he never threw away; the new ones he'd not quite broken in yet; the large bowler type for storytelling and story listening; the hard durable ones for work duty; the little ones for a quick puff just before entering church on Sunday.

Though his own memory of the facts was sometimes hazy, Louis Martel was proud of those he advanced as "positively the truth." He was Acadian, born in the country of Evangeline, the baby in a family of seventeen children. He had lived his early years on a large farm in New Brunswick where hard toil from morning till night was essential for the most frugal food and shelter. School was two miles away and it burned down when Louis was seven. He and his brothers and sisters, still of school age, dutifully walked to another school nearly five miles away for almost a year. When his mother died, most of them stopped going, and Louis did too. Schools were poor, somehow, and often shut by winter weather.

"I never wondered about this," confessed Louis, "or about much of anything else, until I met your Maman." He shook his head sadly. "She was twenty-two, a finely educated creature, and I was nearly nineteen, and sure the world was held in space by two sky hooks. . . ."

His oldest brothers and sisters received various degrees of

formal education. Two brothers went to a classical college for a time. Louis remained at home to work and play on the farm. With such a large family—eight sons, nine girls—a large farm—Grandpère Martel labored long hours and in turn enlisted his grown sons to work on the farm and to fish in the Bay of Fundy, and his daughters to bake, cook, and to work in the fields. When a son married, Grandpère gave him a slice of his farm with an outlet to the sea, and family and neighbors got together and built him a modest framewood house, a barn, and a stone meat house. When a daughter married, sometimes there was and sometimes there was not money for a dowry, but they always had linens, dishes, a crib or two, and good advice on how to care for babies. Education was a luxury, and so was comfort, but common sense abounded.

"You loved God," said Louis, "and served Him. You loved your neighbor and helped him, and you hated all Henglish haristocrats!"

Two of his older brothers fled to more appealing regions, one to the United States, never to be heard of again, another to England, where, Louis always swore on his mother's honor, he had become heavyweight champion of England, under another name of course. A sister, age seventeen, of whom little was ever said, took off one Sunday, right after High Mass, and vanished with an unidentified man.

Louis fled to the Province of Québec, where men were needed in the pulpwood business. From the age of sixteen until he became a carpenter in later years, he worked and lived every winter in camps, chopped wood, and spent the summer in the nearest town, working at odd jobs. Often, however, as a young man, he had returned to St. John to visit his family.

"Acadee!" he said, and sighed. "Sweet Acadee!"

"What's that?" asked Félix.

"Acadee," explained Louis, "is the land that no longer is, a second Garden of Eden that now takes in Nova Scotia, the Bay of Fundy, St. John where I was born, New Brunswick, moves north through the Province of Québec and the State of Maine to the St. Lawrence. . . ."

"The English," said Thérèse, her thin face tense with emotion, "came and burned houses and stole the cattle of six thousand Acadians, and deported them, separated families . . ."

"Military necessity," stated Maurice with great calm.

"Papa, did you hear what he said?" she exclaimed, horrified.

"Acadee!" sang Louis. "Sweet Acadee! All God's children—the English too! Yearned for this land of dreams come true! This Acadee! This Acadee!"

"The story, please," begged Thérèse.

When pressed, Louis would admit that it was while working in lumber camps that he got his first education. Here, he learned to fight with bare fists, to play stud poker, to drink straight whisky with tea chasers, to logroll in competition, to race in the snow in a potato sack, to skate in a race blindfolded, to smoke uncut tobacco, to make herbs and roots yield their mysterious Indian cures for anything from frostbite to melancholia, to predict the weather by tree bark, to make castles from maple sugar, to jig and square-dance to fast violin music, to holler the big wahoo of a laugh that can scare the bears at night. . . .

"Did this big wahoo of a laugh," asked Félix, "scare the bears, Papa?"

"Yes," he said, "the bears, the devil, and all bad things of the night."

Maman moved impatiently in her chair.

"But he never learned to read and write," she pointed out.

"Poor Papa!" said Thérèse.

"I was rich," affirmed Louis. "I had all the forests to myself, which no one had yet put into one book, the whole forests and their mysteries, and my friends. . . . Wonder what happened to all of them! We went out together every Saturday night to the nearest town—there were no movies then—and we went out looking for fights or Indian girls. . . ."

"*Bon*, Louis," snapped Maman.

"Indian girls?" Laurent asked.

"That will be enough," announced Maman.

"That's when," said Louis, "I fell in love."

"Yes, Papa," gasped Thérèse, "tell us the love part."

"And," added Maurice, "the Indian girls!"

"I meant," corrected Louis, "that's when I met your Maman. . . ."

Cécile Bolduc was the youngest of three daughters, born of the first bed of Napoléon Bolduc. He was a well-to-do landowner in the village of St. Michel, in the Province of Québec, and was rumored to have spent some time in Montreal at a university. A sharp horse trader, a civic leader of sorts, he aspired to political preferment in the Provincial government, and he had chosen to belong to the Liberal Party— whatever that meant then, or means now.

Failing the chance to shine in a larger arena, he contented himself to tarry for a while as Mayor of St. Michel. Rosaline and Marie, Cécile's two older sisters, went to convents, graduated, married farmers and raised large families, and no doctors around. Upon graduation, at eighteen, Cécile remained in the convent as a novice, and later, at twenty, took temporary vows—for three years—of chastity, poverty and obedience.

"Maman was a Sister!" screamed Emile. He turned toward her with a new awe. "A Sister, like the Sisters at the Academy?"

"Yes, *mon chéri*," said she. "For a little while."

She asked Thérèse to bring her the family album with the fat leather cover and the silver brocade designs, and she displayed for all to see a portrait of herself in her nun's habit taken just before she left the convent to re-enter the world. She looked so young in the ill-fitting, long robe of black serge, her face barely peeping out of her dark veil and guimpe.

Emile was deeply impressed. But this year Thérèse posed a new question.

"Papa, did you meet Maman before, or after? I mean, did you fall in love before or after she left the convent?"

"After," said Maman quietly.

"Before!" roared Louis.

In the fall of his nineteenth year, and before returning to camp for the winter, Louis Martel, purely by chance, came to St. Michel.

"I don't know why I happened to come to this village," he admitted to his children. "Perhaps to look around—I'd never been there before—perhaps to look for work, perhaps to raise a little hell . . ."

"Yes, yes?" urged Maurice.

"Maurice!" said Maman.

"In any case," Louis continued, "Monsieur Bolduc—Maman's Papa—gave me a job of work weather-stripping the doors and windows of the convent where the Sisters taught school. During winter they and their girl students caught one damn cold after another. . . ."

Maman cleared her throat.

"Your Papa," she said, "has always had a *fixation* about good weather stripping for doors and windows. That's why, no matter what else you did not have, you always had warmth every winter."

The effort tired her and she closed her eyes.

"Maman," Thérèse asked quietly, "should I prepare you for bed?"

Maman opened her eyes quickly.

"Why, *chérie?* I'm very comfortable."

"But, Maman, you'll tire yourself, and you've heard the story, you were there. . . ."

Maman laughed.

"It's never quite the same, with your Papa telling it," she said, then she became very quiet, and a muffled moan escaped from her closed lips. Louis blanched as he held on to Marie in his arms, and he looked out at the snow-filled window. Laurent and Maurice stood up and went up to their Maman.

"Cécile," ordered Louis, "the boys will help you to bed."

Thérèse bit her fingers and turned to Félix and he yawned and she was impatient with him for not understanding, and Marie was fast asleep in her Papa's arms. Laurent and Maurice put their arms around Maman and helped her up and slowly walked her to her room, and Thérèse went in and stayed with her while she went to bed. Then she came toward Papa, took Marie from him and put her to bed.

"Thank you, boys," said Louis, and when Thérèse returned, he said: "Thank you, Thérèse. You are all of much help."

She bit her fingers again.

"I want to do so much more for Maman!" she said tensely.

Me too, thought Louis, but nothing can be done until God has finished fixing up this particular soul, and it always takes a long time. He knew that, and his children would have to learn that too, as he'd learned from his days in Acadee, that nieces and nephews came in their own sweet time, that the fixing of a soul took as many different time lengths as there were individuals. . . . What delayed God, no doubt, were the final touches. . . . That's what his own Papa used to say to impatient parents-to-be, and his Papa, and his Papa's Papa had said. . . .

"You were about to go to work in the convent," said Maurice politely.

"Yes," said Louis, "but Laurent, you better get ready to

leave for the doctor. I think God may knock off work early, tonight. . . ."

And so yesterday was today again, and Louis Martel, armed with his tool chest and materials, invaded the sanctity of the convent where few men had entered, before or since. It was a job, like any other job, and he weather-stripped all day—dormitories, refectories, the chapel, the assembly hall, the sewing room, the lavatories, the classrooms, and wherever he went the Mother Superior went with him.

"Like John the Baptist," said Louis, "she went ahead to prepare the way for me."

Around four, he entered a classroom where a nun bent over her desk, correcting papers probably, her head almost hidden by her veil. Mother Superior coughed once, the nun rose quickly, and when told what was going to happen, she nodded assent and sat down at her desk. And then Mother Superior was called away.

"I took a sly glance at this nun's face," said Louis, "and I'm here to tell you, my children, that I dropped my hammer!"

Thérèse sighed audibly.

"She was," continued Louis, "the most beautiful creature I had ever seen, a real beauty of a *Canadienne*, and here I was, all alone with her in the same room!"

"Yes," said Laurent, coolly, "but she was a nun then!"

"There was peace," said Louis, "in her gray eyes, and shyness in her manner, and holiness to the tip of her fingers, and her complexion was milk-white. . . . She had a brown beauty spot on her left cheek—just as she has now—and this peace inside her shamed the restlessness in my heart, and then, I swear, she raised her head and smiled. . . . Just a little, mind you, and a project was formed in my heart, my children. . . ."

"Did she smile at you, really?" Thérèse asked, a doubt in her eyes.

"Her eyes did, Thérèse, and then she asked—I'd been standing there staring at her—she asked with the most beautiful articulation, in good French, you know, 'Monsieur, has he finished his project yet?' And I said: 'No, Sister, monsieur has, so to speak, just begun!'"

He returned the next day to finish up. *Bonguienne!* There were two nuns in the classroom, Sister Bolduc and another nun, a stout one she was. Both teachers stood at the blackboard and wrote copywork for the students on it with red and white chalk. He set about to finish up the last window and then stopped to gaze in wonder as the two nuns occasionally brushed chalk dust from their long dark habits and wrote highly stylized calligraphy lessons on the blackboard. Whatever they wrote was large enough to be visible to any classroom of students, but even then, now, here and there, they improved the flourishes on some letters with careful erasures and retracings. Once Sister Bolduc turned toward Louis, absent-mindedly working on the back-room window. Caught staring again, he pounded the hammer on his thumb. But she merely asked him, in a commanding voice, to do something for her.

"Monsieur! Can Monsieur see this from where you are?"

"Yes," said Louis in low tones.

"Well, Monsieur, will you kindly read it?"

"That I can't do, Sister," he muttered.

The two Sisters looked at one another in consternation. The other nun, the stout one, strode back to the rear, frowned, and now Sister Bolduc also walked to the rear, stood near Louis and gazed sharply at the blackboard.

"I cannot understand it!" she remarked crisply. "Why can't you read the sentences on the blackboard from where you are? Can you see all right?"

"I can see all right," said Louis, "but no matter where I stand, I can't read."

He laughed suddenly. This was a good joke, to turn the tables on these black-robed inquisitors, and he forced himself to laugh again. The two nuns did not laugh at all. They stared sadly at one another.

"It is unforgivable!" announced Sister Bolduc.

"I'm doing all right," said Louis, darkly.

"Think, Monsieur," said Sister Bolduc, "how much better you would do if you could read and write. Today, everybody must be educated, even young women. But to a man, it is a necessity of bread and shelter. Education, Monsieur, is a wonderful adventure!"

"Is it, now?" asked Louis.

"We must start at once," announced Sister Bolduc.

She pointed her finger toward him, and now sharply toward the blackboard, and then indicated he must follow her as she strode to the front of the classroom; dumbly he followed behind her.

"Your name, Monsieur?"

"Louis Martel, Sister."

"Eleven letters," she concluded quickly. "Your first and last name make a total of four distinct syllables . . . Lou—wee—mar—tel!"

She chalk-printed his name several times on the blackboard, enunciating each letter in turn and very slowly to bring out the four sounds of his name in full. Then, without a word, she handed him the chalk. It was then he realized that she was, after all, just a female, only five feet two; he towered over her, and one big great yahoo of a shout—the kind used to scare bears away at night—would certainly cause her to faint. That would surely frighten the hell out of her, scare them both out of their wits right then and there. . . . This too would be an adventure!

But he didn't shout. Sister Bolduc's eyes stared directly at him—they seemed to guess his secret plan—and her right hand emerged out of her long sleeve and her index pointed toward the blackboard. It was a command that was meant to be obeyed. He took the chalk and painfully began to copy the letters as she pointed them out to him and she enunciated again each letter and each fully rounded sound, and he repeated the sounds, and this was not bad. . . . And then Mother Superior was there and her eyes summarized the whole situation in a single glance. Sister Bolduc took one quick step toward her.

"Monsieur cannot read or write," she shot out in self-defense.

"He never went to school," added the stout nun.

"I see," said Mother Superior, slowly counting the windows that were finished, and the one remaining that was not. "It is a pity," she said, "but now, I think it is time for all of us to go back to our own labors."

That too was a command, and the two Sisters hopped to, and vanished, and he picked up his hammer.

"You are doing, Monsieur, a good piece of work," said Mother Superior, as she stood and waited near the door.

Louis muttered under his breath.

"What did you say, Monsieur?"

Louis was suddenly silent.

"Well, Papa, what did you say?" asked Emile.

"What I meant to say," said Louis, "was for the old crow to vamoose, but she stayed there, watching me all the time, and when I had finished, and finally left, I bet that Mother Superior thought she had seen the last of me, or that I had seen the last of Sister Bolduc. *Bonguienne*, my children, if I had. . ."

Laurent swiftly passed the index of his right hand across his neck and thus quickly cut his own head off. Thérèse gasped in horror.

"We wouldn't be here!" she announced to all.

"And neither would I," added Louis.

Louis Martel spent that winter in a lumber camp among other men only slightly more educated than he, yearning in a vague way for the great adventure to begin, wondering how and if it would ever. . . . Every day, from sunup to sunset, he chopped, sawed, trimmed, rolled and piled cordwood. In the evening, he sat by a lamp near a hot stove, his heavy shoes off to let the heat come through his heavy wool socks, and gazed for hours at an old prayer book. He saw not only the sacred images, but he studied the mysterious text that made sense to the learned.

It was a prayer book, for sure, for it had a cross on the leather cover, and pictures of Jesus, and Mary, and Joseph inside, and the whole ceremonial of the Mass. For long evenings, he gazed, mystified, frustrated, and yet enthralled by this magic only the initiated could freely evoke, these symbols which spoke, sang, soothed, gave you the words to pray to God, and inspired the fortunate ones who held the key to their silent power. . . .

For long hours also he copied painstakingly the printed symbols over and over in a copybook, in the growing excitement that, though he personally did not know what message they concealed, he could rip the veil open any time by asking any learned friend to read back to him the symbols he himself had formed, and his own mysterious scribblings would speak out loud words neither he nor his learned friend had ever seen before. . .Well, Messieurs, this was magic indeed!

Each night, before he went to sleep, he said his prayers, those his Maman had taught him by rote, and soon he began to make up his own special prayer arrangements, and he prayed for Sister Bolduc, that God might keep her well and sassy, and he threw in a few good words for the other one, the stout nun, and even for Mother Superior. And he prayed for others also. The world had now become divided between those who could read, like the Sisters at the convent, and all the others, like himself, who could not, and he prayed even more for the latter, as being more in need of Divine pity.

That spring, with the money he had saved, he went to St. John to see his aging Papa, and did not get to St. Michel until July. When he arrived at the little railroad station, the town was empty. He very nearly took the next train out, if there had been one that day.

"Oh, no!" whispered Thérèse hoarsely.

There was no valid reason to be in this particular village, even under the pretext of resuming his lessons, much less to go roaming around the convent. In July, of course, it, too, was deserted.

"Pa, it was a girls' school!" screamed Thérèse.

Further, Sister Bolduc had probably forgotten all about him. Against this lack of sense, there persisted a sweet memory —a short little female who would not be scared away—and a foolish yearning for this adventure Sister Bolduc had spoken about with such enthusiasm and this—he knew not why— this enthusiasm was precious. The memory of it spurred a great pride in himself, and it grew as he walked aimlessly the one main street of St. Michel, past the church, the convent, the city hall, the one general store. That same day he got work from a farmer, and the family put him up in the spare room. And he worked on the farm, and waited. For what? He did not know. It was the darkest period of his life.

At night, alone in his room, he thought long thoughts. Was this a pause without apparent purpose, a long dry spell that God often imposes on the young before they are off toward the great adventure? Was this loneliness, this prison of me by me, the jailer, also a part of learning? Couldn't learning itself of many things be the slow release of me, the prisoner, by me, the learner? Wasn't this here, the great adventure? And, beyond books, perhaps, but with them, if you were lucky, would not seeing Sister Bolduc again, even from a great distance, and knowing her, and listening to her, be the greatest adventure of them all? And becoming very smart for her sake?

For several days he spoke to few persons, and to no one about his great yearnings. Assuredly, the savants would snicker at his ignorance and worse yet at his unbecoming desire for knowledge. Men of equal ignorance would belittle his strange nonconformity. He knew the loneliness now, twice compounded, of him who knows nothing, and knows too well he knows nothing. One particularly lonely Sunday night, he remembered his Papa's maxim.

"Five minutes, inside a quiet church," he often said, "on your knees, in prayer directly to God, will soothe anything from a broken leg to a broken heart."

"That was good advice, Papa," whispered Thérèse piously.

"Damn right it was," agreed Louis.

Around eight o'clock, Louis Martel entered the Church of St. Michel, right after Vespers. He remained in the church less than two minutes. He had seen her!

"Who?" asked Emile.

"Maman!" announced Thérèse impatiently.

"Now, let Papa tell it," said Laurent with authority.

"I saw this young woman," continued Louis, "very short, wearing a long blue dress with some fancy silver trimmings and a big floppy hat, just as she was leaving the church. I wasn't sure who she was, but I was certain I had seen her before. Same gray eyes. Same beauty spot on the left cheek. Well, I figured right quickly that if I could get close to her—stand right near her—and compare height, you know? Well, let me tell you this! She stopped walking, as she left the church, to look up at the darkening sky and I edged up to her with great care, and then my heart told me it was Sister Bolduc!"

Thérèse giggled. "I bet Maman thought you were—well—one of those fresh village sports!" she said.

"It's a wonder," remarked Maurice, "that she didn't cry for help."

"Well," continued Louis, "it was Sister Bolduc all right! She was Mademoiselle Bolduc now! Out of the convent and into the world. I approached to a respectable distance and I tipped my hat to her in the old-fashioned manner. She pursed her lips at this and fixed me with a withering schoolmarmish glare. Children, it was a preview of the Last Judgment!"

"Maman?" asked Thérèse. "She gave you a mean look?"

"Yes. That glare," said Louis, "would have set a lion to trembling at fifty paces. But not me! Smoothly I said: 'Mademoiselle Bolduc? If I am wrong, Mademoiselle, forgive my gaucherie, and I shall depart without a trace. . . .'"

"Please do, Monsieur," she replied crisply, "and adieu!"

Promptly she began to walk away.

"I am," roared Louis, "eleven letters that make a total of four distinct syllables. . . . Mademoiselle, I am Lou—wee—Mar—tel!"

That stopped her. She hesitated. She turned toward him, a doubt and a fear in her gray eyes. Her lips tightened a bit.

"Oh!" she gasped. "You are not the Monsieur . . . ?"

"I am. . . ."

"The Monsieur . . . who weather-stripped our class windows?"

"The same, Mademoiselle."

Her lips broke out into an open smile.

"I am so pleased to see you again," she said, "and forgive my rudeness. And what are you doing now, Monsieur?"

"I am waiting."

"Waiting?"

"I am waiting, Mademoiselle, to get started on the great adventure you spoke about. . . . I too want to learn. I want to learn the many things there are to know, and everything possible to know. When can we start, Mademoiselle?"

"'We,' Monsieur?"

"Can we start soon?"

She stared directly into his eyes, then seemed to understand, and lowered her eyes, then walked away a few steps, and now her eyes began to dart quickly in all directions but there was no one else about. She turned toward him.

"It is not possible," she said softly. "As you see, I have left the convent. My health was not too good. The doctor said it was neurasthenia."

"I am sorry," he said, "but I would not tax your strength."

"No matter," she added quickly, "for my Papa is a very strict man. He would not tolerate strange men lurking about. . . ."

Louis stiffened.

"Mademoiselle, I know your Papa. I have worked for him, and I hope to work for him again. And I'm no stranger to you, for I knew you when you were a teacher and afraid of no one. . . ."

"I'm not afraid . . ." she began.

"But I shall learn," continued Louis, his voice rising, "many things. If not from you, Mademoiselle the Teacher, I shall learn from someone else, and some day, I shall be worthy of your company. . . ."

"Oh, but Monsieur, you are not unworthy, just . . ."

"Ignorant! See these . . ." And he displayed his painful scribblings of the past winter. She took them and studied them. "I too can write!"

"Yes, you can. But you have difficulty with your *g*'s. And

your *v*'s. It is very good, I must say. Very good, indeed. Do you understand what you have written?"

"Not a word."

"It is a pity."

"When do we start, Mademoiselle?"

Cécile Bolduc tapped the notebook against her left hand. She pursed her lips and a smile came over her face. She glanced toward the empty street that ended at the forest, and into the darkening firmament of the dying day. It was a warm evening, and it was very quiet. Nearby a cricket ticked off the passing minutes.

"When can you start, Monsieur?"

"Now."

"*Bon.* We must therefore ask my Papa. For the permission."

Napoléon Bolduc did not warm up quickly to Louis. Only when one of his barns needed repairs did he begin to speak politely to him, and Louis did the work at night, for nothing, during his free time away from lessons with Cécile. Then her Papa found many other tasks around the farm, enough to keep Louis away from Cécile much of the time.

When he hinted, one day, that the City Hall needed some repairs, Louis offered to do the job, but only for pay. And he did, and now Cécile's Papa suggested many others, and one day Louis found himself with over a hundred dollars saved, and Napoléon Bolduc offered to invest the money for him. Nothing doing, said Louis. Then Papa Bolduc tried to sell him a horse.

"A good horse it had been twenty years before," said Louis to his children.

"No?" said Félix. "Grandpère tried to fool you?"

"He tried," said Laurent.

Louis examined the horse a moment and laughed out loud, right in Papa Bolduc's face, so that he too had to laugh finally.

Then Papa Bolduc offered to sell him a part of his farm on easy terms. He had no sons, he said, and he could give him a good bargain, and then he quoted the Gospel that whoever did sow, so also would he reap.

"I shall neither sow," said Louis, "nor shall I reap. I shall be a builder of homes for the sowers and the reapers."

"Papa," interrupted Thérèse, "how did you propose—that's what I want to hear!"

Louis was quiet, then he spoke up.

"Within two weeks," he said, "your Maman and I had reached the sweet agreement, which, as you know, must in good time be sealed in heaven. . . ."

"Please, Papa," she begged, "what did you say at the great moment?"

Again Louis hesitated.

"I said: 'Cécile, I love you, with all my heart, and in all the world, everybody else.'"

Laurent looked away. Félix and Emile listened quietly, but Thérèse's eyes misted. Maurice smiled happily.

"And Maman?" pursued Thérèse. "What did she say?"

"'Louis,' she said, 'you have my heart forever. . .'"

Papa Bolduc sensed this, and now he offered him a goodly parcel of land at no cost whatever, if only he would farm it. Louis shook his head slowly at this. There were, he said, two kinds of *Canayens*, those who worked their farms, stayed put in their counties and were buried there, having never seen the world, and the others, the adventurers, the *coureurs de bois*, who must forever see what lay on the other side of the next mountain.

"I aim to travel," he said, "even if only by foot."

"What else do you want?" suddenly stormed Papa Bolduc.

Louis took a deep breath.

"I want the great honor," he said firmly, "of Mademoiselle Bolduc's hand in marriage."

"Why did you have to ask him?" Maurice put in aggressively.

"It was in the ancient custom," said Louis softly. "Well, the *bonhomme* threw an old-fashioned fit!"

"He did?" asked Thérèse, and her lips trembled.

"Yes," said Louis, chuckling to himself, "and for a time a storm raged in his face."

For days he had only curt words for Louis, and to this Louis replied with aloof respect. One evening, late in August, when Louis and Cécile sat on the front porch, in the dark, in silence, not touching hands since they did not have permission, Papa Bolduc came out suddenly on the porch. Silently he stared at his large farm lands. Perhaps he was wondering why God had given him only daughters, and no sons. Cécile got up and walked up to him.

"Papa," she murmured, "you have not yet given your answer to Monsieur Martel. Our happiness waits patiently for your blessing."

"You want him?" Napoléon Bolduc raged. "Why, he's got nothing and he wants nothing! Nothing at all!"

"He has everything, Papa," Cécile replied, "he has my heart."

"You'll have nothing else!" roared her Papa.

"And I have," she continued, "the best man in the world any girl could want. Now, Papa, both of us will need your blessing very much. *Alors*, Papa, make a decision, and make it now, and make it a good one."

He turned promptly toward Louis the better to size him up once more. The hardness seemed to fade from his face.

"Any man," he concluded slowly, "who knows so much about horses can't possibly be a complete damn fool!"

"Oh, he's very smart," said Cécile quickly.

"So be it," said Papa Bolduc, "and I shall give you both my blessing!" The two men shook hands.

"We shall need that," said Louis.

The banns were published. Cécile got a good dowry. One evening, in October, Papa Bolduc threw an old-fashioned *noce*, and Louis outdanced all the young bucks in town until the sun rose on four feet of snow, and they were married in the Church of St. Michel, and then he took his Cécile in his arms and carried her to a brand-new sleigh for two, with tinkling bells, that he'd bought with his savings, as well as a fine mare. Napoléon Bolduc protested to Louis. The snow, he said, was thick and deep, and they should wait until tomorrow. And they did, they waited a few hours, and to kill time, he took her for a bobsleigh ride. . . .

The next day, the snow kept falling, thick and wet, and he discussed this with Cécile. She was ready to go, and they did, and he drove her over ice and snow to New Brunswick for a one-week honeymoon with his family.

Thérèse suddenly giggled.

"Maman always said she ate nothing but herrings over there!" she exclaimed. "It was a week of Fridays!"

Then Louis drove his bride to Maine, where men were needed, and he took whatever job he could get, lived where they could, free-roaming from Millinocket to Portland. As Christmas approached, he got a job near Berlin, New Hampshire, and all he could get for shelter was a shack he built himself at night with stray lumber. . . .

And they spent their first Christmas there, but though it was a square shack of unfinished wood, there was a good fire going, and he had weather-stripped every nook and corner of it. . . .

Thérèse chirped in.

"Yes, and Maman remembers it every year. 'That first Noel,' she says, 'we were so close to God, to one another, to nature and to complete earthly happiness, and we had nothing, absolutely nothing but love in our hearts for each other and the whole wide world. It was truly a *joyeux Noel!*'"

"I promised her a chime clock," recalled Louis, "and that's the first thing I bought her!" He turned toward the chime clock on the wall. "And there it is."

It was a tough first year, as he tried to get and to hold jobs, as an apprentice-carpenter now, always moving where the work was, then, as a carpenter. Cécile was alone every day, nearly always in new surroundings, and she cooked, ironed, scrubbed, and, often, merely tried to keep warm. He worked all day, and worried for her, but Cécile's cheeks now took on a rosy color—the neurasthenia vanished—and when he came home, she gave him a shot of whisky, his supper and his pipe, and then read to him by the light of a kerosene lamp.

When he was not too tired physically, she taught him again and again how to write and to read his own name. And then, Laurent was born, and everything seemed to change for the better.

"God is kind," said Louis, "to those in love, and when a man marries, Providence puts his name down on a special list."

"Maman's crying!" announced Félix. "I can hear her!"

Louis jumped to his feet, and then listened. There was a sharp cry, and then a long moan, then another, this one low and piteous, half muffled. Thérèse began to tremble, and Félix's face grimaced. Louis put his arm around him, then winked toward Laurent who, in no time, was dressed warmly against the cold and the snow.

"Hurry, Laurent," ordered Louis.

Laurent left, and Louis went in alone to see Cécile. There was a Madonna in white on the table near her bed, and a lone votive offering. Cécile's fingers were damp over her rosary beads.

"*Chérie*," murmured Louis, "Laurent has gone for the doctor."

"*Bon.*"

"I feel that we will do all right, *chérie*."

"*Bon.*"

"Cécile, we wait for this baby with gladness."

She was breathing heavily.

"Louis," she panted, "the children? Who is with them?"

"Well. . ."

"Stay with them, Louis. The Rosary. . .I've just begun. . ."

He returned to the kitchen. The children stared at him.

"Everything is just dandy," he said. "And now, where were we?"

Maurice interrupted.

"Should we not get one of the ladies we know to stay with Maman? I can ask."

"No," said Louis. "We need no chatterbox, we need a doctor, and now, where was I?"

Louis became an apprentice-carpenter, then a full-fledged union carpenter, and then later, a boss-carpenter, and then, again, in later years, a contractor. He neither prospered, nor starved: he only did all right. Later, he and Philippe Buisson, a brother carpenter, became friends and partners. He drove the car Louis could not, and Louis smoked out and found the jobs both needed wherever they could be found, once as far as Pennsylvania. No matter where they worked during the week, both came home every weekend to their families. After a while there was Maurice, and then Thérèse, and then Muriel.

"Muriel?" asked Emile.

"She died," contributed Maurice, "when she was a baby. Cholera."

Little Muriel, thought Louis. God had fixed a soul for her long ago, and He'd given her this soul, unlike any other, and she had been baptized Muriel, but the body was not finished.

. . . Her milk never reached her stomach but that it became like a poison inside her. She grew frail and cried all day long, and Maman promised, if she survived, to go to Ste. Anne de Beaupré. . . . But God soon asked for the return of this soul that she might sing with His other angels in Paradise. That's how he had explained it all to Cécile over and over when Muriel had died, and it had snowed that night too. . . .

And then there was Félix, and then Emile, and then Marie, and soon now, there would be a brand-new little Martel. And every night of their lives, Maman reserved a period of silence for homework, or family reading. She read to them biographies of the great men of the Church, of France, of Canada and of the United States.

Nearly all the children could read fairly well by the time they entered school for the first time. And all of them could do their sums, for Louis, somehow, became a whiz in mathematics. None of this, however, was ever quite good enough for Maman.

"We shall learn," she said once, "to speak the English as well as the French. . . ."

"The Henglish?" Louis asked with contempt. "Why, that's the language of the Protestants!"

"Shame on you!" stormed Maman. "It is the language of Shakespeare, of Milton, and of those who make money in the business world. You, Louis Martel, shall speak English, and speak it well!"

Louis winked at the children, and shook his head in grave doubt.

"To speak to God in Henglish?" he asked. "Sounds wrong to me."

"And you wanted to learn many things?" asked Maman with passion. "In this house, we shall learn to speak French well, and we shall pray to God in our native tongue, and we shall speak the English, the language of our new country, and speak it well too!"

Louis did learn to speak English, after a fashion, but all the children, from their earliest years, could and did speak both French and English, alternately, at will, and well. And they grew strong and healthy, and they came closely one upon the heels of another. Maman was never too strong, and soon she felt something else was needed.

In the early days, after they settled in Groveton, she paid the grocery bill once a week, on Saturday morning. It was the custom, then, at the Excelsior Meat Market, for the grocer to take and count the money due him, and then, graciously, to fill a paper bag with a good supply of candy, "free for nothing." It gave her an idea.

She got Louis to build her a large functional blackboard, over which she placed a print of the Blessed Family, and on this blackboard she wrote in her fanciest calligraphy the names of each of her children immediately after their baptism. During the week, whenever indicated, she placed a mark, in white chalk for a good deed, in red chalk for a bad one, opposite the child's name. By solemn agreement with the grocer, the child with the best showing—a profit in good marks—got personal possession on Saturday morning of the whole bag of candies to dispose of as he or she saw fit.

Fair allowances were made for a child before his First Holy Communion, but very few after that, and none after Confirmation. Not until marriage were their names to be removed from the blackboard. Maman often gave fair warnings in a soft, even voice, or firm hints. Never once did she raise her voice to secure discipline and good behavior in this house full of rambunctious children. Whether the act committed by anyone was reprehensible or commendable, she stopped immediately whatever she'd been doing, approached the blackboard, and solemnly placed the mark of her judgment upon it, oppo-site the name, or names, concerned.

As the children grew, the act itself of passing speechless judgment never failed to bring on a great silence: in time it became a sacred ritual. Each of them, as they grew, at least once, scorned the blackboard and what it meant, but when Louis came home, on Friday night or Saturday noon, he cast a steely eye on it first thing, and this no one could ignore. He often raised his voice when he began to count the red marks, but never his hand. For the blackboard was also the key to his happy friendship. Whether bad or good, each child got his agreed money allowance, but too many red marks caused Louis to display a mountain of sadness whenever he had to tell one of his children: "For the moment, you are not my friend. Next week, perhaps, but right now, no!"

There was, suddenly, very little time for Louis's education. He had to forego reading and writing, but he organized, as he went along, his own homespun system of mathematics—he needed it every day in his work! This system forever chal-lenged deciphering by everyone, including Cécile.

"Your Papa," she said once, "can figure costs of construc-tion from blueprints, and come closer to the right answers than many a better educated man. The Lord Himself alone knows how he does it. And he never makes any mistakes!"

"The Lord," asked Laurent, dubiously, "or Papa?"

Now, the moans from Maman's bedroom seemed to increase, broken by bitter little cries of distress, and Louis decided that the time had come, maybe, to consider asking one of the ladies in the house—one of Maman's friends—to come and talk women-talk with her. When he heard a knock on the door, he said out loud: "We are saved!"

Two snowmen came in, one carrying a black satchel. He

was Doctor Lafrance. He was tall and thin, and sported his good clothes, his mustache and his authority with cool elegance. He had brought into the world Thérèse, Félix, Emile and Marie. While he took off his coat, Louis served him a quick shot of whisky against the cold and the ever-present threat of *la grippe*. Now, he walked quietly into Maman's bedroom, and came out immediately, with a quiet, confident look on his face.

"Hmmmmmmm," he mused, looking at everyone. "Well, then, Thérèse, I need an assistant here."

"Me?" she nearly screamed.

"Yes, yes. You! The only woman in the house!"

"*Bon*, Doctor Lafrance," she agreed, as her face took on a special radiance.

Doctor Lafrance put his arms around her and took her into the bedroom.

Every time Maman groaned now, and whenever Lafrance came out and snapped orders, and returned to Maman, Louis turned toward his children and spoke calm words.

"Now, my children, observe how a good doctor goes about his business. It is good to watch a man who knows his job doing it well. Watch a good man at his work, for this is Art! Now, I know your Maman will be all right."

Still rubbing his hands from the cold outside, Laurent came up to his Papa.

"Should we not recite the Rosary?" he asked.

"Hell, no!" exclaimed Louis, suddenly frightened. "That's for the dying, and I'm concentrating on the living. . . ."

When Doctor Lafrance came out again, he said, this time, that it would be best to get a nurse. . . . Madame Martel would need a nurse tomorrow, anyway, he knew one down the street, not expensive, Laurent could go and get her, he might as well get her now, and this nurse was very good in cases like these. . . . Laurent dressed again and was gone.

Now, Thérèse came out, her hair ruffled, beads of perspiration on her forehead. . . .

"Papa," she said, "the doctor said I was a good nurse. . . ."

"Yes," said Louis, and he hugged her, "and thank you."

He looked around at his children. They were sleepy and yet no one moved toward his or her own bedroom. Nowhere was there a listening mind and heart for any story, just sheer worry and fear. . . . There was just sheer worry and fear in his own heart, as if the world of snow and ice and illness had submerged, once again, as it did every winter in Acadee, the home he knew as a boy. . . .

Acadee! Sweet Acadee-ee!

It was one o'clock. Emile dozed, his head and arm on the kitchen table, and Maman was having a hard time. Only Thérèse seemed to keep up her composure and alertness, as she bustled around, fixing tea for the doctor, and the nurse, a tall, thin and wordless woman. Now she fixed a tea-whisky for her Papa, and her brother Laurent, who'd been in and out of the snow. Several times Louis suggested to them that they go to bed, but they did not move, and when they did not, he said he sure appreciated their company.

Now Maman's moans were low, continuous and weaker.

"I think," said Maurice suddenly, "we should get Father Giroux!"

"Why?" asked Laurent. "Maman went to confession, received, just yesterday."

"Well," said Maurice, "a priest around is a sign of good fortune. Isn't that right, Papa?"

"Right now," he said slowly, "all we need is a doctor, and we have him. Besides, good Father Giroux is not at his best in the darkness of a sickroom. Like an undertaker he looks, ahead of the timetable. . . ."

Laurent and Maurice giggled. Thérèse smiled. Félix stirred

and Emile woke up, stared toward Maman's room.

"Maman will be all right," Louis announced, "and soon I want you all to go to bed. Now, my sweet Thérèse, fix me another of those excellent tea-whiskies, and I'll tell you why your Maman will come through this very well. . . ."

Félix opened up his eyes fully, and Emile shook his head all the better to see. Louis sipped on his tea-whisky.

"Near the end of our first year," he began, "it was July, I do believe, and we lived then in the White Mountains. Well, one night, in the middle of the night, it began to thunder, and when it thunders in the White Mountains, my children, it's like the Devil himself on horseback with a toothache. . . ."

The children settled to listen.

"Well, sir, your Maman has always been afraid of thunder, and that night those loud claps of thunder really terrified her. As it was the custom in her village, during big thunderstorms, she got up and sprinkled holy water into all the corners of the two-room apartment where we lived. . . . Now, once that was properly done, she came back to bed and immediately went to sleep like a baby. Your Maman has great faith in holy water, and she is right, for wasn't the house safe for the night? Well, sir, the next evening, I came home from work and reached for my bottle of whisky—for a quick nip before supper. . . ."

"Oh, oh!" said Laurent.

"Well, sir, I cast my eyes where my whisky bottle was kept. There was the holy water bottle brimful, and my whisky bottle bone-dry."

"No!" gasped Thérèse, scandalized.

"It was a delicate situation. You see, your Maman knew I enjoyed that little nip before supper. In fact, she usually served it to me herself. This was the problem: if she knew, she would have wondered how the house had been so well protected. Thunder, to her, is the voice of God direct, when in a bad mood! On the other hand, I knew she enjoyed serving me a drink—we were still fresh-married. . .”

"*Tonnerre!*" exclaimed Maurice.

"Well?" gasped Thérèse.

"Well, sir," continued Louis, "before I knew it, with a great big smile of love in her eyes for me, and blind to anything else, your Maman had poured out into my shot glass a large nip of holy water. 'Here, *mon amour!*' she said shyly and handed it to me."

"Papa!" exclaimed Thérèse, pity in her voice. "Poor Papa!"

"I was caught! I reached for the glass, and raised it toward her and said: '*Santé, ma chérie!*' and bravely gulped the stale but sacred water, as best I could. I know today that God understood my sacrifice and so, my children, your Maman will be all right. She's the only creature I know who's been toasted in holy water." He chuckled at this. "And now, to bed!"

The next morning, at dawn, one by one, the children came running out of their cold rooms to finish their dressing near the hot stove. First thing they saw, each in turn, was the nurse, in a plain white smock, tall, thin and wordless. Laurent and Maurice looked at one another, then nodded in agreement, and Laurent cleared his throat, but Thérèse simply walked up to her.

"Good morning, nurse," she said.

As if awakened by this, she answered, "Good morning," and then she smiled. She pointed toward the table and the children saw that she was ready for them with flapjacks, French toast, maple syrup, tea and milk. Now suddenly, Thérèse became shy—this nurse seemed so cold—and she sat at the table and the others did the same, and they ate and looked at one another, asking with their eyes the terrible question, and signaled to Laurent—was he not the oldest?—to ask the terrible question. He cleared his throat, but Louis himself came bouncing out of Maman's room. He was clean-shaven, there was a glimmer of a tear in his eyes, but his voice sang out.

"My children, straight from heaven she came, a precious little bundle of a girl!"

Everyone cheered, except the nurse.

"And Maman?" asked Thérèse.

"Didn't I promise you she'd be all right? Well, she is!"

Everyone cheered, and the nurse smiled.

"*Mon Dieu!*" she murmured. "It's only another baby!"

"Ah," said Louis, "but this is a Martel baby!"

He went up to the nurse, put his arms around her, squeezed her, and then, while the children roared in delight, he gave her a big wet kiss. She blushed.

"You are a crazy family!" she announced.

"Papa!" screamed Thérèse, "can we visit? Can we, please?"

"For sure!" said Louis.

For sure, my children, you can visit, but Maman is resting, and so is the new baby from the long voyage to this earth, and, my children, it is the time for the quiet moment and for the use of the tip of the toes, and time to go in, as if in church at High Mass, and to go in turn, one by one, Marie, the youngest to be first, and then Thérèse, and then the boys, and to say: "*Bienvenue, p'tite soeur!*" but to themselves, not to the whole world—yet. For these two are tired from the long night. Oh, yes, one might kiss Maman, but gently, and the baby too, very gently. . . . And while they did this, it was time for him to unwrap the silver cup for the new baby, as he had for all the others, and he did, and now he put it on the table for the children to admire. . . .

Then, one by one, the children returned and began to fill up the kitchen with their chatter, before getting ready to go to school. Oh, sure, they all agreed they had a nice, sweet little sister, and suddenly they agreed also that she should be called Cécile.

"Cécile?" asked Louis.

Oh, yes, they said, and he said nothing, and now the outcry became unanimous, persistent and loud. He lit his pipe, then suddenly he remembered, put his pipe out, and reached for the box of cigars in the armoire, and lit one. His face a total blank, he then handed one to Laurent. His first-born took it with his five fingers spread out, as if it were loaded.

"Cécile, eh?" he asked his children, and puffed on his cigar. "So be it!" he conceded, and again there were cheers. Cécile, he thought, was the first and only one in my life, and this Cécile. . . . she shall be the last.

"So be it," agreed Laurent, lighting his cigar with a frightened air.

This settled, Louis then reached for the bottle of whisky and put it on the table near the baby silver cup. Now, wasn't that an idea, he thought. He poured the whisky into the silver cup, as the children laughed, then he turned toward Laurent, thought better of it—after all, this boy was still going to school—and then he raised the baby cup in a toast.

"To little Cécile!" he said, "and may God be as kind to her as He has been to all my children!"

Frantically all the children reached for their tea or milk and raised their cups and glasses, and also a chorus: "To Cécile!"

Félix was the first to drain his milk down and Louis thought he heard him whisper something to Emile. He hadn't quite heard what he said, but Emile heard it and he choked in laughter as he finished his own drink.

Louis poured more whisky into the baby cup—he estimated it held about a shot and a half—and he raised it again in a toast.

"To Cécile!" he said. And with this seventh living child, he resolved, Cécile and I have finished our work. Out loud, he said to Laurent:

"Amen!"

"Amen!" agreed Laurent, puffing warily on his cigar.

Marie came over to her Papa to be picked up. He did, and kissed her nose and her forehead, and hugged her. Little Marie, he thought, is no longer the queen, and to be dethroned like this, it hurts. And he kissed her again and caressed her cheeks, and she rested quietly in his lap, a serious expression on her face. . . .

He looked toward the kitchen window. Night winds had etched on the windowpanes snapshots of the North Pole, dazzling skating rinks, whitened forests, advancing icebergs, and frosty angels' wings. . . . What a night for a little girl to travel to earth! And, *bonguienne*, it was still snowing. Emile was standing in front of him. He was up to something, for the smile he hid behind his lips was not a Sunday-go-to-Mass smile. . . . He patted his cheek gently, anyway. . . .

"Papa," he asked, "Félix says . . . the baby is a little girl, yes?"

"Yes, son, the baby is a girl." Now he waited.

"Yes, and Félix says that little girls. . ."

"Yes, Emile . . ."

". . . that little girls are a pain in the ass, and . . ."

A big yahoo of a laugh it was that Louis Martel let go, and it scared away the bears, the devil and all bad things of the night, it even invited the children to laugh gaily also, but it woke up Maman. And little Cécile too, for there soon arose from within Maman's room a thin wail. . . .

The children were putting on their warm clothes to go to school, but they stopped to turn toward Maman's room, and to listen, and to wonder, and so did Louis Martel.

2. The Pledge [1921]

"This is the night," Louis Martel told himself.

It had been a long hot summer to abstain from all strong drinks, and beer too. And tonight, on this Saturday, the nineteenth day of August, at six o'clock, in exactly forty-five minutes, the pledge would run out its time, and he would drown this thirty-day dry spell with one, two, and perhaps three shots of whisky. No, he would never take another pledge in his life to abstain. . . . Never again!

He sat in the kitchen in his easy chair calmly waiting for six o'clock to come around on the chime clock he had bought in the first year of their married life—Maman had liked the chimes so much and it had cost a lot of money, but what the hell! And he saw that it was five-sixteen. . . . Maman checked the meat in the stove and Thérèse, now fourteen, sliced the peaches and sugared them for the shortcake.

Laurent sat next to him and read the *Sporting News.* At eighteen, he had now graduated from high school, worked with him as an apprentice-carpenter, brought money home and officially courted Hélène Pelletier, age seventeen, the shy, moon-faced daughter of the owner of the house where they lived. . . . Once he had surprised them in a close embrace in the hall between both floors. They had not seen him, and he had refused to see them, but he'd told Maman.

"Those two!" she'd said, amused.

"Reminds me of Adam and Eve!" Louis had answered. "There'll be something doing when the leaves begin to fall."

Suddenly it was five twenty-eight. In the chair near the kitchen table, Maurice, the current family reader, read aloud from *A Life of Napoléon*. Near him, fresh from a hasty scrubbing, their hair painfully combed, sat Emile and Félix. They listened to Maurice, more or less. Marie also listened and sucked her thumb, but Cécile rocked in the little rocker near her Papa and made words silently that imitated Maurice's.

It was still five twenty-eight. *Bonguienne*, had it stopped? No, it ticked-tocked away, soon it would be six, and never again would he take such a foolish pledge. Well, not foolish, really. It would be too bold to say that. However, had it been necessary? At the time, yes. It was the only thing left to do for Thérèse. She was now helping her Maman set the table. She looked good today, now that she was fully recovered and God had done it because he, Louis, had promised. . . . Her legs needed some fat—she was all legs and shoulders and bones—her hips were as flat as a boy's, but graceful as a deer. What a change from thirty days ago, less thirty-two minutes. . . . When she came up to him, near to tears, chilled to the bone, on a hot July afternoon. . . .

"Papa," she said, trembling, "I'm cold and sweating, and I feel ill at ease all over!"

A shot of whisky in hot tea, and he ordered her to bed. Dr. Lafrance came. He took her temperature. His eyebrows jumped, and he turned to Maman. She explained that Thérèse had gone swimming that morning in the cold waters of Metaska Pond, that she'd been all steamed up from running wildly with her chums. Temperature: 103-plus.

Dr. Lafrance tried everything he knew. He asked for another doctor and they both tried everything they knew. Nothing they did brought the temperature down. Thérèse began to talk incoherently.

"Lou," said Dr. Lafrance, "I don't know what ails your little girl, but we'll see." He rubbed his cheek and a frown appeared on his forehead. "For sure, she'll need a nurse. Somebody must be with her all night. Get this prescription filled, and I'll get you a nurse."

"*Mon Dieu!*" said Maman.

"Now, now," said Dr. Lafrance, "she'll be all right. Even if I have to get on my knees and start praying."

He used the last expression lightly, but it always had the result of preparing people for the worst.

"I'll do the praying," said Louis, "you trot your ass and get the nurse."

Maman began to sob.

"Now, Madame Martel," said Dr. Lafrance impatiently, "I always put things at their worst, you know that."

She agreed quietly but continued to sob. Muttering to himself, the doctor assembled all the family in the kitchen, sat down in a chair near the large kitchen table and called in turn for Laurent, the oldest, and then Maurice, Félix, Emile, Marie and Cécile, now aged two. He told them each to open their mouths, to say "Ah," he scrutinized their throats, their faces, placed his hand roughly on their necks, felt their throats, thumped their chests, made them cough and listened; he took their temperatures and when Cécile began to whimper he patted her derrière, then hugged her and gave her a large Canadian penny he kept for such occasions. . . . Then he picked up his little black bag.

"I'll be back later tonight, Lou!" he shouted, and left.

Maman wiped her tears and turned toward Louis. All of them began to walk slowly toward Thérèse's bedroom.

"Well, Louis?"

He shrugged his shoulders helplessly.

"Influenza!" she announced firmly, as if this were a command to him to do something right away.

"No," said Louis slowly. "No, no, no!"

"Yes," said Maman, "I have seen *la grande grippe* before!"

Louis stood against the wall leading to Thérèse's bedroom and let his head fall slowly against his chest. Everyone crowded around him. *La grande grippe!* He saw 1918 again. Three years ago. So many people had died in a matter of days from the dread epidemic. He saw again a white casket—Whose had it been?—Yes! Boudreau's little girl. Children who go to God in their years of innocence are buried in a white casket, a symbol of purity. Was Thérèse too old already, or would they use a white casket?

"Dear God!" said Louis aloud. Well, now, what could a man do? A man could start with the Sign of the Cross. He did. "Dear God," he said, "make her well! Make her well again, because You can do it. And if Thérèse recovers, and you make her well and sassy again, I promise anything—anything! I know! For thirty days I shall not touch liquor—hard liquor, I mean—If this be Thy will, that she get well, my heart will be very grateful. May Thy will be done, of course, but make her well, and Amen!"

"Amen!" said Laurent.

"Please, God?" begged Maman.

This done, Louis stood up, his full six feet two, and turned his head toward everyone. He was very calm. He smiled—just a bit.

"If anything can fix up Thérèse," he said with finality, "this ought to do it."

The nurse arrived half an hour later—a big-boned woman with an efficient roughness of manner. Dr. Lafrance came in again at midnight. He checked Thérèse, muttered a few brusque words to the nurse—he was physically exhausted—and then left, announcing that he would come by early in the morning. Then, as an afterthought, he ordered everybody to go to bed. That's what was wrong, he said, folks never went to bed enough, and soon enough! More cure in bed, he barked, than in any pill!

At nine, the following morning, he knocked at the door, and while he poured himself a cup of tea, the nurse breathlessly told him that the temperature had dropped to 99—the poor little girl had perspired streams all night. At six that evening, she was out of danger. And at that precise moment, Louis reached for his bottle of whisky. . .

"Louis!" Maman nearly screamed. "You promised!"

"*Marde!*" he answered.

He stopped dead in his tracks, as if struck by lightning. But he kept the pledge, lest God return the fever to Thérèse and punish him for not keeping his word. And now the pledge was done and finished and he sat in his easy chair. All month long he had encouraged himself with one single sentence.

"It will taste better for the waiting."

The clock said it was five thirty-four. Come to think of it, had the pledge been really necessary? Dr. Lafrance had said later that his medicine had broken the fever. Well, he hadn't known about the pledge, but suppose'n his medicine had really cured Thérèse? Suppose'n the pledge had been nothing but another prayer, and Thérèse would have been cured anyway? He'd gone all these hot summer days with the great thirst unquenched—for nothing? Could such things be? After all, a man need not read the Latin, or the French, and the English, for that matter, to ask the big solid questions. . . .

Five thirty-five.

After all, a pledge was really a contract—like any other contract—but this had been one with God. If He did something for you, you pledged yourself to do something unpleasant that would please God. It was sort of a bargain. Now, the solid question was: did God really enjoy the sight of an honest man abstaining from an honest drink of whisky after an honest day's work? Could not God cure Thérèse simply because it was a wonderful thing to do in itself? Ah, that was the big question in any language. A frightening question, and better to let it be.

Five thirty-six.

Let it be. It was bad luck to ask, even within yourself, certain questions. Something bad always happened right after. Some of the questions Maman was asking herself, for instance. Only she was doing the asking good and loud, about the schools. The parochial schools her children were attending. They were good Catholic schools, Louis thought, but Maman did not. Not good enough for her. The Sisters spent too much time with the children in church, in processions . . . and not enough in classrooms, at the job of learning. Well, it was bad luck to fight the priest, and the sisters, everybody knew that. That too was big question. That was the big question: when did you do as they told you and when did you tell them they were full of wood shavings?

Five thirty-seven.

There was one thing he'd never understood, anyway. Regularly, during homework, children had to figure how much time it took to fill a bathtub with water with three faucets of different sizes: Faucet A, a large one; Faucet B, a medium one; and Faucet C, a small one; or used one and not the other two. . . . Impractical. In all his years of housebuilding, he'd never seen a tub with three such faucets. . . . Another thing. Never mind. It was bad luck to argue with the priest.

Let us dwell upon pleasant things. Ah, yes! That batch of

applejack he and Pete Young had cached away in the cellar, below, at this very moment. And just about ready for tasting. Now, surely, there was nothing evil about that!

Five thirty-eight.

How Pete Young hated to spend hard cash for liquor! Well, since he had the stills and the yen to experiment in distilling alcohol from most anything, particularly from choice, ripe apples pressed into cider, what was wrong in that? Besides, he and his wife were an elderly couple retired on a modest income, who lived a few streets from the Martels on Chestnut Street. He had once been in plumbing supplies and Louis had purchased much material from him.

"A Protestant, a Henglishman, and an honest man," Louis thought. How long was it now since they had become firm friends on sight? Years. Pete was a pillar of the Pine Street Congregational Church and that was excellent, and Louis went to Sacred Heart, and that was excellent, and they had understood one another right away, as men who enjoyed the same jokes understood everything else. When they decided that in an era of legalized dryness it would be fitting and proper for them to make their own drinks, their friendship became sealed.

They formed a partnership. Assets: Pete's two stills and Louis's knowledge of the best apples to make good cider; liabilities: Pete's wife objected not only to the manufacture of alcoholic drinks, but to alcohol as well. Now they had a barrel of applejack, and a few days before they were to test it, Pete told Louis that his wife had begun to sniff around. To save their assets—their first batch—a bold move was necessary—a move to a safer place than his backyard.

And so Louis had invited Jacques Pelletier, Hélène's father, to join the partnership. He owned the house where he lived, Laurent was courting his daughter, and he had a large cellar that no one was using at the moment. And, last night,

Pelletier, Pete Young and Louis had loaded the batch into a barrel and into a Ford truck and quietly delivered it into the cellar below, behind a discarded chiffonier.

"What now?" Pelletier had asked. "Can't leave it here."

"We'll split it three ways," said Pete, "after we test it."

"When?" said Pelletier. He was a property owner and he knew the Law.

"Sunday night," said Louis.

"I can't be here," said Pelletier uneasily.

"We'll save your share," said Louis.

It was five thirty-nine.

Maurice read on and on. Napoléon, now, had fought his first battle with his famous artillery, had won his first bit of glory, had entered into the great days of the Consulate, and the campaign of Egypt. This reading was in line with Maman's current program to introduce her family to the great men of the world—Caesar, Alexander, Charlemagne, Genghis Khan, Louis XIV, Abraham Lincoln, as well as to the great Saints of the Church—Vincent de Paul, François de Sales, Jeanne d'Arc. Occasionally, Maman broke the pattern by reading herself, quietly and with proper gestures, one of the great French or English novels not on the Index.

"Forty centuries gaze upon you," read Maurice in monotone. And Emile and Félix gazed in turn on Napoléon as he stood before the Sphinx of Egypt and urged his Republican troops to do battle against the enemy.

Now Louis abandoned Napoléon to his fate in Egypt and returned to Groveton, Maine, and his eyes rested on the old clock. Emile brought him back to Egypt quickly.

"Papa," he asked, "Napoléon, was he a brave man?"

"Do not interrupt, Emile," said Maman.

"He was a brave man," said Louis, "and he had a lot of soldiers. A brave man is one who, without soldiers, is brave before the big, solid questions. . . ."

"Napoléon! Napoléon!" muttered Thérèse, bored.

"Shush!" said Maman. "You were very quiet the other day when I read *Les Misérables*."

"Oh, that!" exclaimed Thérèse. "That was real life, that was sublime!" And she embraced a tablecloth fondly.

Maman walked up to Maurice, took the book gently away from him and handed it to Thérèse, who gasped.

"It's time for you to be the family reader," announced Maman. She went to the blackboard and put a white mark against Maurice's name.

"Maurice reads very well," she concluded.

"Yes, he does," said Louis, smacking his lips. Silently he noted that, *bonguienne*, suddenly, it was almost six o'clock.

Thérèse now began to read the chapter that would lead to Napoléon's great victory at Marengo and complete control of France. She over-pronounced each word, slurred a few, became completely stumped before one or two, but no one laughed, for this was a grave infraction of the rules, punishable by three red marks. If one wanted to laugh, or one simply had to laugh—a thing which in itself was never discouraged—one must leave the room immediately and go and laugh quietly somewhere else. Now Thérèse was going full steam ahead toward the coronation of Napoléon at Notre Dame when the ceremony was stopped short. Félix jumped up to go and open the door.

"It's Father Giroux," he stated simply, and stood there immobilized.

"So," said Maman, "invite Father in!" and she wiped her hands against her apron and a big smile came to her face.

Father François Giroux, a tall man in his fifties, slightly given to fat, white hair, soft spoken, wore his clerical mufti and Roman collar with old-fashioned dignity. A quiet man, he usually kept his hands to his side and gestured at the most with short nods and shakes of his head. Though he'd been named curé of Sacred Heart three years ago, he had been sick most of the time, and was, as far as his parishioners were concerned, very much a "new" priest.

"Ah, Monsieur Martel," he beamed toward him, "you don't know me, but I have heard about you, and only good things, I assure you!"

"People will gossip," said Louis, smiling.

"I hope," said Father Giroux, "that I'm not interrupting supper." He sat down wearily in the nearest available chair, which happened to be Louis's easy chair.

"Ah, no!" purred Maman. "Besides, Father, of what importance is that?"

"Man," said Louis coolly, "does not live by food alone, but when he's hungry, it helps."

"Will you take something, Father?" Maman asked quickly.

"No, no. Thank you, Madame Martel."

"Tea, perhaps?" said Maman.

"Or perhaps something a little stronger?" suggested Louis.

"No, no tea, thank you. I've come because September is so near and the special school money is due." He allowed the rest of his thought to be understood without words. He was tired. He had climbed stairs all day and had perhaps repeated the same speech many times in the last few hours. Maman turned toward Louis.

"I have it," said he, reaching deeply into his pants pocket for the folding leather pocketbook. He took out four dollars—one each for Maurice, Emile, Félix and Thérèse—and handed them to the priest.

"That was fast," said he, relieved. "I wish I had it as easy everywhere. Therefore, thank you twice, Monsieur Martel."

"We know you have many other calls to make," said Louis

gently, going for the door with great speed.

"Father. . ." began Maman.

"Not now," snapped Louis, his eyes shooting bullets at her.

"Father," said Maman, "we contribute to the special school fund, and we do so gladly, and we send Maurice and Thérèse to St. Michel's High School, and Félix and Emile to the Academy. . ."

"Not now, Cécile," said Louis. "The supper will get cold."

"And," continued Maman, "we were wondering if the curriculum does not leave something to be desired. . . ."

"The curriculum?" gasped Father Giroux.

"Yes," said Maman, more firmly now.

"In what way, Madame Martel?"

"In this way. I wonder if it couldn't be changed a little bit."

"Changed? Madame Martel, now, let me tell you. . . ."

"Right now, Father, allow me to tell you, please. You see, I taught school before I was married. . . ."

"Oh, did you, now?"

"Yes, and I think, Father, if you'll forgive me, that too much school time is devoted to things, at St. Michel's and at the Academy, which, while meritorious in themselves, do not strictly come under the heading of reading, writing, mathematics, history, and other purely educational subjects."

"For instance?"

"You know what I mean," said Maman quietly.

"You mean," said Father Giroux, "religious holidays, and time off for religious services? Surely, you don't mean that?"

"I do," said Maman. "That is precisely what I mean. These, and other extracurricular activities, should be done, but after school hours."

Father Giroux looked at Maman kindly, then at Louis, then let his eyes rove slowly over the children who listened intently. He smiled.

"It's an old complaint," he said finally. "I have heard it elsewhere before I came to Groveton, and yet our Catholic graduates compare more than favorably with public school graduates. . . ."

"Not with me," said Maman crisply. "I'm not satisfied with the way my own children read—I won't mention names right now, before them—but they begin to read and write long after they should. I know because I look into it regularly, and furthermore, they are not learning sufficiently the English language. . . ."

"English?" snapped Father Giroux. "Why, they have an average of half an hour a week."

"Not enough in an English-speaking country," said Maman coldly.

"And they don't get enough math, history, science, civics for any civilized country. If I did not teach my children myself, they would not do well at all. Not well enough for me, in any case."

"Madame Martel . . ." the priest began.

"You see, Father," she continued implacably, "I do think they ought to learn their Catechism, but the boys should have a chance at good vocational training, and the girls at housekeeping and cooking. . . ."

"All that takes money," shot in the priest quickly.

"It takes also imagination," said Maman, "and less days off from strictly schoolwork."

"Would you have them come to school on holidays?"

"No," said Maman, suddenly shy, "but you add up the full school hours they have in school on schoolwork, and the hours they spend away from school for special religious ceremonies, retreats, saint's birthdays, priest's birthdays, and compare them with a public school. . . ."

"Surely, you don't plan to send your children to a public school?"

"Father, I'm determined that my children will have the best in any school that is prepared to give them the best."

"Surely, Madame Martel, you don't object if the good Sisters and teachers take the children to religious ceremonies when they happen to fall on school days?"

"I do. Let them go before or after school hours."

"I agree with that," said Louis suddenly.

Father Giroux threw up his hands in the air impatiently.

"Father, I mean what I say," continued Maman. "Some day they will marry and for that they must know their religion, but they will have children, I hope, and for that they will have to earn a living, and for that they need a well-rounded education, the best available to them."

"And," concluded Father Giroux sadly, "you don't think they are getting that?"

"Father, please believe me. You are new here. Give me your word you'll look into it. That is all I ask."

"I shall do just that," said Father Giroux firmly.

"Good," said Louis jovially, "very good," noting that it was already half past six. This time he opened the door.

"Now," said Father Giroux, as he sighed in relief from the thorny subject and changed his position in the chair the better to face Louis, "there is something else. . . ."

"Something else?" shot out Louis with a dead voice. He closed the door. He very nearly slammed it.

"I believe," said Father Giroux, "that . . ."

Louis stared at the priest, at the middle button of his black vest, but he was hearing nothing. The voice of the priest was a distant cascade of empty words coming with monotonous rhythm against his ears, but he was hearing nothing. Just for this long delay, he would put three full shots of whisky into his glass. He would drop large chunks of ice into it and mix it sparingly with ginger ale, stir it vigorously and drink it in silence. He might chase the whole thing down with a cold, foaming glass of beer. . . . He would drink this down. . . . Maybe he could do it right now! No, better to drink it later, away from this chatter. . . . He might even test the applejack tonight, just for that . . .

"And so, Monsieur Martel, what do you think?"

"I think. . ."said Louis. He stopped suddenly and turned toward Maman. She was looking at him, and her smile was like an iceberg. There was a giggle visible at the top, on her lips, but underneath, only suspected, was a great big guffaw.

"This campaign," went on the priest, "would originate among decent men of the parish. It is a shame that, in this city, pay day, which should be spent purchasing the needs of the family, has become a day of anguish, as the breadwinner stops at the saloon, or at the illegal distributor, or worse yet, at the home manufacturer, and spends a goodly part of his earnings to drink, to get drunk and to lose his reason. . . ."

Louis's face became a dark, dark cloud. This was, indeed, the last straw. A man's castle was built of little liberties, little indulgences, little pure sins, rewards for avoiding the big, dirty sins, retaining walls against the nosiness of some people. . . . This was the last straw!

Marie suddenly smiled at Father Giroux. He stopped talking a moment to pass his hand over her cheek. He smiled affectionately at her, and Marie blushed and ran into Maman's arms.

"You have a nice family, Monsieur Martel," he now continued softly. "You are blessed by God, and I happen to know that you do not drink, is that right?"

The time had come. Louis cleared his throat. Not fast enough, however.

"Not now," said Maman. There was piety on her lips, but laughter begged to break out in her eyes.

Father Giroux turned solemnly toward everybody.

"Oh, I have heard. I have heard that you took a pledge on your own against the curse of drink . . ."

"But, Father . . ." began Thérèse.

"We must not interrupt," said Maman kindly.

"Now," continued the priest, "I too believe in a campaign of pledges—we could have buttons printed for the men to wear, and placards to be put into stores—a pledge whereby men would swear off forever . . ."

"Forever?" barked Louis.

"Forever," continued the priest, "to abstain from . . ."

"Forever," remarked Louis dryly, "is one . . . one long time."

"It is," admitted the priest, "but such a campaign would have tremendous moral and financial effects. Think of the money, now thrown away in liquor that dulls the senses. . . ."

"Indeed," agreed Maman primly, not daring to look at Louis.

". . . Money," continued the priest, "that could be saved for a new winter overcoat, or put into savings, or kept for family emergencies. Think of mothers able to feed their children better, think of the better schools we could build. . . ."

"Indeed," agreed Maman, smiling now toward Louis.

"And think of the family with the father in good health, at home, every Saturday night. . . ." concluded Father Giroux.

"With or without liquor," said Louis firmly, "I'm home every Saturday night! Isn't that right, Cécile?" Where was his lifetime companion and partner in this fight?

Maman got up quickly—her lips frozen in an impish grin— excused herself—this was too much!—and vanished into another room. Louis knew he could hear her giggle, holding to her sides she was, and he knew that Father Giroux could hear her too. Push me, Louis Martel, and you'll find you've struck a stone wall!

"Now," said the priest. He looked directly at him. "What I

want from you, Monsieur Martel, along with other decent men of your caliber, is a solemn pledge in church, that you will abstain from all liquor . . . that is, hard liquor."

Louis cleared his throat once more.

"That pledge," he said calmly, "I shall not take, Father."

He put his right hand into his left and shook it.

Father Giroux was taken aback, then slowly he lowered his head, and there was a long silence. Louis decided he would not break it first. Then Maman suddenly returned, pushing Emile ahead of her. He was a thin boy with a high forehead and an alert manner. Maman placed him squarely in front of Father Giroux, and there he stood respectfully, wondering why. Maman assumed a light tone of voice.

"Yes," she chatted on, filling the silence, "when Emile was baptized, the holy water formed a silvery cross on his head. Temporarily, of course. He was hairless, so the cross was either an accident or . . ." And she raised her eyebrows.

"Or a sign," suggested Father Giroux kindly. He looked toward Louis and his blank face. A wall, that's what I am, a reinforced concrete wall, he answered back without words.

"Maybe," said the priest kindly, "but one must wait for God to show the way, Madame Martel. One must not push the child."

"Or anyone else," added Louis.

"Oh, no," agreed Maman, "but he shows such remarkable aptitudes. Already, he's a little theologian!"

"Besides," added Louis, "look at that high forehead. To me, that's boldness, imagination, tenacity. How can he become anything else but a priest or a crook!"

"Louis!" said Maman, in alarm.

"Surely a priest then," said Father Giroux, laughing heartily.

"Maybe a bishop!" exclaimed Maman, looking at Emile with pride.

"I hope so," said the priest matter-of-factly. "I see I'll have to speak to you privately," he added with that certain look toward Louis and Maman. Maman told Laurent he was in charge of the blackboard and then led the priest and Papa into the *parloir*. When the door was safely closed, and the children could not possibly hear, the priest composed himself.

"We have had," he announced, "in the parish, last night, an unusual death. A Monsieur Dumais."

"Oh!" sympathized Maman.

"Poisoning. Bad alcohol," continued the priest.

"Applejack?" asked Maman, with a dark look toward Louis.

"It is not known yet," said the priest. "Now, Monsieur Martel, as a result, a few decent men are meeting tomorrow night at the school auditorium of St. Michel's High School, and I would appreciate it if you would come too and bring some of your many friends. . . ."

"He will, certainly," said Maman quickly.

"Nobody speaks for me, Cécile," announced Louis.

"These decent men," continued the priest, "will take a mass solemn pledge neither to drink, nor buy, nor manufacture alcoholic spirits, including beer and wine. I ask you, Monsieur, will you join us?"

"Father," said Louis firmly, "exclude me out. I cannot honestly say that I'll never again take a hard drink. In fact, I know that I will take several come next Christmas, or if the flu attacks me, or even tonight, if I feel like it. . . ."

"Now, Monsieur Martel, drinking in excess is a mortal sin. . . ."

"Also poor judgment."

"Liquor is an evil thing!"

"No, it isn't."

"Even if the Bishop said so?"

Louis turned toward Maman. The death of a man was a frightening matter, and Maman was frightened. Well, he was not. Who knew what that man had drunk? Well, he, Louis Martel, was not frightened by this propaganda. A wall he said he was and a wall he would be.

"Has the Pope," he asked, "said so? In so many words?"

"No, but. . . ." said the priest quietly.

"He's an Eyetalian," said Louis. "He likes his guiney red, too!"

"His Holiness," stated the priest calmly, "has often expressed his sorrow at the families ravaged by the drunkenness of the father. . . ."

"Has he ever said that drinking was a mortal sin?"

"No, not just like that."

"Then, Father, we shouldn't be more Catholic than the Pope. His Holiness is infallible, Father, but you and I are not."

"Louis!" said Maman, shocked.

"He's quite right," said the priest humbly. "I'm not infallible, but I consider it my duty to warn my people."

"I agree with you on that," said Louis more calmly now, "but don't scare 'em out of a few drinks for fear of mortal sins. A shot of whisky at the right time and place peps up and tones the soul of Man. Meaning no disrespect, Father, but when you leave, I do believe I'm going to have a drink, for there are days when nothing else will quiet a man's spirit."

"You are a hard man to convince," admitted Father Giroux. "You're like a cement wall!"

The priest chuckled and then slowly got up from his chair. Louis chuckled also, politely.

"Father, will you have some tea?" Maman asked softly.

"No, thank you, Madame Martel. *Bonsoir!*" he said, and gave everyone a nice warm smile and shook Louis's hand. "And may God bless this home!"

And then Louis closed the door, and the priest was gone, and Maman set supper on the table. In two strides Louis reached into the armoire where the whisky was kept, and served himself two shots in one glass, tilted his head back and swallowed all of it at once. He looked blankly into space, then slowly chased it down with a cold glass of beer.

"Papa!" Thérèse sang out happily. "You can drink again?"

"Yes," said he, gasping happily.

"Can I have a shot?" asked Laurent suddenly.

"No," said Louis. "It's not a holiday."

"When will I be allowed to drink like you?" insisted Laurent.

"When you get married," said Louis, enjoying his own joke. "That's when a man needs it."

"Why is Father Giroux against it?" asked Thérèse suddenly.

"Because!" said Louis. "Some folks can't drink, and they should not, and Father Giroux is their man. Me, by the grace of God, I can do it sensibly, I like it, it likes me, and Father Giroux is not going to blackmail me before my family into taking no damn temperance pledges."

"Personally," said Maurice, "it makes me feel good, Papa, when you take a little shot, light your pipe, smack your lips, and fill up the house with the aroma of your tobacco, and then put away a large glass of cold beer. I know you feel good, Papa, and I feel good, and so it must be a good thing."

"Yes," agreed Thérèse, laughing. "I like to see Papa's Adam's apple go jumpity-humpity-jump."

"It's jumping for joy," said Louis.

Maman finished putting supper on the table.

"Personally," she said, "in all the years I know your Papa, I've never know whisky to do him, or us, any harm."

"Nor dull my senses," added Louis boastfully.

"And I've never seen him drunk," said Maman.

She sat Marie and Cécile at the table, and all the children bowed their heads quickly, and Maman, last of all, the better to steal a glance at Louis. He smacked his lips and bowed his head.

"O Lord," he prayed, "we thank you again for the food we're about to eat—at long last! . . ."

Thérèse giggled. Maman frowned.

"And now, Amen!" he added curtly, and he began to cut the meat and to serve his family with all speed.

"First come, first served," he announced. "Eat as soon as you're served, lest any one of you perish from politeness. Food, my children, is not sinful—yet!"

He checked to see if all had been served, and then, as usual, he served himself, last of all.

Later, when all the children had taken their baths, kissed their Papa and Maman on both cheeks, said their prayers and gone to sleep, Louis poured himself a large cup of tea, fortified with whisky, and a small one for Maman, with brandy, and he turned to her. She drank her tea-brandy slowly.

"How on earth," he asked, "did you know we had applejack in the cellar?"

"Oh, do you, Louis?" And she broke out into laughter.

"We'll split it tomorrow night," he explained. "We are not publishing it in the newspapers, of course.'

"And not inviting Father Giroux, either."

"I say now," said Louis, "now that the children cannot hear, that that priest tends to everybody's business but his own."

"So long as he tends to the schools. . . ."

"And I say that a good stiff drink would do him great good in his holy work, and I say that, out loud, that God may hear me."

Maman finished her tea-brandy and yawned.

"It will make me sleep well," she murmured.

She left him at the table and finished little chores around her kitchen.

"Cécile," he announced, "after all, a man has so few rights, never enough fun, and so many fears. . . ."

Maman came back to him and put her hand over his shoulder and before she knew it, he had pulled her over on his lap.

"Obey the Commandments," said Louis. "Love God, love thy neighbor, but when you've done that, Cécile, you know what other commandment they should add?"

"Oh," said Maman sleepily, "another commandment you're going to give us?"

"Yep," he said, squeezing her to him, "thou shalt love God, thou shalt love thy neighbor as thyself, and thou shalt not fear!"

"It is a hard commandment," she said lightly.

"If only I could observe it myself, for there is a great and unknown fear that strangles us Catholics and only a great and abiding love of God that saves us. . . . You know, I bet God in Heaven doesn't give a hoot who does or does not drink, whether a little girl does or does not wear a veil over her head when she enters His church, who eats meats or fish on Fridays, who comes in late for Mass . . ."

"That drink," she muttered, "it makes me sleep."

"I bet," he continued, "that God cares very much if a man lives his life in dignity and pride, hurting no one if he can, above all himself. Cécile, I have a sneaky feeling that, very often, God gets a laugh out of us, and our crusades and our pledges . . ."

"That drink," she muttered, "it makes me want to sleep. . . ."

He picked her up gently and began to carry her to the bedroom.

"That drink," he murmured, "it makes me want to play. . . ."

Suddenly she chuckled against his shoulder.

"Tonight, Louis?"

"Yes, my lovely one. Fear not! Tonight, surely, Father Giroux will not return!"

At the nine o'clock Mass, the next morning, Louis heard Father Giroux thunder against the evils of drink. He repeated, in effect, to his congregation what he'd told the Martels the evening before. But now, of course, there could be no answer; however, Louis decided, tonight, *bonguienne*, we split and taste the applejack, and maybe there would be some laughs with Pete Young over a few swallows.

And so, that evening, after supper, he began to walk around the apartment restlessly while Maman gathered the children around her for a family reading of selected translations of Cervantes' *Don Quixote*. Suddenly Louis winked at Laurent, and both started for the door.

"Going out?" asked Maman.

"Yep," said Louis.

"With Laurent?" asked Maman, mystified.

"Yes," said he quietly, "and for that we need passports?"

"Where to?" asked Maman, opening her book and staring at him.

"For man-work," said he with finality.

Maurice jumped up.

"Can I go too?"

"Sure," said Louis. "Why not?"

"Me too!" shrieked Thérèse.

"No, *mon amour*," Louis purred. "This is man-work."

Thérèse made an ugly face.

"Men have all the fun," she stormed.

"No," said Maman soothingly, "all they have are their little boys' secrets. Now, Thérèse, *chérie*, maybe you can serve us a drink of Moxie, yes? That's my sweet, gentle Thérèse. Now, if you are all ready, I'll start reading. . . ."

When the men were out of the kitchen, and in the stairway leading to the cellar, Louis stopped his two sons. He put one finger on his lips, and winked at them both very slowly.

"Now, men, this is the lowdown," he whispered. "Pete Young is downstairs, waiting for us. He's been there over an hour waiting for us. Tonight we split the barrel of applejack three ways, and we may need men to hold the kegs and generally help around. Of course, all this is strictly between us men, get it?"

Laurent, who was as tall as his Papa, nodded solemnly, and Maurice, with his bright, darting eyes, agreed gleefully. Then Louis led them to the door of the cellar. He knocked twice and opened it slowly, peered into the darkness and then he sniffed.

"*Maudit!*" he exclaimed. "What a stink!"

"Applejack smells like that?" Maurice asked happily.

"Guess it does," mumbled Louis, "but then some of the best things in life do."

Slowly now, he went down the narrow steps to the cellar and walked around on the cement floor, both hands before him, feeling his way in the darkness, just barely seeing the outlines of a sink against the wall. Laurent and Maurice trailed behind him. Louis struck a match against his overall pants.

"Pete!" Louis called out. "Pete!" he called again.

"He's not here," said Laurent, "not in this darkness."

"He's got to be here," announced Louis. "He said he would be."

"Well, he's not," said Maurice, suddenly nervous.

Louis walked around the cellar very carefully, and then he nearly stumbled over three small wooden kegs, about a foot high, full of a reddish liquid. In one of them lay a stirring stick, and he picked the stick up and stirred the liquid speculatively while Laurent lit a match also and bent near the keg to examine it more closely.

"Put that match out," commanded Louis. "Maurice, find the light switch. I'm going to test this stuff myself. I don't know how to make it but I know what it should taste like."

"Pa, should you?" asked Laurent.

"Sure, I should. One of those kegs is all mine."

Maurice felt his way around the cellar to the light switch on the wall, and suddenly a flood of light invaded the cellar.

"Pa!" screamed Maurice.

At his feet lay Pete Young, face up, eyes closed, his thin gray hair ruffled, mouth open, legs and hands stretched out, as if he had been violently pushed down. His straw hat rested, soiled and crushed, a few feet away. There were reddish blots leading from Pete to the three kegs, and the barrel, that now stood empty in front of the chiffonier. Quickly, Louis knelt over Pete. What had Father Giroux said? Who was the man who'd died of alcohol poisoning?

"*Mon Dieu!*" he whispered.

He felt his pulse.

"I feel nothing—much," he murmured. A Monsieur Dumais. That was the name of the man who had died of alcohol poisoning.

Maurice put his hand gingerly on Pete's forehead.

"His head's still warm," he announced.

"It is?" asked Louis. But then, all that applejack in him! He'd be dead and warm—for days. He bent his head near Pete's heart. "I hear nothing—nothing," he concluded tensely.

Maurice picked up a piece of glass from the floor and put it close to Pete's mouth. For what seemed like a long, long time they waited, and then a slight moisture gathered on the glass.

"He's alive," announced Maurice, "but I'd better get a doctor."

"Get Lafrance," said Louis crisply. "In this situation, we must look for friends."

Maurice sped up the steps and was gone. Louis took Pete's wrists and began to rub them, all the time searching for an answer to all this around him, and when he found none, he suddenly slackened Pete's suspenders and removed them from his shoulder, opened up his shirt front and unbuttoned the top of his pants.

"Pete," he said in a hoarse voice, "you old son-of-a-bitch, wake up!"

"Pa," said Laurent, "maybe he drank some of that apple-jack?"

"So?"

"Maybe he's—poisoned?"

"Applejack," announced Louis, "is not poison."

"Maybe he's dying," said Laurent in sudden panic.

Louis stood up, his lips compressed in desperation.

"I don't think so. Any way the doctor will soon come."

"Maybe," said Laurent, "he's had an attack of the heart?"

"Maybe."

"Maybe," said Laurent, "he's just—drunk?"

Suddenly Louis shouted as softly as he could.

"Laurent, you're going to 'maybe' me into a full-blown fit!"

"Maybe," said Laurent, "I should get him a priest?"

Louis raged quietly.

"And that man a Protestant? If applejack's not killed him now, a priest is sure to do it."

They looked down at Pete. He hadn't moved a muscle in all that time.

"We should get your Maman here," said Louis. "She would know what to do."

"Maman?" asked Laurent, a grave doubt in his eyes.

Louis nodded. Laurent began to move eagerly.

"Take care!" said Louis. "Do not scare the others."

Laurent ran up the steps only to come head on with Dr.

Lafrance coming down the steps with Maurice. Both were out of breath.

"Lou," said the doctor, "what's the trouble?"

He pointed at Pete. The doctor bent quickly near Pete and felt his pulse and stared at his watch. He put his stethoscope to his heart and listened. He opened Pete's eyes and stared at Pete and Pete, in turn, blindly stared back at him. Then he unlaced Pete's left shoe, pulled off his sock, took a safety pin out of his black bag and began to jab Pete on the sole of his foot. Pete felt no pain. He never twitched nor recoiled from the repeated pin pricks on the tenderest part of the sole of his foot.

"Well?" asked Louis tensely.

"Coma," announced Dr. Lafrance. "I think."

"Coma?" asked Laurent.

"Coma, that's before death," said Maurice.

"Not necessarily," corrected the doctor. "Just coma."

Louis passed a hand over his face. His forehead was damp, as if he'd been working all day in the sun. First, there would be the ambulance, and their questions. And, perhaps, the undertaker and his questions. And the police and their questions. He could see the undertaker. Slowly he would come down the cellar steps, ask a few polite questions. He would solve the problem of taking Pete out of the cellar by putting him in a bag to carry him out—Poor Pete—folded in two on his way to his Protestant heaven, and the police investigation. . . . Dr. Lafrance studied Pete coolly now and then studied the cellar stairway also. . . . Maybe he too thought of the ambulance, maybe he thought also of the police investigation. . . . The one Father Giroux spoke about. . . .

Oh Lord, said Louis to himself, bring him back to life, and do it, here. In this cellar. Not in the hospital, where they have forms to fill out. Not in the ambulance, where they have reports to make out. Not in the operating room, where doctors ask themselves all kinds of questions. But here, dear Lord, and if You do this for me, O Lord, right here I mean, I pledge another thirty days away from all hard liquor, applejack specially. On second thought, Lord, make that sixty days, and put beer also on that list, but make him recover here. Now!

Dr. Lafrance had poked a needle into Pete's arm and injected him and now held a cotton against the puncture. Then the door opened and Maman was there, her left hand to her cheek in shock at these cellar proceedings. Without a word, she came toward Pete, knelt near him and passed a hand softly over his forehead.

"I saw Dr. Lafrance come down here," she said.

"Madame Martel," said the doctor, in greeting.

"Poor man!" said Maman. "An attack of the heart?"

"Could be," said the doctor. "I don't know."

"Too much to drink?"

"I don't know. Could be."

"Bad liquor?"

"Maybe."

"Poor man!" said Maman softly. "Father Giroux should be called. Maybe he would say a prayer over him. . ."

"Over my dead body," said Louis. "This is no time to antagonize my friend Pete."

Dr. Lafrance picked up his little black bag.

"Well, Lou," he said, "we'll just have to get an ambulance and take him up for observation."

Louis cast a quick glance toward him, and then toward the stairs.

"You think so?"

"I know so," snapped Lafrance, "and quickly."

Louis got into action. He motioned to Laurent to help him, and together they picked up a keg, full of reddish liquor, carried it to the sink near the wall and poured it down the drainpipe where it splashed, gurgled, and vanished. The doctor picked up a tin tumbler, scooped up some of the liquid from the second keg and sipped it.

"Applejack!" he announced positively. "Good too!"

"Yep," said Louis, and then, alone, he picked up the second keg and took it to the sink also. Maurice grabbed a pail, filled it with cold water and splashed the area to clean the reddish stains on the cement floor. Then he got another pail full of water, and on his way back stumbled near Pete, dropped the pail to the floor. A jet of cold water rose and fell and splashed on Pete's face. Pete sighed. Everyone stopped dead in his tracks.

"Do that again!" commanded Louis.

Maurice raced for another pail of cold water and Maman grabbed it from him. Now she stood over Pete and doused her hand in the water and sprinkled some over Pete's face.

He sighed again. Then he moved his head to one side and stayed still again.

"Keep on doing what you're doing!" commanded Louis.

This time Maman tipped the whole pail over Pete's face slowly, and allowed a gentle stream to splash over his eyes, his nose and his mouth. Suddenly she dumped the rest over him.

Pete turned his face away from the frigid jet. Dr. Lafrance suddenly bent near him and put the stethoscope to his heart. Then he reached again for the safety pin, and aimed carefully and jabbed him good and hard on the sole of his left foot. Pete moaned. And now he opened his eyes, closed them again, and then opened them quickly and saw Louis bending over him.

"Lou," he said in English, "what the hell's up?"

"You!" said Louis in broken English. "You're 'hup.'"

"Me?"

"Yah," said Louis. "We were on the virgin to give you hup!"

"Somebody," said Pete slowly, "kicked me on the head."

"Sure of that?" asked Lafrance.

"Sure," said Pete, mumbling suddenly, "I was dividing the stuff into three equal parts into three kegs. . . . I stirred and poured and stirred. . . . Came down here around three o'clock. . . ."

"Yah?" said Louis. "I bet you've been here all day!"

"And, somebody kicked me!"

"Applejack," announced Dr. Lafrance. It was a final diagnosis.

"No," insisted Pete, "I never had a drink of it."

"No fooling, now, Pete?" said Louis.

"No," insisted Pete. "I swear I never touched the stuff." Then he saw the two empty kegs. "My God!" he gasped.

"You never drank any of it?" asked Lafrance.

"Well," said Pete slowly, "I stirred and poured, and sure, of course, as I poured, I took a sip or two, just to test it, and, yes, I tasted it. But I never drank those two kegs! I didn't!"

"Just tasted it?" asked Louis.

"Tested it!" corrected Pete, getting mad. "Why not? I had a few swallows. Been waiting a long time for it. It's very good. Let's all have a taste. Say, what time is it? What happened to the afternoon?"

He started to get up, and Louis helped him. When he finally stood up, he shook himself and his pants fell to the floor. He swayed a moment, trying to understand this unexpected turn of events, then quickly pulled up his pants.

"I apologize," he said toward Maman.

"You'd better go home," said Dr. Lafrance, "and rest."

"Sure," agreed Pete, "but first, let's have a wee shot of this grand applejack."

"No," said Louis, "and besides, we threw away two kegs. Down the sink. We think it is poison!"

"You threw it away?" whined Pete.

"Yah," said Louis. "I threw yours away, and mine also. . . ."

"What?" said Pete.

Then he seemed to reel under a dizzy spell and Louis grabbed him. Maman motioned to Laurent. He threw the contents of the third keg in to the sink. Pete was very sick and never saw this.

"A few swallows of applejack," he mumbled in disbelief.

Louis picked up Pete's straw hat, put it on his head and walked up the stairs holding him by the waist and together they walked slowly down the street to his home on Chestnut. At his home, Pete turned to Louis.

"Coming in for a drink?"

Louis took off his hat and scratched his head.

"Can't. You see, I just took another pledge. To save your Protestant carcass. I thought for sure you'd cashed in your chips."

Pete laughed and put his arms around Louis.

"Well, thank you, Lou, but you didn't have to do that."

"I know damn well I didn't," said Louis, "but I did."

Pete laughed.

"How long this time?"

"Sixty days!"

Pete whistled in horror.

"Lou, I'm not worth it, but then . . . sixty days—we can start another batch and have it ready about that time. . . . But listen, Lou, don't go around thinking you saved my life. Not with that pledge. Forget it! Speak to—what's his name?— Father Giroux. He'll fix it up for you. . . ."

Louis frowned. He shook his head.

"No, this one is between me and God. I'll deal with Him direct. There must be something I'm doing wrong!"

The first weeks of September were days of nervous warfare between Maman and Father Giroux. In the first three days of school, there was exactly one hour of schoolwork—attendance records—and the rest was given over to a start-of-the-year retreat with long hours of church services and two sermons a day. On the morning of the fourth day, Maman walked to Sacred Heart Academy where Félix and Emile were in fifth and third grade respectively, and requested the Mother Superior to have her sons returned to her forthwith. The Mother Superior explained that they would have to be fetched from church, since this was the last of the Retreat Devotions, for this very afternoon, regular schoolwork was starting in earnest, one could be sure of that. . . .

Maman was adamant. She thanked the Mother Superior and informed her that she was withdrawing her sons from the Academy—now. The Mother Superior was shocked. Children might be expelled, but they did not withdraw. Well, Maman said that this time it was the school that was being withdrawn from. Félix and Emile were produced and Maman walked them out of the school and to their home where she sat them down at the kitchen table and gave them herself a session in mathematics, grammar, reading, and writing. And a short lecture.

"There is a time for everything," she concluded, "and this is the time of your education. You know what I mean?"

Emile and Félix nodded solemnly.

The next day, Maman walked up to St. Michel High School and asked for the Mother Superior. Same business as the day before, and same shock. For the time being, Maman said, Maurice and Thérèse would not return to school. And again, she took Maurice and Thérèse home, where they joined Emile and Félix in a joint session of mathematics, grammar, reading and writing. And a short lecture.

"There is a time for everything," she concluded, "a place for everything, and for the time being, this is the time and place for your education. My children, you know what I mean?"

All four nodded solemnly. They knew this was a fight and they also knew on which side they were.

Later that night, she began to worry a bit. Louis smoked and listened.

"I know," she said, "that before God I'm right, and I'm going to fight this to the end."

He sipped glumly a tall glass of ginger ale, unspiked, and stared gloomily at the old chime clock.

"Should we fight the priests, and the nuns?" he asked.

"Yes, when they are wrong. They have been wrong before. This is not a matter of morals, but of practical sense. You said yourself, Louis: 'Thou shalt not fear!'"

He took a small sip of his unspiked ginger ale.

"*Bonguienne!* Do you know, Cécile, that Pete Young has never taken any pledges, like I do?"

"Oh, well," said Maman, smugly, "he's a Protestant, and their religion is just not like ours, that's all."

Louis smiled sadly.

"Wouldn't it be one hell of a note," he mused, "if when we died, and got into Heaven, somehow, Pete with his religion, and me with mine, came out even, and nobody up there would be able to tell the difference?"

"Now, Louis," said Maman, "you talk like a pagan tonight!"

"That's because this drink, here, is not a Christian drink!"

A week later, Maman enrolled all the children with a private tutor—an elderly retired teacher—who was competent but poor. He was overjoyed at this unexpected source of income. He already had a class of sixteen pupils—Protestants, two Jews and some Catholics expelled from parochial schools. He charged low rates and hinted that invitations to supper would not be unwelcome. And the Martels became the talk of the town.

Father Giroux did not make any move for two weeks. Maman began to fear she had outmaneuvered herself, for this tutor did not and could not issue diplomas. She remained steadfast for everyone to see, however, even when some of the kids reported that there had been some changes in the schools: all religious activities now took place *after* school hours. Then, Father Giroux wrote her a short note. He had, he wrote, checked into things and she had, in part, been right. Would she now return her children to school? Had not this gone far enough?

Without batting an eye, Maman now removed her children from under the tutor's care and trotted them herself to the Academy and to the High School, after a short lecture about behaving, not like conquerors, but like Martels who knew how to behave well in all cases. Alone with Louis that night, however, she let go.

"Thou shalt not fear!" she gurgled with joy.

Louis toasted her in ginger ale, unspiked.

He kept his pledge. For sixty days he touched neither whisky, nor wine, nor beer. And Maman observed him, and felt sad, and thought this was too much for any honest man to bear, and when his temper grew short, and he apologized for it, she kissed him, hugged him, and favored him in many ways.

And, one afternoon, late in October, the pledge was done, a new batch of applejack was nearly ready for splitting—Dr. Lafrance was the fourth partner this time—and the work week was finished. Louis and Philippe Buisson, his partner on the job, picked up their tools and walked slowly out of the half-finished hospital they were building. There was an obscene noise of breaking timbers and crashing cement forms, and a cloud of dust enveloped them. A hoarse voice shouted: "There are two men down there! They're trapped!"

After the first shock of astonishment, everyone jumped to the task of removing two-by-fours and broken plaster, coughing and cussing and shouting. Now a frantic activity developed near the door to the basement, to reach the men under the twisted lumber and cracked cement forms.

"Lou," Buisson shouted, "here! Down there!"

"Who's working down there?"

A voice shouted.

"Mr. Martel! Your boy's down there!"

"*Mon Dieu!* It's Laurent! *Mon Dieu!*" muttered Louis.

The middle floor, apparently, had collapsed and sent crashing to the basement cement forms supporting the inner structure.

"They don't have a chance," wailed a voice.

Louis reached the entrance to the basement. It could hardly be seen for the dust now slowly settling. Men were trying to open the door.

"Out of my way!" shouted Louis, and he and Buisson picked up a four-by-four and rammed it into the door. It did not budge. Once more, and now it was pushed an inch. Louis raised his right foot and kicked it open. He spat dust and shaded his eyes and began to walk down the stairway to the cellar—and then, suddenly, the dust seemed to clear and he saw the two men in the basement, dazed, with dirty faces. They walked around blindly in the dust-filled basement.

"Laurent!" Louis shouted.

His son waved at him, as if to ask: What happened?

"Thank God!" whispered Louis.

When they reached home, his girl, Hélène Pelletier, wanted to know all the details. Laurent had been hit on the forehead and he had a bloody gash, and Hélène took a long hour to fix that up. Maman looked at Louis and Philippe Buisson—he'd come in for a short drink with Louis—and protested that there were too many of these accidents to please her. Louis nodded, and then took Buisson down to the cellar. He took a dipper and served him a shot of applejack, and then took a large one for himself. Now they talked quietly. Suddenly, Buisson exploded in laughter.

"Say, Lou, you know what you kept repeating while you were trying to reach Laurent?"

Louis tilted his head back and took a copious swallow of the applejack. He shook his head in amazement that it could be so tasty, so strong, such good applejack!

"Didn't have time to talk."

"Oh, but you did! You kept shouting: 'No pledges!'"

"I did, *hein?*"

"But you were praying too, Lou, I hear you!"

"Sure, I was! I said: 'My God, help me! Help my son! But I want it for nothing! For nothing! This one, I want it on the house!"

3. The Bad One [1923]

Father Joseph Lebois had a problem.

That was the October of the year Thérèse was sixteen going on seventeen and expected to do very well in her last year at St. Michel's High School, and Laurent's marriage to Hélène Pelletier was just two weeks away. Father Lebois, recently of Berlin, New Hampshire, had just been assigned as the new parish assistant to Father Giroux at Sacred Heart Church in Groveton, Maine. And he came one night to the Martel apartment, with his problem.

Louis Martel had become fond of Father Lebois the very first time they'd met. This young priest, thought Louis, assumed that if you wanted to do the right thing for God and country, the Church, or to help people in need of help, everything would turn out in the best possible way if only you had enough *savoir-faire* to have somebody else do it for you. It was a pleasure to see this priest work. His was, of course, the philosophy of a naïve child, which the world needed, and the methods of a gang leader who could also quote the Latin. In any case, Louis mused, he doesn't mind getting his feet wet for our Lord.

Maman was delighted to see him. She had had her way, to some extent, in tightening up schoolwork in Sacred Heart parish. She was now at peace with its administration. In any

case, a visit from the priest was always an honor. She promptly served him a cup of tea.

"Sugar? Milk?" she asked.

"A little dyamite?" suggested Louis.

"Ah, yes, a little dynamite," he said, "and thank you."

Father Lebois was tall, slim, well built. He looked like an
athlete, and had been, at one time, sought after by "Les
Canadiens" for a professional hockey career. He still was good
at it, and on cold days he could be seen chasing the puck
around on the ice with the choir boys. As a priest, however, he
was still known as a hockey player: he could handle a stick
well, he could and did bring the puck past the opposition,
right up to the goal. He never shot a goal, however, for he was
better known still for his ability to pass the puck to someone
in a better position to score a goal. He was—well—a very
good puck-passer.

Maman introduced him to Laurent, her oldest, Maurice,
now eighteen and very tall suddenly, to Félix, Emile, Marie
and Cécile. Thérèse was at choir practice. After his tea, Father
Lebois took out his pipe, Louis handed him his own tobacco
pouch, and soon both men smoked contentedly.

"What a grand family you have, Madame Martel!" the
priest exclaimed.

"Thank you, Father," said Maman, "and they are doing well
in school. . . ."

Louis waited for the priest to show his hand, but there now
came some polite talk with Laurent, soon to be married, and
with Maurice who was part-time helper at the Excelsior
Grocery Market. They talked about Thérèse who seesawed
daily between becoming a teacher, like Maman, or a nun, or
a movie star, and who never missed Rudolph Valentino whenever the Great Lover rode his white steed across the Empire
Theater screen on a Saturday afternoon.

"Some movies are good," said Father Lebois, "and some movies are bad."

Yes, thought Louis, this hockey player, and priest, could also skate on both sides of the rink at the same time.

"Oh, yes," said Maman, "and we watch the movies they see. They are not allowed to see stories with . . . you know . . . where the leading lady acts like . . . well . . . a street girl. . . ."

Father Lebois nodded quietly, and turned to talk. He spotted Félix and began to discuss with him baseball, boxing, autos, and, of course, hockey. Emile, Maman pointed out, would probably become a priest. Already he was an altar boy. . . .

"And here," she said, "is Marie, who is six, and Cécile, who is our baby. . . ."

"Ah," said Father Lebois, "Marie, and Cécile. And, Marie, what are you going to do when you grow up?"

Marie revealed a deep frown, and stared at the priest.

"A street girl!" she cried out in defiance.

Maman reddened. Father Lebois choked a smile. And Louis shrugged his shoulders. This too will pass away, he wanted to say, if only we make nothing of it. Maman went to the blackboard and put a red mark against Marie's name, and the latter frowned again.

"And you, Cécile?" the priest asked, fearing the worst.

Cécile hesitated, scratched her derrière, and said nothing. Now, suddenly, Father Lebois seemed in a hurry. Maman told Laurent he was in charge. Then she invited Father Lebois to step into the *parloir*, and the priest smiled in appreciation of this distinct honor. Though muscular and tall, the young priest moved deliberately always, but after Maman had closed the door, and she and Louis were alone with him in the quiet of the *parloir*, he began to speak. He spoke so fast they could ask no questions. Before they knew just what the problem was, they were in the thick of it.

"She is an orphan," said Father Lebois, pouring his words without letup, "truly an unfortunate waif of fortune, the ill fortune of her parents. The father—he was Canadien—was killed in a street fight before she was ten and her mother died two months later. I knew her mother: truly she was a saintly woman, my own mother will testify to that. An aunt, a sister of her father, in New Hampshire, finally took the little girl into her house, but she is an unwanted child; there is no peace there for the child. And now this aunt says she can't handle her any more. She says that Sophia is a bad one, has gotten herself into bad company. The aunt does not want her in her house any more. . . . And right at the start of the school year. . . ."

Louis turned to Maman. He was lost. What was this leading up to?

"It is a very sad story," said Maman vaguely.

"Right now," continued Father Lebois, "she is with the Sisters. In Berlin, but it is temporary. They have no place for her, really. Their shelter is for younger—much younger—girls. The Sisters have written to me—I was their priest for a while. There is no money, and no hope of money from the aunt. But I'm determined that she'll graduate from high school, if she's to make a life for herself. Don't you agree, Madame Martel?"

"But, of course," agreed Maman vaguely.

"This aunt," shot in Louis, "is simply throwing her out?"

"It amounts to that," admitted the priest. "She is a sister of the father. It is a sinful thing she is doing. . . ."

"It is, Father," said Louis, "but why tell us about this?"

"Yes, Father," asked Maman. "There are so many unfortunates, and so many sinful things . . . why this one?"

"Ah," said the priest, "but this one I know personally. I have lived with these facts, in this special case, and the heart in such instances leaves the conscience no peace at all, and I must do what I can do. . . ."

Louis, Louis Martel told himself, observe the technique of an expert. It is a pleasure to watch, but note well that you, or someone, is being set up for a long, long pass.

"Is there no family," asked Louis, "that will take her in?"

"An excellent question!" said Father Lebois. "And to it there is a sad answer. The aunt is the only relative, and she has never forgiven her brother for marrying somebody else but a Canadienne. . . . The mother of this poor little girl was Polish. . . . This child is unwanted. There is—well—some bad feelings. . . ."

"Shameful!" said Maman suddenly.

Now, thought Louis, there should be some reference to the Sermon on the Mount, or a glowing picture of the virtues of this little orphan. This young Father knew his business. Now, watch. . . .

"Of course," said the priest, lowering his head, "I must tell you, since you will want to know, and I must be absolutely frank with you, that Sophia is—well—reputed to be a bad one."

"Bad one?" snapped Louis. No, this smart man was taking the wrong approach. Who can sell a bad apple?

"The good Sister," said the priest, "tell me she really is, as the aunt alleges, a bad one, a hard child to govern. Weeps all the time. Fights. Really fights with her fists. Sulks. Won't take care of her clothes. Won't do anything at all until she's good and ready to do it."

"I'm pained to hear this," said Louis, eying the priest. Now, Monsieur Lebois, what other maneuver will you pull?

"Poor little girl!" exclaimed Maman.

"What would you advise a young priest," said he, "in a situation like this? Frankly, Monsieur and Madame Martel, I have come only for this."

Louis gazed at his pipe. Now, that was real clever. Maman would fall for that. Here, here it comes.

"*Mon Dieu!*" said Maman. "She needs a good home."

"That's it," agreed Father Lebois violently, "and thank you!" Now he calmed down very quickly. "I have to find her, as you say, a home, a good home." He turned and fixed his eyes steadily on Louis. The counterattack was probably best.

"We're full up here," he stated firmly.

"Otherwise," added Maman, "we'd be glad to help."

"More tea," said Louis. Hell, I've got a houseful of kids right now. Perhaps for a few days, at most a week, to help out.

"It would be," continued Father Lebois implacably, "a matter of a few weeks only, at the most. The good Sisters in Berlin assure me that by that time they hope to find a place for her, somewhere. . . ."

"Will you have more tea?" said Maman quietly.

"It wouldn't be so bad," continued the priest quickly, "if she had her diploma. Why, I could find her employment and a home right in Berlin, or elsewhere. But they don't want her at the high school either. . . ."

"Nobody seems to want to help this girl but you, Father!" exclaimed Louis, getting irritated by all this.

"I know the Sister Superior in Berlin, and she is a high-booted Napoléon," the priest went on at high speed, "and if Sophia is a bad one, why, they feel they don't want her to agitate the others. Now, of course, if I could find her a home right here in Groveton, Father Giroux is the high-booted Napoléon at St. Michel High School. . . ." He ended this with a quiet smile of power and then began to survey the *parloir*, probably looking for a spare bed, thought Louis.

He realized his pipe had gone dead and he lit it again.

"Well. . ." he offered slowly, "we're full up here. All the bed space is taken up, two to a room as it is now, that is until Laurent marries. But right at this time, Father . . ."

The priest squared his shoulders and slowly enunciated the

next sentence. Near the goal, after the series of smart stick-handling, he was now ready to pass the puck.

"To you who have so much," he said, "the Lord asks for just a little bit. Are we going to keep Him waiting?"

"At least two weeks," replied Louis swiftly.

Maman pursed her lips. She too was scheming, but if she weakened, he was lost too.

"This," she asked, "would be for only a week or so?"

"At the most!" announced the priest earnestly. "And if the good Sisters cannot find a place, why, we'd all have to trust to Providence. . . ."

"And an extra bed," added Louis. "Now, let's see. If Laurent moves in with Félix and Emile, into their room until he marries—and that's two long weeks from now—and Maurice sleeps in the *parloir*, that'll give us an extra room, and an extra bed with this loveseat. . . ."

"My loveseat!" exclaimed Maman, scandalized.

". . . And," continued Louis, "if we can talk Thérèse into sharing a room with Marie, that would leave Cécile, alone in the little room. . . . This might make room for . . . for this little girl. . . ."

"Yes!" said Father Lebois, his mouth open. "That's good!"

"Good," agreed Louis, "but not wise. We've got to keep the boys away from the girls. . . ."

"Oh," said the priest.

"Oh, yes," said Louis, "it is a fact of life."

He took a pencil and a used envelope, and drew a rough plan of his apartment. In the square now occupied by Emile and Félix he wrote in 10 and 12, the one assigned to Marie and Cécile he jotted down 6 and 4, in the square representing the room of Maurice and Laurent he wrote in 18 and 20, and in the room given over to Thérèse he scribbled 16. Then he began to erase all these figures. He moved Marie and Cécile out of their room and moved them into Thérèse's room.

"It's all right, Cécile?" he asked Maman.

"So far," she replied, frowning in concentration.

Louis then moved Maurice and Laurent to Marie's former room.

"They'll be crowded," commented Maman.

Then Louis moved Marie and Cécile into the room formerly assigned to Maurice and Laurent. Maman approved with a smile. Then he again moved Maurice into the room occupied by Félix and Emile, left Félix there, and moved Emile out.

"And where does Emile sleep?" asked Maman.

"In the *parloir*," said Louis.

"Where? On the loveseat?" asked Maman sadly. Her new loveseat!

"On the loveseat, where else?" asserted Louis. "After all, Emile might become a priest!" he added, and turned toward Father Lebois. The priest nodded solemnly. Louis wrote 16 in the large front room and thus restored Thérèse to her old room.

"That," he concluded, "will make the boys' large bed available for Thérèse's room. It's a large double bed."

"For two weeks," said Maman, passing a loving hand over her loveseat. "And Emile is not a boy who's hard on things."

"And this little girl?" Louis asked. "How old is she?"

"Just seventeen," said Father Lebois sadly, "and already the boys chase her. It's a pity, but she is also very beautiful."

"At seventeen," Louis murmured, "everybody is beautiful!"

He wrote in 17 in the room now also assigned to Thérèse.

"Yes," agreed Father Lebois, studying the plan over Louis's shoulder. "It will be good for Sophia to share a room with someone her age."

"Now then," continued Louis, "when Laurent marries, perhaps we can make new arrangements, if she is still with us. . . ."

"That's a good plan," said Father Lebois, beaming.

"And this will be good for Thérèse also," said Maman, "and if this little girl, Sophia, comes into our house, she'll be family. . . ."

"That would be fine," said the priest, suddenly very calm.

"Subject to the same rules and regulations," snapped Louis.

"And to the same love," added the priest.

"That goes without saying," said Maman.

Louis suddenly frowned. When had he said he would do all this?

"Well, now, I haven't said yes yet," he objected. "I'm only thinking with my mouth open. As you see, Father, we are crowded. . . ."

"Monsieur Martel," said the priest quietly, "that's exactly why I picked you. There's always room for one more child at the table of a good family."

"For," threatened Louis, "if Laurent weren't getting married. . ."

"Yes," said the priest soothingly, "and your son is marrying a nice Catholic girl of excellent parents—Hélène Pelletier. A fine family!"

"A fine family," agreed Louis, "and they'll have nice children, I know!"

"If it pleases God," added Maman.

"And if it weren't for that," continued Louis, "this business would be out of the question. I would say, 'No! Positively!'"

"And I wouldn't question your good judgment," added the priest emphatically.

"Because," continued Louis coldly, "to make room at the bottom, or in the middle, there's got to be movement at the top. If my children don't start moving out and into their own nuptial beds pretty soon, there won't be room in here for new ones to spring out of my own, including orphans."

"God provides," said Maman, suddenly delighted.

"Yes, Madame Martel," said Father Lebois, getting up to leave. "God arranges all these things."

"If He does," Louis snapped, "why didn't you pass Him the puck?"

The priest, however, looked directly at Louis once more.

"And you'll make a home for Sophia?" he asked.

"Yes," said he firmly. "I don't give in easily, but when I do, I hold back nothing!" Now, he had said it. How could he be such an easy mark?

"Yes," added Maman, strangely excited by this turn of events, "this little girl is welcome to what we have to give."

"One more thing," said the priest in a low voice. "There is no money."

"There is no need," said Louis proudly. And there it was. He was now committed. Since when had his home become an orphan asylum? No matter. He would do his best for this little girl. A bad one, was she? He would see. Hell, two weeks at the most. It would pass quickly. . . . He'd been taken in, that was clear!

There was not much time to prepare the children for Sophia's arrival—less than a day and a night—but Louis and Maman did their best. Laurent was too busy getting ready for his own wedding to be overly concerned, as he and Hélène Pelletier had to paint and furnish their new apartment. Maurice and Félix took it all very calmly, though they spent a little more time than usual before the mirror combing and recombing their black hair. Emile looked forward to sleeping alone in the *parloir* and reading late at night.

Marie and Cécile were enthusiastic, but when Louis outlined his plan, Thérèse became moody, and when he was finished, she began to pout. She did not make any comment, nor did she join in the general fun and frolic of moving things from one room into another. When the large bed was finally set up in her room, which she was to share with Sophia, she suddenly spoke up.

"I bet she can't even speak French!"

"I bet," said Louis, "you can't even speak Polack."

"Polish!" corrected Maman quietly.

"I'm French," said Thérèse with sudden passion, "and the French language and French culture are the highest in the world!"

"They are very high, indeed," said Maman, "and you can be proud that you are of French blood, but Sophia can speak French and English and Polish too, but that does not make her better or worse than you, unless . . ." And Maman raised one index toward her.

"Unless what?" snapped Thérèse.

"Unless," continued Maman, "you prove yourself better before God—where it counts—with a little humility!"

"Isn't it better to be French?" Thérèse shot out.

"It's perhaps better," murmured Louis tenderly as he placed a rough hand over her silky black hair, "than being a Henglish haristocrat, but it's no guarantee that the sun'll shine . . ."

"Papa!" Maman cried out in warning.

". . . out of your derrière!" finished Louis.

"But she's a bad one!" raged Thérèse.

Louis cast a glance toward Maman.

"Why do you say that?" she asked Thérèse.

"Because . . . because that's what they all say!"

"Who are they?" snapped Maman.

"All the kids!"

Maman looked toward Louis. It was going to be harder than expected. Oh, the terrible, terrible telegraphy of children, that spanned the long centuries, the barriers of countries and the walls of languages. . . . Louis went up to Thérèse, put his hand under her chin that she might look him directly in the eye.

"And besides," he said evenly, in a low voice, "she's Polack!"

"Polish!" quickly corrected Maman.

"Let me tell you something," said Louis, "that I have pounded nails with Polacks . . ."

"Poles!" said Maman quietly.

"And Wops!"

"Italians," said Maman quietly.

"Italians," conceded Louis, "and Dutchmen and Swedes and Canucks . . ."

"French-Canadians!" said Maman haughtily.

"And all of them," continued Louis, "pray to the same Lord that you do, my precious future little nun, and they all do in their own lingo, and some of them are dumb as hell sometimes, and sometimes smart as hell, but all of them all the time are in God's heart and mind, like you and me!"

"I know that, Papa," answered Thérèse, near to tears.

"Do you, now, my pretty one?" he asked softly. "Maybe you think you do, at Mass, when your heart is full of Sunday-morning love and your tummy with flapjacks, but do you know it on Monday morning?"

Thérèse's mouth formed a quick answer, but she couldn't speak; her lips began to tremble. She turned toward Maman for support.

"Papa is right," said Maman firmly.

"And let me tell you something else," he continued, taking a deep breath. "Before I married your mother, when I was a lumberjack . . ."

"Oh, that story again!" Thérèse nearly screamed.

"Yes, that story!" said he in a firm voice. "When I was a lumberjack, one night, I stopped for a drink at a saloon, and an old Indian came in. He was from up North, and these Redskins never were known for their beauty. I must tell you that, without hesitation. This particular one was so ugly it made you want to sit down to compose yourself!"

There was some laughter, and he laughed also.

"Well," he continued, "this ugly-looking Indian—I tell you he had lost all the cheeks in his face—well, he wanted a drink. Just as I did, for, as you know, the great thirst assails all men, Indians too, just as does the great hunger of the stomach, and that other hunger of the flesh, the greatest hunger of them all . . ."

"Never mind, Louis!" snapped Maman.

"Anyhow," he continued, "Indians were not allowed to buy drinks at the bar. . . . Did you know that?"

"It made them wild," Maurice contributed quickly.

Quietly Louis turned toward him.

"It made them as wild," he asserted, "as it did any green-horn who drank too much! Well, sir, this Indian, uglier yet because of his thirst, just stood there, two feet away from the bar, his mouth parched, his eyes fixed now on the colored bottles on the shelves, and now on anybody who would buy him a drink—you could do that, all right—and so I bought him one, and then another, and we conversed, man to man, and behind that long nose, and beady eyes, and dried-up cheeks, there was, I'm here to tell you, a smart brain, and do you know what?"

"What, Papa?" shot in Marie, admiringly.

"He gave me some of his secrets!"

"Secrets!" screamed Cécile in great wonder.

"Yes, mademoiselle! That night, we became friends, and the next day he took me into the woods and showed me exactly where to find the herbs and the plants that cure the maladies that mystify the doctors. . . . These herbs you boil, you see, and you drink the juice . . ."

"Ugh!" commented Maman, making a face of disgust.

"All right for you," said Louis, looking hurt, and turning toward Maman, "but it cured your backache when for weeks Dr. Lafrance could do nothing for you! But the point—the point of this—the moral, my children! This Indian had two beautiful daughters!"

"The ugly Indian?" asked Marie, breathless.

"With no cheeks?" screamed Cécile.

"Yes! It is a thing to remember that some of the most beautiful blooms emerge from the damnedest swamps! He had two lovely maiden daughters!"

"*Batege!*" exclaimed Maurice.

"What were their names?" asked Marie, enthralled.

"And I tell you," continued Louis, "I was introduced to them that very night. . . ."

"So?" Thérèse asked very coolly.

"Papa, their names, plea-ea-se?" shouted Marie.

"Did they have cheeks?" screamed Cécile.

"Oh, yes," continued Louis, "and one fine day, both of them came softly walking through the village, in their moccasins and fine Indian dresses of many colors—both were slim, round-faced, dark-eyed, and graceful as elks. . . . And all the village sports came out of their hiding places, as if this was the circus, and went chasing after them. . . ."

"I bet," said Maurice, biting his fingernails.

"But not one of them," said Louis, "could get a tumble. . . ."

And Louis brought his right hand down sharply, like the sudden drop of the guillotine.

"Their names?" begged Marie.

"Oh yes!" And now Louis remembered. "The prettiest one, with the singing voice, was Mockingbird, and the other, the frightened one, with the troublesome eyes, was called Moon Shadow!"

"Moon Shadow!" Marie whispered.

"*Eh, tonnerre!*" murmured Maurice.

"Well," continued Louis, "they were pippins, Indians or no, and I say that a pippin is a pippin in any country, and in that town I was the only fellow for which they would smile, they would talk to, whose jokes they found funny. Only Louis Martel! Only I could take them out, and I did, and that's a fact!"

"Both of them?" asked Laurent, his mouth open.

"One at a time," explained Louis. "That was before I met your Maman, and each in turn. I, Louis Martel, treated them both like princesses, which they were in manner and decorum, and I had them laughing, in stitches, all the time, and they made me a belt for to wear on holidays. . . ."

"Yes, Pa," interrupted Laurent, "they were pippins, but in this case, what is the moral?"

"This!" And Louis took a deep breath. "If I had married either one of them, it is a fact that you'd all be beautiful Indian children!"

The younger children laughed in delight.

"We couldn't drink in a bar," countered Maurice thoughtfully.

Louis raised his right hand toward heaven solemnly.

"It could have happened!" he declared.

"But Papa, it didn't," said Thérèse coldly, "and we are not Indians, and that's a fact too."

Louis took a deep breath, frowned, sucked on his dying pipe.

"What Papa means," said Maman quietly, "is that Jesus stated: 'Suffer little children to come unto me!' He opened His heart to everyone. He didn't particularize!"

"That's it, damn it," barked Louis. "He didn't particularize whether they were Polacks . . ."

"Poles," said Maman.

"Or Wops . . ."

"Italians."

"Or colored, or Jews, or Canucks . . ."

"Or French-Canadians!" said Maman impatiently.

"Or, for that matter," he concluded, "Protestants like Pete Young!"

Maman said nothing.

"That's right," exclaimed Emile brightly. "He did not particularize!"

"I know damn well that's right!" shouted Louis. "And furthermore, in this particular instance, I am putting down both feet on the floor in regards to this young girl who is to live in this house. I shall be very strict with the marks!"

"With Sophia too?" taunted Thérèse.

"With Sophia too," added Louis, "as with everybody else!"

Ah, the magic of that blackboard! How often, Louis thought, he should thank Cécile! For the mere mention of it seemed to calm Thérèse down immediately—and everyone else.

When Sophia Lewicka was brought to the Martel home, Louis Martel carried her two suitcases and one bundle of clothes into the kitchen where the entire family waited. He introduced her slowly to all. Maman came to her and gave her a nice, warm hug, but Sophia, slim, with blue eyes, blond hair, a fixed stare, stood near the door, her arms at her sides, not knowing what to do next.

As per previous instructions, Laurent and Maurice shook her hand and carried her bags into Thérèse's room, Marie, Cécile, Félix and Emile mumbled in turn that, yes, indeed, she was welcome, and Thérèse, without a word, showed her where the bathroom was and the room where she was to sleep, and then steered her back into the kitchen. Louis then excused himself and went out, and Maman went back to her stove, consciously tending to her supper. For an awkward moment, the children faced one another, and then turned toward Sophia, who still stood frozen near the door. At this moment, Laurent snapped his suspenders once or twice, and bowing slightly toward her, pointed toward a chair near the dining table.

"Please, take a chair," said Laurent. "My Papa says, when you are resting everything else, the tongue speaks easier."

The children laughed.

She moved toward a chair and Maurice quickly held it for her, and she sat down. Maman took one sly look toward her, and forced herself to continue with her supper preparations. The children stared hard at her blond hair. Now, thought Maman, the weather should come up for serious discussion. . . .

"The weather," commented Laurent, "has been getting colder all the time." He sat down near Sophia and looked into her cold blue eyes. She said nothing.

"Yes, indeed," agreed Maurice, "the weather's been something," as he saw that Sophia was a real pip.

Marie and Cécile giggled toward Sophia and crowded near her at the table, and then everybody sat at the table also. Thérèse sat on the other side, facing Sophia. Sophia sat, her face still without expression, and stared at them with cold eyes, until suddenly she spotted the blackboard. At the bottom of the list of names, printed in letters equal in size to the other names, was her name: Sophia.

"What's that for?" she asked, a cloud of suspicion in her eyes.

That broke the ice. All of them competed with one another in words to tell her, and as quickly as possible.

"It's a peculiar idea of Maman," tartly concluded Thérèse. "Kind of silly, don't you think?"

"I don't know," said Sophia in a low voice.

"I think it's silly," said Thérèse finally. "As if we were all infants. Don't you think it's idiotic?"

"I don't know," murmured Sophia.

"I wish," Thérèse snapped, as she watched with one eye her Maman busily working at the stove, "that for once I was in a family without an idiotic blackboard! Just once!"

Cockily she glared at Sophia, and then turned sharply toward her Maman, but she only pursed her lips in great concentration on her supper preparations, and worked steadily, without hearing a word, it seemed, as if she had become suddenly deaf.

"Maybe," Thérèse hinted, looking sideways toward Sophia, "you can ask Papa to take your name off. . . ."

"Why?" asked Sophia in sudden panic.

"Because . . ." said Thérèse. "Just because."

"No," said Sophia in a low voice.

"You like it?" asked Marie hopefully.

"I don't know," said Sophia lamely.

"You'd like to win a bag of candies!" shouted Marie in triumph.

Sophia turned toward Marie.

"No," said Sophia, "because if I ever won, I'd give it away. I don't like candies very much."

"You don't?" asked Cécile, deeply shocked.

Laurent cleared his throat, snapped his suspenders once, and when Cécile suddenly reached with her little hand into the large sugar bowl, he looked sharply at her, but she had withdrawn enough sugar for a mouthful and now she ate it smugly.

"I didn't like the blackboard once," he announced, "but as you grow older and begin to assume responsibility . . ."

"Well, well!" purred Thérèse, "look at the little papa, all of you! He's not married yet, and already he's gone over to the opposition!"

"Yes," laughed Maurice, "just because you're going to live with a wife, this does not make you a patriarch, you know!"

Sophia turned toward Laurent. She cleared her throat. She was making a real effort.

"You are marrying soon?" she asked.

"Yep. In two weeks."

"God bless you!" she whispered.

"Thank you," he said. "I wish you, too, much happiness."

Sophia smiled a bit, and then there was a silence that lasted a minute or two. Cécile fidgeted, then turned a smiling face toward Sophia. Suddenly she got off the chair, picked up a broken-down doll off the floor—one arm was missing and her eyes were pushed in—sat down again near Sophia and then gave Sophia her doll. Sophia took it and made a pretense of looking at it and then being shocked at the wounded doll. Cécile giggled.

"I wish," Marie gasped suddenly, "I were getting married!"

"You're too young," said Thérèse.

"And I was wearing a long veil, and Maman cried because I was going away. . . ."

"You'd make a nice bride," said Laurent, "and if it weren't that I'm already promised . . ."

"Hooked," said Maurice, "by a pair of dark eyes!"

"In any case," announced Laurent, "we'll have a blackboard in my house!" He looked toward Maman. This, she heard, and she turned to look at him in turn. She nodded agreement. It was a victory that had been long in coming to her. Laurent, my first-born!

"Not in my house," said Félix, who at eleven was nowhere near marriage. Suddenly he was surprised. He'd gotten in a word edgewise.

Then there was a short pause.

"I don't know," said Thérèse, entranced by her indecision. "Maybe I would, and maybe I wouldn't."

"Maybe I would," repeated Marie, "and maybe I wouldn't!"

"I would," said Sophia suddenly.

"Why?" asked several voices.

"Did you have it in your house?" asked Thérèse pointedly.

"No," said Sophia.

"Then, how would you know?"

"I don't know," replied Sophia.

"That's it, you just don't know," said Thérèse with finality.

"I know this," Sophia replied, looking directly at her. "I like to be told where I stand. I like that! I like to know that!"

"Don't you know anything?" Thérèse asked sharply.

Sophia's blue eyes suddenly glittered.

"I know something you don't know," she snapped.

"No foolishness now," said Thérèse casually, "and what's that?"

Sophia suddenly brought up both closed fists forward.

"I know that you're lucky," she asserted, "and you're too stupid to know it!"

"Me!" screamed Thérèse.

Sophia held her two fists forward, ready to use them. Laurent and Maurice exchanged regards of admiration.

"Yes, you!" asserted Sophia.

Maman stopped working near the stove. She listened a minute, without looking, pursed her lips. Painfully, she then decided to go on doing what she had been doing. So long as they were both only exchanging hot words. Was the League of Nations doing any better?

"What do you mean?" cried out Thérèse, suddenly taken aback.

"I mean this," said Sophia, slowly lowering her fists, "that

. . . that it's nice to have your name on a blackboard. Somewhere. It's nice to know that what you do, good or bad, means something. To somebody. To anybody. That's . . . all I mean."

"Right," agreed Laurent. He sighed and looked at Maurice. There would be no scrap, after all.

"It means something, all right," commented Félix.

"It means a bag of candy," argued Cécile.

"It means," said Laurent smugly, "that you know where you stand."

"Oh," said Maurice, throwing out his chest and flexing his muscles, "you know damn well where you stand."

He gasped at his own words and everyone turned toward Maman.

She put the ladle from the pea soup pot on the stove, peered anxiously into the large pot where steam was rising to the ceiling, wiped her hands on her apron and slowly walked up to the blackboard and quickly chalked a red mark against Maurice's name. Taken aback, he now gazed at Maman with cold eyes. In the silence that followed, Laurent smiled quietly, Félix smiled, Emile was noncommittal, Marie made faces at Maurice (and Maman did not see that!) and Cécile counted all the red marks and white marks with her outstretched finger and got all mixed up. Sophia looked up toward Thérèse and there was a message of peace in the barely perceptible curl of a snicker on their lips. . . .

Louis returned then and put three large bottles of Moxie into the icebox, noticed that Sophia seemed to feel at home, and then turned toward Maman. Had his smart and decent children been smart and decent? No, Maurice had not. He looked at the blackboard, turned toward Maurice and looked at him as he pretended to study his fingernails.

"*Alors*, Maman?" he asked.

"Yes," said she.

Slowly now, Louis added up the plus and minus marks, and a deep silence crept into the kitchen. He shook his head. He picked up the eraser and at one stroke wiped all the red marks—and there was a short cheer. Next he picked up the white chalk and opposite each name he put one white mark, and one for Sophia too. Everybody cheered. And Sophia smiled for the first time and settled more comfortably into her chair.

Maman had prepared a supper of hot pea soup, boiled beef, home-fried potatoes, carrots, with a side dish of beets. For dessert there was ice cream, and tea and milk. After supper, and while the girls, and Sophia, cleared the table and washed the dishes, the men, that is, Louis, Laurent, Maurice, Félix and Emile sat around while Maman read in French, in her best teacher's diction, items from *Le Messager*, the local French-Canadian daily, and then, in English but with traces of hesitation, from the Groveton *Daily Herald*.

And then the girls were finished, and Louis served them each a tall glass of Moxie, and then he served the boys, and then he poured himself a shot of whisky, and lit his story-listening pipe. And Maman read them the story of young Adam Dollard, scieur des Ormeaux, whose selfless heroism and bravery and death, at Long Sault, with sixteen of his companions, saved the French colonists in the early days of French Canada against scalp-hungry Iroquois.

Maman read this epic, reminiscent of the Alamo, with vigor, rising intonations and dramatic pauses. . . . Once, Emile was seen to duck suddenly, as hundreds of Iroquois lunged screaming toward the fort held by the intrepid Frenchmen. . . . And Louis, holding to his pipe as a weapon, ducked and fought back, one with the defenders, as all of them, except one who managed to escape, were attacked, always by overwhelming numbers, and finally slaughtered to a man!

"And before going," Maman added, "they all had made their peace with God!"

It was past nine when the story was finished, and Maman kissed Marie and Cécile and Emile, and they in turn kissed their Papa on both cheeks, said their prayers and went to bed. Any whimpering meant a red mark and cheerful conformity meant an added squeeze from their Papa. At ten, Félix was bidden "*bonsoir*" and went through the same routine, and then Laurent, Maurice and Thérèse also. Maman now went to Sophia and took her in her arms. Sophia froze. But Maman hugged her, though her hands remained to her side. Now Maman kissed her on both cheeks.

"*Bonsoir*, Sophia," said Louis.

She nodded quickly at him and Maman escorted her to her bedroom.

Louis lit his pipe. Now, was she really a bad girl? What did anyone mean by bad girl? A bad girl was a girl, he had once heard, who went to bed with any lumberjack for the price of a brace of cordwood. Well Sophia was not *that* kind. Would Father Lebois permit her to sleep with sweet, pure, pestiferous Thérèse? No.

What other kind of bad girl was there? There had been his own sister. At seventeen, she had run away with a man, right after High Mass. Had she been a real bad girl? The man came from the brilliant world and his sister had been fooled. Was that real bad? If we think so in this world, may God forgive us in the next!

It's just that . . . a virgin of seventeen is a damn nuisance to some, and so is a boy of eighteen, and so is a keg of dynamite. But the greater pests are those who can see but a thin line between holiness and whoredom, and no pathway between. . . . The Creator Himself put the dynamite there. He expects explosions. Who are we to seek anything else?

O Lord, thank you that I'm no longer seventeen! Thank you that I'm spared from the frightened wisdom of those heavy in years who won't allow you in peace and comfort to make your own favorite mistakes—the ones they would like to repeat! Thank you to spare me now from those who remember not the hot cauldron that prevents the young from sitting for long anywhere at any time, who forget with what force unknown passions seek and must find outlets before one is ripe, who now remember in tranquillity only passions spent and misspent. . . . Thank you, Lord, and grant me humility.

Thank you, Lord, to remind me that you made parents out of people, and that from such can be born neither geniuses, nor criminals, nor idiots, but too often embarrassing hunks of ourselves. Thank you, Lord, and help me help this little bad one. . . . And while You are at it, help me help myself too!

He smoked his pipe and nodded in agreement with his own conclusions.

That next morning, Thérèse was commissioned by her Papa himself to take Sophia to St. Michel's High School and to register her. He warned Thérèse there might be difficulties.

"It is a task I don't envy you," he told her.

"Why?" asked Thérèse, suddenly alerted. "She's got as much right as anyone else. She's Catholic!"

"Sure," purred Louis, "but can you manage to get her in at this late date?"

"We'll see about that!" promised Thérèse firmly.

"Well," he hesitated, "I guess I'll have to depend on you, *mon amour!*"

After Sophia and Thérèse left together, he donned his work clothes, winked at Maman, and went to work, whistling. Sophia was admitted, of course, for Father Giroux, "the Napoléon of the school system," had been there before himself and greased the way. When the two girls came home that after-noon, Thérèse informed Maman that, yes, it had been hard, but she, Thérèse, had led her by the hand and Sophia had been admitted finally. Maman smiled and put a white chalk mark opposite Thérèse's name.

And then the two girls found that their clothes had been washed, and lay in a basket, damp-dry, to be ironed for the next day. Sophia picked up her clothes—Maman had emptied her suitcases—all the clothes she had in the world—then turned to Thérèse.

"I don't have to wash them," she announced. "See, they are all washed already!"

"Oh, yes," replied Thérèse casually. "Maman does all that," and she sat down royally in the nearest chair.

"You both do the ironing," said Maman calmly.

"I've never done that," said Sophia, hurt.

"Then you'll learn how," said Maman firmly. "Thérèse is very good, and she'll teach you."

"Maman!" Thérèse whined, but she did.

Supper time, once more, and though Sophia felt more and more at ease, she still spoke very little, and then only a few well-chosen words. After supper, and homework, Maman announced that this time she would read something different.

"Something peaceful, I hope," said Louis, lighting his pipe.

Slowly and distinctly, this time, Maman read the life story of a young girl, destined to become world famous, certainly not for great deeds as the world measures them, Maman explained, but for greater acts in the eyes of God. Thérèse Martin was born in France in 1873, the youngest of four sisters. Her family was well-to-do but average. When she was but five, her mother died of cancer. Early she resolved to give her life into God's service. "Heaven for me," she wrote later in her life, "will be doing good upon earth!" Félix yawned and slowly felt his pitching arm. Thérèse and Sophia were all ears. Cécile and Marie sat on their Papa's lap and listened.

As a young girl, Maman continued, and still in her very early teens, and yet convinced of her vocation, Thérèse pressed, against some of her family's objections, and against even those of a canon and a bishop, for permission to become a nun.

"Just a youngster!" protested Louis.

Thérèse decided, Maman continued, to petition Pope Leo XIII himself, and one day, when in his presence, she did. She begged permission to enter the Carmelite Order at the age of fifteen. Permission was granted and she became a Carmelite nun when she entered the Carmel of Lisieux in 1888. Too young to know her own mind, thought Louis, but then, at that early age, faith is at its purest, and the yearning to serve shines the brightest. . . .

She underwent a rigid postulancy. Then she became very ill, and while a convalescent, she wrote her famous book, *Histoire d'Une Ame*. At twenty-four, she was dead of tuberculosis. "So young," said Maman, "and so beautiful, and so saintly, and hence why her impact was, is, and will be world-wide!"

Then Maman went on to explain why this was so. Not so much because of the miracles attributed to Thérèse, or because she prayed for snow when she entered the Convent, and that it snowed that day, or that she wrote a book that captured the hearts of many. No, said Maman, the world was now turning more and more to her, and the Pope was considering her beatification, and then eventually her canonization, now in 1923, because, perhaps, of Thérèse's way of life. "I shall spend my heaven," said Thérèse of Lisieux, "doing good on earth!"

Sophia stared straight ahead at the crucifix on the kitchen wall. Louis was sure the light in her blue eyes came from tears held back too long. . . . Thank God, he thought, I'm not seventeen, when you're no one and want to be everyone, when tears and laughter come for the same reasons and for no reasons that you understand, when you love and hate what you want and loathe, when the reality of what you see is deep, deep black and nothing but a great sacrifice, and the noblest deeds can square off the disquiet that haunts you for evils you have no memory of committing. . . .

And now, they came, the tears down Sophia's cheeks, and her shoulders shook a bit and more tears came, and Maman looked up suddenly at her. Each, in turn, the children saw and then pretended not to see, for she wept silently. Louis stood up. Maman nodded to Laurent and he shepherded the others out of the kitchen. Louis took Marie and Cécile to bed.

"I don't know," he told them. "Something very sad hit her, all of a sudden, I guess."

That night, he slept in the *parloir* with Emile. He made himself a bed on the floor and Emile slept on the loveseat. Maman took Sophia to bed with her.

The next night, Maman read one of the adventures of Arsène Lupin, the great French detective, and held the whole family spellbound. One by one, again, all the children kissed their Maman and Papa. Almost casually now, Sophia kissed Maman on both cheeks. Suddenly she turned toward Louis.

"Good night, Monsieur Martel," she said, and smiled.

Louis looked up severely at her. He waved his index at her, indicating that she too should come and kiss him. Slowly, she approached him and pecked him quickly on the right cheek, and edged away.

"One moment, please," said Louis. "The left cheek? It will be lonely!"

She pecked at his left cheek and fled to her room, giggling.

When the children were all in bed, and quiet, Louis was relieved to be able to get back to his own bed. Still smoking his pipe, he flipped off his pants, and undershirt and underpants, grabbed his long nightgown and poked his head through the opening, puffing and blowing smoke all the while. He knelt by the bed, crossed himself, holding his pipe at a respectable forty-five degree angle from his mouth, and prayed intensely and briefly, quickly made the sign of the Cross and jumped into bed, yawning, still puffing on his pipe.

Maman had already put on her long, neck-high laced cotton nightgown and now, she too knelt near the bed for her prayers.

"It is going good with Sophia, *hein*?" said Louis.

"Good," said Maman curtly, not wishing to be disturbed during her devotions. She closed her eyes and lowered her head to concentrate.

"She's not a bad girl at all!" commented Louis.

"She's a good girl, yes, yes," agreed Maman, yawning, opening her eyes; she suddenly gave up, and rested comfortably on her knees by the bed. "Until last night," she added, "Sophia belonged to the bird kingdom."

"Now," said Louis, "what in hell is that?"

"The bird kingdom," insisted Maman. "Before, when I hugged her, did you notice how her arms remained by her sides? She wasn't accustomed to the hugging and the kissing. Didn't know how. She had no arms. Like a bird. No arms to embrace or to return a caress. Never had caresses and never gave caresses, until last night, or perhaps so long ago with her own mother, she had forgotten. . . ."

"Yes," mused Louis, "the bird kingdom. No hugging, no kissing. It's enough to make anybody bad, your respectful servant included," he added with a laugh.

"Louis," she snapped, rising from her kneeling position, "that was a mighty short and sweet prayer you treated yourself to tonight. It seems to me your prayers are getting shorter and shorter every night."

"Getting older and older every night," said Louis, "and in

many respects, this man, here, is not the man you married."

Maman slipped into bed beside him, settled herself comfortably against the small of his huge frame and sighed.

"However," she purred, "I notice that you still have an eye for the creatures at church every Sunday morning."

"I take notice," said Louis evenly, "that you take notice of that."

"It need not be taken notice of, particularly," she said, her head reared back in mock anger. "It strikes one's face that you scrutinize and analyze all the pretty legs that pass by everywhere. . . ."

He sighed contentedly. He knocked his dying pipe against the shaving mug by his bedside table, and dropped the pipe into it. Then he raised himself on an elbow, bent his head near Maman's, kissed her ear and then tickled her in the ribs. Maman gurgled, giggled, and moved away.

"My dear Cécile," he said, with a chuckle in his throat, "my dear, dear *amie*, the best one any man ever had. . . ."

He began to stroke her back gently, and she purred.

"On the left side, now," she begged.

"It is you I love," he continued, "and I love eternally, but when the day arrives that I stop gazing with fine appreciation at a passing pair of pretty legs, don't put me to pasture like an old horse. . . ."

"No?" said Maman.

"No!" said he. "Shoot me!"

"Oh, you!" said Maman.

She sighed, turned toward him and put a sleepy arm around his neck.

"*Bonsoir*, Louis," she mumbled. Her head sought out and found the accustomed spot near his shoulder and rested there.

"*Bonsoir, mon amour*," he mumbled, yawning.

"It is you who is the bad one," she murmured gaily.

And then, slowly, they let go of all the burdens and the joys of the day and slept.

Sophia made out. Soon she had her first quarrel with Félix, and her first red mark, and their dramatic reconciliation. Soon also she and Thérèse shared secrets they shared with no one else. One week, she had the unenviable record of seven red marks. Once also, she got the bag of candy and promptly gave it to Cécile, as she had promised, and found out that this entitled her to two white marks for the following week.

Two weeks after Sophia arrived, Hélène Pelletier became the bride of Laurent at Sacred Heart Church, Father Lebois officiating. There was a breakfast and dance at Marceau's Dance Hall, and Louis danced with the bride and Maman danced with the groom, and the newlyweds went to Boston for their honeymoon, and when they returned their small apartment on Maple Street was ready. . . . And Emile moved out of the *parloir*. Nothing else changed, and the months went by. . . .

Sophia made out. One Saturday night, she and Thérèse stayed outside the house, on a front porch, down the street, until eleven-fifteen. Louis was awfully mad at both of them.

"Papa," said Thérèse boldly, "we did nothing wrong. There were two new fellows we'd never seen before, and we talked. . . ."

"We talked and talked," said Sophia. "Is that bad?"

"No," said Louis, "that is not bad. . . ."

"Besides," she added, "we didn't know it was that late, and I have no watch. . . ."

This stumped Louis a moment. He reached into his pants pocket and took out two one-dollar Ingersoll watches. First he listened to the ticking of one, and then of the other. Then he handed one to Sophia. Both girls broke out into giggles, and Louis smiled also.

"Now," he stated simply, "we understand one another."

Another time, they gave themselves away. They found themselves talking excitedly before everybody about a movie they had seen. It was one Maman had forbidden them to see. Very specifically. Then and there she gave them both two red marks.

"Censorship!" cried out Sophia.

"No," said Louis. "Disobedience."

"Same thing!" cried out Thérèse.

"Don't press the point," warned Louis. How could Maman know if this movie was bad for the girls, for surely Maman had not seen it herself. Perhaps the priest had said so in church. Had he seen it himself? *Bonguienne*, concluded Louis, maybe he, Louis Martel, would have to see it, and decide this. After all, maybe it was a real whipper-snapper, and why miss it? But, in any case, children must obey their parents! And stay away from dynamite!

But Sophia did very well. She found the use of her arms. Twice she used them to push Maurice away when he got kiss-hungry and tickle-bent in the kitchen hallway. He never tried again. On the other hand—and Louis saw this himself by accident—the shy boy, once, who took her home after a school dance, found it very easy to hold her and kiss her in the hallway, near the door of the Martel kitchen.

"Don't break it up," he told the embarrassed pair, "on my account."

He smiled at them, as Sophia blushed and the boy quickly departed. It was only later that Louis remembered that it was Sophia who held the shy boy. . . .

One fine day, she will graduate, thought Louis, and so will Thérèse, but something else will surely come up, for life is one damn thing after another, with young girls around the house, and young boys fully aware of it. One fine day, it should ease up, and parents could pick up their medals for conduct above and beyond the endurance of man.

One fine day, both she and Thérèse spent an afternoon shortening their skirts, and then rather brazenly came skipping into the kitchen where Maman was preparing onion soup.

"Not for Sunday Communion, I hope," she commented.

"What's wrong with them, Maman?" asked Thérèse with passion.

"They look 'fast' to me," said she, shrugging.

"But, Maman," screamed Thérèse, "all the girls are wearing them above the knees. . . . Yes, they are, Maman!"

"Yes, Maman!" screamed Sophia. She stopped short, aghast at what she had said. She put a hand over her mouth quickly.

Maman smiled.

"If you wish," she said simply.

Sophia flew into her arms.

"We can wear them?" she begged.

"No," said Maman.

About this time, Louis came in from work. Both girls turned to him as to the Supreme Court. He gazed judiciously at their legs.

"Nice legs both of you chickens have," he said. He put his hands under the kitchen faucet, lathered them and began to whistle an old song.

Thérèse, with this unexpected support, began to parade gingerly around the kitchen. Louis wiped his hands.

"However," he said slowly, "those skirts are just about the right size for Marie and Cécile."

"But, Pa!" implored Thérèse.

"Those skirts," he said, "are too short to be truly elegant."

"But, Pa!" said Thérèse. "The boys like to look at legs."

"Thérèse!" said Maman, her face very stern.

Louis slowly poured himself a shot of whisky, then raised his right arm, as he always did, on great occasions.

"That is true," he admitted, "but believe me, my little sirens, if you want the boys to keep looking, don't overexpose the merchandise!"

Sophia gurgled in laughter.

"Maybe he's right!" she exclaimed, and Louis bowed to her with a smile.

Sophia Lewicka remained at the Martels' nearly nine months. Both she and Thérèse, who were now inseparable, graduated from St. Michel's that June with honors. Thérèse got her first wrist watch, an expensive present by her Papa's standards. Father Lebois gave Sophia the same present, which he got at a wholesale price from a local jeweler. Maman gave them both a silver cross with a silver chain, and they were to use these at several dances that June at Old Orchard Beach. Maman liked the silver cross and chain so much herself that she expressed a wish for one too, and Sophia promised her one when she made her first money. . . .

Late in June, Sophia left the Martels. Father Lebois took her to Boston where a job in a Catholic hospital awaited her. She wrote "home" every week for a year. She often spoke of a visit back to Groveton. Then she became a postulant nun in the order of the Sisters of Charity. Two years later, on their twenty-fourth wedding anniversary, "the bad one," as they still called her, sent "Maman" a new silver cross and chain, and to "Papa" an expensive pipe. A big one. "For story-listening," Sophia wrote.

They never saw her again. For Sophia Lewicka who, it seemed, had barely entered and passed through their lives, and yet somehow had found and given affection there, was now Sister Martha and attached to a hospital in the West. She would never come "home" again.

Each Christmas, and at each family birthday, there was

always a cheerful note from Sister Martha, and the assurance of her continuing prayers and lasting love. First Maman, then Thérèse, then Marie—as the years went by—wrote to her, always on behalf of the entire family, and gave her the minutest details of their changing lives. And Louis, who listened to the letters as they were received, and as they were written in answer to them, never failed to add: "You should put in there also that the pipe she sent me is still a good pipe—never heats up—and that I put my arms around her and give her a big squeeze, even though she is a Sister, and all that folderol."

One night, Father Lebois came, and gave his report to the Martels.

"I have seen her!" he said. "The institution where she works—night and day—is for children with frightful diseases, children whom nobody but the good Lord Himself, or His servants on earth, look upon with love! . . . You should see their eyes light up when she tells them her stories of laughter. . . . Or gives them a bath! Or feeds them! Monsieur and Madame Martel, I do believe she is a saint!"

"Perhaps," said Maman, "it all came about from reading the life of Sainte Thérèse, that night, long ago, when we wanted to love her and hoped that she would love us . . . ?"

"Perhaps," said Louis, "but something surely lit up in that little girl that night. Maybe we had the kindling, but no doubt God gave us the spark."

"Perhaps," said Father Lebois in quiet wonder.

Sophia's name was never removed from the list on the blackboard, even after she died suddenly at the age of thirty-two of an unknown disease. For one year, the family wore the conventional mourning, as if indeed they had lost a sister. But even before that, Father Lebois's report had caused Louis to think much about Sophia.

A saint? he wondered. Perhaps, and perhaps not. Surely not

because a little forsaken girl needed a big job of giving and had found it. . . . Then all mothers with many children, and a big job of giving, were saints, without the benefit of brass bands. Yet, if Sophia was a saint, this had happened in his house. . . . That night, surely, Providence had caused the little girl to pause. . . . Father Lebois was a kind man who, perhaps, exaggerated. . . .

However, if Providence had foisted this little troubled guest upon him, in all fairness, Providence perhaps had also decided to pay him off in this rare coin. . . . If this was so, how frightening the task, and how rewarding too the joy of the adult's blind groping to guide the young heart! Little Sophia Lewicka, an elect of the Lord? *Bonguienne!* If so, Messieurs, who else, these days, could say he'd been kissed by a saint?

"She was a bad one," he finally concluded for the benefit of his family, "the kind that gets and deserves a mezzanine box in Heaven for the big show." He lit his pipe and added: "I think she'll remember us all when we have to meet St. Pete, and save a few choice seats in the balcony for the likes of us."

4. The Inheritance [1925]

"When a man marries," said Louis Martel, "right away Providence puts his name down on a very special list."

His voice boomed out toward Laurent, who had married Hélène Pelletier two years ago, toward Thérèse, eighteen, who ironed the week's laundry, toward Félix, Emile and Marie, occasionally working at their homework on the dining table. Laurent was visiting tonight, and reading a picture book with Cécile, six, who sat on his lap. Maman sat near her new, polished kerosene stove—just two weeks ago Louis had given it to her for Christmas—and thoughtfully examined numberless pairs of woolen stockings, too many of which had holes in them. Louis's eyes, however, were riveted on Maurice, and he meant business.

Maurice was just twenty, and for a year now had been intolerably in love with Muriel Jolicoeur. This Christmas they had become engaged. He had had a good job at the Excelsior Grocery Store. Two days ago, the manager had released him. It made no sense. Maurice was a whiz in math, and all the women shoppers spoke of his helpfulness and cheerfulness. Oh, the manager had been unhappy about it. He liked Maurice also, but poor business was poor business.

Marde! thought Louis. There were just as many stomachs to feed in bad times as in good times. But then, all other grocery stores within fifty miles had done the same thing, and Maurice had scoured beyond that to find another job. Now, he had reached that state of mind, Louis knew, when a jobless man questions, not the facts of life as they are, but what his precious soul will sell for before any takers.

"If there is one thing I believe in," continued Louis, booming out his voice, "it is that Providence keeps a sharp eye for brand-new husbands. Yes, my children, I do believe in that!" And, he added to himself, if I don't believe in this, what can I believe?

Maurice fixed him with a stare of incredulity.

"Do you mean," he asked slowly, "that I, a jobless fool, should marry now? At this particular time?"

"Young people," stated Louis firmly, "should marry when they are young."

"But, Pa, I'm broke!"

"You may never be any richer," said Louis, "but you sure as hell aren't going to get any younger."

"But, Pa, who's going to pay the bills?"

"Providence," Louis began, "is the guardian . . ."

"Providence," interrupted Maurice, "is not handing out pork chops this year!"

Félix, Emile and Marie laughed. Thérèse looked up from her ironing, and Laurent nodded slowly toward Maurice.

"Yes," continued Louis, "I do believe Providence keeps her eyes out for new husbands. Now, take my brother Jos. Your own uncle Joseph. Had nothing all his life. Lived with relatives, or anyone who would take pity on him and put him up and feed him. Poor Jos had only the clothes on his back. . . ."

"And he just got married, and . . ." teased Maurice.

"Well, sir," continued Louis, "he met a girl as pitiable as he was, and they got married, yes. . . ."

"A rich girl, I hope?" said Laurent.

"No. Your aunt Constance—it must be said—was neither rich, nor very bright either. Well, sir, somebody gave him an old farm up in Canada nobody else wanted. Rocky ground. Nothing would ever grow on it but trouble. Well, the day after he was married, Jos went plowing this field and before noon he had found one, two, three, four American silver dollars. . . . That pepped him up. . .That's all he needed to get going. . . . Two years later he sold the land to a mining concern for a pot of gold!"

"Oh, Pa," snorted Maurice. "What movie is that from?"

"And I do believe," continued Louis calmly, "that Providence placed these silver dollars there—just for him! As a sign!"

"Oh, Pa," remonstrated Laurent, making a face, "please!"

"Now, wait!" commanded Louis. "This sparked my brother Jos. Marriage sparks husbands to do things, to try things, to hustle. When I heard about my brother, I realized I had discovered a new force in life, like electricity. . . ."

"Now, Louis," said Maman curtly, "you did not discover that."

"Every man," he stated, "makes his own discoveries. To him they are genuine discoveries, and I made my own. When I was married, I had nothing and yet nobody's stomach ever hung low in my house. Sure, we've had some close shaves—wouldn't be good sport otherwise—but, I say to you, what the hell?"

"Louis," said Maman, "your language!"

"Things are different now," said Maurice, stretching his long, strong arms and then letting them fall limply to his side, "things are tight and money is scarce, and you can't afford a new baby every year. . . . Let alone a wife!"

Laurent nodded toward Maurice, bit his fingernails and stared at the floor. Hélène was pregnant, and home, resting, tonight.

"Louis," said Maman, "it is true. People don't live on big farms now where there was always food, and there was shelter, and there was plenty of work, and mutual help, and a young couple had their own place to themselves to fix up, and where they could, and meant to stay the rest of their lives. . . ."

"Things are rough now in Maine," said Maurice. "It is a fact of life."

"A fact it is," added Laurent, "and hospital babies cost money, Pa, and where is the work coming from, I ask you?"

"From you!" shouted Louis. "When you see the pullet you like, you marry her, bed her and pluck her. Money! You worry about that later. *Eh, maudit!*"

"Louis!" cut in Maman sharply, "this time I give you an order, *hein?*"

Louis's face hardened. He got up from his easy chair, started to walk around restlessly looking for a pipe, any pipe, and then realized he had it in his hands. Slowly he filled it, tucked it down with a thumb deformed from pounding nails, pouring cement in wooden forms, and measuring spruce and ash and pine to fit within one-sixteenth of an inch.

What could a man do for his children, these years of economic depression, for Maurice and his sweet little girl with the musical name, Muriel Jolicoeur? Should a father stand by and say nothing, while the years drifted by, leaving them both as dried and bitter grapes on the vine? Nowhere does the land wait for the farmer, nor does the school of fish for the fisherman. This day, this hour, this minute is going, going . . . Poof! It is gone! Gone, Messieurs, into eternity, and if you are young, pray, what have you done with it?

He reached into his overalls pocket for a wooden match, scratched it the length of his rear, put it to his pipe, sucked on it and blew a big smoke ring toward Cécile.

"Allo, my pretty one!" he purred toward her.

"Allo, Papa!" she replied softly, shamelessly smoothing her dark, long hair, and carefully fluttering her eyelids, and then as he had patiently taught her, she gave him a quick, subtle wink.

In the pause, Laurent announced casually that it was eight o'clock and time for him to go home. Hélène wanted to go to confession tonight and she would just about make it before nine. Sunday was her Novena Sunday to Ste. Anne, and tomorrow, Saturday, was a very busy confession day at Sacred Heart, and she did not want to get caught in the rush. Maman said it was time for Cécile to say her prayers and to go to bed.

"Just now," said Cécile, hurt, "when Papa is acting up?"

Louis winked at her and she slid out of Laurent's arms, ran and threw herself up at her Papa as he fell slowly back into the easy chair, curled her around his shoulders on his right, and put his big fingers gently over her eyes to close them, and in a few minutes she slept, her straight little nose nuzzled dangerously close to his red-hot pipe.

"I never saw," he said in a very low voice, "so many grown-up young men so scared. . . . Not even when, as a young man myself, a bunch of us were caught in a forest fire. . . ."

When Cécile moved a bit, he gently rocked her in his arms. Félix looked up from his copybook and waited. Thérèse rested her ironing hand and waited. Maman shook her head sadly. Everybody looked so gloomy, thought Louis. As if the planet Earth was scheduled to crack up at noon tomorrow!

"No sir," he continued, "never saw healthy young people before, who were in love, as you are with Muriel—that's the one with the large dark eyes and the soft-spoken voice—is that right, Maurice?"

"Yes, Papa, she's the one."

"I see her often at nine o'clock Mass," said Maman. "Always neat, never twittery."

"Well," said Maurice, "she's not twittery, Maman, but she's scared, like I am."

All right, all right, mused Louis, so we are scared. And yet, shall we resign from life? Something had to be done, and *bonguienne*, he would have to be the man to do it.

"I can understand why some people are scared," he said, warming up to his subject, "but a Martel! Never!"

"Why a Martel?" asked Félix, dropping all pretense at homework.

"Because!" asserted Louis. "*Bonguienne!* Why, Martels came to these shores hundreds of years ago, in a wilderness beyond imagination, facing angry Indians, ferocious animals . . ."

"No ferocious animals," corrected Maman. "Bears, perhaps."

". . . and nothing to eat," he continued, "except what they scoured around for themselves!" What did they eat anyway then, besides salt pork and fish and game? Louis suddenly asked himself.

"Yes," said Maurice, painfully concealing his boredom.

"And furthermore," continued Louis, "especially for Martels—all Martels everywhere—to be scared is just plain ignorance, when there's a good chance that soon Martels will come into real big money!"

Even Maman turned toward him. And he told them, that night, the wild, wild rumor, the wild, wild legend that had enough of the truth to be wholly believed. . . . Oh, there had been rumors before, vague, sporadic, and Louis had never spoken of them officially, but tonight he did, because, as he explained, for long no one had been able to prove them true, and now it was just as hard to prove them false. . . .

For this legend had a firm foundation in the facts of French-Canadian history. Everybody was agreed on that— even Maman, and she knew her history—though, in this case, much of it revolved around word-of-mouth tidbits from those who had perused old archives. Why, just recently, in a Québec court, a decision of law had opened up all kinds of possibilities that gave the legend a legal basis for the wildest realities. That is, as Louis was quick to point out, for only those whose families had come to French Canada in the very earliest days of the French colony. Also, as he pointed out, for those who knew their genealogy!

"The D.A.R. my neck!" he had said every Thanksgiving, and he said it again. "Why, when the Pilgrims came here for their turkey, we French-Canadians were already frying mountain trout all over the East Coast!"

"Chauvinist!" said Maman, with a smile.

"All right," he said, "but French-Canadians don't know how to brag. When someone compliments one of our daughters, we reply: 'No, she's not hideous!'"

Maman laughed. She then nodded toward him.

"You are perhaps right, Louis. We apologize too easily for what we are. Perhaps it's just that we merely cling to ancient forms of courtesy. Maybe . . ."

"Maybe," snapped Louis, "it's because, in the past, we've kissed too many asses!"

"Now, Louis, and right in front of the children!"

"I'm sorry. . . . But we have no reason to apologize to anyone. Certainly not to any Henglish haristocrat. By God, we don't!"

"Of course not," said Maman quietly. "Our record, as a people, is a proud one."

They had come—the Martels, the Bolducs, and others, from France—to the new, wild land—New France, they called it—and they had meant to stay, to raise their families, to cultivate the land and to enrich it. And they had done just that. And then, England and France had fought for the land, and France had lost. . . .

"A sad, sad day," Louis admitted. "But then the kings of France, like all kings before or since, were just as empty-headed as those of England."

"The present English kings are nothing," Maman pointed out calmly. "Just figureheads. Don't get mad at them!"

"I don't," he said, suddenly pounding the kitchen table. "All Henglish haristocrats are worth less than a fart in a high wind. Sure, they can lay cornerstones, but men build the bridges for the people to use. . . ."

And then, New France became Canada, and then the United States rebelled against "Henglish haristocracy" and made overtures to Canada to join in the fight for freedom from kings and their oppressive or unnecessary rule. . . . Canadians of both English and French descent turned down the invitation. . . .

"A sadder day, yet, that!" exclaimed Louis.

In time, however, French-Canadians had become a distinct cultural entity, both in Eastern Canada and in New England, whose more than five million people freely bridged the borders of Canada and the United States. Solid citizens, under whichever flag, they saw no reason, however, for relinquishing their hardy attachment to the Catholic faith, their strong traditions of family life, a common French language, respect for personal idiosyncrasies, and consolation for a vanished but glorious past in a genealogy that harked back to the France of the Sun King. How was all this to enrich the Martels? Very simple.

When the first French colonists came, some were granted *seigneuries* by the Kings of France, and some were given possession of tracts of land. The first Martel in the New World, Louis also by Christian name, was granted 50 arpents, so the story goes, on land which was now within the confines of the City of Québec. Because of the temporary needs of common defense, at that time, against Indians, and later, Englishmen, several religious and governmental installations were permitted to squat freely anywhere on the lands. Now, over three hundred years later, this same land of the Martels was tightly covered and occupied by business, government and religious real estate development.

"Invaders!" Louis would mutter darkly.

They were invaders, however, of long and honorable standing on tracts of land that was now worth large sums of money to their historically rightful owners. Who these were legally was something else again. How much the land was worth nobody knew. Every time the worth of this land was discussed, Louis simply threw his hands up in the air.

"You can't calculate it!" he would remark crisply.

For fifty cents, you could write to Québec, or Ottawa—somewhere—and secure a complete genealogy of your family. Thus Louis could trace his family history from his father, through the first Martel in New France, all the way to Normandy. He had recently secured several of these genealogies, and his children read them over and over to him—and no skipping, because Louis remembered dates, names and places if they had been read to him only once. Any tome that retold the stories of those early Québec and Montreal days was precious data that he now knew by heart.

A few days after he revived the legend, and it flourished with new strength every passing day, Emile came home from school one afternoon with some electrifying news.

"Papa!" he declared breathlessly, "there was a Charles Martel who was a great Frenchman, perhaps the greatest. . ."

"Yes," said Louis calmly, "but many of them have been."

"Oh, but this one," gasped Emile, "this one was the first to repulse the Mohammedan invaders when they threatened to destroy France. He gave them a good licking!"

"A Charles Martel, huh?" pondered Louis. "Well, could be. When was all that, Emile?"

"In 732 A.D.!"

He turned toward Maman.

"Did you know this?"

"Yes."

"And you've kept this intelligence from me?"

"It's taught in all schools," said Maman primly. "Surely Charles Martel is not related to you."

"Could be!" said he. "Now, if I'd had an education, I'd have dug up all these facts. A worse crime than being uneducated is to be both educated and asleep over a gold mine!"

Maman shook her head in impatience.

Every night now, the subject of the inheritance was first on the kitchen table for discussion—right after homework, and sometimes as a part of it. Suddenly Félix developed a keen passion for geography and history, previously his two weakest subjects. Marie invaded libraries for any and all accounts of the discovery and growth of North America. Emile read the accounts of the Jesuits and Recollect missionaries. Thérèse and Laurent and Maurice pored for hours over digests of law on inheritances, wills and land rights.

And Maman? She rejoiced. Once again, she could escape into the adventures of her favorite detective: Arsène Lupin. Louis smoked his pipe and damned himself for not being able to read the written facts himself. He knew many things, however, that were not in the books.

His own father, Louis Martel, senior, had been proud of the fact that one of the first, if not the first, Catholic marriage performed in New France had united a Martel male with a Brouillard female. It was to this first family of colonists, or one of the first, that was granted the land that was now a part of the city of Québec, and this land, once mostly virgin forest, had been the incentive and the reward—for Martels and others—to colonize the country.

Martels, and others, had cleared this land and settled on it. Dispossession of it was therefore a grave historical injustice, in Louis's opinion, and in the opinion of those, who, around Groveton, began to listen to him and to believe in his case. In truth, the Martels had multiplied, and thus helped to colonize Canada, and Maine for that matter. And Massachusetts, Rhode Island and Michigan, too.

Louis's Papa had been a strong believer in large families. He himself had had seventeen children. As the youngest one, Louis could remember his aging Papa's concern when his brothers' and sisters' families numbered a mere nine, or seven, and, sometimes, as few as five children. His Papa would often shrug his shoulders sadly and mutter to himself.

"This race of ours is dying out!"

Yet all Martels had an enviable record, from the earliest days to the present, of marrying young, breeding long, successfully, and late in life. Childlessness rarely happened and was therefore always a Divine comment of some kind. A reading of the Martel genealogy, it seemed to Louis, revealed that Martels were planted generously from Labrador to the coast of Louisiana. Some were legislators in the Provincial governments, and a few at Ottawa. Some had achieved political recognition in the United States. Many were priests, one at least was a bishop, two were bankers, many were businessmen and rich farmers, some were nuns, a few had spent time, or were reported now to be, in jails. All who had married had been prolific. And all, of course, could also claim an equity in the Martel inheritance. Wait! Now, this family fertility could prove to be a damn nuisance!

He thought this one over a long time. One night, he decided.

"In union," he told his family, "there is strength. Together we can make the government give us our land. . . ."

"Or the money," chirped in Thérèse.

To this everybody, except Maman, agreed heartily.

"Can I go to the movies?" Félix asked, tactically striking when he thought he had a chance.

"No," said Maman. "Once a week is enough. As it is, there is in this house too much fantasy now!"

Several Martel Family Committees had already been formed by now in some places in Canada, and Louis immediately formed his own Groveton Martel Committee, with Thérèse as Secretary, and himself as President, "pending," as he said, "regular elections." There was a Hector Martel Committee in Woonsocket, Rhode Island; a Guy Martel Committee in New Bedford, Massachusetts; a François Martel Committee in Lewiston, Maine. A plethora of Martels were united for action in St. John, New Brunswick. Most of these Committees, however, functioned so loosely and idled so much of their time painfully sorting out and adjudicating first lines of consanguinity and rehashing old tales of Martel wonders that nothing much was done. Then, a Father Doucette, regionalist historian, wrote a few letters, indicating his interest in the case.

Things now went into high speed. Forgotten were the records of births, marriages, deaths and the whisperings of unofficial and official scandals. Father Doucette, a good man and a scholarly one, had begun to write letters, out of curiosity, but the documents people said he had found had spurred him on in earnest. The Québec Court decision of 1924 was a fact no one could ignore, for this epochal judgment had recognized ancient seigneurial land rights granted by a Ruler of France, long after the seizure and occupation by an English king. Well!

That spring there were times when strong rumors swept and nearly overwhelmed the Martels. The Canadian Government, it was said, was in a dither over this rightful claim. It was no longer a question of whether or not to settle a just claim. No. It was the dilemma of when and how equitably to divide up the loot. This spread so fast and was believed so fiercely that one Martel, who had just started to work in a bank in Millinocket, told the president to go jump into the Penobscot River, resigned, and went home to wait for the government man to come with the check. Others thought this somewhat premature.

As president of the Groveton Martel Committee, Louis prevented anything as wild from developing. Every Sunday, after High Mass, he held court near the rectory of Sacred Heart. It was there his cronies joined him every Sunday for an exchange of the latest news, and a pipeful of uncut tobacco. And for Louis, that's where the trouble started.

For there was a Léon Brouillard, and his family, in Groveton. This was, thought Louis, a hard, cruel fact. The conclusion could be dangerous. If a Martel had first married a Brouillard, long ago, all Brouillards were also entitled to some equity, according to Anglo-Saxon law, the law of Canada, where the money, if any, was coming from. It helped some, but not much, when Louis began to "talk up" French law which, as everyone was agreed, was the law that obtained when the deeds were signed by a king of France. Under it, a female had few, if any, rights at all. In law, the Law is supreme, argued Louis, even if it is not justice.

Every Sunday morning, however, Léon Brouillard placed a vociferous claim. He too felt entitled to some of that money, and he stood his ground with Louis. Often the two men would grow very angry, and faced one another, red-necked, until Father Giroux, hearing the loud voices, would come walking casually toward the group. It went on, thus, for a long time. Also Léon Brouillard stuttered. It took him forever to state his case. Louis had only to fix Léon with a cold, hard stare for him to stutter even more. Finally, Louis asked

Thérèse to read some Brouillard genealogies, and he listened, staring at the wall, unseeing.

"I guess," he concluded at last, "we'll just have to cut in the Brouillards also. Justice is justice, even when not legal. If only he didn't stutter. I wonder what the first Martel male ever saw in a Brouillard female!"

But then, things got worse.

While Father Doucette wrote his rather conservative reports, more descendants, cousins of either the Martels or the Brouillards came forward. First, the Gendrons, then the Bouthilliers, and later, the Hamels and the Peloquins. All lived right in Groveton. All could and soon did produce their own genealogies. Cryptically these revealed that somewhere, during the many decades, one or several of them had bedded with and brought forth descendants from Martel offshoots. They too had been fertile. And for their fortuitous drop of Martel or Brouillard semen they now expected repayment in kind.

"Blood money!" exclaimed Louis.

"Won't be much money left," whispered Thérèse.

"Not enough to buy pork chops," added Maurice.

One Sunday in May, Louis came home around one o'clock. He had attended nine o'clock Mass and had remained near the rectory until now. There had been the usual discussions and arguments, but when he entered the kitchen, he smiled grandly toward Maman, grabbed her, whirled her around, then went directly toward the armoire and took out a bottle of whisky. Maman gave him a quiet look and then went back to preparing her dinner.

Now Louis began to whistle, as he lit the stove and put a kettle of tea over the fire. When the tea boiled, he poured three shots of whisky into a tall glass, then poured the tea into it, threw one tablespoonful of maple sugar into the hot drink, waited a second or two for the ingredients "to get acquainted," then he passed the glass to Maman to test it. She took the glass carefully, took a small sip, fearful of burning her lips, and then nodded assent. In deep silence, the children read the funnies.

He sat down in his easy chair and drank it slowly, his Adam's apple doing a happy jig in his throat, his eyes transfixed upon the crucifix on the kitchen wall.

"How was the sermon, Louis?"

Good. The sermon had been good. Maman went on preparing dinner. The sermon had been very effective—that is—until the last ten minutes when he had nearly dozed, but no matter. Today he felt very happy. He had found the solution. There had been two collections, true, at the nine o'clock Mass, one for Chinese missions, and one for the new parochial school, but that was all to the good, and what was money, except to be spent?

"Did you see Laurent and Hélène at Mass?"

"No, they go to St. Francis."

"Why?" asked Maman, frowning. "That's not their parish."

"I know that."

"But why?" persisted Maman.

"Over there," he explained, "it's a short-sermon church and a one-collection parish. But I saw Father Giroux this morning, and he was so pleased with my solution that he shook my hand before everybody!"

"What for?" asked Maman. She opened the oven and poured gravy over the roast. "Have you become a peacemaker, Louis?"

"Well, Father Giroux said to me: 'Monsieur Martel, you are a Talleyrand!' I don't know the man, but in any case, I'm going to have another drink."

"Talleyrand," said Maman, "was a French diplomat."

"Is that the truth?" And Louis did a happy jig right then and there.

"Diplomat," said Maman, "your dinner is ready."

For Louis had found the answer to the problem of the proper distribution of the Martel inheritance—the riddle, which, it was said, was ruffling the best Anglo-Saxon legal minds at Ottawa. And now, at this Sunday dinner, he would inform his own family.

Maman called the children to dinner. Thérèse had changed from her blue Sunday dress to everyday wear. She helped Maman set the table. Maurice, Félix and Emile sat at the table and waited. Marie reached into the sugar bowl, got herself a handful of maple sugar, passed some to Cécile, and ate some herself before Maman could see them. Then Louis sat down, his bronzed face barely concealing the glow of the tea-whisky. Everyone lowered his head. Maman rushed to table and sat down just as Louis, mentally composing his prayer, cleared his throat once, and began.

"God bless the food we have here today, and keep this home together in love and charity and prosperity. Amen!"

Everybody said, "Amen!" and Cécile said it twice.

"And protect our inheritance," suddenly added Louis.

"Amen!" said Thérèse.

"Cut the meat," said Maman, "and make small pieces for Cécile."

Louis sharpened his tools noisily. His face glowed—toward everyone.

"Good roast beef," he said, "good whisky, a good night's sleep, and the Catholic religion, that's what makes a man . . ."

"Cut the meat," said Maman.

"No potatoes for me," said Thérèse quietly.

"You don't eat enough," said Maman.

"I weigh too much," asserted Thérèse.

Louis cut meat slices and deftly dropped them on plates that Maurice quickly placed before him.

"In the days when I was a young man," said Louis, "when my eyes were alerted for likely members of the opponent sex, we didn't judge them by whether or not we could lift 'em."

"Papa," said Maman, "cut some more meat."

"Yes, Papa," said Emile, "don't make us languish!"

Louis put both elbows on the table and looked at Emile.

"That's a fine word, 'languish,'" he remarked slowly. "Now, I know you'll become a priest, some day, or a diplomat, like your Papa."

Later, when he had finished his second portion of chocolate ice cream, he told them of his ingenious plan.

". . . And so, I suggest, and I propose that the big split shall be of equal shares among the Martels and the Brouillards, and of quarter shares to all first cousins of these two families. . . ."

"Equal shares?" asked Maman, taken aback.

"Yes," said Louis, fighting back, "with all the Martels and the Brouillards!"

"With *all* of them?" shrieked Thérèse.

"*Batege!*" shouted Maurice. "Equal shares and quarter shares with all the children and grandchildren! There won't be enough!"

"Correction!" said Louis, pausing to light his pipe, and looking as judicial as he could. "Equal shares, yes—not for all members of these families—but . . ." And he paused dramatically. "For all the *heads* of families!"

"Heads of families!"

"MALE heads of families!" said Louis, accentuating each syllable. "Father Giroux said himself that this was a solution worthy of a Solomon. Wished he'd thought of it himself. And it is wise because it's fair!"

Maman pursed her lips, smiled, and then began to pick up the dishes. Thérèse was so crestfallen that she forgot to help Maman.

"Explain it, Louis," said Maman. She stopped and studied her three sons and her three daughters. "Let's see how this money we have not yet touched, and may never see, will be divided among those who are already disappointed about the unknown amount to be distributed all over Canada and the United States."

She suddenly burst into laughter. Louis raised his head toward her and fixed her with his coldest stare.

"My children," he said, "there is something worse than men of little faith, and that is a woman of no faith at all. I know of no more terrible misfortune that could befall any man!"

Maman began to put the dishes into the sink, smiled to herself, but said no more.

"Now," continued Louis, "this is it. To give an example. I, as a male head of a Martel family, will get a full share. . ."

"Of what?" asked Maurice.

"Of the sum total, that's what!" asserted Louis. "That means that Laurent, who is also a male head of a family, will get a share equal to mine, and that's only fair, though he's not been a head for a long time, nor has he worked at it as long as I have."

"You are a diplomat," said Maman, handing dishes to Thérèse and Marie, and gently pushing them toward the sink.

"And Monsieur Brouillard," asked Marie in a low voice, "he is a male head?"

"Yes," conceded Louis, "a stuttering male head!"

"And if I become a priest," protested Emile suddenly, "I'll never become a male head?"

"If you become a priest," said Maman primly, "money won't matter, *chéri*."

Louis roared. He asked his question of the whole wide world: "Who's a diplomat now?"

In the months that followed Louis's discovery of the solution to the distribution of the inheritance, things went on just about as they had before. The cost of living remained unbearable high, jobs were just as scarce, and the mills, as the saying went, were "very dull." There was only one thing that was different, somehow.

That June, more than the usual number of young people bought engagement rings, published banns, secured wedding rings, bought furniture, and married. The boys rented summer formals and the girls wore their mother's refashioned wedding dresses and it was very gay. . . .

June is always a busy marrying month, but this year sons and daughters of the Brouillards, the Bouthilliers, the Gendrons, the Hamels and the Peloquins, as well as of other families, swelled the marriage statistics. Sacred Heart throbbed with *Lohengrin* and *Ave Marias!* Oh yes! Maurice Martel married Muriel Jolicoeur, of the large dark eyes and the soft-spoken voice. And all the Martels and the Jolicoeurs danced until dawn. . . .

True, for three weeks after, he and his bride lived on the fourth floor of a poorly furnished walk-up apartment, ate beans and tea for breakfast and most of their other meals, at night, either with her family or at Louis's house. Then Maurice got a temporary job as a grocery clerk in Portland, and then he moved to Augusta for a permanent one. Two years later, an opportunity opened up: assistant manager in a large grocery store. Six years later, he was the manager. These things happen, of course, with or without a legend to spur them into being.

It has now become blurred, this legend, the possession of those who remember only a past glory, and the object of gentle scorn from those who are the future. The first still browse over genealogies on long winter nights, at weddings or at funerals. But the latter are the contemporaries of the Martel grandchildren, and they sport new cars, home freezers, hi-fi sets, and dwell in split level houses. Most of them also have been blessed with large families of healthy children. Too much committed to the present to look backward, they trust to God, and to their own sweat, for the future. Without the inheritance, all have done well. Many have done very well, and all of them practically from scratch. This, perhaps, they have forgotten. Very good.

"A man's memory," says Louis Martel, "should be as good as his forgettery: you can't tackle the frights of today if you've got yesterday's fears in your back pocket."

A few months after Maurice and Muriel were married, however, Maman, who was noted for her memory, cornered Louis late one night as he was filling up his last pipeful for the day. She turned on him suddenly.

"Louis, the famous inheritance? Whatever happened to that?"

"Inheritance? What inheritance?"

Maman's lips curled in mockery and her eyes shone in victory.

"Aha! All that money! All that talk! All that historical research! And Father Doucette! What happened to your grandiose attacks upon the Government of Ottawa? *Hein*?

Louis smoked in peace, and said not a word.

"Just talk, Louis?" she persisted. "Nothing but talk?"

"Well," he said at length, "about many things one can never be sure, except that the more one lives, the closer one is to the end of one's days, and one must go on working, and eating, and sleeping . . ."

"Just talk, *hein*, Louis?"

"And one must, on the first trip around, grab the drink from the tray, lest when it comes around again, the tray be empty. . . ."

"Oh, Louis!" she shouted. "You're impossible!"

"So?" he asked suddenly. "Will not Maurice get his inheritance?"

"Which one?" Maman asked, and burst into laughter.

"The only one! The one each man blueprints and grabs for himself. And by the way, how old is Thérèse?"

"Eighteen. Soon, she'll be nineteen."

"Any good offers yet?"

"These days are hard on young men. They have no money. . . ."

"And less imagination!" Louis added sadly.

Again Maman burst into laughter.

"*Mon Dieu!*" she exclaimed. "For Thérèse, what big plans are you concocting?"

"Don't really know," he confessed. "But it gives one to think, does it not? There is one thing I do know. Somewhere there is a young man in a fog. Unaware is he that he is for Thérèse. Already, Providence has put him on a special list. . . ."

"I hope so," she said, enjoying this, "and I'd like a peek at that list."

Louis Martel was deadly serious.

"Once," he announced, "I too was on that list."

She became immediately serious.

"Oh, I do believe that to be true!"

"Of course, it's true!" he exclaimed. "For some class of people there's simply got to be a kindly Providence. For the blind. For those who've taken too much to drink. For the absent-minded ones, and window-washers, and railroad men! For new husbands! And for nice girls modestly waiting at home for a husband! And good thing for them there is such a Providence!"

"Yes, Louis," murmured Maman.

He threw his hands up in the air.

"Who the hell else would take on the job?"

5. The Rosary [1927]

"The night," said Emile, "is the hardest time of all!"

He was now fourteen, and Louis suddenly turned toward him.

"The first night, especially!' continued Emile. "And so tonight, at nine o'clock, let us agree to recite the Rosary together, the family in the kitchen, and Maman in the hospital."

Louis looked again at his son. For the first time, it seemed, in a long time. *Bonguienne!* Children had a way of surprising you.

"Very well, " he agreed.

"The Rosary, of course, will not hurt Maman's chances of getting well very quickly," Emile concluded, "but in that way, we will all be together and we will tell Maman and she will not be alone. . . ."

There were some fifteen other patients with her in the women's section of St. Anne's General Hospital, but this was her very first night away from home, and this was a cold and rainy February night. . . . And at nine o'clock, in the ward, the lights went out. . . .

At nine promptly, Louis took out his Rosary beads and knelt near his easy chair, facing the print of the Holy Family. They were all there who could be: Laurent, his wife Hélène, heavy with child again, Thérèse, twenty and still single, Félix, Emile, Marie and Cécile. Maurice and Muriel had not come yet. They all knelt where they were, leaning near a chair or a table, their left hands covering their faces, and their right fingering their beads.

"Hail, Mary," intoned Louis, "full of grace . . ."

". . . blessed are thou amongst women," whispered Maman.

". . . blessed is the fruit of thy womb, Jesus," recited Louis.

". . . Holy Mary, Mother of God," the children intoned, in reply.

". . . Pray for us sinners . . ." whispered Maman.

". . . Now, and at the hour of our death! Amen!" replied the children.

". . . Hail, Mary!" said Maman, "full of grace . . ."

How suddenly it had come, the pain in her side! She had not cried out, at first. There had been so many other things to do at the same time—the confirmation dress for Cécile— Félix had a tooth that ached, and he should have that taken care of—and Louis had not been able to find his pipe again. She had not cried out at all, come to think of it, though her side ached and she was sure suddenly she would faint! When she realized that, she decided she must not frighten the children. She tightened herself up inside, and sat down, her forehead damp, and waited to be alone with Louis or one of the older children. It happened to be Félix. He was sixteen.

"*Chéri*," she panted, "a secret! Tell Papa I'm not well. Not well at all. A secret, Félix! Tell Papa."

He came. Tenderly he lifted her and carried her to their bedroom. Dr. Lafrance came. He examined her. Louis asked no questions. He was afraid to. But then, Dr. Lafrance did not appear worried.

"Right now," he said, "let her rest, Lou. It may be overwork. If the pain returns, however, we'll have to see."

A day passed. The children competed with one another to nurse Maman and to bring her cheerful conversation and presents and flowers. On the second day, during the night, the pain returned, fierce, burning, and would not go away. Maman kept her hands over her mouth until Dr. Lafrance came. He gave her a sedative. Louis spent the rest of the night sitting up in the kitchen, or napping, alert in a moment if Maman called.

At breakfast the next morning, Father Lebois came.

"Monsieur Martel," he said jovially, "you need a shave, and a drink." And he put his arms around his waist. "Louis, I know a lady who can help around the house. A Mademoiselle Thibault. Shall I ask her to come?"

"Oh, thank you, yes," said Louis, "but my wife should be in good health soon, I pray."

"I pray, too," said Father Lebois, "but not right away."

"No?"

Father Lebois sat down and looked serious.

"Louis, I have just spoken to Lafrance. Madame Martel should be in the hospital."

"Hospital? Is it that bad?"

"Now, now! People go to the hospital to get better!"

"Is she that sick, Father, that she must go?"

"She must go," said Father Lebois.

Louis thought it over a moment.

"If it must be," he finally assented.

Now Father Lebois came closer to Louis.

"Another thing. I'd like to give her the Sacraments."

"Oh, no!" said Louis, shocked.

The priest smiled slowly. He put a hand over his shoulder.

"Now, Louis, the Sacraments don't kill people. In fact, the sick person is the better for it. I know!"

Louis stayed home that day. Once the children were at school, the ambulance came and took Maman to the hospital. Dr. Lafrance would wait no longer. Later that day, Father Lebois came to see her and stayed a long time with her. He heard her confession, gave her Communion and the rites of extreme unction. First to see her that evening were Louis and Thérèse. She had slept the entire day, without sedative of any kind and sat up in bed now, cheerful in a quiet, subdued fashion. They spoke of many things of no importance and found it easy to do so. Dr. Lafrance came in and they left the room together. Suddenly he turned toward them.

"One would think," he said, "that the last rites, as they are called, are the bells announcing the end. Well, they are, in many cases. In this one, and I've seen this many times, the patient seems to have been given a new mysterious peace within. A better medicine than we have found, so far!"

"Besides that, how is she?" snapped Louis.

"We are doing," said Dr. Lafrance, "all we can."

That first night, the first one without Maman at home, was one Louis wished he would never see again. And yet, Emile's suggestion had made it bearable, and she would get well again, God willing. . . .

"Hail Mary, full of grace . . ." he intoned.

". . . The Lord is with thee . . ." whispered Maman, fingering her beads.

". . . Pray for us sinners . . ." responded the children.

And every night that she spent in the hospital, at nine they recited the Rosary together and there were times when they felt very close, that soon Maman would be well again, and there were times when, admittedly, the monotony of "Hail Marys" invited the mind to rove wildly and to conjure up other scenes and other times . . .

"Hail Mary, full of grace, the Lord is with thee . . ." said Louis.

". . . Blessed is the fruit of thy womb, Jesus!" whispered Maman, sleepily.

". . . Now and at the hour of our death. Amen!" responded the children in singsong.

Laurent looked up at his Papa and wondered how could a man take and absorb fully without a long cry of anguish the sickness of the woman he had loved so long, unless he had a strong faith . . .

"Hail Mary," said Maman wearily, and then she smiled and whispered: "Louis! Louis!" It was at night that she missed him most, his rough gentleness, his supply of laughter and his strange need of it, his slow, painful education in many things, but above all, his uncluttered mind that made him see and teach, in his own way, what she had not known. . . . "Hail Mary!" And her mind wandered and she rejoiced in its wanderings. . . . To the year Democracy invaded the Martel household. . . . When their Papa taught what he did not feel obliged to practice. . . . When the older children began to fight to achieve an identity of their own . . .

. . . She was reading to them the History of France and rather forcefully re-creating the stirring events of the Revolution of 1789–1795, when the Bourbons fell, and their Papa rejoiced, and when liberty became license and their Papa frowned. . . .

Laurent, the oldest, listened to this with great attention and then made some researches on his own. Long after Maman had passed from the Revolution to Napoléon's Empire, he still repeated with passion the words: "*Liberté! Egalité! Fraternité!*"

One evening, in a plot with Maurice, he offered to read something from a school textbook to the family. Beaming, Maman quickly approved, and Louis settled in his chair to listen. Loudly, with proper emphasis, Laurent began to read: "When in the course of human events it becomes necessary for one people . . ." He read on and on, and Maman smiled her agreement throughout this reading of the Declaration of Independence. ". . . Let Facts be submitted to a candid world," proclaimed Laurent.

And Laurent read on, putting his own emphasis where he wanted by the tone of his voice, the calculated pause. . . .

"A Prince," he nearly shouted once, "whose character is thus marked by every act which may define a Tyrant, is unfit to be the ruler of a free people."

"Great stuff, that!" raved Louis. "That's telling off those Henglish haristocrats!"

Maman, however, thought it best, for the sake of variety, to introduce the *Fables* of Lafontaine as a gentle diversion, but Laurent persisted. Maurice nodded in agreement, and Thérèse smiled. At first Maman dismissed this "revolution," as she put it, as "the normal crisis of the first-born." But, one day, Laurent began to ask disquieting questions. And during the silence of homework!

How come, he asked, when he or Papa failed to pick up and hang up their clothes, he got a red mark, and Papa didn't? How come, he pointed out, when he or Papa let go with a certain four-letter English word, or a certain five-letter French word, he got a red mark and Papa didn't? Was there, he concluded loudly, a rule of justice for young persons and another rule of justice for Papas? Were children half-citizens and half-slaves? Maurice nodded. Thérèse beamed, and Maman pursed her lips, smiled to herself, and turned to Louis.

"*Alors*, Papa," she said, "make a decision, and make a good one, and make it now."

"I say that Laurent has got me in a corner," said Louis slowly, "and I add that I don't like it."

And the children roared.

Louis, however, sought legal relief from Maman that night when they were preparing for bed.

"You're the finely educated one," he said sharply. "Is this part of the adventure one has to endure from educated sons and daughters?"

"Yes," said Maman, "and Laurent is a very good student."

"That may be," he said, "but at this rate you and I may be educated out of house and home."

"No, we won't!" she reassured him. "He who fears the spread of ideas invites mediocrity . . . and Democracy is the greatest idea to come to Man!"

He thought this over for a moment and stroked his chin.

"Well, now," he demanded, "now that we are all equals and brotherly in this house, who's going to be the boss? I'd just like to know?"

"You!" said Maman simply.

"It's good to hear that!" he snapped.

"And tomorrow," added Maman, "your name and mine go on top of the blackboard. . . ."

"Well," exclaimed Louis, "I'll be a monkey's ass!"

"And that," snapped Maman, "gets you your fist red mark. There is only one kind of justice. We must practice what we preach."

He pouted for a while.

"Guess, after the women, the children will want to vote too!"

She tickled him in the ribs.

"Is that so bad? This Democracy?"

Not so bad at all, especially when he began to think that a little more of the same would go a long way, in the Carpenters Union, in the City Hall, in the State and in Washington, in the local school government, in the Sunday collection. . . .

On the third night, Maurice and Muriel came to see Maman, and that night, at nine, they joined the family for the Rosary.

"Hail Mary, full of grace . . ." Louis recited.

"The Lord is with thee," whispered Maman.

"Pray for us sinners," responded Maurice with the others, and suddenly he looked up and saw the back of his Papa's neck where the gray line was slowly winning out over the black. . . .

"Now, and at the hour of our death. Amen!" whispered Maman.

"Amen!" said Maurice. Pray for us sinners, he thought, and wondered if his Papa ever thought of that afternoon, long ago, when he and Laurent were just boys in their early teens. . . . He wondered too if Maman remembered. . . . On the way down, this afternoon, by car from Augusta, he'd told the story to his wife, Muriel, and now he wondered when his own son, Albert, would be old and wise enough to hear it too. . . .

"We were about sixteen or seventeen," he told Muriel, "and Papa took us to a ball game near Metaska Pond. We'd taken the trolley—it was about three miles to the ball park—and after two miles, the trolley tracks ended, and we had another mile or so to walk, and we walked on the lonely road when suddenly a car came along—that was long before Papa got the Oakland—and Papa waved his hand for a ride. . . .

"This guy was drunk as a lord, but we found this out only after we'd clambered into his car. Well, he started his car at thirty miles an hour—it was a touring car—and in no time he was whizzing down the country road, now to the right, now to the left side of the road, barely missing a horse and buggy on the way, and I was scared we were all going to get killed. . . .

"After a minute, Papa tapped this guy on the shoulder—hard—and told him calmly that he wanted off at the next turn in the road. 'No,' said the drunk, 'you wanted a ride, didn't you?' 'Yes,' said Papa, 'but now I want to get off!' 'What for?' said the drunk. 'To pee!' said Papa suddenly. The drunk seemed to sympathize with that, and he stopped the car suddenly, nearly throwing us out. After we were off, Papa told him he shouldn't be driving in that condition, and the driver told him to go to hell, and Papa tipped his hat and replied: '*Bonjour, Monsieur!*' and the drunk took off in the lonely country road. Papa said later he should have tied him up to the nearest tree.

"And there we were, stuck in the middle of nowhere, and it was dusty and hot, and Pa was dying to get to the ball park—you know how he loves to see the two teams warm up—and we started to walk down that road, and Papa with his long strides soon had us ten feet behind him, and then a second car, this one a real big job—probably the only other car on the road that day—comes along. . . .

"It took Pa only a minute to get in the middle of that road, and while he waved us off the road, he waved his hands like mad in a friendly way toward this big car, but this car—a Packard, I think—just honked and honked and Papa had to get off the road in a hurry as the car swept by, leaving us in a cloud of dust and heat. . . ."

"That was mean," said Muriel.

"That was Father Pinsonneault," said Maurice. "You know, old Father Pinsonneault?"

"Oh! He probably had a sick call."

"Yes," said he, laughing, "a sick call with a canoe and a fishing pole. That's where we saw him an hour later."

"No?"

"Yes! Papa just stood there, on that road, looking with unbelieving eyes at what he had just seen, first looking at Laurent and me, and then looking at the back of that big car. Then at the top of his voice he began to cuss!"

"Oh, no!"

"Oh yes. It was the most eloquent cussing I'd heard. Papa was truly eloquent that day!"

"What did he say?"

"He stood there!" said Maurice, once more picturing his father as he was then, tall, tense, and mad as hell, his dark hair shining with sweat. "I'll remember it as long as I live. He waved his fist at the dust and he pronounced his judgment in a terrible, terrible tone: 'My children,' he roared, 'there will be more joy in Heaven when the drunk gets there than when old Pinsonneault crashes in. . . . For, in truth, I say to you, that it will be harder for a priest, riding a Packard, to get into Paradise, than for a drunk, in a rat trap, who stopped for us when we were by the wayside!"

Muriel laughed gently.

"God will forgive him," she said.

"Who?" asked Maurice. "The priest or Papa?"

"Our Father, who art in Heaven. . ." recited Louis, starting on another decade of the Rosary, "give us this day our daily bread. . ."

"Thy Kingdom come!" said Maman, and she chuckled, sleepily.

"Thy will be done," recited Louis.

"On earth. . ."and Maman chuckled again. She chuckled because she could see a tall, thin, skinny cop. Papineau was his name. "Clothespin, he was called!" she whispered. He wore a blue jacket that reached to his knees. . . . Clothespin! Dear, dear Clothespin!

"Blessed is the fruit of thy womb, Jesus," recited Louis.

"Holy Mary, mother of God," responded Félix.

"Pray for us sinners," responded Emile.

Maman chuckled again. Yes, Emile and Félix were then little boys, and little sinners, too.

. . . And that night, the children sat around the kitchen table doing their homework when Papineau, the policeman, came and knocked at the door.

"It's me, Papineau," he said.

Again, she saw Félix and Emile swiftly slip right out of their chairs, out of sight and under the table. Papineau, tall and as thin as Saint Francis, his blue jacket reaching to his knees . . .

"As we forgive those," recited the children, "who trespass against us . . ."

"Clothespin!" whispered Maman to herself and chuckled.

"Monsieur Martel?" Clothespin asked, as he removed his cap.

"Yes," said Louis, "and what's your trouble?"

"Maybe it's mine," he said in his thin voice, "and then maybe it's yours. You see, we've been getting complaints about some boys going over to the lumberyard on Christopher Street by the river, and raising all sorts of devil out there. . . ."

"Do you know who the boys are?" asked Louis.

Clothespin looked around the kitchen at the entire family and seemed to be counting heads, and then he counted two pairs of shoes sticking out, just beyond the table. Everybody kept very quiet. Clothespin turned toward Maman, and then Louis, and all three looked at one another with blank faces.

"Roughnecks!" he said roughly. "That's who they are!"

"Bad boys," agreed Maman.

"They deserve a good talking to," admitted Louis.

"We know who they are," repeated Clothespin.

"Any of my boys?" asked Louis quietly.

"Well," said Clothespin evenly, "these boys are real smart at running away from me. So, I couldn't rightly be sure. You see, they tie a fifty-foot rope to the bottom log at one end of a long woodpile, and stretch the rope to its full length, and then they wait for hours, until I happen to walk past my beat, and when I come by, swinging my stick, that's the time . . ."

". . . they pull the rope!" finished off Louis sadly.

"Why, yes," said Clothespin, surprised at this, "and all the logs, one after the other, come tumbling down in one great big roar. . . ."

Louis passed a hand slowly over his face, probably to hide a smile.

"I can hear it now," he admitted, "for it makes a great big noise. Like thunder, sort of."

"Just like thunder!" admitted Clothespin.

"And you know, perhaps, who the boys are?"

"We know who they are," said Clothespin firmly. "They are roughnecks, and from bad families. I'm almost sure they are not your boys, Monsieur Martel, because I know you would not tolerate such behavior. . . ."

"I agree with you, Monsieur Papineau, for if they were my boys, I'd be ashamed of them. . . ."

"And I know what a man like you would do to them," added Clothespin, winking at Louis.

"And you're right," said he, winking back.

"Because," continued Clothespin, turning toward Maman, "one boy, tonight, got a broken leg—nice family too—they live on Groveton Road—and he's in the hospital now, and no family, as you know, can afford that very much. Some of the logs rolled over him."

"Oh, *Mon Dieu!*" gasped Maman.

"Broke the leg in two places," stated Papineau coolly.

Louis thought this over a moment.

"Probably used too short a rope," he concluded sadly.

Maman's face grew grave, however, as she observed Clothespin's attempt to appear officious only to achieve an ascetic and sad expression. He was the thinnest and skinniest cop in all history of crime-prevention and detection. She loved him at that moment, and forever after. I shall pray for him, she resolved.

"Thank you for telling us," she said. "We appreciate it."

"I just thought," said Clothespin sadly, "that you'd like to know what some boys are up to."

"*Merci*," said Louis. "I'll warn my own boys about it."

Clothespin winked once more, sadly, and left. Louis then asked Félix and Emile to come out and to show themselves. He then handed them each a red chalk and silently pointed to the blackboard and each put a bad mark against his own name. And then they waited—for doom itself to come.

"That's all," said Louis. "And it's for cowardice!"

"For what?" asked Félix, becoming braver.

"What did we do?" asked Emile, playing it sweet.

"You hid under the table, that's what," said Louis, "and that's enough. Another thing. If you must try that deviltry, make sure you use a hundred-foot rope!"

"Yes, Papa," said Félix.

"And for God's sake," he added, "when you pull the rope, stand clear!"

"Yes, Papa," said Emile.

"Pray for us sinners," responded the children.

"And when you pull the rope," whispered Maman, "for God's sake, stand clear, my children!"

She began to weep. Oh, what a weakness! *Mon Dieu!* And she knew it, the weakness of a child, but she wept, and she felt better and now she said to herself that she wanted to go home right now, to sleep in her own bed, where Louis took up most of the space, and to see her children. Who on earth was doing for them what must be done? She wept and did not care if it was a weakness, she wept on. The Gray Sister came by in the dark quietness, leaned over and put her cool hand over her hands and her prayer beads.

"Madame Martel, have you need of anything?"

For a long moment, Maman nodded quickly without being able to say a word.

"I want," she finally gasped, "to see my children!"

Now she wept unashamedly, though this nun was very young.

"Yes, I know," said the young nun. "I know! I understand!"

She placed a hand over hers and sat by her bed and held her hand for a long time.

On the fourth day, Napoléon Bolduc, Maman's Papa, and her two sisters, Rosaline and Marie, arrived from Canada. Louis had asked Thérèse to write to them that Maman was, well, pretty sick. Over the years, Grandpère had threatened to come for a visit, and now he was here. Aunt Rosaline and Aunt Marie, now in their fifties, complained of various ailments, but Grandpère carried his seventy-six years with a straight back and a steady refusal to accept the slower life-speed everybody was willing to map out for him. Louis met Napoléon Bolduc at the station and rushed him to see Cécile, while Rosaline and Marie went to his house to look after the children. Maman was overjoyed to see her Papa. He kissed her on both cheeks, wiped a tear from his deeply tanned face. She kept him for the full hour of visiting time.

"Now, Cécile," he announced, "with all those children, this is no time to be sick, understand?"

"Yes, Papa."

"Now. Have you been a good girl for that nice man you married?"

"I have tried, Papa, I have tried."

"Then, hurry up and get well, Cécile. I have plans for your children. . . ."

Maman raised herself on her elbows.

"Papa," she warned, "better ask my husband before you decide anything. Louis has not changed. . . ."

Grandpère laughed. Outside, he cornered Louis.

"She does not look in the best of health," he said.

"No. We have a good doctor."

"*Bon*. Now, let us see your children. . . . I never spoiled my own children, Louis, but I'm going to spoil yours. . . ."

"Go ahead, Grandpère. Every child should inherit at least one grandfather. That's the only thing they are good for. . . . To teach them how to break the rules, and get away with it."

Grandpère chuckled and Louis did too.

Visiting hours in the wards at St. Anne's General Hospital were from seven to eight weekdays, and two to three on Sunday. At the next opportunity, Rosaline and Marie went to see Cécile, and the three sisters had a long session of reminiscing. Grandpère, however, stayed at the house to get acquainted with the miracle of his American grandchildren, and great-grandchildren. Marie and Cécile dogged his footsteps and unashamedly searched his coat pockets, as they always had Papa's, for pennies, candy, chewing gum, and anything else that might lay hidden there. As a defense, Grandpère had a large supply of maple sugar angels, and he handed them out generously.

One day, Grandpère sharply observed Hélène, Laurent's wife.

"When is the little one expected?" he asked.

"Any time now, Grandpère," said Hélène lightly.

Grandpère's face darkened.

"Somebody dies, somebody is born," he mumbled. "Somebody is born, somebody dies. Everything evens out in the long run. It's simple mathematics. You have a good doctor?"

"Oh yes. Doctor Lafrance."

"That's good, but I know something better."

"You do, Grandpère?" asked Laurent. "Please, tell us."

And both approached him with grave attention.

"Just this," he began, "that I wish you," he turned toward Hélène, "only glad thoughts. It is good for the child-to-be."

"Thank you, Grandpère," said Laurent.

"With Madame Martel so sick," said Hélène, "it is not always easy to do."

"Exclude," insisted Grandpère, "all other thoughts but glad thoughts. Do this that the child to be born shall be of sound mind and body, and his blood free of poisons."

"Yes, Grandpère," said Laurent. He smiled gently toward him.

Grandpère laughed suddenly.

"Old men are often old fools," he said, "and I'm no exception. Now, do you believe what I have just told you?"

"If I did not," replied Laurent quietly, "I would say so!"

Taken aback, Grandpère gave him a quick look.

"By damn," he said, "I believe you would."

A few moments later, alone with Louis, Grandpère turned to him.

"Louis," he said, "you have taught your children the rules of ancient courtesy before an old man's queer ways."

"They are not badly behaved," admitted Louis, "but then, Grandpère, we have had your blessings these many years, and I, your gentle, lovely daughter. . ."

And for a moment his voice broke, but when little Cécile came running between them with a smile, he recovered quickly.

Hélène was delivered of a nine-pound baby boy the next morning, in another wing of St. Anne's General Hospital. He was promptly baptized Jean-Paul Napoléon Emile Joseph Martel. Muriel was godmother, and Grandpère Bolduc himself was the godfather. A few days later, the baby was brought home, and a four-generation photo was taken, Louis holding Jean-Paul, Laurent standing near him, Hélène sitting in a chair on the other side, and Grandpère Napoléon proudly commanding the entire scene. The photo was rushed to Maman, framed, and put on her bedside table.

Later, in the Martel kitchen, Grandpère looked somewhat sadder.

"Somebody is born," he mumbled, "and somebody dies."

"Yes," agreed Louis.

"It is simple mathematics," continued Grandpère, "but it adds up to true immortality, Louis."

"Yes, Grandpère, and will you touch a drop or two for the new baby?"

"I will," said Grandpère. "In fact, I'll have a double shot. Never hurt me before, and with age comes a new freedom. To Jean-Paul!"

"To Jean-Paul," said Louis, "and to his children, and grand-children and great-grandchildren!"

"Yes," said Grandpère, "and that's immortality!"

He drank his double shot in three gulps.

"*Salut!*" said Louis, and then he drank his shot.

"*Salut*," agreed Grandpère, "and this is damn good whisky. Got any more of it?"

"Yes, and I'd be honored to serve you another." Well, well, thought Louis, this *bonhomme* was not an ogre, after all.

Grandpère smiled, took the glass Louis offered him, and began to look at him very closely. Then he gulped his drink in one swing of his arm.

"Louis," he said, "I bet you once thought me a son-of-a-bitch!"

"I did."

"Well, Louis, I only wanted to set you up, to help you, but I was, let us admit it at last, a son-of-a-bitch!"

Louis drank his shot of whisky also with one swing of his arm.

"Grandpère," he said, "I don't really think so now, and I say so because for me that is the truth. . . ."

"I was hard on you," said Grandpère. "You were taking my last one, and I could have helped you. But! We just didn't understand one another. . . ."

Louis put his hand on Grandpère's shoulders.

"No, we didn't, and that's no sin. One generation should not attempt to pass comment upon another; they don't speak the same lingo. I know. I have children too now. . . ."

At this Grandpère twinkled in sudden discovery.

"It's your turn, Louis!"

Louis nodded.

"I bet," he said, "my children often think of me as an old bastard too, set in his ways, and as stubborn and blind as King George the Third. But then, Grandpère, it's only fair. . . ."

"Yes," said Grandpère, enjoying this, "it's your turn!"

"However," said Louis, serving him another drink, "when I get as mulish as you were, I want somebody to kick me in the ass!"

Grandpère sat down. He laughed so hard he nearly spilled his drink. And Louis sat down hear him, laughing too.

Seven days after Maman was admitted to the hospital, she underwent an operation.

"She'll feel better for it," Dr. Lafrance had predicted serenely.

After the operation, Louis paid a short visit to Maman. She was still under sedation. On his way down the hall from her room, he ran into Dr. Lafrance.

"Well?" said Louis.

"Louis," said the doctor, "do you want the dream or the reality?"

"I want nothing but the reality."

Dr. Lafrance nodded his agreement to this soberly, as if he had expected nothing else. He pushed Louis gently toward a window and now stood facing him.

"My good friend," he announced, "the reality is bad."

"Bad, huh?"

"Very bad. In this case, Louis, medical science is helpless."

He put his arm around Louis, but he brushed it aside.

"How about another doctor?"

The doctor shook his head.

"Do you think I haven't done that, Louis?"

Once again he put his arm around him. This time Louis did not push him away.

"We are going to do all we can," he added slowly.

Louis shook his head to all this ritual.

"That's a tough reality," he said finally, twisting his hat in his hands. "Like a sneak blow to the body.

The two men stared at one another. In the early days Lafrance had delivered his babies and Louis had paid his bills in repairs on his house. In later days, and firm friends now, they had enjoyed together many a poker session, and a private joke. Today, they simply stared at one another.

"I wish I could do something," said Lafrance.

"You can," said Louis, swallowing hard suddenly. "Tell no one yet. No one, understand? Above all, the children. They will need to be prepared, and there is time for that, isn't there?"

"And, Madame Martel?"

"There is no need to tell her," he said, tapping his forehead with his index, "she knows."

"How can she know," said Lafrance gently, "she's been under heavy drugs. She has no pain. How can she know better than I?"

"She knows. She knows like she knows many things. I knew it, too, but I was nursing the dream."

"Lou, I'm sorry. Is there anything else I can do?"

"There is. Chase all the pain there is away from her."

"I'll do that, Lou."

"I hope Cécile has finished with all pain. From you or God now I can ask for no more, and certainly for no less. However, as I say, may His will be done."

"Yes," said Lafrance.

"But," snapped Louis, "let it be done—without pain."

Two days later, Maman had recovered sufficiently from the effects of the operation, and Louis came to see her, alone. He wondered if anyone could read his awesome secret, written large in his chest, and in his heart, and wondered too if his cheerfulness did not in fact give him away. . . .

Maman spoke little of the operation, but now she spoke of something else, and spoke of nothing else. . . . Because of the visiting rules, it had been agreed *en famille* that a list must be drawn allowing each adult member to visit in rotation. Emile, however, who was not quite fourteen, and Marie and Cécile, aged ten and eight respectively, had to be excluded from this list. Maman had never failed to ask how they were, as well as Michel, age two, son of Laurent and Hélène, and Albert, baby son of Maurice and Muriel, and then she asked pointedly when they also would come to see her. With the hard logic of the sick, she soon wanted to see precisely those who were denied visiting privileges. Therefore, one night, Louis Martel knocked gently on the door of the office of Sister St. Claire, Superior of the Hospital. He removed his hat, and briefly and humbly stated his case. The thin lip lines of the tall, thin nun never moved.

"I understand," said Sister St. Claire.

"I knew you would," said Louis.

"However, we have our rules," she said, "and they are made for the welfare of our patients. These rules must be kept. You understand?"

"No, Sister. But I'd like to."

"We have different rules in rooms for private patients. But we have no private rooms right now, and we won't have maybe for some time. The rules are different, but rules are rules."

"And who makes these rules?" he asked, in genuine curiosity.

"I make them," said the Sister.

"Do you ever break them?" asked Louis, his face flushing.

"Sometimes," replied the Sister, "but not often. And not now."

His face became very tense and hard. He made two steps toward the door.

"Wanna bet?" he shouted.

Sister St. Claire rose.

"I never gamble," she replied.

"You should, Sister! Win or lose, it would be good for your soul."

"I know what's good for my soul, Monsieur!"

He thought this one over for a minute, then decided he would try something else—somewhere else. He put on his hat and made for Dr. Lafrance. The doctor smiled weakly and admitted his own helplessness. He said plainly that he couldn't antagonize the Mother Superior.

"I need her in my business," he asserted.

"In that case," Louis said, "Madame Martel is leaving this prison, even if I have to take her to a Protestant hospital."

"Louis, they have the same rules."

"Then, I'm taking her to a private hospital!"

"Louis, you can't be serious."

"Wanna bet?" said he, his voice rising. He went directly to the rectory where Father Lebois was sipping hot wine and soaking his feet. Two nights ago, he had trudged in the snow, without his rubbers, on an emergency visit to a sick parishioner. He had a sore throat.

"Monsieur Martel," he said in a hoarse voice, "I cannot interfere at the hospital. I should be there myself, in bed, but I'm not going if I can help it. Sister St. Claire is outside my jurisdiction, and in a manner of speaking, it is one of the great consolations of my life."

"Afraid of her, too?"

"Yes," admitted Father Lebois. "She is the Mother Superior, a real saintly woman, a holy Amazon, you might say. I don't think you're going to make her bend. She does not bend easily."

Father Lebois shook a finger in warning.

"You want to bet?" Louis asked.

As the days went by, Maman began to scan her arriving visitors with growing agitation. One night, she looked directly at Louis and specifically asked once more to see the younger children. And, once more, he recited the rules. Now, she began to weep into her prayer beads.

"Do this little thing for me, Louis. Is it so much to ask?"

"No, it certainly is not."

"Then, why can't it be done, Louis. You can do it!"

"It's against the rules, *chérie*."

"Do this little thing for me, Louis!"

His lips tightened.

"Cécile, they forbid visits to young children for good reasons, I guess. But if I can, and if they come, it must be a glad visit. Do you promise that, Cécile?"

"I promise. There will be no dramatics. I promise! But do this little thing for me, please?"

"I will do it," said Louis, his face relaxing.

The next evening, at ten minutes to seven, Louis Martel came tearing into the reception room of St. Anne's General Hospital, his heavy shoes hitting the floors like the clatter of cavalry. In his right arm, he carried little Cécile, and his left hand swung forward, his fist tightly closed. For the occasion, Cécile wore her Confirmation dress of white and a large picture hat; she clutched a bouquet of roses in her hands and presented a somber look in her dark eyes. A Sister ran toward Louis and there was a sharp question in the upraised index of her right hand. When she reached him, he bent near her, and against the dark veil that covered her head, he whispered one word.

"'Pendicitis!"

"Dear me!" said the Sister. "Follow me!"

He did. She led him down a long hall, then stopped abruptly.

"Wait here a minute, Monsieur. Don't worry. I'll be right back!" And she trotted away.

"Thank you, Sister," said Louis.

He waited a bit, as she had told him, smiled at Cécile, then started to walk in long strides toward the second floor stairway. It was deserted, so he strode up the stairway in long steps, and on top of the stairs, he met the second floor nurse. She held a pad in her hands and checked papers at her desk. She stared at him.

"Yes?"

"'Pendicitis," said Louis.

"Oh, yes. Who is your doctor?"

"Doctor Lafrance, Nurse."

"I see. Well, wait here a moment. Now, I'll take your name . . ."

"Say," Louis snapped, "what's this running-around you

people are giving me? It's 'wait here!' and 'wait there!' What's going on here, anyway?"

The nurse stared at him, and slowly began to back away, an unanswered question in her eyes.

"I'll be right back," she promised as she ran down the steps.

Louis waited a few seconds, and then walked quickly down the long hall, entered the women's ward, strode past the ladies in bed, receiving their adult visitors, came up to Maman's bed, and deposited Cécile in all her starched splendor into Maman's arms.

"'Pendicitis!" announced Louis with a wink for Maman.

"I got 'pendicitis," said Cécile, covering her mother with kisses.

"Me too, *chérie!*" giggled Maman, gazing happily at her last-born. They had a very nice visit.

When Dr. Lafrance heard about it—he was wearily signing a death certificate—he sat down and laughed. It brightened up his whole evening. Father Lebois, making his night rounds, rejoiced also, but not openly. After all, he observed, such happenings were bound to disrupt any well-organized institution, even if run by iron hands. No one, however, expected a recurrence, and the next day babies were born, operations were performed, beds were made, and meals were served, but there was much sudden laughter in the women's section during the day, and as evening approached, a few mothers began to express hopes that their own younger children might come to visit them too.

That evening, again, Louis came tearing into the reception room of St. Anne's General Hospital, his heavy shoes hitting the floor like the clatter of cavalry. This time, he carried in his right arm Marie, and in his left arm a package containing a fancy pillowcase for Maman. Marie, who was not much bigger than Cécile, plainly looked scared, and kept looking toward her Papa for reassurance. Again a Sister came quickly toward him with a sharp question in her eyes. Again Louis bent near the veil that covered her ears.

"'Pendicitis!" he whispered.

The Sister bent forward in a fit of giggles, and turned away to come face to face with Sister St. Claire. As Louis later put it, "She had suddenly sprung out of an ammonia bottle."

"Yes, Monsieur Martel?" she asked crisply.

"I want this child to see her mother. Now!"

"Put the child down," she said, "and come with me."

He did as she ordered, but slowly. Furiously his mind searched for a good countermove. Sister St. Claire briskly walked up a flight of stairs and into a quiet corridor. He followed. Suddenly he guessed, and realized he had won his fight with the holy Amazon. That very afternoon, Maman had been moved into a semi-private room, and toward it now, Sister St. Claire led him and Marie. She opened the door, smiled coldly, and left. It was a very small room, with two beds, but Maman was alone and it was private. Marie rushed toward her. They exchanged hungry kisses.

"Sweet Marie, have you 'pendicitis too?"

"No, Maman, I just miss you so much!"

Thus Father Lebois, Dr. Lafrance and Sister St. Claire had been forced to face and solve the problem. It had called for an emergency conference.

"This man," said Sister St. Claire, "is an emotional idiot."

"'Pendicitis!" exclaimed Father Lebois, and Dr. Lafrance had then bravely joined in the laughter.

"Hospitals can stand a little jollity," Lafrance suddenly asserted. "It stirs the juices."

"That may be," snapped Sister St. Claire, "but our work here is that of tending sick bodies, making beds, bathing patients, giving medicines, administering and enforcing the rules that will assure our patients protection, rest, the best medical care, attention. . . .”

“And love and charity too,” said Father Lebois crisply, “and of all these, let us first have love and charity!”

“And a few more cases of ’pendicitis!” added Dr. Lafrance, chuckling softly.

One Sunday afternoon, Emile got to be alone with Maman in her private room. They had a long quiet chat.

“You should do as you choose,” said Maman, “not as I would like, for you yourself will have to answer to God and Man. . . .”

“Yes, Maman.”

“But if, as you say, you believe you have the vocation, then do become a priest. . . . At fourteen, it is time to think of it. . . .”

“It’ll cost money, Maman, and if I don’t have the vocation, Papa will have to spend a lot of money for nothing.”

“For nothing!” said Maman sharply. She sat up straighter in bed. “Get the education—a good classical education—in the humanities—and even if you never become a priest, no matter what else you do become, you’ll be a fuller man for it!”

“Yes, Maman.”

“To become a fully educated man,” she continued, “whether or not you are a priest, is a sound objective in itself. There’s no loss there at all. And there’s not enough money to repay for the good life it will open up for you. I wish all my boys could go to college. And the girls too!”

“Yes, Maman.”

“And if they do not, their children will! The life of the fully educated man develops always into a glorious journey with never-ceasing discoveries. Remember that, but of course, if you do become a priest, a good priest, I shall be so proud of you—so very proud of you, my little Emile!”

“I shall celebrate my first Mass for you,” he said simply.

"And Papa too. Don't ever forget Papa."

A frown came over his face and Maman saw him push back a rebellious lock of hair over his bold forehead.

"But," he interposed, "will he want to spend all that money for me and my education? Perhaps he does not understand. After all, he never even went to school, you know."

She settled herself more comfortably in her bed and studied him. He was near the age of crisis, a religious boy, but a boy with a sound boy's normally bad habits, and some good ones too, and then she remembered that the traditional coolness had appeared between Emile and his father. He spoke polite but short words to his Papa. The direct approach was always the best, she concluded.

"Emile, do you ever feel ashamed of your Papa?"

"What? Me, ashamed of Papa?"

"Yes, Emile. That is what I am asking?"

"Oh, no! Never!"

"I have been ashamed of him," said Maman quietly.

"You, Maman?"

"Yes. In the first years of our married life, I was. That is why I want you to acquire learning so passionately."

"That is why I do also!" he nearly shouted.

She recognized the signs.

"Then, Emile, why not admit it?" Her voice was suddenly sharp.

He lowered his head.

"Yes, Maman," he finally confessed. "I too have been ashamed of Papa. Sometimes. But only for not knowing how to read and write. Or to endorse a check. I have been ashamed every time he took such a long time to sign his name. I have been ashamed, but I also felt mad at myself for it!"

"I know, because I hated myself for it too!"

"But then," he added, "there are so many wise things Papa

knows. He has much learning in his head and in his hands, and I also feel proud of him. Only sometimes, he acts as if education was a lot of tomfoolery—you know?—unimportant and trivial!"

"That," she said, "is the pride of the man. Would you brag of your illiteracy? Would you not hide it behind sly remarks? Let him fool himself, Emile, but don't let him fool you. However, a man can become fully learned in many things and yet never go to school. Your father is that kind of a man. He can't read books—no!—but he can read people. Emile, my son, that is a lot more difficult and just as useful. Some educated people have read many strange and esoteric books but cannot read the everyday people they love. . . ."

"But, Maman, do you think Papa will want to. . . ."

"But he will!" Maman exclaimed. "It is a promise he made to me long before you were born. And Papa keeps his word. When we were married, after I left the convent, and I talked of my life as a nun, he said that if any one or more of our children ever wanted to give themselves to God's service, he would spare no expense or sacrifice. . . ."

"He did?"

"He promised it to me again yesterday. And now, let's have no more worry on that account."

"Maman, you always take care of everything! I love you so much!"

"If you do, are you too big a boy to give me a kiss?"

"Oh no, Maman!"

"Or to hug me?"

"No, Maman, never!"

He did, and then she pointed to a black leather book with gilt edges by her bedside.

"And now, would please read to me. At random. It's *The Imitation of Christ*. You know it?"

"Oh, yes."

"You read so well, and it would give me so much pleasure."

"Yes, Maman, and I'd like that too, very much."

He opened the book at random, and where his eyes fell, he began to read.

"Love keeps watch, and sleeping slumbers not, wearied is not worn out, pressed is not depressed, deterred is not confounded, but like a living flame and burning torch, it breaks its way upward. . . ."

As the days passed by, Dr. Lafrance increased the dosage of drugs, and Maman slept, and when awake, was very often incoherent. There were times when she spoke of herself in the third person, as Sister Bolduc, and reprimanded her girls for gossiping. Suddenly one night, her mind seemed to clear. Louis was alone with her, and he told her Thérèse was due to come also, a little later.

"She has many fellows, she's over twenty now, but no proposals yet," she announced firmly. "Not yet!"

"She'll marry soon enough for me," said Louis quietly.

"Louis, don't let her become—a martyr—an old maid."

"I won't. I'll see to it."

Then Maman closed her eyes and seemed to try to compose her thoughts. She fingered her prayer beads.

"Louis, I can't help worrying. The children. They are still so young."

"They will be all right. Before God, I promise you that."

Maman's face became troubled again, and he reached for her hand.

"Louis," she said suddenly, "if I should not come home, please marry—again."

"What a silly thing to say!"

"I say it because I mean it. Marry again, and marry soon."

"Me! At my age. An old fool! With grown children?"

"Not only for the children, Louis. For yourself!"

Louis sighed in visible impatience.

"Now, Cécile, have you any likely candidate?"

"Louis, *mon chéri*, listen to me and listen well. . . ."

"Now, why don't you rest quietly instead of sawing more wood than we need?"

She pursed her lips and shook her head firmly.

"Find a good woman, Louis. One who loves small children. That's important. Who'll be kind to you as you've been to me. Who won't attempt to change you into a different man, who can make good, tasty pancakes . . ."

Now she stared fixedly at the white hospital wall. Louis knelt beside the bed and took her hands and kissed them.

"Cécile, you have my heart, my love, and I'll have no other."

"You are a man with a warm, passionate nature, Louis. I have such nice memories of that! A demanding lover, but kind always!"

"Now, now, Cécile. . . ."

"But marriage is your home, Louis. You must promise you'd marry again—soon?"

He got up . . . Suddenly Cécile had become so very small, as if he were seeing her from the other end of a telescope, like a doll in a toy bed, and he stood so very far above her, and then all of it broke up in watery patterns, and he wept silently and walked out quickly, seeing no one, except the large bouquet of roses Thérèse carried so carefully in a large vase. She stopped to stare at him, frightened, in the hospital corridor.

"Don't stand there," he said gruffly, surprised at this himself, "leaving your Maman alone in there!"

"Yes, Papa," she said slowly and went inside.

"See, Maman, what I have for you?" she soberly told her.

"Yes, but first bring me a kiss. I need a kiss right now."

Her visit was short. Soon after, Maman again became incoherent. She laughed several times gently to herself, and once exclaimed in delight: "Louis, *mon méchant!*" And then again, she was in St. Michel, in the convent, painfully spelling out words for long-forgotten school girls and scribbling forever and ever on a blackboard: Louis Martel. . . .

Thérèse listened, alone, respectfully, for a few minutes, then knelt by her bed, and she prayed for a long, long time. Now, Maman slept and suddenly Thérèse looked at her. Her face did not move. Her cheeks seemed to have shrunken somewhat, but her eyes seemed to flutter, and then she felt the strong arms of Nurse Monique Beaulieu and saw her Papa looking down at her. She had fainted.

"You'll be all right," said Nurse Beaulieu.

Thérèse turned toward Maman. She slept fitfully now.

"Papa," she whispered, "I know. . . ."

Louis took her in his arms and held her for a moment.

Nurse Beaulieu announced that it was nearly nine o'clock, anyway, and time to go home and get a good night's rest, she would watch over Madame Martel, and would take good care of her. . . .

"A short prayer?" begged Thérèse, very tiredly.

Louis and Thérèse knelt briefly, and Nurse Beaulieu tactfully stepped aside a moment.

It was nine o'clock and the family had gathered again to recite the Rosary. Everyone was there; Maurice and Muriel were staying overnight. Grandpère and Rosaline and Marie were there, but Louis and Thérèse were at the hospital. Neighbors had called daily with prepared dishes and Mademoiselle Thibault was getting ready to go home for the night.

When the door opened slowly, another neighbor was expected but it was Louis, his face drawn, his eyes moist. When he spoke, however, his voice was firm.

"Children," he said slowly, "I have the saddest news of my life. Your Maman waits for us in Heaven!"

Thérèse slipped in from behind her Papa. Her eyes were brimming with tears, but she tried to imitate his tone of voice.

"There was no pain," she added slowly, but her voice broke.

Aunt Rosaline suddenly welcomed Thérèse into her broad chest, and Aunt Marie took both Marie and Cécile into her arms. Félix just stared straight ahead, and Emile swallowed hard, and quietly covered his face with a handkerchief. Laurent reached for Hélène's hands, and Maurice got up and started to walk around, looking briskly for something in the *parloir*. Muriel quietly followed him, waiting for the moment that would come, and when it did, she quietly embraced and held him. Grandpère Bolduc put both arms on Louis's shoulders. He nodded calmly at him, and Louis nodded back, and then stared at the floor. Grandpère studied the state of shock which was quickly taking over everybody. He reached into his pocket and pulled out his prayer beads. His voice was firm.

"I shall begin the Rosary."

Slowly he knelt where he stood, leaning on the back of a chair, his gray features raised toward the crucifix on the kitchen wall, and his voice, at first low and constrained, now intoned the "Our Father" in a tone that became more and more commanding, and then it fought its way over and surmounted the muffled weeping until in the returning quiet it could be heard easily, soft and yet resonant, as other voices joined in the decades of "Hail Marys."

"Glory be," said Grandpère, "to the Father, to the Son, and to the Holy Ghost!"

"As it was in the beginning," came back the voices, "as it is now, and shall be forever after!"

His eyes riveted on the crucifix, Grandpère continued at a steady pace the decades of "Hail Marys," while the others, their heads bent toward the floor, responded in muffled tones. Occasionally, there would be a slowdown, as each began to react in his own way to the finality of death, but others took up the sudden voids. Grandpère never faltered: his voice never ceased to be a gentle exhortation to all to come through with the answers. . . .

In the middle of the Rosary, Father Joseph Lebois slipped into the kitchen silently. He had wanted so much to be there when the news struck the Martel family, and he had run up the stairs in a big hurry. When he saw that the Rosary was well begun, he too knelt, misty-eyed, and joined the others. When Grandpère saw him, he handed him his prayer beads with a bow, and the priest took over, for Grandpère was now weeping silent tears, but his head was still turned toward the crucifix. . . .

Maman was buried in Sacred Heart Cemetery, located two miles north of Groveton next to a forest of pines, the kind that she had loved all her life. She rested in the family plot, near Baby Muriel, and only a few feet away from the shrine to the Virgin Mary whose arms rose heavenward in constant protection over the graves.

A month after she died, Louis placed a modest tombstone over her resting place. And on their wedding anniversaries thereafter—they had not quite made their twenty-fifth—he never failed to place a bouquet of roses at the foot of this tombstone. It read in full: "Mme. Cécile Martel, daughter of Napoléon Bolduc, beloved spouse of Louis Martel, mother of 8 children: 1879–1927. May His will be done!"

And for a long time Mademoiselle Blanche Thibault came every day to care for the younger children, and every night

Thérèse hurried home from her job at the Groveton Trust to cook supper for the family. And after the homework was done, Thérèse took upon herself the task of reading stories to the younger children, and, of course, control of the black-board. The prescribed mourning period of one year of no dancing, no music, no movies, and the wearing of dark clothes only complicated her task, but she set about it with dull diligence. For instance, all the children had to be outfitted with dark suits and dresses, and it was not always easy to comply to the letter, despite fear of gossip, especially with young children in the house.

February, March and April dragged along. Then, one Sunday in May, right after Mass, Louis made a trip to the cemetery—it was a clear, warm day—and he stayed a long time at the foot of Maman's grave, and when he came back to his house he had something special to say.

"This sadness for Maman," he explained, "is a sadness she would be the first to oppose. One must go on working, eating, sleeping, growing. . . . And at this time, breathing the freshness of spring, and, once more, accepting the release that comes only from belly laughter. . . . As for myself, I told Maman, this afternoon I'm going to a ball game, and who wants to go with me?"

Thus, the mourning period ended officially, but even then, there was not much laughter in the Martel home. Every night, after everyone was in bed and the house very quiet, Louis sipped his nightcap, alone in the kitchen, but even this lacked the punch to hit the spot that hurt the most.

6. The Opponent Sex [1929]

That summer, while the world inflated itself toward the big October bust, Louis Martel's pride inflated him to welcome back home from the seminary his boy, Emile, now sixteen, and well on his way to becoming a priest. For sure, he still had a long way to go, Louis thought, and one never knew about such things. Was not Groveton dotted with boys who had started out the same way and were now garage mechanics, or dentists, and married? But not Emile! He seemed to know where he was going and he had always known. . . .

Two years ago he had entered the seminary near Montreal, and every summer and Christmas vacation since, he had made the long trip home to Groveton—alone. Even in his first year, and now particularly in his second year, he had won many prizes—citations, and gold pieces he always gave to his Papa—for excellence in French Literature, Latin, Greek, Religion, and Elocution.

"This boy," Louis often said to anyone who would listen, "does not shave yet, and already he's a savant. Speaks the Latin, some of the Greek, and much of the English." Then he would add, for the laugh: "And pig-Latin French!"

There was still great need, this summer, for laughter and comfort. Maman's death, over two years ago, had forced Thérèse into a mother's role toward Marie and Cécile and Félix too. She also worked full time at her secretarial job at the Groveton Trust. And this had been tolerable until, six months after Maman died, Antoine Bouchard began to pay court to her. More and more now did the family depend on Mademoiselle Blanche Thibault, a gentle, unmarried woman of thirty-two, who still came in by the day. She was quiet, easy on the children: they loved her. "Mademoiselle" was a success. Then, suddenly, she married and moved away and came no more.

"The Lord gives," thought Louis, "and the Lord also takes."

Hélène, Laurent's wife, took over the care of Marie and Cécile during the day, but they were spoiled by the entire family—specially by their Papa. That year he had a surplus of love to give and of grief to assuage. Secretly, the family rejoiced when one night it was learned he had dated "a widow who lived on Park Street." Emile's forthcoming vacation, however, seemed to overshadow even this.

Recently a convent of Dominican Sisters had been built across the street from Louis's house, and now, Oak Street seemed a fitting place to receive a vacationing seminarian. For a week before he was due to arrive, Thérèse and Hélène and Félix swept, washed, painted and fixed up the apartment, as if the Bishop himself was coming. Marie and Cécile helped also. The crucifix in each room was gently dusted. A luminous Sacred Heart and a small altar with real candles were installed in the front room, reserved for Emile.

He was met at the station on a Saturday night by the entire family. When he jumped off the train, in his dark suit and gray cap, he spied his Papa and ran toward him, his right hand extended.

"*Bonjour*, Papa!" he shouted.

Louis ignored the outstretched hand, placed his hands on his shoulders, embraced him, and then kissed him on both cheeks.

While everyone else did the same, Emile's cap fell to the

ground, and everybody laughed. Maurice, come to Groveton for the occasion with all his family, and Laurent, picked up his two suitcases, and the ticket for his trunk, and while this was being done, Emile handed out holy medals to everyone. "Blessed by His Holiness!" he said over and over. And then, the entire family walked up Pine Street to Oak Street, Louis leading, and bidding a happy greeting to friends and strangers alike. Félix and Maurice drove their cars alongside the parade and occasionally tooted horns that invited anyone who became tired to jump in and take a ride. There were no takers. Who needed transportation this evening?

Emile was, suddenly, much taller than last year, almost as tall as his Papa, and yet he looked much like his Maman— same gray eyes, same little mouth that opened sparingly to correct the incorrect, or crinkled in laughter at the incongruous. His forehead was even balder and bolder than ever, a fact which, to Louis, remained an assurance of his future. He glanced at him many, many times on the way to their house, and that evening.

"The Lord takes away," thought Louis, "and the Lord also restitutes!"

That evening, there was a *veillée*, way into the night. They sat around in the kitchen in a wide circle of straight chairs, and ate cake, and drank cold cider and lemonade—mere pretexts for the sheer pleasure of talking to one another—together—and all at once.

Around eight, Antoine Bouchard, Thérèse's *ami*, came, a tall, good-looking young man, rather thin, who sat quietly to one side and listened. Emile sat in the chair of honor and freely gave the latest tidbits of his seminary life. The family listened with deep attention—for this was a view into another world—and once, when Hélène had to put Jean-Paul in bed, she begged Emile not to go on speaking while she was gone.

Tonight, Marie and Cécile would be allowed to sit up late.

The seminary, Emile explained again to his family, was really a group of buildings of red bricks, linked together by quiet walks through a garden-like campus. It was located about two miles from the nearest point of worldly contact and its life of scholarly and religious dedication was ringed on all sides by a five-foot-high and two-foot-deep privet hedge. There was only one entrance to and exit from the seminary grounds and that was in front of the Administration Building, and the Father Superior's office windows surveyed and commanded all approaches to it. No student was allowed alone outside the area ringed by the privet hedge, at any time, under penalty of expulsion.

"Only to retrieve a baseball!" added Emile seriously.

Emile had chosen this life, he continued, and it was good. There were no movies, no news of scandal and disaster, no stock market reports, and, come to think of it, not much of anything but study, prayer, and one hour daily of sports. All seminarians wore blue, knee-length military coats of a quick-fading serge, tied around the waist with a blue sash, and a cap with a straight visor, somewhat similar to that of the French Foreign Legion, and indeed, they paraded to and from classes and buildings in formations of two by two. The food, he made clear, was frugal and unimaginative, but it never failed to make its appearance before him three times a day without any effort on his part.

The school year lasted a full ten months, seven days a week. He slept in a dormitory, barracks-style. Once a week, there was hot water for a bath. Emile thought this was sufficient.

"I don't," Thérèse said laughingly.

The life was Spartan, explained Emile, and it was carefully filled out to prevent any free time for distractions or temptations. There was a Prefect of Studies, who saw to it that you studied, and a Prefect of Discipline, who saw to it that you behaved. Once a week, he went to confession, and every morning he attended Mass at five-thirty, and received Holy Communion. Occasionally, especially on holidays, there were school excursions to visit rare old churches, old folks' homes, orphanages, hospitals, and during the baseball and hockey season, sport contests with other seminaries.

Emile talked on and on, and once or twice, resolved delicate questions such as what constitutes a mortal sin, or why the Church does not, can not, and will not approve of divorce.

"Emile," said Louis suddenly, "you remember Pierre Nadeau?"

"Yes, Papa. The free-thinker?"

"He says he is," said Thérèse smugly, "but he is only bragging."

"Well," continued Louis, "he stuck me with his stories about how we are all grown up to man from the monkeys. What about it, my little theologian?"

Emile swallowed once, easily composed himself and raised his right hand, his index pointing heavenward.

"The theory of evolution," he said, "is much *au courant* at the moment. Many believe it has value. The Church, however, teaches, as She always has, that Man came from God."

"That's right," said Thérèse passionately. "That Nadeau! He's a show-off!"

"Well, now," insisted Louis, "if he's dead wrong, I want to know and tell him. But I want to tell him *why* he's wrong. That's why I send you to the seminary. Is it true that we came, first from an amoeba, as Nadeau puts it, then from the fish, then from the crocodiles? He calls it 'evolving.' Nadeau claims that we evolved upward from the fish to man."

Emile smiled, waited for silence to settle, and then thundered out the answer.

"If we were once fish," he asked solemnly, "then became crocodiles, then evolved into something higher, and became monkeys, and then again, evolved into something higher than that, and became man, then, Papa, ask Monsieur Nadeau how come man has not evolved into something higher than man lately?"

There was applause.

"Hah," said Louis, beaming, "education! It's wonderful!"

"How do you say 'boy' in Latin?" suddenly asked Marie.

"*Puer*," Emile replied quickly.

"And how do you say 'girl'?" Marie asked again.

Emile hesitated a moment.

"That depends," he said slowly, smiling at her.

"Depends on what?" Louis asked.

"It depends, Papa, on certain things."

Louis's eyes sharpened.

"Well, tell us, my little professor," he insisted, sipping on a lemonade, spiked with whisky, and laughing gaily.

"It depends upon," said Emile vaguely, "whether she's married. . ."

"Yes," said Louis.

". . .or whether she's a virgin, I guess," finished off Emile lamely.

In the dead silence that followed Antoine Bouchard gave Félix a cigarette and they exchanged shrugs of deep understanding. Louis cleared his throat.

"For sure," he remarked blandly, "education is a wonderful adventure! Your Maman was right."

Later, much later, but slowly, Laurent, Hélène, Maurice, Muriel, Félix, Marie, and Cécile said *bonsoir* and went to bed. Most of the children were already dozing, or in various stages of helplessness. Precisely, at eleven, Antoine got up, shook Emile's hand, said he was glad to have made his acquaintance, made a few friendly observations, and walked out, leaving the door to the hall open, and then Thérèse swiftly followed him, also leaving the door open.

"Antoine is a nice fellow," said Louis, apropos of nothing.

Emile stared at the opened door.

"What are they doing?" he asked. "Are they going somewhere?"

"No," said Louis, "they are saying *bonsoir*."

"In the hallway?"

"Yes. It's private there."

"It's late for that, Papa."

"Never too late, my boy," said he.

"What are they doing in a hallway at eleven at night?"

"Kissing, I hope."

"You permit this type of courtship?"

"What type?" he asked suddenly.

"Well," hesitated Emile, "that type!"

"There's no set type," Louis explained, "except the type that works."

"I don't know about that!" argued Emile, disturbed.

"Well, I do," said Louis with finality. "Ask me!"

Then suddenly Thérèse returned, alone, flushed, her eyes darting wildly toward her Papa, then toward Emile, then toward the floor. She was now a tall, sturdy young woman with dark glossy hair, clear gray eyes that seemed to seek refuge behind generous eyelashes. She had a beauty spot on her left cheek—like Maman's.

"Well," she whispered happily to no one in particular, "that's that!"

Louis looked up toward her.

"Sounds like the end," he concluded.

"No, it is the beginning, I think," she whispered. "Before Christmas, Papa, perhaps before Christmas!"

Louis got up, placed an arm gently around her waist, rubbed his stubby cheek against hers. She giggled and tried to free herself from his reach, and when she did, she slowly came back to place her arms around her father, and then she looked at Emile.

"You like Antoine?" she asked hopefully.

"He looks like a nice young man," Emile said thoughtfully.

"My little Thérèse!" said Louis. "What beautiful babies you'll make!"

"Oh, Papa!" screamed Thérèse in unconcealed delight, and then she blushed, and now broke into a fit of laughter.

"Well, my pretty one," teased Louis. "Are you still ahead of him?"

"Of course," recited Thérèse, smiling widely, "I never give him the kiss he expects . . ."

"That's right," said he, "and . . ."

". . . And never fail to give him the one he doesn't deserve!" finished off Thérèse in a singsong.

She pecked her Papa on the cheek, and then bent near Emile, who still sat quietly, and kissed him wetly on the lips.

"*Bonsoir, p'tit frère!*" she sang out, her eyes staring vacantly ahead into her own dreams.

And now the kitchen was quiet. Louis pulled up a chair and straddled it, the better to face Emile.

"We come," said he slowly, "to the serious side. You are still of the same decision, to become a priest?"

"Oh yes, Papa. And I thank you."

"And I thank God for such a son as you. Your Maman would be proud of your marks in school, and all the prizes."

"My first Mass will be for her."

"In heaven, she's proud of you."

"And, Papa, I pray for you every day, because this education—it costs a lot of money."

"It does," said Louis, patting him on the knee easily, "but when you begin to make some substantial collections and business is good in your own church, I'll be waiting for you in the back. . . ."

"What, Papa?"

Louis chuckled.

"I say this for the joke. If you become a good priest, a caretaker of souls, not just a bookkeeper, there is not enough money to pay for such a thing."

"Yes, Papa. That's what I want to be, a good priest, perhaps a great priest."

"Good is good enough. That's all I ask, that you become a good priest. Any male can become a priest, son, but one must also be a man."

"I think," said Emile lightly, "that I'll be a missionary in China!"

Louis shrugged his shoulders vaguely.

"Be what you will, and what God wills, and it will be satisfactory to me. Meantime, you take care of the spiritual and I'll handle the material. But tell me, are you happy?"

"Happy?"

"Yes. Happy. Content. Getting laughs. Enjoying life."

"Oh yes, Papa."

"If you tell me so, I believe you. What I mean, to be frank, is, are you having any fun? Real fun. I think sixteen-year-old boys should have a lot of fun. It's good for the liver and it's not sinful, you know."

"We have a lot fun, Papa. We play hockey, baseball, ping-pong, charades, and sometimes. . .we even raise a little hell. . . ."

"Ah?"

"Oh, yes. Oh, the stories I could tell you. . . if it weren't too late."

Louis settled more comfortably into his chair.

"For these stories, I could stay up all night, and tomorrow night too. . . . Speak on. . . . I'll just light up my pipe."

"Last May," Emile began, "we gave a play and it was before the folks of the village, you know, and it was for everybody, and even women and girls came to the play—it was for our library fund—and you know, Papa, I had never noticed before how many young women come to these plays?"

"Probably a good play?" suggested Louis.

"No," said Emile darkly. "I thought it rather sugary."

"Ah! Too bad."

"Anyway, after the play, we were invited to mix—I mean, to mix really—with all the gentlemen as well as with the ladies and even the girls, mind you! Right in the seminary!"

"Well," said Louis, "God created man, and woman too."

"I know," said Emile vaguely.

"Only thing," added Louis, "he made them opponents."

"Well," continued Emile, "her name was Juliette, and she wore a corsage of lilacs. And lilacs smell very sweet, I think! I don't know why I did it, I just don't know at all, but I asked her if she would give them to me. Know what she said? 'Maybe, yes! And maybe, no!'"

"That's the way God made them, all right."

"And so, when she left the reception hall, near the little theatre, and went outside, I followed her, begging for the lilacs, and when she walked slowly outside the seminary grounds proper, I followed her! I didn't realize what I was doing! Over and over I asked her for the corsage of lilacs and she kept saying: 'Maybe, yes! And then, maybe, no!' and smiled, and yet appeared so sad to refuse, that I found myself right on the street with her. . . ."

"That's against the rules. . . ."

"Strictly, Papa! But I never thought at all, never gave it a thought! And as we chatted, the time seemed to fly right by. . . ."

"I know," said Louis slowly.

"The time just flew, Papa. So fast, and I didn't seem to care. . . ."

"I know."

"Then suddenly, I remembered. . . . It came to me that it must be, at least, after midnight! Then and there, I panicked! There was only one door to get back into the seminary, and that door was plumb in front of the office of the Prefect of Discipline, and the Father Superior himself. I snatched the lilacs from her hands—never even said *bonsoir*—and ran into that one door to meet my punishment. Expulsion! That's what it could have meant. If that had happened, Papa, I would have died of shame before you!"

"Only," amended Louis, "if you got caught."

"But I didn't!" whispered Emile. "For when I reached the door, Father Martin . . . he's my father confessor . . . he was sitting in the office, reading his breviary. He looked up and smiled. Imagine!"

Louis thought this over a moment.

"I thought," said Emile gravely, "he would storm at me. No! He only smiled."

"How old is this priest?"

"Pretty old, I guess. Over forty, at least. Well! I mumbled, '*Bonsoir, mon Père!*' and explained I'd gone out for some lilacs. I felt like an idiot, saying that, since it was not quite the truth. And he replied quietly: '*Bon!*'"

"That's all he said?"

"That's all. He got up, closed his breviary and gently pointed the way to the dormitory. The next day he said nothing to me about this, nor did he ever again. It was a close shave, having him there instead of the Prefect, or the Father Superior, and very exciting, but I wasn't caught, Papa!"

Louis suddenly turned to him.

"And, my future priest, what is the moral of all this?"

Emile laughed wisely.

"The moral? Not to leave the seminary after midnight! Or at any other time!"

"No," said Louis.

"No?"

"No. You can read Latin, but you can't analyze this adventure. Oh, you were caught, all right! I'll bet a golden footrule that Father What's-his-name, once or twice, when he was young, went after his own lilacs too. . . ."

"Oh, no, Papa. Father Martin is a saintly man!"

"Oh, yes, but a man. He knows, and what's more important, he remembers. . . . He remembers about young men, and the terrible power of the sap that runs through the bloodstream in the spring of the year when one is sixteen. . . . Oh, you were caught, all right!"

"Oh," whispered Emile.

"The moral? This wise old priest let you fight it out by yourself! All the privet hedges meant to keep you inside were as nothing to a . . . a tiny bunch of lilacs. He only said: '*Bon!*' If you win the fight, no speech is necessary. If you lose, no speech is worth while. That, son, was the best sermon any priest ever made, and to top it off, it was damn short!"

"Oh, yes!" agreed Emile.

"See, you knew the moral all along. And now to bed, and don't forget your prayers. Big picnic tomorrow, right after High Mass. Say, you like swimming, don't you?"

"Yes, Papa."

"Good. Latin is a fine thing, I know, but swimming can be fun."

Louis got up and stretched. Emile did also.

"Papa," he said suddenly, "it's good to be home."

Louis put a hand on his shoulder.

"*Bon,*" he said.

Metaska Pond is a beautiful but small body of water, south of Groveton, one of the many small lakes in Maine, entirely surrounded by cottages. Most of those built around Metaska Pond were the work of Louis Martel himself, especially his own, two rooms and an attic, with a large screened sun-porch that faced the Pond. He had built it on weekends, and on Sundays, when no one was looking.

This first Sunday of Emile's vacation, Félix drove the entire family there in his Papa's car. Thérèse and Antoine came together in his car. Both cars were laden with baskets containing potato salad, pickled eggs, and red beets, baked ham, cole slaw, tomatoes, olives, blueberry pies, bananas, oranges, two large watermelons, several bottles of Moxie and many more jugs of lemonade and cider. And as soon as they arrived at the cottage, Louis took the jugs to the pond, tied them to a long series of ropes and dropped them into the lake waters to keep them chilled.

The first to get into his swimsuit, Louis was also the first to jump into the water. Aware of this, Marie and Cécile bounced in right after him. They paddled around and frolicked and swam for a while and then they had three short races and Marie beat him once, and Cécile nearly beat him the second time. Then they dried themselves quickly and came back to the sun porch. He set up his hammock outside the cottage, securely tied it to two oaks, got into it and fell asleep.

Antoine and Thérèse began to set the table for the picnic, and Cécile to help them. Marie grabbed a broom that was much too big for her and furiously swept the cottage. Félix coaxed Emile away from Montesquieu's *Grandeur et Décadence des Romains*, and urged a swim upon him, and then Antoine announced he would join them.

As was the custom, the men went up to the attic to change into their swimsuits. Antoine and Félix were nearly ready when, suddenly, they stopped to stare at Emile. For a brief moment, he stood, stripped of all clothing, and struggled nervously to cover himself with his swimsuit. Both men gaped at him, and the soiled strip of cloth, like a tiny belt, around his waist. It lasted only a moment, for Emile was now safely inside his suit.

"What's that?" asked Félix. "That thing around your belly?"

"Nothing," asserted Emile.

"You had an operation?" asked Antoine kindly.

"No, it's nothing," said Emile, flushing, and he ran ahead of them out of the cottage and to the lake.

Later, Thérèse, looking slim and unprotected and suddenly exposed in her navy blue wool swimsuit, with a bright red belt at the waist, spread the picnic food on the wooden table on the sun porch. She gave Cécile and Marie glasses of milk, hummed a song, and set up the wicker chairs around the table and told Marie to wake up Papa. She tickled his nose and twice shouted like a bear and soon he was awake and now he remembered! He darted to the lake to recover his cider and lemonade jugs. He served himself a long, cool cider drink. They ate and chatted. Antoine told Emile about the high cost of living and Emile confessed that he had little chance to think about money at all.

Later, Louis took Marie and Cécile into the nearby wood for the traditional family game: to discover treasures like Indian pipes, mountain laurels, lady's-slippers, jack-in-the-pulpits, and so many others God Himself fashions every year and hides here and there that their sudden appearances be the cause of joy and wonder.

Later in the afternoon, Marie and Cécile napped on the beach near the lake. As usual, Félix was off to the other side of the lake on a long, long hike. He liked to keep himself in the best possible physical shape. Louis went back to his hammock to nap. Thérèse washed the dishes and Antoine helped, between tomfooleries, and then they sat together in a large wicker chair. Emile picked up his Montesquieu, turned his chair away from them and resumed his reading. Slowly now, Antoine brought his arm around Thérèse and squeezed her closer to himself. She smiled at him, and let her head fall slowly on his shoulder. Suddenly she sat up, and Antoine had to readjust his sitting position.

"*P'tit frère*," she said, "what's that?"

Emile looked up from his book toward Antoine.

"You've told her?"

"It can be seen, Emile. Through your swimsuit."

"What is it?" asked Thérèse.

"It is nothing," said Emile. He returned to his book.

"It *is* something," insisted his sister, half rising. "We're all family here. If you are sick, someone's got to know."

"I'm not sick, Thérèse, I assure you."

"Then, what is it?" she persisted, rising and going toward him, her arms on her hips. "I wish to know, Emile."

"It's nothing for women to look into," he said finally.

"Or laics," added Antoine.

"Correct," snapped Emile.

"If you say so, I believe you," she said, "but you don't have to be shy in front of me. When you were a little boy, I took care of you . . ."

"Thérèse," snarled Emile, "I'm not a little boy. . . ."

". . . and when you wet yourself or got sick to your stomach, I took care of you, and you had too many secrets even then, and now you live with priests all year round, and priests, after all, let's face it, are only men and men can be dumb, can't take care of themselves, why, Papa is that way too. . . ."

Emile laughed at her.

"Go on. Papa took care of you."

"No! Maman did, and you have no Maman now."

Emile lowered his book and faced Thérèse. Antoine spoke up.

"Well, you're not his Maman now. He's not a baby. Calm yourself."

She pursed her lips.

"Is it a medical thing, or not? That's all I want to know."

"No," said Emile, heaving a sigh. "It is a religious thing."

"Oh," said Thérèse, taken aback.

"Now," said Antoine impatiently, "will you mind your own business? I think I know what it is. When I was sixteen, it was suggested to me also. It's a vow. About girls. Not for me, boy, not for me!" and he squeezed Thérèse awkwardly.

Thérèse reddened. Her forehead creased into a series of question marks, then an impish smile came to her lips.

"It has to do with the sins of the flesh?" she gasped, unbelieving.

"Not exactly," corrected Emile with confidence now. "It represents a solemn reminder that whoever wears this garment around his loins has taken an obligation of chastity."

"What?" screamed Thérèse.

"That's what it is!" stated Emile, again on the defensive. "I took this vow last May after a retreat. Isn't it wise to gird your loins against the temptations of the flesh . . . ?"

"You, *p'tit frère?*" asked Thérèse, her hand covering the shock in her face.

"Yes! Me! Am I made of altar marble?"

"You! A boy of sixteen?"

"Yes," asserted Emile, with a slight stutter now. "You girls don't know anything about it. You don't even realize the danger to men's souls from your careless actions. . . ."

He picked up his book and began to read with determination.

She turned to Antoine and he smiled, and she calmed down. She sat near him, her arms gently folded in her lap. She studied Emile quietly, as if to understand all this, and for a moment, decided to let it go as a great mystery. Now, quickly, she could remain silent no longer.

"Are girls such evil things?" she asked, mystified.

Emile put down his book.

"I don't mean to imply that," he said gently, "but a great bishop once said that it is easier to abstain from the flesh completely than to partake of its delights wisely."

"For the bishop," agreed Antoine, "that may be a smart move."

"But, *p'tit frère,*" pursued Thérèse, "at your age! To take such an obligation of conscience! It makes too much too soon of such a small thing!"

"*Bonguienne!*" cried out Emile. "It is not a small thing!"

"*Bon!*" If you say so, Emile," she agreed quickly, and again she folded her arms in her lap. Emile took out a pipe, filled it, struck a match against the chair, lit it and sighed deeply.

"One can smoke in the seminary?" asked Antoine.

"Oh, sure," said Emile. "On Feast Days only. I like the aroma. Somehow, it evokes glad things. . . ."

"And home?" asked Thérèse.

"Why, yes. Come to think of it, I guess it does, Thérèse."

He returned to his book and she gazed at him. Antoine gently pulled her toward him and she relaxed in his arms, her eyes on Emile.

Beside her, out of the corner of her eye, she could feel Antoine. He shook with quiet laughter. She dared not look him in the eyes, and she knew why. Soon they would be married. They had not said the final word, but it was almost final now. . . . She knew both of them waited for the moment of mutual discovery they put off every night they held one another in close embrace, when the flow of their fleshly yearnings almost overran the measure they'd set up for themselves . . . . Emile had a point!

After such moments, Antoine always shook with laughter, as if he needed this for a sedative. . . . She too smiled a bit then, but a bit sadly. Why couldn't the yes-yes of the senses, Papa had once asked, make peace more often with the no-no of the soul?

She studied Emile, while Antoine still shook with laughter, and now madly she poked her elbows in his ribs. There was a plea in her eyes. She was telling him not to laugh, how tragic it was—and how wonderful, too—about her younger brother. Again she saw the curtl of a smile on Antoine's lips and her own lips made out the command to stop it. He did and then she took his hand and placed it slowly near her breast and closed her eyes. Antoine became very quiet.

Unaware, Emile read on about the decline and fall of the Roman Empire.

When they all returned home that evening, about nine-thirty, Thérèse saw to it that Marie and Cécile went to bed early, and right away so that she could return quickly to Antoine. But the door to the *parloir*, when she got there, was closed. This was not fair, since this was the agreed courting place, and besides, from within, she could hear male exclamations of laughter. It was Antoine and Félix, of course. Those two got along just fine. . . .

Too fine, her Papa often said. A young man who comes to court a girl, and finds too much to laugh about with her younger brother can become derailed on the delicate railway to romance. The courted sister runs the big risk. . . . Thérèse stood near the door and listened. The men's laughter could be heard all over the house. There are times, surely, in sisters' lives, in the interest of all that is sacred and noble, when they should be allowed to murder their younger brothers. . . .

Emile had gone to bed early, and now Louis occasionally

twirled the dials of his radio, and adjusted his earplugs all the better to hear above the guffaws. Tonight, he had announced earlier, he was going for distance. California, for sure, and perhaps Mexico. . . . He sighed in great impatience suddenly, took off his earplugs, and turned toward Thérèse who still stood near the closed door to the *parloir*, quietly tense. One could hear the loud laughter coming from within, but Thérèse was not laughing at all.

"For all that laughter," Louis asked, "it must be a good joke, no?" He stared at the closed door. Both listened to the laughter a moment.

"Do you know the joke?" he asked finally.

"No, I do not," she snapped. Her eyes blazed.

"Do you suspect?"

"I do! It is about Emile."

Louis stood up. He glared toward the *parloir*. In three bounds, he made the door, knocked once, and pushed it open. Thérèse was right behind him, and both looked hard at Antoine and Félix.

"Tell me the joke, Messieurs," he commanded. "Me too, I'm in the mood for laughter." His eyes glared at them.

Félix came toward him, a smile still on his face.

"Pa," he began, "what is fun is fun, we mean no disrespect, but it is like this . . ."

And he told him about that thing which they had seen around Emile's waist—the strip of cloth—that made him secure from womanhood. . . . Again, he giggled as he spoke. Thérèse bit her lip. Louis did not laugh. He slapped his forehead. Now he bellowed.

"At sixteen! A chastity belt?"

"Well, not exactly," said Antoine.

"Are you sure of this?" asked Louis.

"It is only a very small cloth belt, Monsieur Martel,"

explained Antoine, "but I saw it, with my own eyes, I saw it."

"My good God," thundered Louis, "it'll cut off his blood circulation!"

"I thought," said Thérèse, "he was sick, or something."

"You too," screamed Louis, "have seen this thing?"

Thérèse turned scarlet. She groped for words.

"Through his swimsuit, Monsieur Martel," explained Antoine in a quiet tone.

For a moment, Louis was lost, as he looked at the three of them. Antoine chuckled to cover his embarrassment. Then, he stopped.

"I thought it was funny," said Félix sadly.

In one step Louis was out of the *parloir* and into the kitchen. "Emile!" he shouted.

Thérèse came quickly toward him.

"Papa," she whispered, "here, we need a pinch of tact, yes?"

"Yes," agreed Antoine. "Fun is fun, but. . ."

"Emile!" Louis shouted again. "Come out here!"

Emile darted out of his room and stared wildly at everyone. With hair disheveled, he pulled a bathrobe over his long nightgown, and looked frightened. Louis put an arm on his shoulders.

"Come with me," he commanded, "to my bedroom."

There, he told him he knew everything about the vow, and that "bric-a-brac around the belly." He wanted to know who had suggested he wear such a thing.

"The priest. The priest who preached the retreat. He said it would be a symbol."

"Aha! A symbol! Well, take off the robe, and the nightgown, please."

"In front of you?"

"You haven't got anything I haven't seen. But this—er—symbol! Ah, that, I want to see. And now."

Emile undressed, slowly at first, and then more quickly, down to his scapulary cloth medal, and, of course, to the soiled, rumpled tape-like cloth that ringed his midsection.

His Papa took a good look at it and started to stroke his chin. Emile dressed very quickly.

"This is, no doubt," said Louis sadly, "the eighth great wonder of the world."

"The priest who preached the retreat," Emile explained, "spoke of this symbol as a reminder against the temptations of women. And for that, Papa, it is a protection. . . ."

Louis nodded in agreement.

"That I do believe! And as it gets dirtier and smells more and more of you, it protects better and better. Right now, good or bad, no woman would come within loving distance of you."

"It smells, Papa?"

He looked at his son and remembered that Maman had asked him once to be especially careful with Emile. "He is the intellectual in the family," she had said. "He will always be the first to grasp the meaning of life, and the last to absorb its reality." Now, how could he, Louis Martel, unlearned, talk to Emile Martel, the future priest? Well, by God, he is my son— a boy yet—and if I only remember that I love him, love him, I can be generous with the facts of life. . . . He reached for him and hugged him.

"To me," he roared in laughter, "you smell good. I understand! I don't think you're planning to seduce one young girl every day. . . ."

"Oh, Papa, that's the last thing in the world. . . ."

"I know it is, and in the seminary, you don't even get a chance. But the seminary, that's only the training season. . . ."

"What, Papa?"

"It's nothing yet, but life is the unexpected. . . . Life, one spring evening, is a girl who happens to come strolling along with a bunch of lilacs. Do you see?"

"Oh, that!"

"In the seminary, it's a man's world. . . ."

"Of course, Papa."

"It's outside that counts. That's where the ball game is played. Outside, there'll always be women—and for myself, I say thank God! But a woman in the flesh, warm and tender, and full of sweet plots, is—well—a problem of reality. You may win her, if you have a mind to, with symbols, but, even if you try, you can't make her vanish with symbols. And why should you?"

"Pa! Because. . . . You know very well! Women are tempting. I know!"

"Thank God they are! What are we afraid of here, Emile? Too much tenderness? Is that lust? Too much love? Is that against the Commandments? Too much of the softness of the female that softens you and me, as we need to be?"

"Yes, Papa, that's where the danger lurks. . . ."

Louis smiled and shook his head in surprise.

"And I thought it was the other way around! Well, I've yet to meet a woman who eats men for breakfast, for they too have a soul to save, Emile, just as precious as yours. . . ."

"Of course, Papa."

"But the Creator made the female creature into a sweet tune that stirs a man's bones and makes him spring and jig to fast time. . . ."

"I cannot think like that, Papa."

Louis signed, and pulled up a chair.

"Sit down, Emile."

He looked for his pipe, found it, filled it, put it in his mouth, studying him all the time, then suddenly put it back inside his shirt pocket. He would not smoke. He must speak quietly. Please, God, hand me the right words, right here, as on a platter.

"You see, Papa," asserted Emile, "I'm afraid to lose my vocation."

Louis pondered this for a moment.

"And if you did, then what?"

"I'd die of shame. For the sake of Maman, and you too."

"Yes," admitted his Papa, "it is a big load, a truly big load you are hefting." He decided to light his pipe. He offered him his tobacco pouch and Emile fetched his own pipe, filled it, and both smoked a moment in silence.

"Emile," Louis said suddenly, "you may not know this, but you do NOT have to become a priest."

"Oh, Papa!"

"Well, you don't. And if you decided to chuck it, at any time, I would not fall into a dead faint. The world would go on. . . ."

"I guess so."

"I'm sure of it. Nor would you collapse, or go to hell by registered mail. Son, you do NOT have to become a priest. And if you so decide, would you be bold enough to say so, good and loud?"

"But, Papa . . . I think I do have the vocation!"

Good, and he had done his best, and God was witness to what he meant to do. What logic could one use to make him use the logic to see his own way clearly, but, *bonguienne*, freely also? Did anything else matter? He would try again. He must.

"Son, the call of the priesthood is not a disease some catch, and others escape. It is a contract with God and His Church, but I do believe it works both ways. Only those are called who wish to be! For, if you are not free to choose, we are not talking here about a vocation, but a trap, and God knows nothing about this. . . . Emile, my son, you are free to choose. . . ."

"What, Papa?"

"You are free, Emile. Free! Do you understand?"

He looked up suddenly at his Papa, the sudden recipient of a strange gift.

"Free, Papa?

"Sure as hell you're free, as I am!"

Emile laughed suddenly, then a frown came over his face.

"Free?"

Louis nodded, then walked out of the bedroom toward his radio. Félix had gone to bed, and now, at long last, Antoine and Thérèse were alone in the *parloir*, and both could be heard whispering in the semi-darkness when Louis and Emile passed by. Emile went up to his Papa. He made his voice into a whisper, too.

"These two—they are settling the great problem?" he asked lightly.

Louis smiled.

"That problem!" he said. "It is never settled, for above all, they too are afraid, as you are afraid. The problem of fear is never settled, but, in there, Emile, there are two of them facing it, and you, if you become a priest, you'll always be alone, alone with God. . . ."

"It is enough," said Emile firmly. "No need to be afraid with God's grace."

"But you are afraid, a little bit?"

"Sure. The priest told us to be cautious."

"But not to be cowardly, he didn't. For the priesthood is a matter of courage. It is not just books in Latin, giving hell and collecting money, it's to help people, all kinds of people, that they too will not be afraid, and sometimes to help people who are a lot smarter than the priest is. . . . That takes a special kind of courage, Emile. . . ."

"It does, Papa, it does."

"And the priest works at his trade among all manner of men, and, *bonguienne*, women too, the good-looking and the ugly-looking, the slinky ones and the fat ones, and there is love and hatred and meanness, and the mortgage payments on the church and the school, and children to be baptized, and people to be buried, and confessions to be heard and ceremonies and the love and respect of people, deserved and undeserved, and the great hunger of the flesh that might, at any time, but for the grace of God, knock you on your . . ."

"Ass!" Emile finished off soberly. "But I am free, as you say. Free. Free to choose?"

Louis sighed. Maybe, after all, he had done it.

"Yes, you are. Did you not know it?"

"But, Papa, I want to become a priest. Very much!"

"*Bonguienne*, that suits me fine!" said Louis, slapping his knees.

"Free, huh?" repeated Emile, his face lighting up.

"Not quite," said Louis. He extracted his penknife from his back pocket, flicked open the smallest and sharpest blade, and handed it to him.

"What for?" asked Emile.

"For to cut off that damned contraption around your belly!"

Emile took the knife, peeked around to see if anyone would see, opened his robe, reached inside his nightgown, took the knife and sliced the cloth tape, and pulled it out. For a moment, he did not know what to do with it. Louis pointed at the trash can and Emile dropped it in.

Louis turned on his radio. It immediately began to whistle and screech, and soon a staccato voice poured forth from the earplugs. He gave one to Emile and put the other to his ears, and began to dial gently. Now he winked at Emile.

"You speak Mexican yet?"

"No," he laughed, "just a bit of Latin, English and some Greek."

"No Mexican?"

"No, Papa."

"Too bad," said he, twisting the dials. "Then I could find out if I have Mexico or not. But then, no one can know everything, not true?" Then he added, "I can't speak Mexican either."

Suddenly there was a sharp whistling within the earplugs and both winced.

"Papa," said Emile, rubbing his ear, "I don't really know very much of anything—yet."

"Oho!" laughed Louis, ruffling his hair. "My son, Emile, at sixteen, he is a true philosopher!"

"No, but some day, I will be, you watch and see."

"I know it, Emile. I just know it."

Louis twirled the dials some more, and cocked his ear as he held on to the earplug.

"Now," he exclaimed, "where in hell can Mexico be tonight?"

7. The Courtship of Monique [1930]

It was one o'clock—the sun was at its highest—when Louis Martel arrived at the fair grounds. The ball game between the Groveton Norths and the Groveton Souths had already started. After four innings, the score was nothing to nothing. Hastily he made his way up past the grandstand and the open bleachers toward the right field, with his folding chair, his sun glasses, and his large thermos of cold beer. He stopped at the edge of the first base line near the right field position, opened his chair, fixed his glasses, took a small swallow of beer and sat down. A good crowd had started to overflow from the seats into the edges of the outfield. Some sat on the grass, some stood, and others walked casually around.

If it's an artillery game, he decided, I'll stay here and watch those long fly balls sail by. If it's a high strategy game, with artistic pitching, I'll move back of the plate. In the trees beyond the outfield, birds chirped. From above, the sun settled warmly on his forehead. And the pepper-talk from the infield, fifty feet or so away, tickled him. One should have, in a ball game as anywhere else, a lot of pepper-talk. Félix, his son of nineteen, was playing second base, and as soon as he saw his Papa installed, he redoubled his own pepper-talk. It was hot but there was a breeze.

It was good, Louis mused, to be alive on this Fourth of July, free, healthy, single, and wise to the plotting wiles of plotting widows, to be a lively forty-eight, with children and grand-children, all healthy, some shy, some sassy, but all brought up respectably, to be a family man and yet, for the moment, to have no one around to tell you what trees made the best shingles. He took a large swallow of cold beer, sighed, thanked God for his peace of mind, and then he saw her!

From left field toward the right field, around the outer edges of the playing field itself, she walked slowly, staring straight ahead, walked, unaware of the ball game, walked to within ten feet of him, turned, and slowly walked back toward left field. And then again she turned around and walked slowly toward him, her knees bouncing gently against the long red dress, her dark hair slightly ruffled by the breeze. Now she paused fifty feet away to look at the players. She was alone, though some had waved at her and she had smiled at some, but she was alone, and she was not more than thirty, with a full face, calm dark eyes, white skin—*Canadienne,* for sure—and for a moment, he was sure he had seen her before. He forgot to look at the game.

Bonguienne! What a womanly woman! What a marvel of a woman, this marvel of God's mysterious earth, this creature of the female side, this counterpart of a man that made them both awkward when asunder, and when joined the sweet proof of Providence's perfect blueprint. . . . She began to walk away from him, and then she stopped, and then started to walk again, her head erect and her steps sure, alive, nervous. . . . Messieurs, have you ever driven a well-mannered but sprightly mare?

Left flank. Right flank. Slowly. Gently. But ready to buck! Always ready to buck! Slowly. Gently, and now the twitching of the mane, ready to buck, ready for the deviltry to begin. . . . Left flank. Right flank. Messieurs! What a womanly woman! Now she turned again toward him, and walked. Right flank. Left flank. She was simply taking in the sun, and the air and the Fourth of July and his breath away. Who was she?

A sudden cheer rose and forced him to look at the ball game. Félix was on second base, panting, looking toward him, brushing his suit. Louis waved at him, but he would never know, nor would he ever admit that he'd never seen the ball Félix had slugged, nor where it had landed, nor—he again turned his head toward the red dress—who this womanly woman of perhaps twenty-nine was, nor would he ever know—perhaps. Someone asked him what inning this was, but he didn't know. . . .

Now she stood apart from the crowd, her long red dress in contrast to the whites, the blues and the yellows of other people. A little boy dropped his blue balloon and it floated up and down near her on the grass and she ran for it, missed it once and then caught it and handed it to the little boy. No, there were no rings on her fingers, unmarried, unbetrothed, and a look of yearning toward that little boy, a womanly woman, yes, but unfulfilled. *Bonguienne!* He must know who she was, and he would. She was only ten feet away.

He might offer her his chair. I'd rather stand, Mademoiselle, I assure you. Or a cold glass of beer. Homemade, you know, in the old-fashioned manner. He might just ask her what the score was. No, that sounded *mal élevé*, somehow. And then Félix was at his side, and he was limping.

"Pulled a muscle, Pa. I'm out of the game. Did it in the eighth inning!"

"Too bad. Take my chair."

"*Non, non,* Papa. I'll lie down right on the grass."

"That was a good hit, Félix. You've got the right swing," he said. "I'm sorry you hurt yourself."

"Thank you, Papa," he said. "I think I did it in the eighth inning."

Félix stretched on the grass, and then suddenly leaned on one elbow and stared at the lady in red and tipped his cap at her. She smiled, waved a hand swiftly at him, and then Félix reclined fully on the grass. Louis took a large swallow of beer, his eyes seeing but unbelieving. Daughters, he had always known, could mystify you, but sons, never!

"Félix, my beloved son," he purred, "that lady? You know her?"

"Yes, and then again, no, Papa."

Louis took another swallow of beer. Now, this was son-talk. The thermos was now nearly empty. He must calm down about this. That silly answer demanded gentle probing, and this affair, before a mere boy of nineteen, would require diplomacy.

"You salute her, and you don't know her? Is that courtesy?"

Félix leaned on one elbow again.

"It seems, Papa, that I know her from somewhere. She knows me too. And yet, her name escapes me. Who she is, I don't know, and who I am, she does not know either. To ask her now, after what seems years of acquaintanceship, What, pray, is your name? would be discourteous. She smiles at me often, and to hint that I don't know who she is, might kill a very pleasant little game."

Louis jammed tobacco into his pipe. Diplomacy, be damned! Tomorrow, you die, today you meet her! He lit his pipe and sent a barrage of blue smoke toward her. He turned to Félix.

"Félix, I want to meet her. Do you understand me, Félix?"

"Sure, Papa," he agreed, and took a more comfortable position on the grass.

"Not in limbo. Right now!"

"*Bon*, Papa."

Félix got up. Papa picked up his chair and his thermos.

"Pa, she's gone."

Indeed. She was nowhere to be seen. The ball game was breaking up and the crowd swerved and veered in all directions. No use trying to detect her in that moving, swirling crowd. Louis smoked his pipe, a hard glint in his eyes.

"*Eh, maudit!*" he said between clenched teeth.

"I'll find out who she is," Félix offered, "sometime."

Yes, yes. Sometime. These nineteen-year-olds had all the time in the world, and no genius to put it to work. Hit a two-base hit, and the effort killed them. They did not understand that a man of forty-eight learns to pace himself more wisely, while watching for the main chance. These young kids? Poop, poop, and they were done. Félix was limping alongside of him, slowing up his own stride.

"Call up Laurent," he told Félix, "to come and fetch us in his car."

While Félix phoned, Louis began to calm down. What was not to be was not to be. One must resign oneself to the inevitable. If Providence, which arranged these things, had written that he would never see her again, he would not—it would never happen—but if Providence had it all arranged, it would happen, for sure, somehow, somewhere. . .

All the time, he met widows everywhere, but this had nothing to do with Providence, he was sure. You said, "*Bonjour!*" to them, and right away, they began to talk, and talk. God, he was positive, would not send him, nor anyone else, the chosen one all fitted with a chatty commercial. They turned up near him at Mass every Sunday, at the boxing matches; some sought his advice on house building, some offered to mother his Marie and Cécile, and others invited him for cozy home-cooked meals. . . .

Nice women all, thought Louis, who had lost their husbands, as he had lost his own life partner, but they pressed too hard for what he had left to offer. . . . Some were too young, and all talked too much. What a man needed, he resolved, was a woman who could listen, who . . . What did a man like him need a wife for, anyway? Because . . . because it is written in the Ancient Books that it is not good for a man to live alone. . . .

"It was an accident!"

That's what Louis Martel said, a few weeks later, that July afternoon when it happened. They were building a bowling alley and skating arena, down on Washington Street, and he was in charge of the job. And, of course, he felt responsible. Designed to be four stories high, the building was half completed when the scaffolding upon which two carpenters were working began to collapse over the sidewalk. . . .

He was inside the building nearby. Without thinking, he reached over and grasped and held on with all his might in his right hand the two-by-four nearest him, and this seemed, for a precious moment, to shore up the scaffold, but then it crumbled some more, and he held on, again with all his might, though he could feel the muscles of his arm and hand ache with searing pain. . . . But it was enough. The two carpenters jumped into the building, and Louis let go, and the scaffolding crashed to the sidewalk, four stories below. . . .

"An act of heroism," everybody agreed.

"An accident," said Louis.

Out of it, he got compensation, insurance, a paid medical bill, a severely sprained right hand and a six-month enforced holiday with pay and honors. He decided, however, not to waste his time.

"I don't know," he told everyone, "what I'll do with all this time, but I promise to do something big! Real big!"

Dr. Lafrance took charge of the case. There would be, he said, some medicine he could give him, and there would be some Louis would have to fashion for himself. This, Lafrance said, would consist of long hours daily of exercising his hand back into shape. He must come and see him every Wednesday at his office.

Félix went with him the first Wednesday, and when he opened the door for his Papa, there she was! The lady in red was now the nurse in white.

"*Allo*, Félix," she said pleasantly. "And, oh, Monsieur Martel, there you are! The doctor will be with you in a moment."

Louis nearly blushed. She knew them both!

"I saw you at the game, Fourth of July. But I guess you don't remember me!"

"But, Mademoiselle . . ."hesitated Louis.

". . . And I know why. I'm Nurse Monique Beaulieu . . ."

Of course they knew her. She'd taken care of Maman in her last weeks on earth. And also of Cécile and Marie, with their appendectomies, a year ago. Remember her? Of course.

"But in white," thundered Louis in deep apology. "Only in white!"

They would have to wait and she appeared to be ready for time-killing talk. Louis had never seen his son so talkative before. It was the question she asked, perhaps?

"You play many sports, Félix?"

"Yes. Hockey, football, boxing, all manner of good exercise. . . ."

"Exercise! That is the best thing. . . ." she said slowly.

Félix rattled on.

"My Papa here taught me about all sports, particularly baseball. I can still remember when Papa took a bunch of us to a small playing field, in back of some houses, one afternoon, and before we started to hit the ball around, he got us together and he told us to play fair, and that . . ."

"You play ball yet, Monsieur Martel?" she asked with a smile.

"Only with my left hand," he answered, lifting his right arm in a sling. She frowned in sympathy at his bandaged right hand. Félix continued.

"Now, Papa told us, you see those windows in those houses over there, in left field? Well, if you happen to hit one and break one of those windows, do the right thing! Walk right up to the owner and tell him, like a gentleman, that you broke the window and want to do the right thing, understand?"

"Very proper," said Monique Beaulieu, a trace of a smile coming upon her lips. "And when your father came to bat, and hit one, and broke a window . . ."

"He dropped his bat," blurted out Félix, "and beat us all out of the park!" Then he and the nurse had a good laugh at Louis's expense. He laughed also, and yet he wished that a special day would be set aside, each year, so that fathers could quietly strangle their own sons.

Thérèse put the phone back on the hook, gasped and then asked the operator—quickly—to give her Laurent's phone number, that she might talk to his wife, Hélène.

Thérèse had married Antoine Bouchard in August, a year ago—Emile had assisted as altar boy before going back to the seminary—and she and Antoine now lived in a fashionable suburban area, up Chestnut Road. Antoine, of course, as they said, "had gone up in the bank," an officer, no less, and they had to afford Chestnut Road, even though she sometimes felt out of touch with great events in Groveton itself. And once again, she was probably the last to hear of it.

Hélène answered. Yes, Jean-Paul and Réné were in good health, and Laurent and Michel also. And how was Antoine? No, Thérèse was not pregnant—not yet, my God!—and neither was Hélène, but then, did Papa have a new girl?

"Antoine just phoned!" said Thérèse breathlessly. "And he said that someone had seen Papa at the Empire Theater last night."

"With a girl?"

"With a young girl!"

"Oh, yes. That was Monique Beaulieu. . . . She was the nurse who's been so nice to Jean-Paul, and to Marie and Cécile. . . ."

"Hélène, they were holding hands in the movies!"

"Yes, well, they go every time the program changes. . . ."

"But, Hélène, Papa is forty-eight! And she's—well—not quite twenty-seven."

"Thérèse," Hélène began quietly, "your Papa has made up his mind. He told Laurent. He's going to marry her!"

"No!"

"Oh, yes. He told Laurent all it will take is a little diplomacy!"

"Poor Papa!" said Thérèse.

After she hung up, Hélène took René in her arms. He had just begun to walk. And she sang him a little song.

"Poor Thérèse! Poor Thérèse! Poor Thérèse! With no little babies, she has to worry about her Papa!"

Maurice, in Augusta, picked up the phone, and when he had heard the entire story from Thérèse, he said, no, positively, he would not come right down to Groveton to straighten everything out.

"Why not?" asked Thérèse. "He's your Papa too."

Maurice chuckled a few moments—on her telephone time.

"If Papa's got himself a young *minois*, he being a single man and all that, and he's having himself a time of it, you're crazy to worry. Call me for something important, will you? Oh, ask him if she's got a friend, and I'll be down pronto!" And he hung up.

That same evening, Thérèse drove over to speak to Laurent and Hélène. As they often did these days when no woman presided over the Louis Martel home, Marie and Cécile were visiting. They sat in the living room, listening to the radio and the adults sat in the kitchen.

"I can understand," admitted Thérèse, "that it is lonesome for Papa, living alone, but I can't see him falling for such a young girl. . . ."

"She is thirty-two," said Laurent firmly.

"And the children?" whispered Thérèse.

Marie and Cécile came bouncing in. Hélène frowned at Thérèse.

"I know!" Cécile announced triumphantly. "You're talking about Papa and his girl!"

Thérèse stared in embarrassment toward Laurent.

"Yes, we are," said Hélène quietly.

"I know!" whispered Cécile. Marie nodded quietly.

"How do you know so much?" asked Thérèse, and wondered, indeed, how come everyone knew what she was just learning.

"I know," said Marie. "Because! Because whenever Papa has a date with her, he puts sweet-stinky smelling stuff in his hair. That's when we know he has a heavy date! And he sings! He sings around the house!"

Laurent chuckled.

"And besides," and she let this go with full force, "he dyes his hair!"

"No!" exclaimed Laurent, enjoying himself.

"Yes! Yes!" sang out Marie, and then she giggled in personal joy. "And the other night, he could not find the bottle, and he did not sing at all around the house, and he looked, and he looked. . . ."

"He looked," Cécile added, "under the bed, under the

chairs, everywhere, and he could not find the bottle."

"I hid it," said Marie casually.

"Why?" asked Hélène. "Why do that to Papa, *chérie?*"

"Because!" she affirmed.

"Because!" repeated Cécile.

"I don't like her!" stated Marie. "I hate her!"

Later, Antoine and Thérèse were going to bed.

"Me? Me, speak to your Papa?" he said. "Of all the men I know, including my own Papa—may he rest in peace!—your father is the one man who can handle himself best. . . ."

"She is twisting him around her little finger. . . ."

"Oh, no, she is not. If I know your Papa, he is twisting her around his own strong arms!"

"Antoine!"

He opened the covers of the bed and she slipped inside and he tucked her in, smiling all the time to himself. Then he got into bed on the other side.

"*Chérie,*" he said, "quiet down. Why don't you write to your brother Emile. . . ."

"Thank you, 'Toine," she kissed him, "I will. I will!"

"Sure," said he, still smiling to himself, "maybe you ought to get the Church's side of all this. . . ."

Emile wrote as follows:

"In all countries, under all climates, there is only a certain age below which one may NOT marry. This is Canon Law. *Primo.* It is also Canon Law, *secundo,* that with the previous stipulation, and others, not referring to age, after that, the sky's the limit. Here, the Church is more charitable than the world. . . .

"You ask me, dear Thérèse, to pray for him, and I shall, as I do every day, and for you also, that you may see the logic of it. *Sic posit!* Rejoice that she is young! The way these things happen, it could have been otherwise for Canon Law does not forbid a union with one old and ugly. . . . In either case, *tertio*, it is none of our business, except to wish Papa well. . . .

"Marie wrote also, and told me that Papa is dyeing his hair—coal black, as it used to be. If God understands more and more *re* the use of lipstick, I'm sure He can take in a good hair dye job too. I yearn to see him again soon, with coalblack hair, as it used to be, for to me Papa will never really grow old. . . ."

She wept over the letter, and turned to Antoine.

"I just don't want Papa to be unhappy, that's all I want."

That summer and early fall, Louis, his right arm and hand in a sling, courted Monique. The talkies had come to stay, and this was a blessing for a man who could not read, for the silents had been misery, except Charlie Chaplin. Monique loved the movies, vaudeville, and dancing. And she taught him the new steps, until he found that these newfangled gyrations were but easy variations of those he had jigged to violin music long ago. They often went dancing, Louis with one arm literally in a sling.

During this leisure time, every morning he went to Mass, spent some time in Municipal Court to find out about the Law and to listen to good cases, took long walks and checked on all of Groveton's new buildings going up, or coming down, stopped daily at Bordeaux's Barber Shop to find out the news that never got printed. Afternoons and evenings, when not out on a date, he played cards with Marie and Cécile. One night a week, he had a date with Monique. He seldom spoke about this, and then only to Laurent.

This is my business, he told him. He told Laurent other things. He told him he now could almost do anything with his left hand his right hand once used to do for him: he was now, by God, a switch-hitter. This had been Monique's idea. She had taught him, patiently, but with stubbornness. In or out of her uniform, she was firm toward the duty to be performed, energetic, a dynamo. "A dark-eyed skirted dynamo," said Louis, "but a dynamo!"

"You see this?" he told Laurent, tapping his belly. "Slim and solid. I owe that to that dynamo. You see this?"

He took a pencil and deftly manipulated it between the fingers of his right hand, and then of his left hand. "With either hand now, I can tie my shoelaces, shave, hammer nails and saw wood. Exercise! That's what did it! And Monique!"

Much of her duties toward him, at first, he explained to Laurent, consisted in taking care of his sprained and lacerated hand, in changing the dressing, and then later, in exercising it. First, she did it for him, then she taught him how to do it. "The more you exercise it," she told him, "the stronger it will get again."

"She believes," said Louis, "in God, the sacredness of nursing, the gift of life, and exercise! She was the sole support of her Papa and Maman before they died. Her Papa was sick a long time. They left her that big house on Pine Street. It needs repairs. I'm doing it in my spare time. Exercise! She likes to take long walks winter or summer. Every morning and every evening she takes bending exercises, shoulder exercises, leg exercises, breathing exercises, derrière exercises. . . ."

"Pa, you going to marry her?" Laurent asked gently.

Louis looked away for a moment, and then turned toward Laurent.

"Yes!"

"Then, it is settled?"

Louis smiled ruefully.

"Oh, I've got to ask her yet, and then I'll have to ask all of you, and the whole town of Groveton. . . . *Bonguienne*, Laurent, in a way, it was not my idea. . . . One day, she was exercising my hand and then I was holding both her hands. . . . It comes suddenly to you, the reminder that your allotment of companionship has not run out yet. . . ."

"Papa, I know."

"At first, you resist it, and she resisted it also, as if it were a shameful thing. . . . Ah! But the shame is that one believes one cannot love again! I know I do, and I believe she does, too. Any woman, Laurent, who catches so quickly and laughs so easily at the little jokes you make reveals her secret. . . . She is keeping open the pipeline to her heart. . . ."

One night in September, at a dance, he and Monique were fox-trotting to *Goodnight Sweetheart!* when he began to whisper into her ear. . .

"I love you, Monique, and everybody in the four corners of the world!"

"Yes, Louis, I do too, but there is a problem. . . ."

"The problem is as follows," he said, "and let us see it for what it is. My children need a mother and your training is the best for that. . . . Score for me?"

"Score for you. But, Louis, I'm too young for you perhaps. . . ."

"Do you mind?"

"Oh, no. I like being young, and being with you."

"Therefore, it is preferable that a mother be young and healthy."

"But is that enough?"

"Of the greatest importance, however, is that I need a wife, I need you. True, for that, you have no training, and I train you myself. . . ."

"We'll see who trains whom!" she said with a sad smile.

"It is preferable also," added Louis, "for a man with any

woman that he have a head start of some kind over her. I have it on the calendar."

"But, Louis, I may not be the good person you may think I am. . . ."

"Monique, the Groveton gossips always will work at their trade. Let us concentrate on our trade. I love you in a very special way! How can any past days darken the future you give me?"

"Louis, I want to marry you, very much. . . ."

"We all sleep in the bed we make. Personally, I'm tired of sleeping alone. . . ."

"Louis!" and she laughed at him.

"And I promise that I'll work very hard to make things better for you in all things," he said solemnly.

"Of that I am very sure," she said, and took his hand.

"But, one thing I will not do. I will not take any more exercise than I have to. I will not do calisthenics on the floor, nor run uphill, nor do setting-up exercises in the morning, nor bend down from the waist up. No sirreee!"

She smiled at him.

"But Louis. What will you tell the children?"

He frowned—just a little bit.

A few days later, Félix took his Papa aside.

"Papa," he said slowly, "I hear talk about town. About you. And about Monique. I speak of it because it hurts me."

"And this talk! It is about what?"

Félix began to speak but no words came out right away.

"Mademoiselle Monique . . . They say she's making a fool of you. Forgive me, Papa, I hate even to say it. . . ."

Louis Martel's face tightened.

"Thank you, Félix. You are a good son. Yes, Monique knew a man. He played fast and loose with her. She was hurt too.

Perhaps he was no good and perhaps she was young. No matter. . . .”

“No matter, Papa. . . .”

“For me, I pass the great big sponge over all this. I wipe it off. Like the Confession and the Absolution. If it weren't for the big sponge, Félix, we'd all die of shame before attaining wisdom. Big errors bring on big punishments. She has been punished. Would we add to it?”

“*Non, non, Papa.*”

“The punishment? She cannot have children.”

“*Non?*”

“*Non*, and who would add to this punishment?”

“Not I! Anybody who can turn you into a switch-hitter is first class to me. I think she's a dandy. But, Papa, you must do the great action. Quickly.”

Louis put his arm around his son.

“It is that I'm a little afraid. . . .”

“You, Papa, afraid?”

“I think of Marie who is thirteen, and Cécile who is eleven, and of Monique, who wants to be a mother to them, but not a stepmother, and I have to hesitate. . . .”

“But, Pa, they are just little foolish girls. . . .”

Louis shook his head in doubt.

“Félix, boys grow up into manhood, sometimes, but all little girls come from God full-grown and worldly-wise. All the time they know what is at stake—for them, and they should! They know what is going on between folks—all the time they look and listen—and they sense who deserves their jealousy, or their approval. To be that way is their life's business, but we must respect it!”

Then he decided to take the great step. Diplomacy be damned! Honesty was better and faster and life granted its gifts only to those who reached out for what they morally demanded, or snatched, from that day's choices. He would tell Laurent to blow the trumpets and call a meeting of the Martel clan, and he did, and one night, in October, there gathered in his kitchen Laurent and his wife Hélène, Thérèse and Antoine, Félix, Marie and Cécile. Laurent told them Papa had an announcement to make.

They all sat in the large kitchen, where Maman once had presided to the tick-tock of the clock bought so long ago, and they made little jokes about this and that. Marie and Cécile sat close together. Louis smiled at the entire gathering, lit his pipe, leaned on the back of a chair. He would, he thought, give it to them straight.

"I have decided," he said, "to marry again."

"Mademoiselle Beaulieu?" added Hélène helpfully.

"No one else," said Papa.

A silence followed. To break it up, Louis went on to say that Maurice and Muriel could not come, but they had sent their good wishes. So had Emile from the seminary.

"He's for marriage," said Louis, "for everybody else."

Laurent chuckled. So did Antoine. No one else laughed. Marie began to frown and Cécile studied her, and then she began to frown too.

"Papa," said Laurent quietly, "you know you have my permission."

"Bless you, Papa Martel," said Hélène.

"I wish you well," said Antoine.

"Pa," said Félix, "I think that's just dandy. Besides, she can make flapjacks. Just like Maman."

Marie began to weep quietly, then she burst into tears. Louis went up to her and took her in his arms.

"Now, now, my lovely one, I'm not leaving you!"

"I know," she sobbed, "I know that."

"Then, why are you weeping?"

"Because. . . ."

General conversation broke out. When would this happen, would Monique keep her job, how was Papa's hand, and hadn't this been a hot summer? Marie wept and wept. And Louis began to appear worried.

"It will be all right," offered Hélène to Thérèse, "when she is settled in the house. . . ."

"It's only a matter of time," advised Antoine.

Marie broke out into hysterics.

"What shall I call her?" she asked the whole wide world.

"Call her?" asked Louis, nettled.

Marie turned to Cécile, and they exchanged looks of victory.

"We can't call her 'Maman,'" stated Cécile coldly.

"I guess not," agreed Laurent, turning to Hélène.

Louis sucked on his pipe and found it to be a dead pipe.

"Mademoiselle Monique," he admitted, "cannot replace Maman. No one can do that, and Monique has nothing like that in her head."

"Of course not," chimed in Thérèse.

"She can only be herself," stated Félix.

"Still, I cannot call her 'Maman'!" Marie yelled.

Very slowly now, Cécile too began to weep.

"You don't have to call her 'Maman,'" agreed Louis slowly. "Your Maman has gone to heaven. . . ."

"And I wish . . . I wish . . ." Marie bawled, her face breaking into helpless grimaces, "that she were right here with us!"

"So do I!" screamed Cécile.

"God!" muttered Louis. "So do I. But the reality is that she is not with us. . . ."

Hélène took Cécile in her arms and let her weep a bit and then purred gentle words in her ears and she rearranged the yellow ribbon in her hair, and Cécile stopped crying and began to rearrange Hélène's hair also. Laurent sighed, shrugged his shoulders, and exchanged a look with Félix.

"And besides," added Marie, "she's going to have babies. . . ."

"Lots of babies. . . ." echoed Cécile suddenly.

Louis decided that now, this, this could be the turning point. This was as desperate as it could become, and if experience taught anything, it taught that, if properly used, liabilities could become assets. He turned toward Thérèse. It was she who had been the mother-substitute when Maman had died, and it was Thérèse who was not, yet, a mother herself, though it was not for lack of yearning. He looked at Thérèse, whispering words to her with his eyes, remembering her First Communion dress, the fever that nearly killed her, her first date, the closeness, and yet the shyness between father and daughter, the unspoken understanding always. . . .

And his eyes spoke to her, and he hoped that the message he radioed to her would bring back the answer to the present riddle, for if one gave to one's children in their days of childhood, could one not expect the rewards of their maturing?

He turned and went to the armoire. Antoine had already poured quick shots, and Louis downed his, and so did Laurent and Antoine. The three men exchanged a moment of quiet calm. They knew what they could not speak out, and their wives knew also. For Louis had told the men, *en famille*, and the men had told their wives, *en famille*, and Antoine had told Thérèse, and now Louis again turned toward Thérèse, and he hoped she would remember. . . .

As he'd told Félix, he'd also told Laurent and Antoine that there could be no children, that Monique had, what Dr. Lafrance called "an automatic birth control condition," and that Monique had found it out by accident during a routine health examination. . . . Laurent had been fascinated by this because he had three already, and so had Antoine because as yet he had none. . . . Maybe his Thérèse had the same condition. . . .

Now, again, Louis studied Thérèse and in wordless signals asked her what she had decided. Marie and Cécile were quiet at the moment.

"I imagine," said Thérèse suddenly, "that Mademoiselle Monique would be very happy with a family of children, already. . . ."

"House-broken?" asked Louis.

"Yes, Papa. I imagine she would love to take care of folks who need her. Children, especially."

"Oh, she does, Thérèse, she does," Louis agreed. He must remember to kiss his little Thérèse more fondly and more often.

"Oh, Papa," she replied, "I know what you have in mind. I knew that all along. The children also need a maman. I know that."

Marie frowned and her face contorted and became a weeping grimace again, and Cécile began to weep loudly.

"She'll live here," whined Cécile, "and cook the meals, and fix the house, and tell us when to go to bed and to say our prayers . . ."

"Yes, she will. . . ." said Louis.

"And . . . and . . ." Cécile continued, gasping, "and what to wear, and 'don't do that, Cécile!' and 'don't do this, Cécile!' and we won't be able to call her 'Maman'!"

"Well," said Louis, taking her in his arms, "my little Cécile, what would you like to call her?"

Her face broke into tears.

"I don't know, Papa!"

Louis passed her along to Thérèse.

"Maybe," said Thérèse to Cécile, "Mademoiselle Monique can borrow you? Like I do sometimes, like Aunt Hélène? For a few weeks, you know?"

"That's different," said Cécile, gasping, "borrowing like that is different."

"That's different," agreed Marie. "You borrow us like that to have dinner with you, or to go to the movies, that's very good, but, Papa, why do you have to marry her?"

Louis laughed tiredly.

"I don't *have* to marry her!" he said. "I want to. And if she's going to live here—why—it's the custom to marry. Don't blame me for that. I did not invent the custom!"

Laurent and Antoine roared.

"I'll call her 'Monique,'" stated Marie suddenly.

"No, you will not," said Laurent. "It's not respectful."

"Shall I call her 'nurse'?"

"No," said Louis. "This is going to be her home, not a hospital."

Hélène turned to Laurent. He had no suggestion to offer. Antoine turned to Thérèse. She frowned. She had none either.

"'Mademoiselle'?" offered Cécile. "It's a nice name. Or 'Madame'?"

"No," said Thérèse, "that's too . . . too cold."

And now Louis turned toward Marie. It was she who had felt the loss of her Maman the most—she had been too young, and yet old enough—and he told her in voiceless words that he acknowledged her great loss, for to lose one's mother at the age of ten, Marie, my little Marie, was almost but not quite beyond repair, and perhaps it toughens a little bit against another hurt. . . .

"You don't scare me," Marie suddenly told him.

"*Chérie!*" reprimanded Thérèse. "That's Papa you're talking to."

Louis said nothing. I remember the night you came to us straight from God—you chose to come on a Sunday night when everything was nice and quiet—and we loved you because, right from the start, you had spunk. Your Maman was so sick after you came. And with what courage will you face the rest of your years, dear Marie, with what imagination?

"You don't scare me either!" said Louis to Marie gently.

"I wish I could!"

"With that look," said Louis, "you gain nothing from me. When you smile, you can make me melt so fast!"

A smile came on Marie's face and with effort she chased it away.

"I don't feel sweet," she announced. "I feel mean."

"Sweet or mean," said Papa, his voice now becoming firm, "when Mademoiselle Beaulieu is my wife, that blackboard will be red with marks if you don't behave toward her, as I expect a young lady to behave. Am I understood?"

"Yes, Papa," said Cécile automatically.

"Will her name," asked Marie, playing for time, "be on the blackboard?"

"Should it be?" Louis asked quickly.

"Why not?" asked Marie. On that issue, she would fight!

"What name, then?" Louis shot at her very quickly.

"Maman-Monique," said Marie.

"That's it!" exclaimed Thérèse to Hélène.

"That's good!" exclaimed Louis, and he must remember also to kiss even more fondly than before his smart little girl, Marie.

"Maman-Monique!" said Cécile, tasting the words quietly.

Hélène placed a warm kiss on Marie's cheek.

"When did you think that up? Just like that, *chérie?*"

Marie crossed her legs, wiped her tears.

"Somebody had to," she admitted modestly.

Louis Martel closed the discussion then and there. One step at a time, he told himself, and in time a man could walk around the entire world. . . .

Monique was formally invited to dinner two evenings later. Hélène and Thérèse prepared the dinner and everybody was on his guard. Once and only once, Marie had to address a question to Monique, and she did it deliberately.

"Will you have more tea, Monique?"

"Yes, please, Marie."

Louis looked up from his ice cream dessert and said nothing. No one else deigned to notice it. And he remembered also that one must always leave a competitor a face to save, especially that of a loved one. Adults could always win all the victories against helpless children, if they but applied their powerful laws, but if children were ever to become adults too, they too must snatch little victories from the jaws of constant defeats.

"Monique!" said Marie, biting into the consonants. "That's a nice name, Monique!"

"Thank you, Marie," said Monique, a sly smile on her face.

Louis said nothing, and told himself again to keep his damn mouth shut.

Now the banns were published, and the talk in the town stopped. And Monique visited with the children often, and, at least once each visit, Marie called her by her first name. A few nights before the wedding, just as Louis and Monique were getting ready to go to a movie, and were to take Marie and Cécile with them, Marie became violently sick to her stomach.

Monique looked at Marie, pondered a moment, then told Louis to go to the movies with Cécile—she would be disappointed if she didn't go—and she would stay with Marie. Louis objected but Monique was firm.

When they returned around ten from the movie, Marie was sleeping peacefully. Cécile undressed and crept into bed near Marie and went to sleep.

"How long has she been asleep?" asked Louis.

"Oh, I gave her something."

"Was it something she ate?"

"No. It was too much of everything, and also, that your little Marie is now a woman. . . ."

"She . . . ?"

"Yes, Louis. I gave her first-class nursing care. As if she were a very rich patient. And I put a lamp near her bed. She didn't have one. And I explained what was happening to her. I gave her the candy she likes best. She stared at me, all the time, without a word, not one, as if I were the Angel of Death. 'Monique, this' and 'Monique, that,' and never once did she smile at me. A little autocrat she is, Louis, but we must be patient."

"It will pass, Monique. It will pass, I hope."

Monique stayed with Marie a night and a day, and when Marie put away her fist big meal, Monique left and was gone for a day and a half, and when she appeared in the Martel apartment, she was Madame Louis Martel. It had been a simple wedding. Father Lebois had married them, but there had been time for only a very short Boston honeymoon.

The entire family was there to welcome them back, and drinks were served and toasts offered. Laurent, Maurice and Félix insisted on passing to their Papa all types of good advice.

"Put your foot down," said Laurent, "right away!"

"They don't behave," advised Maurice, "until you train 'em!"

Cécile jumped all over her Papa and he gave her the present he and Monique had bought for her in Boston, and for Marie. . . .

"Where's Marie?" Monique asked.

Then she knew! She hurried to Marie's bedroom. She was in bed, pretending to read under her new bed light. She nibbled on some of the candy she liked best. When she saw Monique she burst into tears.

"Where have you been? I've missed you so much, Maman-Monique!"

8. . . . A Time For Loving . . . [1931]

It was in the spring of that year that Louis Martel first began to hear the stories about Félix. He didn't like them one bit. All the more so because he couldn't make up his mind right away what to do about them.

That Félix should come up for discussion around Groveton was natural enough. In his first two amateur bouts at a local boxing club, he had knocked out his opponents with rights and lefts in the first rounds. Folks now called him "Champ." He was a celebrity. A true switch-hitter, Louis agreed, who had power in both hands. And Mike Callaghan, the local promoter, had immediately signed him to a professional contract.

Not so long ago, Louis thought, Félix had been a quiet, shy young man who led a clean outdoor life and had no bad habits. He and Maman-Monique had gotten along just fine. Both believed in exercise, and Félix kept himself in shape for the sheer love of it. Oh yes, seven days a week he still lugged fifty pounds of ice on his shoulders up stairs and through back lots for the A-I Ice Company in the summer, and coal bags for the A-I Coal Company in the winter. Yes, every Sunday morning, after his daily run, he went home, changed, and reported at Sacred Heart where he stood at a large table, in front of the church entrance, and made small change so that the worshippers might have the right coins for the two collections. Yes.

Once, he spent most of his time in the family circle, except for an occasional movie with some male chums, or a trip to Boston for a ball game, or a hockey match. So seldom did he go out with girls that Monique worried about it.

"You should speak to him, Louis," she had said once.

"What on earth about?"

"You know what on earth about."

"Monique, there are some things you don't have to tell boys and girls. Give them a good religious training, feed them red meat, and if they have the equipment, they'll find one another!"

"He's a little shy," Monique had observed, "but he'll make a good husband when he marries. . . ."

Quiet waters run deep and the turmoil beneath is seldom heard. In or out of the ring, Félix was no longer shy. In March he had met and defeated Battling Kid Jones with a barrage of lefts and rights in the second round. In May the ex-heavyweight champion of Maine, Jack "Knockout" Burns had lasted only three rounds with Félix. Now, the Groveton "Champ" was being carefully prepared for bigger targets, maybe the present heavyweight champion of Maine, Buddy Rocca himself. Prepared in peculiar ways, he no longer stayed home much, and he palled around with a sporting set—and sporting girls.

The tunes your children hum, Maman often said, are the ones parents have taught them. But now Félix was singing strange new tunes. Sure, Louis had fought some in lumber camps and had chased Indian girls—all good, clean fun—but in time, he'd married, settled down and grown up. Nowadays, much money could be made in the ring. Newspapers made a big fuss over young athletes, analyzed their styles, quoted their precious words, and young women surveyed their physiques and talked learnedly of biceps. And young athletes reveled in their years of springtimes that had no winters.

It was all so exciting, thought Louis, to dream of becoming

champion of the world, to be Félix' age when the eye is sharp and the fist obeys the brain so fast and so surely! This year, especially. When every father scrutinized each of his growing boys for a potential Jack Dempsey to rescue the big crown from the insignificant hands of a Max Schmeling. And Félix was a natural. He was five feet eleven, weighed 195, and was built like a brick meathouse. *Bonguienne*, who could blame the boy?

Maman-Monique did.

"Brawling in public?" she'd ask Louis. "Why, it must be some kind of sin!"

"Exercise never hurt anybody," he'd retort weakly.

"A punch in the eye hurts everybody," she'd snap back. "Louis, is that the man your Félix is to become?"

"Monique," he'd answer gently, "for the interest you take in my children, I thank you. For myself, I don't know what he will become. But remember this: you and I can't grow him all the way into old age. I say, let him do some of the growing up himself."

"With these bad companions? In saloons!"

"Monique, you can't breast-feed boys forever. It's past time for me to remind him every time he has to go to the back-house. Box or don't box, it matters very little, but let him be his own man!"

"Poor Félix," Monique always said, in conclusion.

That June, Mike Callaghan was almost sure that come September or December, Félix would take on Bud Rocca for the title. And so Louis was prevailed upon to allow Félix to use his summer cottage at Metaska Pond for training purposes, and Félix moved all his belongings to the cottage. A makeshift ring was built and training started in earnest, just as the summer resorts were opening up. Every night, right after supper, men and boys, and some women too, made the special trip to see Félix Martel spar his nightly six rounds, skip rope, shadow-box, and they paid two bits to see him do it.

Louis went nearly every night, but Monique never did. Instead she paid a twilight visit to Sacred Heart to light a candle. Marie and Cécile were thrilled to have a *pugiliste* in the family. It made nice talk with the boys at the corner candy store. Laurent wrote letters to Maurice in Augusta, and Maurice read them out loud to his friends.

Emile came home from the seminary for his summer vacation and Monique sought support from him—theologically, that is. As usual, he had the answers. Some bishops, he said, had seriously condemned boxing, and others had bought first row seats to some of the better fights. As for himself, he said he would spend his vacation with other seminarians at a boys' camp as a counselor, for room and board. He was eighteen now, completely absorbed in his studies, his future plans, and as Louis thought, in himself. Good and proper, at his age, but *bonguienne*, could he not have gone to see his own brother spar a few rounds at Metaska Pond? Good thing, anyway. Emile would not hear the stories about Félix. And Emile, almost a priest!

One evening in July Louis deigned to comment upon Monique's nightly lighting of a candle at Sacred Heart.

"The candle, Monique? It is for to win, or for to lose?"

She pretended not to hear.

"Monique, all those candles? For to win, or for to lose?"

"For Félix!" she replied mocking him, "Satisfied, *non?*"

"You are betting on a winner," he said slowly, and then he thought he should light a candle too, for Félix, and it would be for him to grow up.

It was at his weekly poker game that Louis got the real low-down. It was strictly a ten-cent limit, straight stud or draw poker, and no spitting into the ocean, or anywhere else. There was Dr. Lafrance, who had brought most of the Martel children into the world, and half of Groveton too; Pierre Nadeau, lawyer and free-thinker, Philippe Buisson, fellow-worker and friend of Louis, and others. They were all long-time friends, who cold say out loud what bitter enemies would never have dared to utter.

"She's a Spanish girl," said Dr. Lafrance, "about twenty-two, I should judge, and though she's not a patient of mine, I'd say she's a very healthy specimen of a girl."

"Oh, she's healthy all right," said Pierre Nadeau, "and very lively," he added quickly. "She dances all night—that crazy sentimental stuff—and goes horseback riding with a fast crowd around Metaska Pond. She's a waitress, I think. Works in a lobster restaurant up there somewhere."

"Oh, she's a nice girl," asserted Lafrance, "but our future champion of the world is not getting his proper rest. Generally, Louis, I would not discuss these things. It is not my business at any time, but now it is. This is a matter of the race. We now have, my friends, a real chance to put up a French-Canadian Jack Dempsey for the big title, one day, but *batege*, he must stay in training. . . ."

"I understand," said Louis.

"I say," said Philippe Buisson, "that she's ruining him. You cannot frolic and fight. You cannot have the skirt in bed all night and the cockiness in the square ring. . . ."

"Oh," interrupted Pierre Nadeau, "I do not say that they are going to bed. I do not say that at all, but if they are, I do say, it's their own business!"

"It's none of my business at all," protested Lafrance, "except that I'm going to bet on Félix, and I tell my friends to bet on Félix, but he can't be training in the cottage, with all the lights on, late at night. Otherwise, it is none of my business!"

"Thank you," said Louis. "You all mean well. I feel like the husband who's the last to find out his wife's been getting her strawberries in another county."

"Mind you," said Pierre Nadeau, "I believe all men are equal, and it is right for the French and the Spanish, and the Catholics, and Protestants, and Jews, to be brothers, but this is a different matter. This is a matter. . ."

"*Marde!*" shouted Lafrance. "With that brother stuff! You crazy atheist! The French, the Spanish, the Irish, the Catholics, the Protestants, the Jews, I bring them all into the world, like plucked chickens they all look, and they all look alike, but now, your Félix, Lou, he is not woman-smart. He's woman-shy. But this filly here, she is man-smart, she's a twister of men, this Lucia Lopez. . . ."

"Lucia Lopez?" asked Louis.

"*Batege!*" exclaimed Pierre Nadeau. "I wish I were younger, because she's the cutest little piece I've seen in a long, long time!"

"At least," Louis murmured sadly, "my Félix has a good eye."

He went home before the poker game ended. He walked slowly, and pondered. This private business, in a cottage, late at night, is it my business? What Papa has the right to sneak a look into his boy's pockets for what he will see therein, or in his heart, or in his secret actions? Well, this Papa had, Louis resolved, provided, of course, he combined this right with tact. Besides, it was his cottage!

That Sunday morning, right after Mass, he turned to Monique.

"You would like a lobster dinner this afternoon, perhaps?"

She said she would, and that afternoon, Laurent and Hélène drove them to Metaska Pond where Louis insisted he'd heard of a very good fish restaurant. They found it, and Hélène and Monique, like two little girls out on a spree, gleefully put on large aprons that covered them up to the neck and patiently waited for the lobster. . . . Louis and Laurent had a smoke and keenly inspected the place, other folks, and then Lucia Lopez passed their table with a large tray, loaded with food, on her way to another table. Laurent looked up at his Papa and just barely nodded his head.

Louis quickly noted that she was small of bones, slim. Nice ankles . . . dark-haired . . . lustrous hair . . . sad, dark eyes . . . generous frontage. A healthy girl—no T.B. here at all. Quick with the hands, efficient, and what a set of restless hips. . . . And when he looked down at the table again, the lobster was there. They ate with enjoyment and rehashed family matters. Later when the women excused themselves, Louis and Laurent had a smoke.

"She's a cute little one," said Louis jovially, "she's got it, all right."

"Yes," said Laurent, "and she gives it away."

Louis turned on him.

"Laurent, remember the bad girl and the Pharisees. They wanted to kill her with bricks because she also gave it away, and *bonguienne*, they nearly did, but He came along and He began to write something on the sand with His stick. Now, what do you suppose He wrote?"

"Their own sins?" he asked, not too interested.

"Perhaps, and perhaps some telephone numbers. Perhaps Jacqueline's?"

Laurent stammered.

"But, Pa, that was before I was married!"

"Jacqueline was *Canadienne*, she gave it away too, so let us be charitable to this young girl, and your brother!"

"Yes, Papa," said Laurent quickly, for the ladies were returning. "Change the subject, will you?"

Some Papas had too long a memory, he thought. But this Papa, thank God, could also keep his mouth shut. Not even

Maman had known the secrets all his sons had had to share with him, the hidden things from their growing years, the deviltries they'd indulged in, the scrapes they'd managed to escape from, with his help, with only slight scratches. . . . There were male secrets, Papa often said, it was male courtesy to keep away from the womenry. So it would be now with Maman-Monique, but so also would Félix have to face Papa for that toe-to-toe, eye-to-eye conference. There was a name for it. When he had a chance, Laurent asked the question.

"Pa, you going to give Félix a calldown?"

"You damn right I am."

As it turned out, Louis did not have to summon Félix. A week later, late one Saturday night, Félix himself came home suddenly, when normally he would have been asleep in the family cottage at Metaska Pond. It was nearly twelve. He had chosen a time when he knew everyone else would be fast asleep. Especially Monique. Louis had just taken a bath and sat in the kitchen for one last pipeful before going to bed.

"Hi, Champ," said he brightly.

Félix smiled a bit, but he looked upset. He began to speak right away.

"Pa, I have some trouble."

"Woman-trouble?" said Louis helpfully.

"In a manner of speaking, yes."

"Well, Champ, what kind of trouble?

Félix sat down and looked at his powerful fists and punched his left one into his right one.

"It is nearly impossible," he said, "to speak it out loud."

Louis lit his pipe, stretched, and then suddenly reached into the armoire and took out the whisky bottle.

"For myself," he said calmly, "I'm going to have some dynamite with a beer chaser. How about you, Champ?"

"Oh, no, Pa! You know I'm in training!"

"In training for what?" he barked. "For the championship of Spain?"

He glared at Félix a moment, then he got two glasses, poured out two shots of whisky, opened a bottle of beer and poured two half-glasses.

"Here," he spoke firmly, "drink this. Tonight it is I who train you. Not Callaghan. I'm the manager, Champ, and I say: you drink this!"

Félix gulped the whisky and then slowly he sipped the beer. Louis did the same. Félix then looked up sadly at him and now shook his head with obvious distress.

"It is big trouble?" Louis asked quietly.

"It is great trouble," Félix replied, almost in a whisper.

Louis's face suddenly darkened. He looked long and hard at him. He sat down and faced him.

"Speak it up," he said, "and we'll talk it down."

"I don't know what to do," Félix blurted out quickly. "It is almost two months now. I see her every day—this girl—and she is—she was a lot of fun. You know, Pa, I appear at ease with girls, but really I'm not. But this girl—she puts me at ease inside where it helps the most."

"I know what you mean."

"We had a lot of fun together, Pa, and it started like that, and then it got out of hand, and now to stay away is cowardly, and to see her is misery, and every time I ask: 'Lucia . . .' That is her name . . ."

"Yes."

"I ask: 'Lucia, is it all right yet?' and every time she replies, 'No, Félix, not yet.' And I want to dig a hole in the ground and jump in and hide for good. These nights, Pa, I don't sleep."

Louis suddenly chuckled.

"This is all?" he asked softly.

"This is all," gasped Félix, "but what do I do?"

"You marry her!" commanded Louis. "And let's have another drink. My God! I thought you spit on a Bishop!"

Félix again punched his fists together.

"There's a catch," he said slowly, looking up at his father.

"There always is," said Louis, smiling. "In this world it is a certainty of the living, and in the next one the relief of the dead."

"She's already married!" blurted out Félix in grave tones.

"In the Church?"

"In the Church. I cannot even do the right thing by her. It's an insult to be gentlemanly and nice toward her when there is much more I must do, and nothing I can do."

Louis thought this over a long minute, then poured another round of drinks. His shoulders seemed to slump.

"That is, indeed, the great trouble," he commented.

"Now that I've told you, this trouble has shrunk a little, but now also I'm sorry to bring you pain. For only that am I sorry. For me it is not too much to suffer—I deserve it—and for my conscience it is a lot, and for you and Maman-Monique—God forgive me!—it is too much. She must never know this!"

"No," Louis agreed. For a moment he thought Félix was going to weep, but he didn't. Louis waited.

"I cannot speak of this to anyone, only you and Mike. To everybody not in this trouble, this is funny. But, Papa, this is not a thing of laughter to feed to men in barrooms. For me, I do what is the right thing—whatever it is—and the cost is nothing, even the championship of the State of Maine. But what is right, Papa?"

"You are late, Félix!" suddenly roared Louis, rising from his chair. "Now, you ask that question, you great big mackerel! Morality is a set of reins. You have to know when to pull up on the reins to a bucking horse!" And he slapped him hard on the shoulder.

"I do what you say," said Félix, rolling with the slap.

"Now you say that!" again roared Louis. "When the great trouble is upon you, you shameless son, you!" Then he stopped suddenly. "But forgive me! Forgive me these words, Félix. I spoke in passion. Nails pounded in anger always split the wood. . . . Forgive me!"

"You forgive me, Pa. I have nothing to forgive you."

Louis sat down again. Oh, that moment of sudden impulse! This is what you had to fear from sons you loved, that sudden surrender to the impulse before the long-denied hunger, and the overwhelming ease of its appeasement. . . . Certainly sons might make mistakes—this you must not fear openly—there is wisdom from mistakes—thus it is one learns! What you have to fear was the mistake that comes from the sudden impulse, comes only once, and costs too much and yields only bitterness. . . .

"Papa," said Félix, "there is nothing that can be done!"

"Always," he snapped, "something can be done!" Of that he was certain, but then, he wondered, what, indeed, could be done in this case. He got up and for a moment could not find his pipe. Then he turned toward him.

"Félix, as my own Papa used to say, 'It's a long, long walk from one end to the other of Acadee, but you'll get there for certain if you just put one foot in front of the other'."

He joined his hands together in a prayerful clasp.

"This is what we do now. First, you need sleep. And for that I recommend a strong nightcap—three shots, for to make you sleep. And tomorrow, after Mass, you'll feel so rotten in the stomach, you will worry about nothing else but that. . . ."

"Yes, Papa," he assented quietly.

Félix sat a while and said nothing. Louis got him another

drink and he drank it slowly. Louis fixed himself another, very slowly, and when he looked at Félix again, he saw that his head was nodding, and his body had slumped in his chair, his legs sprawled before him. His right hand still held on to an empty glass. He began to snore softly. Louis looked down at him, passed a hand a couple of times slowly over his forehead, and then took the empty glass from his hands, then roused him and led him to his bedroom.

Louis Martel did not sleep a wink that night.

Next morning, he was up before anyone else. Cécile and Marie had gone to Communion at the seven o'clock Mass and Monique had given them a hand to get ready, and they woud soon come back for breakfast. Monique had had a cup of tea, and now, as was her habit, studied the tea leaves to see what the future would bring. Oh, she did not believe in it at all, at all, but it was known that sometimes the truth had been revealed there. Félix still slept, and Louis now stropped his razor with an air of detachment, pulled a hair from his head and with a quick motion cut the hair neatly into two pieces. Now he returned to the bathroom to shave.

"Louis," she called out to him, "the tea leaves . . . This morning, they are very optimistic. Oh, what happy tea leaves!"

"That's good," he commented. Sweet Monique! She knew he had not slept a wink, did not know why, and was trying to cheer him up. Sweet, innocent Monique! He turned on the hot water faucet, stirred up a heavy lather in his shaving cup and brushed it on his face with vigor. This always had been a time for singing the old songs he'd heard his brothers sing, back home in Acadee, when they shaved and he'd watched, yearning foolishly for the morning when he too would shave, and sing. . . . He did not feel like singing this morning, any way.

Monique was at the bathroom door.

"Mike Callaghan!" she announced coolly, and pointed toward the kitchen door. "I let him wait outside."

"*Bon!*" said Louis. In three bounds he made for the closed door—he would tell him off but good—and opened it. Mike Callaghan—he had been thin once, perhaps, but now fat had come on all over and he moved tiredly—had a grin on his face—he too needed a shave. Louis did not invite him in, but stood at the door, purposely leaving him just outside the kitchen door.

"Hi, Champ!" said Mike, then noticing the hard glare in Louis's face, he swallowed and asked quickly: "Can I see Félix?"

"He's asleep," Louis began to close the door.

"I must see him," said Mike, putting his foot in the door.

"Why?"

"Why? Because. He's got to go back to training. Footwork. Roadwork, and sparring, and everything. It is decided! He fights Rocca in Portland in December. For the title. The big fight!"

"Right now, this Champ is in no mood to fight anybody!"

"Oh, that!"

"Yes, that!" replied Louis with a mean look.

"Ah, but I have the good news!"

"Good news!" sneered Louis. "You damn promoters! What good news can you have? Get the hell out of here!" Again he began to close the door.

"Yes, yes, Mr. Martel! I'll go home now, but please tell Félix, tell him everything is all right. He can sleep tonight!"

Louis stretched his right hand around his neck and pulled him up close to his own face.

"*Maudit!* What good news?"

Mike began to whisper.

"Well, it is a delicate matter, and out of my line, but the

Champ, he is worried to death, pines away and punches the bag like a girl, and so, me, Mike Callaghan, I do something! I find out! And now, Mr. Martel, about this girl, you know . . ."

Suddenly Louis made the great sign over his mouth, that he should speak even more quietly, so that Monique would not hear.

"Well," continued Mike, "this girl—Lucia—What do you suppose? She goes to the restaurant to work in the morning—yesterday—and in the afternoon, she's off for three hours and decides to go horseback riding, and when she gets off the horse, it has happened!"

"What has happened?"

"It has happened! Just like that! It is all gone, Mr. Martel, the great big trouble. What made it go? Vanish? Horseback riding! And poof! She tells me right away, she wants me to tell Félix, she worries, she too wants him Champ, and she is all right, I made sure of that, and our Champ, he is all right too now, and ready to fight Rocca for the championship of the State of Maine!"

A big grin came over Louis Martel's face; no, there would be no need for the long, long walk through Acadee. He even put his arms around Mike and gently pulled him inside the kitchen. Monique was doing the breakfast dishes.

"Good morning, Madame Martel," said Mike joyfully.

Monique barely nodded toward him.

"Hi, *mon amour!*" Louis shouted at her.

Without a word, she tendered Mike a cup of tea.

Louis chuckled quietly to himself and she stared at him. Félix suddenly appeared in the kitchen, in a pair of boxing shorts. He had slept in them and they looked it, his hair was disheveled, his left eye had not opened fully yet, and he held on to his head.

"I have," he announced, "the big bellyache."

Louis roared in laughter.

"Hi, Champ," said Mike.

"Hi, Champ," said Louis.

"*Mon doux Seigneur!*" exclaimed Monique. "Protect me, for I live in a house of idiots!" She turned on Félix. "Will you look at yourself? Is this how you keep in good shape? You smell of drink in the morning? A disgrace! Look at you! A good Catholic boy like you, nearly naked before thousands of people, trying to knock another human being with blows directed at the heart, the jaw. . . . What would your Maman think of all this?"

Félix sighed. Louis went up to her.

"Monique," he stated curtly, "there is a time for fighting, and a time for loving, and this morning, I say, this boy needs loving, and now we all get ready for to go to Mass. . . ."

"Félix," continued Monique, "you should set your eyes on a nice young girl, not one that hangs around boxing rings, but one that goes to church, and take her dancing, and who knows what would happen?"

"Who knows is right!" barked Louis.

"Oh no," stammered Mike, "for Félix, he will meet Bud Rocca in December. It is almost sure. And nothing's got to interfere with that, huh, Félix?"

Félix sighed again.

"In December?" asked Monique suddenly.

"Yes," said Louis, "for the big fight. It is decided, and what can we do about it? Nothing, Monique, and let us have peace now."

"Yes," agreed Monique, "let us have peace, for there is a time for everything."

She smiled at him, and even at Mike Callaghan.

"*Bon,*" said Louis, "for after all, dear Monique, about boxing, let us admit it, you know nothing."

"I know nothing, but I know it is wrong."

"But you don't know," insisted Louis gently.

"I need not know anything if I am right!"

For a moment, he could find no answer to this, and when he thought he had found one, Cécile and Marie had come in from church, Mike had gone home and Monique had already gone on to think and talk about something else.

As December loomed nearer, Mike Callaghan stimulated the sale of tickets by announcing in an interview that Félix Martel had discovered a new secret punch that would surely defeat Bud Rocca.

"Provided," added Monique to Louis, "there are no complications."

"Complications?" he barked. "What complications?"

She gave him a blank expression.

"About boxing, I know nothing," she admitted.

"From the tea leaves," he suggested, "perhaps you know something the Groveton *Herald* does not know?"

"I do! From the tea leaves!" she purred softly.

This was too much, and he sat down, smiling, to hear all this. He sat her on his lap and held her chin softly.

"On this fight," he said, "my son will fight, but I wish to bet on the winner. Could you know, by chance, know who this winner will be? From the tea leaves, that is?"

"Oh, Louis, don't you know? There will be no fight, no fight at all! That is, from the tea leaves!"

Louis shook from laughter so much that Monique felt as if she were on the roller coaster at Old Orchard Beach.

One night, in late November, when he should have been at the boxing club, training for the Rocca fight, Félix came home right after supper, while Monique was washing the dishes and

Louis was wiping them. Cécile and Marie were out, and this was good, for from the tense face Félix wore that night, Louis knew right away something else had happened.

"Papa, I have to talk with you."

"Trouble?" barked Louis.

Monique wiped her hands and began to walk away into the *parloir* to leave the men alone.

"No, no, Maman-Monique," begged Félix, "please . . . This is for your ears also."

Now he punched his left hand into his right, while Louis stared at him, a big question in his eyes.

"It is a great wonder to me," started Félix, "that some things happen and others do not. Don't you think so, Papa?"

"Often," he said slowly, "I think of just that."

Suddenly Monique smiled quietly to herself.

"Papa," continued Félix, "when I fight before, and when I say my prayers, never once I ask God to win the fight. Never. Now, for this big fight, I pray. . . ."

"And," added Monique quickly, "you light a candle?"

"Yes!" Félix exclaimed, surprised. "I light a candle!"

"Good," agreed Louis, "you take no chance. Nothing bad can come from lighting a candle." He sighed. "Not in church."

"But things can happen anywhere, Papa," protested Félix.

"*Bonguienne*," said Louis, "what happened now?"

"This night," went on Félix, "on my way to the boxing club, I decide to stop at Sacred Heart, and I light a candle and she lights a candle. . . ."

"Who lights a candle?"

"Noelle! She lights a candle too. We are all alone in the big church. It is cold outside and warm inside. At the same time, we light a candle. . . ."

"Noelle?" asked Louis. "Noelle, who?"

"Noelle Meunier! At the same time, we light a candle, and

at the same time, we leave the church, we approach the holy water fount. She dips her fingers in the fount and is about to cross herself. . . . Suddenly, she sees me and she extends her moistened fingers toward me, I touch them to secure holy water from her. . . ."

"It is a good custom," said Monique.

"And at the same time, we cross ourselves, and then she smiles at me, not boldly, she is not bold at all, but as if she knows me, as if she'd known me since our baptism. She smiles at me, and I tell you, right then, fighting Monsieur Rocca is a matter of no importance, Papa, for she lights a candle in my heart too!"

"Meunier, *hein?*" exclaimed Louis, tapping his forehead to remember. "Is that the only daughter of Meunier, the dairyman? A good girl, is she not?" Monique nodded her head violently. "Ah, you know of this complication?"

"I know Noelle," admitted Monique. "She's not quite twenty, well-set and smart. Good little figure and very saucy, but I didn't know Félix had such a good eye."

"That," said Louis calmly, "I already knew, but after the Sign of the Cross, you go to the club?"

Félix cleared his throat.

"Well, that first night, Papa, we talk not a word. Just yes and no. The second night, I talk a lot, and to my foolish words she listens with grave respect."

"At her age," Louis thought out loud, "she has already much wisdom."

"During the next month—" continued Félix.

"A month already?" exclaimed Louis.

"The second month," continued Félix, "she talks a little more."

"You have time for all this, and training too?

Félix punched his right hand into his left.

"No, Papa, I do not. That is the problem."

"So? Is that how a champion prepares for the big fight? Rocca will kill you in the very first round!"

"Papa, listen to me. I do have time to listen to Noelle. She talks a lot more now. But I have no time. . . . See, Papa, when I look at her delicate fingers. I hold them in my hands and I say to myself: tenderness is better than striking another man in the face when I have no hatred for him. When I think of this, I think I have no time to become champion of Maine, of Massachusetts, or of the world, for that matter."

Louis stared at his son.

"This little girl. She asks this of you, Félix?"

He shook his head. He would be patient.

"No, Papa, she asks nothing of me. She takes me as I am. She does not even call me 'Champ.' To her I am Félix. That is a glorious thing, this, that such a nice person should take me as I am, champ or no champ, for in many ways, I am an imbecile. But to her, Papa, I am a champion already." And he suddenly swallowed.

"A complication," concluded Louis toward Monique.

"A sweet complication," she observed.

Now Louis began to chuckle, and once, he slapped his own forehead in astonishment.

"Who the hell is going to tell that to Callaghan?"

Again Félix cleared his throat.

"I did tonight. It was very hard to do and he had a fit. I fight no more, I said, I fool around no more, I work every day, I make love every night, and I have peace inside, maybe."

Louis got up and walked around briskly, smiling all the time, then he sat down. His jaws tightened.

"Félix, this little girl. You marry her?"

"I do, soon, Papa. Tonight I meet her and tonight I ask her. With your blessings, I hope."

Monique jumped up and kissed Félix. He turned to his father, and waited.

"Papa," he said, "did you want me to be champion of the world? I mean, very much?"

"Yes," Louis admitted, and then he shrugged his shoulders, "it would have been nice, but first, I wanted you to be champion of yourself. Now, I say, that if you are a champion to this little girl, I say, marry her. Marry her and raise your own little champions. . . ."

"Thank you, Papa."

"As I say, there is a time for fighting," he added, "and a time for loving. . . ."

Félix suddenly got up, gleefully, and put on his coat and hat. Very calmly, he made his announcement.

"And, *bonguienne*, Papa, my time has come!"

And he was gone. Louis began to smile silently toward Monique. Her face was radiant, shamelessly so. Without asking, she served two shots of whisky and two chasers of beer. He raised his glass toward her, and both drank the whisky in quick gulps, and then slowly sipped on their beer.

"And a time," Louis said very slowly, "for growing."

"Oh my! Yes!" she said, and primly wiped the white foam from her upper lip.

9. That Was a Real Big Miracle! [1933–1934]

It was at the funeral of Madame Clémentine Pelletier, Hélène's Grandmère, that Thérèse Bouchard, née Martel, began to ponder over miracles. Married over four years now, she was twenty-six and still without child. The quips had all been told and retold, in true French-Canadian fashion. Today it was something no one in the family circle joked about any more: it hurt too much. To the time-worn jokes had succeeded a gentle curtain of silence. Even Antoine spoke little of it any more.

Grandmère's funeral brought it all back. All Martels who could be were present, and Thérèse sat in her pew, crowded by her nieces and nephews: they shoved, they coughed, they pushed, they whispered, they bent their heads in prayer, they sneezed and borrowed her hanky, and she was patient, for they also constituted the roster of her private sorrows. . . .

Hélène and Laurent had Michel, Jean-Paul and Réné. Maurice and Muriel had Albert, Lucien, Lucille, Henri and expected another around Christmas. All her High School friends had children whenever, it seemed, they wanted them. Not she and Antoine. No! Antoine was doing very well at the bank, they had a nice apartment on Chestnut Road, and two empty unused rooms that could be turned, in a jiffy, into nurseries. Was it a punishment?

And there was Félix! Just two years ago, he had surprised a lot of people, given up boxing suddenly, and married Noelle Meunier. Monsieur Meunier owned the largest dairy in Groveton. Noelle was his only child, he was a sick man, and more and more Félix had become the man in authority. From a young man, going nowhere in particular, right after his wedding, he'd become a young executive—and well off.

This union of Félix and Noelle, her Papa had said, no doubt was made in heaven, but sealed in the Groveton Trust Company. For this good fortune, what price had they paid? They had little Pierre. Right on the button, nine months later. And now, a year later, what do you think? Sure. Noelle could barely button her overcoat. . . . Of course. From ironing their husband's pants, some women got pregnant. Not Thérèse!

The long procession of cars escorted Grandmère to Sacred Heart Cemetery, and then the long procession returned to Groveton, and most of the Martels went on to Laurent's house for some last words of consolation with Hélène. Louis and Monique brought along Marie, now sixteen, and Cécile, now fourteen, in their black school dresses and white collars. After lunch, they would return to school.

While Monique helped Hélène prepare a light lunch, Thérèse watched as her Papa cast off the funeral atmosphere by playing around with Michel, Jean-Paul and Réné. He tickled them, he made them do somersaults, he played soldiers with them, he took each in turn for a round of boxing, and each in turn knocked him flat on his back and counted him out with loud shrieks. . . . Papa was going through all this because it is good to unbend after a funeral. And because Papa loves children, his own, somebody else's, anybody's, white, black and brown children. . . . How he would love one of my own, mused Thérèse.

Grandmère's passing had been expected, and yet it saddened her, seemed to sharpen the pain of barrenness, for her departure marked the end of an era in Groveton. To hear Grandmère tell about it, her time had been a glorious time to be alive! To believe! To know that God Himself took a hand in things! She would miss Grandmère, and so would a lot of folks who had mocked at her stories. In her time, it seemed, no one spoke of fecundity as a phenomenon: when you married, why, children just came—it was no big event, it was commonplace! And so were miracles, big and small personal miracles!

Twice in her lifetime, Grandmère had been a witness to a miracle. Once, at St. Anne de Beaupré, she had seen a young man, paralyzed from the waist down, suddenly cast aside his crutches and walk with firm steps up the steps to the statue of the Saint. Grandmère often said she had "seen this with her own eyes, seeing . . . a miracle, for sure!"

Later, in Groveton, "with her own eyes, seeing . . ." she had seen a heavy stone that had been laid with solemn ceremony on a street corner for a new church, three times removed mysteriously at night and relaid on another street corner of the town, half a mile away! Finally, the Curé had built the church in the new corner, and this was now Sacred Heart Church!

A miracle, no doubt. Why? Because the original corner was once struck with lightning and thunder, and the building built there later was totally destroyed by fire, rebuilt and again destroyed by fire. "The Lord," Grandmère had calmly concluded, "never was partial to that corner of the town."

Some folks had laughed secretly at some of Grandmère's more fanciful stories, but not Thérèse's Papa. Those two had a special understanding. After all, did she not also have great confidence in the efficacy of Indian herb and root remedies? Foolishness, of course, thought Thérèse, but she and her Papa had much in common. And did she not, as her Papa said one should, take regularly her *tisane* of dandelion against disorders of the blood, the liver and the bile? Foolishness, of course, but then, Grandmère had lived to a ripe ninety-two.

Yes, foolishness, but it was a fact that Grandmère all her long life never really had been sick, and had she not contracted pneumonia, after falling down a flight of stairs, she might still be alive. . . .

Hélène and Monique now announced that lunch was ready and everyone sat at the table, and quietly talked of Grandmère.

"The young women," Louis said, "took their colored pills against woman-trouble, and mooned about all day, but Grandmère, after a hard day's work that would kill me, drank one of her *tisanes*, and suddenly looked better than the whole lot of them. My children, I tell you, those old Indians knew more in their day than we do in ours. If not, why did Grandmère live such a long life?"

"Why, Papa?" asked Marie, politely.

"Because she took her Indian remedies, that's why!"

Thérèse ate sparingly and remembered all those long years of growing-up, and each spring when her Papa came home with stringy roots and stinky herbs which he soaked in boiling water, and let it simmer, and then served to her. . . . The memory of it made her cringe, the thought of the vile, reddish liquid made her ill even now. . . . Well, no more of that. She was free of that, at least, for it must be admitted, both Grandmère and her Papa were old-fashioned, that's all.

The small talk went on, and now Thérèse barely listened. After funerals, they always did it, the folks who were left behind, and it was her Papa who made the calculations. Grandmère, he stated finally, had had ten children of her own, sixty-one grandchildren and ten great-grandchildren. This post-funeral recital of Grandmère's genealogical record depressed Thérèse deeply, and even more when Réné, age two, jumped into her lap and hugged her, for no special reason. She petted him and asked herself what was wrong with her?

After the first year, Antoine had wisely observed that "time cures most ills"—he was always so kind—but now she knew she had become panicky. Two years ago she had consulted Dr. Lafrance. By now he had become somewhat crotchety. He examined them both. Later he shook his head doubtfully.

"Go home, my children," he advised.

"Is that all you have to say?" exclaimed Thérèse. "No pills? No tips?"

"Go home!" he snapped. "There's nothing I can do for you that you can't do for yourself. Tips, you want? Go home, or I'll charge you double for this foolish visit. Tips! Pills! There should be only one man in each marriage bed!"

Whatever that meant! Now, in this, the start of their fifth year of married life, Thérèse observed with terror that Antoine too had joined in the general compact to be silent about this unusual crisis in a family of Canadiens. She would tell no one about the campaign of novenas and special prayers—everyone had given up but she—and about the promise of a special pilgrimage to St. Anne de Beaupré if she were blessed with child. Please, St. Anne—boy or girl!

She had written to Emile, who had three more years to go in the seminary. He had consulted with his more intimate priest-teachers and one had recommended St. Gérard Majella, patron saint of pregnant women. This had been two months ago, and the results, so far, were negative. Father Joseph Lebois, curé of Sacred Heart, had suggested adoption of an orphan child. "You can't lose!" he had said very seriously. One night, she'd told Papa she was lighting a candle to St. Anthony every night.

"Why him?" he had asked, taken aback. "He's the patron saint of lost articles!"

It would take a miracle, Thérèse decided, nothing less than a miracle, the kind Grandmère had seen, with her eyes seen, in her lifetime. Grandmère had seen them, of course, but Thérèse had not, and were miracles still in vogue? Abruptly, she turned toward her Papa.

"Pa," she said, "do you believe, like Grandmère, in all those miracles?"

"Sure do," said he quickly.

"Do you believe that prayers can perform a miracle?"

"Sure do. Don't you?"

"Of course, but I sometimes wonder."

"About what?" said Monique.

Thérèse lowered her head and spoke softly.

"I prayed for Grandmère to get better, and she died. And I prayed for Maman—so hard—I remember it so well—and she died. . . ."

"That's right," said Louis, "and I prayed too, you know. But every prayer that asks for something has two strikes against it, unless you add—and mean it—'Thy will be done!' in case you don't get what you want."

"I know," said Thérèse irritably, "but don't you think my will should be done, once in a while . . . ?"

"It would be nice," said Monique.

"Well, now," continued Louis, "God can do anything He makes His mind to. Everyone knows that, even the Protestants. But the big question remains: does He want to? It's not a can-He, but a will-He proposition."

"I might as well be an old maid," Thérèse shot out suddenly, "and just as empty."

"Yes," said Monique softly.

"I might as well be a nun!" Thérèse sobbed, covering her face with her hands. Réné patted her back and stared worriedly at Hélène.

"Yes," said Louis thoughtfully.

Monique went to Thérèse, as Réné escaped and ran to his mother; and Thérèse looked up toward Monique.

"*Chérie*," said Monique, "I have no children of my own either. It appears that I'm like you. And I'm thirty-five!"

"But," said Thérèse, gasping for breath, "in your case, you had an idea. . . . You knew in advance. . . . But I didn't! I didn't!"

"I'm not any different," she said firmly, "than you are. I'd love to have a baby of my own, though God knows I've thought of Papa's children as nearly my own, including you, Thérèse. . . ."

"Yes," said Thérèse.

"But," said Monique, taking Thérèse's chin in her hand, "I just feel it in my bones that you'll have your wish one of these days. You'll have many children, Thérèse, I just know it!"

"Do you?" asked Louis uneasily, turning toward Monique.

"Do you?" asked Thérèse hopefully.

"I do," said Monique firmly, "and I want to be godmother to the first one. Promise me that?"

And Thérèse smiled, and Monique embraced her, and Hélène began to suggest first names for boys and for girls and they chattered and laughed again, and this was good, for Louis's comment was not heard.

"Good thing they don't sell insurance on that yet!"

Around Christmas, Maurice wrote to his Papa and, among other things, he gave the news that Muriel had calmly gone to the hospital and easily given birth to a seven-and-a-half-pound little girl who had been baptized Blanche. About the same time, Hélène became pregnant again but no one made much of it. Thérèse remained barren. During all the holidays, also, she'd had a long, lingering cold and, one night in January, when Monique was at church and Antoine working late, Louis decided to go and see her at home on Chestnut Place, in their new apartment which had five rooms and modern furniture.

"Where do I sit?" he asked every time he entered her house. And then he gave all the chairs with newfangled shapes a good long look.

"There!" And she pointed at the queerest-looking chair.

"Is it safe?"

"Oh, Pa, don't make fun of progress!"

He sat and folded his arms quietly.

"How do you feel?"

She looked at him distractedly.

"By now," she confessed, "I know it'll take a big miracle."

"Or an Indian remedy?"

"Oh, Pa!" she made a face. "By the way, will you take a Manhattan?"

"Yes, and put some old-fashioned whisky in it."

She served him the drink in a fragile glass on a red tray and placed a lacy napkin on his lap. He promptly folded it into three folds and placed it in his jacket pocket. She took a sip of her drink, a Manhattan also, and nervously lit her cigarette. He noticed this and said nothing, and when he said nothing she blew smoke toward him.

"I have to do something to keep my nerves quiet," she confessed.

"Antoine, does he drink?" Louis asked.

"No. Well, yes. He did once. He just had too much. And he was funny. And lovable. Just like you, Papa!"

"God spare you that," he said with a smile. He sipped his drink and then looked at it and sipped it again. Now he smacked his lips. Quietly she went on talking.

"No, he was lovable, but he gave it up after that night. You see, to get places at the bank, he feels he has to maintain a certain decorum. . . ."

"Oh, yes, yes!" agreed Louis. "If this Manhattan is progress, there is hope for tomorrow. And if you can mix such a good drink, you can do anything, Thérèse, and it is I, Louis Martel, who tells you this!"

She smiled at him. With him around, everything was better.

"But it will still take a miracle!" she commented.

"What kind?"

"A big one! A real big one!"

In March, Laurent drove his Papa to Metaska Pond, as he did every year, to a place both of them knew very well by now—they had gone there every year since he'd been a young-ster—a damp marshy region surrounded by trees of all kinds. And it was always the same story. When they arrived, Louis left Laurent alone in the car and then picked up a large can-vas bag, a pair of scissors and a knife, and went in alone, as he did every year, while Laurent stayed behind in the car reading the *Sporting News*.

This year, briefly, Laurent watched as his Papa vanished into the wood and, briefly also, he became impatient with him. Every year, Laurent had had to go along on this foolish expedition, when his Papa grubbed around, searching for plants of a special kind, roots from certain trees, herbs that would be dried to just the right kind of dryness, and God only knew what else. And all this to make a horrible tea that nobody but the old folks wanted to drink. There was magic, of course, in the sudden discovery of a lady's-slipper—and the delicate bloom was itself magic of a kind—but what magical power did sassafras possess? Or boneset? Once he had asked Dr. Lafrance about these remedies of his Papa.

"*Marde!*" had said the doctor.

"*Marde!*" Laurent repeated to himself. It was bad enough to wait for him as he scrounged around for the ingredients of these forgotten and forsaken Indian remedies, but when the children had been little and defenseless, they had had to drink the tea, smelling as it did of the swamps. Was the stuff really any good at all? Papa was sure it was, and he was no fool. If the shy and royal blue gentian could please the eye, Papa said, why could not other magics of nature ease the pains inside the body and cure it of its ills, and be damned to doctors with closed minds and sharpened scalpels!

Well, his Papa was no fool. He had to remind himself of this. Whenever he and his brothers and sisters had gotten themselves in trouble, it was because they had assumed Papa was wrong, and Papa had been proven right so many times. He had never hesitated also to come to their help, no matter what the trouble was. For this they all had overlooked some of the queer things Papa said or did. Laurent went back to his *Sporting News*. For this now, and may other things, he could very well be patient with Papa.

When Louis returned, he had filled up the canvas bag and two other and smaller bags with what, Laurent assumed, must be roots, and herbs and plants and blooms and assorted tree branches. He smiled at his father.

"Good picking, Pa?"

"The best ever!" he said.

Very carefully he put his bags on the floor near the back seat of the car. When he got home, Laurent knew, he would place all this junk to dry in the shed in the back yard of the house. At certain times, he would take them out, root by root, herb by herb, clean them, boil them into a tea, and give them to anyone who could be induced or forced to drink it. Come spring, there would be a special tea against the miseries of spring, and come winter, there would be another against the miseries of winter. Laurent knew the rhythm well, and so did everybody who knew his Papa.

So did Monique, by now, and one Saturday afternoon, two weeks later, when Michel, son of Laurent, was visiting, Louis went downstairs to the shed, with Michel trailing him. He was about eight, and had coughed all winter. In the shed, he helped his Grandpère cut and clip and clean the herbs and the roots.

"What is this for, Grandpère?" he asked, squaring himself as manfully as Louis did.

"This is magic!" whispered Louis. Then he added: "Partner!"

And Michel's eyes sharpened into a conspiratorial gleam. Together they carried the stuff upstairs where Louis dropped it into a kettle of water and put it to boil. When the potion had assumed a reddish tint, Louis poured himself a tall drink. Monique watched him with cool fascination, but when Michel saw him drink it down, his eyes popped.

"Grandpère," he protested, "are we not partners?"

"We sure are," said Louis, returning to the kettle.

Monique advanced toward Michel. She hugged him and patted his cheek.

"Isn't it time for you to go home?" she asked him. "You never stay this long, and your Maman will worry, Michel!"

It was too late. Louis had already poured a small drink and now he handed it to Michel.

"Smells good," said he, taking the drink in his hands.

"There's a smart child," said Louis with reverence. "Wish all my children were half as smart."

"The poor child!" exclaimed Monique. She gave Louis a mean look.

Michel drank it down slowly, stopped once to wink at his Grandpère, then manfully resumed drinking until he drained it. His face had by now become horribly contorted.

"The poor child!" protested Monique again.

"It's good, Grandpère!" said Michel bravely.

"Good?" asked Monique carefully. "Smells good?"

She turned toward Louis. Now she put all the glasses away.

"It smells good," Michel agreed, "but it tastes like you know what."

Louis returned to the kettle, removed the cover and noticed with satisfaction that the tea had assumed a more reddish brown. He rubbed his hands together.

"That," he announced, "is the staff of life. Where's Michel?"

"Outside. Playing. Or gone home."

"I think he'll want more of this tea."

"Yes," said Monique, "that's why he ran outside as soon as he could, when you weren't looking. Now, Louis, does Doctor Lafrance approve of that stuff?"

"That man!" sneered Louis. "Can't even play poker!"

"But that's not right, Louis. Today you go to a doctor and you do what he says."

He looked up from his drink.

"Even when he doesn't know what he's doing?"

"Do you know better?"

"No, and I charge a damn sight less."

"Do you know more than Doctor Lafrance?"

"Just as little. He can't help Thérèse, either!"

"Oh, Lou, that may be God's will."

"Maybe, and maybe not. Maybe it's only because they don't drink this tea. Who knows? That could be the reason. I know Grandmère drank it, my mother and father drank it, I drink it, and Thérèse does not drink it!"

Monique turned away from him in impatience.

"Lou, you're just being silly!"

"Do you want some? It's nice and hot."

"No, thank you."

"You know, Monique, the old Indian who told me about

this told me other things. Did I ever tell you? He said it could cure anything from migraines to athlete's foot. Anything! He promised me that, and he charged nothing. And it'll cure any-thing—almost!"

Monique suddenly turned back toward him with a strange gleam in her eyes.

"Anything?"

"Well, that's what he said," Louis stated, suddenly uncom-fortable.

"Then," said Monique, "give some to Thérèse! If she'll drink it! Louis, I dare you!"

He suddenly roared with laughter. He exchanged a look with Monique, and then he roared again. He sat down and became thoughtful and sober-faced.

"Well, now, hold on a minute," he said at last. "That old Indian said that if you mixed it in a certain way, you had no papooses, and if you mixed it in another way, you had many papooses."

"With the same gunk?"

"The very same."

"Wonderful!" said Monique coolly, taking a bag of potatoes and beginning to inspect them. She began to peel one.

"He did," said he with a frown. "The only thing is that I don't remember which is which."

"That's convenient," said Monique, reaching for another potato. "The Church can't condemn it or approve it."

"However," said he firmly now, "I'm sure that the way it's mixed right now would be good for Thérèse."

"I bet," said Monique calmly, "I just bet it would," she added, chuckling. She patted him on the head and hugged him and laughed gently at him.

He sat and meditated and puffed on his pipe.

Louis Martel celebrated his fifty-second birthday in April and everybody came, and, of course, Hélène also, her pregnancy very obvious, but no one made much of it, for Thérèse seemed to be even more depressed than before. And so, after Louis had counted the neckties and the pipes he'd received, and the many whisky bottles, he kept Antoine and Thérèse behind—it was easy, they had no children to put to bed—and Monique gave them a cup of tea for the road. Louis came to the point immediately.

"How are you coming along, Thérèse, in your novenas?"

Thérèse looked up in surprise.

"Oh, I haven't lit a candle in over a month."

"That's too bad," said he.

"Well, I've just about given up." Then she turned mockingly upon Monique. "And you were so sure, Maman-Monique, so very sure!"

"I still am," said she quietly.

"Me too," said Louis airily, puffing on his pipe and staring wisely into space. Antoine laughed.

"And what makes you so certain, Monsieur Martel," he asked, "when Lafrance himself can give us nothing but a shrug of the shoulders?"

Louis tapped the tobacco deeper into his pipe.

"Well, no one's asked this doctor for advice," he commented lightly. "And in such cases, I don't give it. I hate pushy people, especially fathers who poke their noses into their married children's affairs."

"Monsieur Martel," said Antoine, "I invite your advice. What would you suggest?"

Again Louis tapped his burning tobacco deeper into his pipe.

"Some other time," he replied courteously. "Some other time."

Thérèse sat up tensely in her chair. She favored everyone with a look of utter impatience.

"Pa, I know you," she said. "You have something on your mind. But you want to make us languish. You want us to beg you, is that it?"

"You may not care to do what I tell you," he said, brushing ashes from his lap.

"I will, Pa, I will," implored Thérèse, "providing. . ."

"See what I mean?" said he. "Conditions, conditions. . ."

"Let us know at least," said Antoine, "what it is, and then maybe she'll do it."

He turned sharply toward him.

"Oh, you too will have to be in on this!"

Antoine guffawed.

"Well, now, how can anything happen otherwise?" he asked.

Louis nearly blushed, then he smiled.

"I don't mean that," he said. "I mean, it will take, for both of you, at least one year."

"A year?" said Antoine.

"What's a year, after all this time?" asked Thérèse lightly.

"A year, and perhaps longer," added Louis, "and don't expect miracles! Big or little!"

"Agreed," said Thérèse, all ears. "What do we do?"

"Good," said Louis, and he motioned Antoine to follow him. He led him downstairs to the shed, and together they brought back a bag, and he gave it to Antoine. Then Louis cut up some pieces of roots, threw them into a kettle full of water, and lit the fire under it.

"Oh, Pa," sighed Thérèse, "I should have known. Those old Indian remedies!"

"Yes," said Louis. "And now, Antoine, watch what I do."

"I nearly died drinking that stuff," whined Thérèse, "when I was a child."

Louis stopped stirring the tea, and let his hands drop to his side.

"Oh, I can stop all this right now," he said calmly.

Suddenly Antoine spoke up.

"She'll drink the stuff," he said firmly.

"And you, too, 'Toine," said Louis.

Antoine paled. Monique burst into laughter.

"You think perhaps I need it?" he snapped back.

"Everyone needs it," said Louis, gently putting his hand on his shoulder. "This speeds up the body's electricity, cleans the bloodstream, purifies the intestinal tract, chases the poisons from the nervous system, clears the head, tones up the muscles, invites you to go to the backhouse, and makes you feel like a bronco. Who'll be first?"

The tea was boiling and the color of it was deep brown. Thérèse seemed to have shrunk into her chair. She looked at Antoine and with her eyes begged for mercy.

"You want the baby," he said calmly, "you drink the gunk!"

Monique laughed and watched Louis, and waited for his next move. He snapped his fingers suddenly. He reached into the armoire where the whisky was kept, poured a pint of it into the boiling kettle, stirred it well with a large spoon. . . .

"That's what the old Indian said!" he exclaimed toward Monique.

He poured himself a tall drink and drank half of it, and then looked up at Monique. Without a word he poured and served her a drink in another glass.

"Here! You can use this too!"

"Oh, Lou!"

"Sure, my pretty one. Show the kids nobody dies from it!"

She gazed steadily at her husband. He was so defenseless with his extended hand, holding a glassful of that stuff, all of his faith and tenderness deposited in a meaningless potion.

Slowly she reached for the glass and deliberately drank it down.

"*Merci*, Louis," she said, making a face.

"I'm grateful to you," said Louis, and then he quickly poured another drink and handed it to Antoine.

"If you hold your nose," advised Monique, "it helps."

Antoine drank it down slowly, making several kinds of faces, and now there was a glass for Thérèse, and she held her nose and drank it down too. Everybody, but Louis, looked at one another, not knowing whether to smile, or to grimace.

"Now," said Louis victoriously, "in that bag there is more. Every night, before you go to bed, you each have a glass, and you do this for the next three or four weeks, mixed just as I have shown you. Then you lay off the stuff for a full month. . . ."

"And then, what?" asked Thérèse, holding on to her nose.

"Then," said Louis, "You increase the dose, and take it for another month. . . ."

"Another month? *Bonguienne!*" she screamed.

Louis was very patient.

"I said," he replied briskly, "that this might take a long time."

"Agreed," said Antoine, but the smell was still in his nose and he shook his head several times against the smell, and the mystery of it all.

Soon after, Thérèse and Antoine said *bonsoir* and left, and when Monique and Louis were alone, he took another look into the kettle, then turned toward her.

"There's a lot left," he said.

"Is there? Well, it doesn't smell as bad as all that. Could I have another?"

"Sure, and me too," said Louis briskly.

He served two drinks and sat down at the table, near her, to have his last pipeful of the day and to talk about many things, as they did every night of their lives together.

"Frankly," she announced, as she sipped her drink, "I'm surprised! I feel a great big, strong coaxing inside of me. . . . A bad-girl need of my husband's shameless arms. . . ." Suddenly she giggled.

Louis put out his pipe and stood up.

"In Acadee-ee!" he began to him softly. "Sweet, sweet Acadee!"

Slowly Monique placed her head in her folded arms, sighed, then put her arms and head on the table and looked up at him with half-closed eyes.

"*Bonguienne!*" she whispered in a low voice. "Hurrah for those poor old Indians!"

Louis had flipped off his shirt.

"Last one in bed," he announced, "is a Henglish haristocrat!"

Spring took a deep sigh and suddenly became summer, and vacation time, but five days a week Louis Martel and his partner, Philippe Buisson, were away from Groveton on the big construction job in Portland, and both came back Friday night, tired, hungry and sweaty. Five days, sleeping in a rented room, living in somebody else's house, made Louis moody and grouchy. He stayed that way until he walked up to his own sink to wash his hands and to sing some old, forgotten French-Canadian love song, and to hear the latest news about his own household.

Tonight, however, he'd be returning to an empty house, for Félix and Noelle and little Pierre had driven with Monique, Marie and Cécile to Berlin, New Hampshire, for a visit with friends there who had a summer place. They would be back Sunday afternoon.

Louis had made his own plans. Poker, and no women around. When they reached Groveton, Philippe, who drove the car whose expenses they shared, let Louis out, as usual,

- 254 -

near Bordeaux's Barber Shop. In the rear, one could buy genuine whisky from Canada that gurgled in the pouring with an Irish accent.

"See you later, Lou," said Philippe. He would play poker too.

Louis waved his hand and walked into Bordeaux's shop. Dr. Lafrance was on his way out, his three bottles safely tucked away in his black satchel. He looked up at Louis, smiled in a peculiar way, and then suddenly did a jig right there on the sidewalk.

"Lou Martel, you rascal!" he shouted.

"Hello, you moneybags!" said Louis, soberly surprised at his unprofessional conduct. "What's the matter with you? Been taking your own prescriptions?"

The doctor stopped, and then put his hand on his shoulder.

"Say, Lou, have you been home yet?"

"No. Nobody home. Family's away."

"Oh," said the doctor, suddenly circumspect. "Well," he chuckled, "it'll keep. See you later." And he was off to his car. He too would be at the poker game.

Before this, however, Louis had a rendezvous to have supper at Laurent's house. Monique had arranged that. Hélène knew how to cook fish with the proper respect and, after boardinghouse fare, that was a pleasant thought. He bought his three bottles, wrapped them up in a copy of the Groveton *Daily Herald*, and walked up Maple Street.

After a good supper of mountain trout and baked potatoes, and apple pie baked with maple sugar, Louis and Laurent sat in the front room and smoked their pipes, and as soon as Hélène could get the boys away from Grandpère's chair and outside the room, she came back tiptoeing toward him, her dark eyes flashing with the delirium of a big secret she alone monopolized.

"And how is Michel's health?" Louis asked suddenly.

"Oh, he's fine," she sang out, "hasn't coughed since April!"

"Well, now. . ." began Louis.

"Grandpère!" interrupted Hélène. "Forgive me stealing the floor from you, but. . ."

"Can't wait, *hein*?" Laurent said, and chuckled.

"No, I can't!" she purred. The baby she was expecting was now very obvious and her face glowed and her eyes danced.

"Grandpère," she whispered, "guess who is with child?"

"You!" said Louis.

"No! No!' said Hélène, her breath pushing out the words.

"Who? Muriel?" Then he added quickly, "Noelle?"

"*Non, non, non!*' she shouted joyfully.

"For the love of God, who?"

Hélène tasted her secret alone once more, and then let it go. "Thérèse!"

"No!"

"Yes!"

"Well," said he, slapping his knee, "I'll be a monkey's behind!"

"Yes," confirmed Laurent. "This time 'Toine's done it."

"Hélène," said Louis quietly, "this warms me up all over." Then he chuckled. "Yes, I rejoice with all my heart."

"It's a miracle, that's all," caroled Hélène. "It's a miracle!"

"Nah!" said Louis pleasantly. "A miracle is a big thing no man can do but God can do." Then he had a quiet laugh within himself.

"Well maybe," agreed Hélène, joining him in his laughter, "but don't you give any of those Indian remedies to my Laurent. He can perform his own miracles. . . ."

And she returned to the kitchen, her little tummy preceding her, and from the kitchen both men could hear her humming a little song. An air of calm victory came into Louis's face, and he winked smugly at Laurent.

"I think," he announced, "I'm going to get me a patent on that drink!"

Laurent gave him his most cynical smile.

"That drink," he said, "and a few prayers and much luck. . . ."

Both of them pondered over this a moment or two in silence, then Louis asked if he might take a bath and a nap, as he always did "against the perils and the trials of the long poker night."

"Besides," he added, "now that Thérèse has her wish, I have to go to Mass and receive Communion tomorrow morning. I promised I would do it right after I knew she was *enceinte*."

Laurent settled himself more comfortably in his chair.

"Pa, you work hard all week, why not go Sunday morning, and sleep late tomorrow morning?"

"No," said Louis. "I promised. Sunday would be one day later than I promised, and a promise is a promise."

Hélène came back, a dishcloth in her hand, wiping a large dinner plate.

"Grandpère, I have your change of underwear and socks here, and a fresh shirt. Maman-Monique brought them over before she left. And your suit of clothes also. I had it pressed. . . ."

Louis released a happy sigh.

"Man marries for many good reasons," he announced to no one in particular, "and for a bit of foolishness too, and sometimes just for the sport of it, but deep down, Laurent, do you know why he marries?"

"To have kids?" said Laurent casually.

Louis looked at him. Laurent sat deeply in his chair, a vacant stare in his face, the fat of his thighs spreading over the seat. He smoked quietly, contentedly, and once scratched his belly.

"No," said his Papa.

"Gee, why?" he asked, expecting almost anything in answer.

"For comfort, son."

"Oh," said Laurent, sitting up.

"Yes! And woman is the great comforter!"

Laurent sat back in his chair again.

"There are days," he remarked, "when you say that all women are the great agitators—won't leave a man a peaceful moment. Make up your mind, Pa!"

Louis Martel shrugged. Perhaps he didn't hear his son. Anyway, he had things to do. He bathed, and then lay down on the parlor couch, and napped from seven to eight-thirty when Hélène woke him up, and Laurent too, for that matter. Louis splashed cold water over his face, shaved, and picked up one of his bottles, and Laurent drove him to Sacred Heart and he went to confession. When he came out, he was, as usual, silent and shy, and Laurent then drove him to Pierre Nadeau's house, where the game was located that night.

Nadeau was an unbeliever, a bachelor, a money-maker, a lawyer, a conniver, but he was also a Democrat, and Papa had known him since both were young men in Groveton. They were friends and asked no unfriendly questions, except across the poker table, where it was every man for himself. When Louis Martel came in, Lafrance, Philippe Buisson, Mike Callaghan and Léon Brouillard were there already, and the game had started. He put his bottle on the table and greeted everyone.

"Here's my contribution," he said simply, rubbing his hands.

Nadeau guffawed. Philippe sat down and roared with laughter. Léon Brouillard stared at Louis in amazement, stuttered a bit, but then decided to say nothing. Mike kept his usual smiling countenance. Lafrance laughed and laughed.

"*Batege!*" exclaimed Louis. "Are you all idiots? Tell me, what's the big joke?"

Lafrance put a bottle on the table—expensive stuff no one

else but a doctor could afford—and gave Louis his bottle back.

"This is my treat," he said.

"It's my share," Louis protested. "You insult me if you refuse!"

"Now, Lou, listen," said Lafrance. "It's my treat, because we're celebrating a special occasion. For you! We've all heard the good news!"

"Oh, that," said Louis, suddenly smiling. "You've heard?"

"Yes," said Buisson, "and forgive me, but gossip is stronger than friendship." Everybody laughed.

"Well," said Louis. "I'm certainly glad for Thérèse."

The laughter stopped suddenly.

"Thérèse?" said Buisson.

"Your daughter, Thérèse?" asked Nadeau, mystified.

"Yes," said Louis. "She's legally married in the Church and she's going to have a little one. It happens, you know."

"Thérèse—she's going to have a little one too?" stuttered Léon Brouillard.

"Who else, my God?" asked Louis.

The roar of laughter that drowned that question stopped when Lafrance put his hand on Louis's shoulder and asked for silence.

"Monique! She's pregnant, too," said Dr. Lafrance.

"My Monique?" said Louis, passing a hand over his hair.

"Yep," said Buisson. "She told my wife—she was leery about telling anyone else, but my wife told me tonight, and I couldn't keep it to myself. . ."

I'd heard it too, elsewhere," said Nadeau calmly.

"And you told the whole town?" asked Louis, mildly irritated.

"Sure!" said Lafrance. "It's good news!"

"Guess it is," said Louis, and he sat down suddenly, and all the men shook him by the hand with some solemnity. Lafrance opened his bottle and poured a shot for everyone.

Léon Brouillard gulped his drink.

"It's—it's—it's—a miracle!" he stuttered.

"It is, like hell," shouted Louis. He picked up his drink. "To my Monique!" he said solemnly.

"To Louis Martel, I say," said Lafrance, and all the men finished their drinks.

Louis started to laugh slowly, and the others joined him.

"I'll be a monkey's ass," he announced.

Lafrance began to feel his shoulders.

"Say, Lou, how old are you anyway?"

"Fifty-two. Give or take five."

"O.K.," stuttered Brouillard, "let's play poker."

"Yeah," said Nadeau, "we ought to be able to take this young buck tonight. He can't be lucky and hit the jackpot in all the places. Who's the dealer?"

They played straight stud poker, nothing wild, except one's imagination, and the money slowly changed hands, at a two-bit limit, and every hour, on the hour, they stopped and paused for a drink, and a joke, and they played now quietly, now argumentatively, and once, facing a poor hand, Louis turned up his cards in disgust, and stared into space.

Well, what do you know, he thought, there's more Martels where the others came from!

And they played some more, and half the second bottle of whisky was gone, and it was midnight, and the cards were bad, and Louis reminded himself that from now on, he must not eat or drink but keep the fast, if he were to go to Communion that morning. . . .

It was now Nadeau's turn to deal. And Louis realized suddenly that the night was nearly gone, and the cards had been bad. Nadeau asked everyone to ante up.

"No luck, Lou?" asked Lafrance.

"Never saw such unfriendly cards," said Louis with a big smile.

"You can't have everything," said Buisson gently.

"One has to be patient," said Louis, "for it is well known that if the money lasts, the cards will change!"

Everything changes! *Tout passe! Tout casse!* When Grand-mère Pelletier passed away, the age of full-blown miracles perhaps vanished also. . . . But what had taken its place? Another change! Man called it a miracle now when he himself performed the magic of his science and left nothing extraordinary for God to do. . . . Today, if a man survived an illness, we complimented the doctor. If he died, we spoke of God's will. . . . O Lord, this is not fair. . . . Not fair at all! No wonder You permit us our workaday miracles. . . . You've got your own special brand, but not for us, not for this age of change. . . . O Lord, for what have we witnessed in this fancypants era of slick thinking but the agony of the imagination. . . . However, everything changes. *Tout passe! Tout casse!*

"Ante up!" barked Nadeau.

They did, and he dealt the hole cards around, then the second cards, face up. Callaghan peered at his and found he had aces, back to back, in hearts and diamonds. Lafrance tried to appear unconcerned about his threes, back to back, in clubs and spades. Brouillard had a queen of clubs in the hole and a seven of hearts showing; Buisson surveyed his jack of hearts in the hole and the ace of clubs, showing; Louis got an ace of spades in the hole and a ten of spades, showing. Nadeau served himself kings, back to back, in hearts and diamonds.

Callaghan bet his ace, showing. Nadeau raised.

"I'll raise you both," said Louis quietly.

"Action, that's what we need," said Lafrance.

They all came in. Nadeau dealt the third card: a deuce of spades to Callaghan, a ten of diamonds to Lafrance, a queen of hearts to Brouillard, an eight of clubs to Buisson, jack of spades to Louis, and to himself a jack of diamonds with his pair of kings.

Buisson passed, on his ace and eight of clubs, high; Louis hesitated, then passed. For sure, he thought, I'll take Monique to Metaska Pond every chance I get this summer and get some sun into her so that she will be well rested for this new child, this new Martel, boy or girl, he or she would be welcomed. . . .

"I'll bet," said Nadeau tensely.

"I'll raise you," said Callaghan with a smile.

"I'll raise you both," said Louis.

"Lou," said Nadeau, "didn't you see my possible pair of kings?"

"I see nothing," said Louis.

They all came in. Nadeau dealt a ten of clubs to Callaghan, a nine of spades to Lafrance, a seven of diamonds to Brouillard, a four of spades to Buisson, a queen of spades to Louis, and handed himself a king of clubs with a grand gesture of slapping it down on the table. Buisson turned up his cards and gave up.

"My pair of kings bet," said Nadeau.

"I'll raise you," said Callaghan coldly.

"I raise you both," said Louis.

Maybe, he thought, Thérèse and Hélène could arrange to stay the whole week at the cottage and get themselves a real deep tan, and the kids too, and he would join them Saturday afternoons—and go to church in the country Sunday morning, and all week long they would be on a picnic. . . .

"Lou," snapped Nadeau, "I raised you too! What do you say?"

"*Bon!*" said Louis. "I shall raise you too!"

Everybody once more studied the cards that were visible.

"Why?" asked Nadeau, contraried. "On a possible black flush?"

"Because!" said Louis. "Because you're troubling that next card coming up."

"Praying for it?" asked Nadeau hotly.

"No, playing for it," said Louis.

"He's bluffing!" announced Nadeau to the others.

"Nobody bluffs," said Louis, "in a two-bit game."

They all came in. Of course, Louis mused, he would have to prepare the other children for this unexpected child—the one everyone knew could never be—that this child be made truly welcome, like a Christmas gift, hidden behind the tree. . . . There might be some feeling among the older ones, for their Papa at fifty-two to be starting another family in a second bed. And Monique . . . Dear Monique! She had never wanted merely to be a stepmother and she had never been. . . . But in her wildest moments, she'd never hoped she'd become the mother of her own flesh-and-blood child! Dear, sweet, patient, loving Monique! How tender he would be with her!

"Lou, crissakes, what do you say?" asked Nadeau. The fifth and last card lay on the table. Louis looked up and saw that Callaghan had a possible pair of aces, and he had dropped out. Lafrance had a small pair of threes showing and he was staying. Brouillard with a pair of sevens had dropped out because Nadeau now had two pairs showing, jacks and kings.

Louis looked at his fifth and last card. He never stirred. He must watch his lips lest they twitch too, like Nadeau's, and his eyes lest they begin to dart about all over the table like Lafrance's, and his hands lest they appear to be reaching to count the pot, as Brouillard's were. Now, very slowly, he peered at his hole card, as if seeing it for the first time, and allowed an expression of deep surprise to come over his face, then one of distress, and then, after looking again, he made his face into a mask of utter blankness. A deep silence had invaded the room.

"He's got nothing," sneered Nadeau.

"It's going to cost to find out," said Louis.

Nadeau exchanged a look with Lafrance.

"I'll pass," said Nadeau slyly.

"I'll pass too," said Lafrance.

Louis began to push money into the pot with both hands. "Never piss or pass in a draft," he remarked.

Lafrance turned to Nadeau.

"Is he bluffing?" he asked.

"If he's got what I think he's got," said Buisson happily, "I've never seen it before."

"He can't have it," stuttered Brouillard. "It's impossible."

"It would be embarrassing," said Buisson, "if he had it."

"And twice as embarrassing," said Louis, "if I didn't."

Nadeau's face twitched. Lafrance turned to him, smilingly.

"He's kidding me," Nadeau shouted finally, "but I've got to push him too. I'll raise you, Lou!"

"You will?" Louis asked. "In that case, I shall raise you too, and raise you, and again!"

He pushed money into the pot with both hands.

Nadeau stopped short. He hesitated.

Philippe Buisson cleared his throat.

"The boys," he said, "are about to be separated from the men."

"I think," whined Nadeau, "that you are bluffing!"

He turned to look at Louis, to try to penetrate into his mind, to read what that bottom card was. My face, thought Louis, is that of an honest man, and that's what you see, Nadeau, and my face is also that of a crook, and that's what you see, Nadeau, for my face, Nadeau, is both what you want to see and what you fear to see, because that's the face I'm giving you. . . . Nadeau shook his head impatiently. Suddenly he pushed money into the pot.

"I'll see you," he screamed, "and you'd better have it!"

"I promise nothing," said Louis blankly.

Now, Lafrance studied the situation, but he quickly came in with money, turned up his hole card, mildly proud of his three threes. No one else was. Nadeau uncovered his three kings and his pair of jacks. A full house!

"Well?" he asked, his mouth twitching, toward Louis.

"Messieurs," he said, his face breaking into a smile of wonderment, "I give you the ace, the king, the queen, the jack and the ten, five of 'em, and all as black as a haristocrat's ass!"

Then Louis raked in the pot, picked up the cards on the table, tore them all slowly into bits and flung them out grandly through the window into the rising morning sun.

"Messieurs," he said softly, "I bid you a good morning, and kindly stay away from swinging doors!"

The six-thirty Mass at Sacred Heart had just got under way when he entered. He passed by the poor box, slipped a clean dollar bill through the slit and hurried to a seat in the quiet church, already warming up from the morning sun. A few minutes later, he got up and went to the altar rail, received Communion and returned to his seat. He knelt, took out his Rosary beads and began to recite them slowly and with increasing efforts at concentration, but he kept losing count. With his closed eyes he could only see three flapjacks, golden with black burnt specks around the edges, swimming in maple syrup, a steaming cup of tea, and a royal straight flush in spades!

This was no way to pray, he reproached himself, and tried again to concentrate. He put his elbows on the back of the seat in front of him, and put his hands in his face to invite deep, deep concentration and he let his thoughts flow freely, between the earthly things and the things of the spirit, and he told himself that this afternoon he would see Monique, his wife with child, they would rejoice together in this child to be, and thank you, Lord, and he would see Thérèse, also with child, and that would be most pleasant, too, and, thank you, Lord. . . .

Thank you, Lord, for all you've given me, and mine, though, for certain I've never pestered you for such grand favors. . . . Thank you for the necessities, and for the surplus you've thrown in for good measure. . . . Thank you for Thérèse and that little miracle. . . . And thank you for Monique and our baby-to-be, though You know, dear God, that was no miracle at all, hardly. . . . In any case, a small one, at best. . . .

Thank you, dear Lord, for all the frosting on my cake, but now, dear God, when you made that last card a king of spades . . . when You dealt me that royal straight flush in spades, O Lord, that was the kicker, the sweet thrill that comes to few of us in one lifetime, the magic beyond man's contriving. . . . For that was a miracle, no doubt, and a real big one, O Lord, and for that I thank you most of all! Amen!

And now Father Lebois said, "*Ite, Missa est!*" and he blessed the assembly and the Mass was over and Louis made the Sign of the Cross, genuflected in the aisle, went over to Armand's Place, had his three flapjacks, swimming in maple syrup and his two cups of hot tea. Then he lit his pipe and walked up Pine Street toward home. It was a warm clear morning.

"This," he said to no one in particular, "is the day of my life!"

He walked on, and into Oak Street, and to his house, and up the stairs to his own empty apartment, undressed and went to bed immediately to sleep in his own bed the sleep of the just.

10. Jeune Fille [1937]

It was Friday night, and the house of Louis Martel was filling up fast with the immediate family for the *noce de famille*, the intimate celebration to send off his daughter, Cécile, age eighteen, from maidenhood into womanhood with proper and traditional cheer. It was June again in Groveton, Maine, and tomorrow, in the Church of the Sacred Heart, Cécile would be united in Holy Matrimony with Tom McLaughlin.

Father Lebois himself would officiate, her sister Marie would be her maid of honor, and Louis Martel would escort her to the altar, and the ceremony would take place at eight o'clock in the morning, the most desired time of all. A long time ago, when she was but twelve, Cécile had announced that she would be married exactly as it was all going to happen tomorrow.

Louis had laughed gaily then at his last-born from his first bed when she'd first expressed this fantasy, but now it was about to happen, in real life it was going to happen! He would give her away, as the expression went. But why must he give away this sweet possession, granted him long ago from passionate impulses, and give it away within the rituals of unconfined gladness? Because he must. It is so ordained.

He sat down for a moment in his crowding kitchen, then got up and walked around the apartment and chatted with everyone, and now he stopped again in the kitchen, face to face with the old chime clock that had rung every hour, on the hour, since the days he had bought it as a gift to his own bride, Cécile Bolduc, so many years ago. It was quarter to six. He hummed a little song to himself: "Acadee! Acadee-ee-ee!" and slowly filled his pipe. He had never returned to Acadee, after his own honeymoon, the land of hardship and of dreams that come through elsewhere. Would he go again before he died?

"Tomorrow," he announced to no one in particular, "I'll lose another one. It's in the nature of things!"

In the nature of things it is also that you are born from pain, you grow up through turmoil and you die too soon, but you marry always in a frenzied joy, as it should be, but Lord, why do we go through these acts over and over, except that we must! Since his days as a boy in Acadee, he had seen it again and again, the old story but always new in the flush of the moment, baptisms, marriages, and yes, funerals, and always in church! Once when he'd been a young man, it had been an adventure, just to be alive. . . . O Lord, where are the calendars of my youth? Why must time rob you of your children in the month of June? Hadn't it always been so? Yes, and it would always be so. . . .

For June—any June in a French-Canadian setting—is the time when in all churches, every morning between six and eleven, except Sundays, every half hour, a young girl, all in white, and her father, and her bridesmaids, walk down the aisle to meet her young man at the altar before their families, their friends—and the world. There, both kneel on a satin-covered prie-dieu, attend a nuptial mass, receive communion, listen to a sobering lecture on the responsibility of matrimony, exchange their vows, kiss modestly, and then dash gently, in sweet release, to the rear of the church to meet family and friends for photos, as well as to pass by another young girl, her father and bridesmaids, on their slow way to the same satin-covered prie-dieu.

Tomorrow, they would all arise at six, and those who would receive would forgo breakfast, and the others would take a *petit déjeuner*. Papa and Monique would eat, but Cécile and Marie would not. And then, bedlam would slowly develop into a frenzied, happy, disorganized circus during which everything would seem to go wrong and somehow turn out all right. The men would dress self-consciously in their rented summer formals, and the bridesmaids would arrive and Monique, Marie, Thérèse, Hélène, Muriel, and Noelle would converge on Cécile to dress her up in time for the photographer who would surely arrive at the same time as the florist, the limousines, and the last-minute delivery boys with gifts for the bride. . . .

Monday the Groveton *Daily Herald* would say that the bride wore "a gown of imported lace with a high neckline and full skirt of imported tulle with appliqués of lace extending into a chapel-length train." Since Marie herself had written the story for the *Herald*, there would also be a list of the names of all those who would be present, and the final observation that the happy couple would make their home in New York City.

Tomorrow, there would be the sudden panic, and the unexpected calm, and the rush to the church—and Cécile would take Papa's strong arm and he would smile at her—and then the slow cadenced walk up the aisle, and Father Lebois, waiting, waiting, who had known Cécile when she was so very small, so long ago, and yet only yesterday. And then breakfast at Marceau's Dance Palace, the toasts, the dance of the bride and groom, and her Papa's reserved dance with the bride, and the children running wild between the dancers, and mothers of children, flushed from an early drink, looking to their husbands, once again, with the glow both once knew on another June morning, only yesterday, and yet, so long ago.

And then there would be the long, long wait, as the bride and groom spent an appropriate amount of time with each of their guests, before their departure for the honeymoon, and yet, never in a hurry, never any sign of any desire to leave, lest too much haste be a discourtesy to all, in the ancient rules of politeness, and appear unseemly. Not until five in the afternoon would they be free, and then only upon the urgings of parents, and only after the bridegroom would have undone the mischief his best friends will have done to his car, or his baggage. . . . By five, Cécile and her new husband would be gone. . . . gone to New York. . . .

"Tomorrow at this time," Louis mumbled, "the last-born from my first bed will have flown the nest."

No one, not even Monique, who heard, made any comment. But Tante Pauline was listening and she heard. She was a sister of Louis, and had come for the wedding. Long ago, her husband had left her—disappeared completely from the scene—and she had had to go to work in a cotton mill. She had raised her one child, a daughter, with her own two strong hands. And now the daughter was married, and gone too. Pauline was tall, like Louis, gaunt and thin, lived in Woonsocket and seldom visited Groveton.

"You slave for them," she lamented, "and then they leave you!"

Few heard her. This was a houseful of children. Laurent and Hélène had brought Michel, Jean-Paul, Réné and Denise, nicknamed "Chou-Chou." Maurice and Muriel—both looking fatter—had arrived that afternoon by auto from Augusta. They had brought along Albert, Lucille, Lucien, Henri who was seven and spoke all the time, and Blanche who was four and shy and always smiling, and Roland, the baby. Also there were Thérèse and Antoine with Anne and Jacqueline, two happy little dolls. Félix and Noelle had brought their own three cowboys: Pierre, Jean and Robert. And, of course, there was little Louis, born to Monique two years ago. . . .

Right now, little Louis was in a bad mood. No one, in all this excitement, was aware of his existence—at the moment. He strode sullenly toward his Papa and tugged at his trousers. When that did not work, he began to whine loudly. He was a sturdy little boy, a little slim, with dark, darting eyes.

"Louis," said his Papa, "you behave now!"

Little Louis stuck out his tongue at the world.

"Play with me, Papa?"

Louis picked him up.

"If you're a good boy," he said, "tomorrow I'll take you for a walk in the country."

"A long, long walk, "Papa?"

"A long, long walk."

"For sure?"

"For sure!"

Now, of course, all the children wanted to be picked up by him, and he lifted each in turn, calling each of them by his right name, and he inspected them all for muscles, and teeth, and gait and temper and alertness, and they in turn inspected his pockets and found a large Ingersoll watch, a Rosary that needed fixing, a pocket knife, a pouch of strong-smelling tobacco, assorted sticks of chewing gum, and old theater stubs. . . . While this went on, he inspected their parents. . . .

Félix looked prosperous, and still in good shape. Maurice slept in a chair. Muriel, his fruitful wife, was pregnant again. Tall and gaunt, Laurent chatted with Félix's boys. Hélène and Noelle and Monique and Thérèse went about with the preparations of the family dinner.

Thérèse, now thirty, had filled out voluptuously since the

arrival of her two little girls. Antoine and Félix discussed with verve the high cost of living and the fortunes of the Red Sox. Busy at the stove, near Monique, was Marie, now twenty, a student-nurse, good-looking, single, unpromised and unconcerned. Now and then, she caught one of the running children in her outstretched arms, Anne or "Chou-Chou" or Jean or Pierre or little Louis, and hugged them madly in turn.

These days Monique often whispered to mothers of susceptible sons. "Such a sweet girl! Too sweet—just to be a nurse!"

Louis had announced once loudly that she was too fussy.

"Papa," she had replied, "there's a depression."

"Maybe," he'd answered, "but better for two to starve together than for anyone to starve alone."

Only one was absent. Emile was away, in the Grand Seminary, and, in time, would celebrate his first Mass for Maman, as he had promised long ago. No one thought he could come to the wedding, except Cécile, who had written him a long, entreating letter in which she had suggested nothing less than a special intervention of the Cardinal himself. . . . "Please, Emile, do this little thing for me!"

The loud banging on the kitchen door brought on a silence, and through the silence came a voice that sang out the rowdy chanson: "*Bonhomme, bonhomme, tu n'es pas maitre dans ta maison quand nous y sommes!*"

"*Mon Dieu!*" said Louis. "It cannot be!"

Monique covered her mouth to hide her emotion and ran to the door. Two strong arms reached to lift her up and swing her around, her petticoats flying to the breeze, exposing her knees to the delight of the children. It was Emile, in a dark suit and panama hat. He embraced her, let her go, and came bouncing into the kitchen.

"I hear," he shouted, "there's going to be a wedding!"

"Emile, my son," shouted Louis.

"And I've come to kiss the bride!"

He went directly to Louis, kissed him on both cheeks, and while he went around and shook hands and kissed everyone, Louis could only stare at the floor and bite on his unlit pipe. Now, Emile turned to his Papa.

"Is this not," he asked, "the house of Louis Martel, the man of four syllables?"

"It is!" said Louis.

"If it is," replied Emile, "how come there is no medicine handy for a weary voyager sick from the great thirst?"

As if his arrival had been a signal, Monique poured whisky shots in tall glasses, frosty with ice, and then she poured steaming black tea into the glasses and served the men and the ladies, and they stood and laughed together all at once. Now the children were served glasses of ginger ale and the glasses clinked and the ice tinkled and Louis gave the signal and then began to sing *Allouette*, and they joined in the chorus, and he sang it loud, and then he sang it low, and then he sang it fast, and he clapped his hands, and made faces for the children, and he sang it to the end, demanding always a stronger response, until the very finish.

Emile raised his glass—freshly refilled and still hissing from the clash of ice and hot tea—and looked at everyone in turn.

"To Papa," he toasted, "a good judge of liquor, a scholar in the true sense of the word, and a connoisseur of the opponent sex!"

"*Salut!*" came back the chorus.

"Here's to a long life," said Félix, his face already flushed, "and a merry one, a quick death and a happy one, a good girl and a pretty one, a cold drink and another one!"

"*Salut!*" came back the chorus.

"Here's to love!" sang out Marie suddenly, "that lies in a man's eyes, and lies, and lies, and lies!"

"Marie!" gently reprimanded several voices.

"Here's to a steak," said Louis, "when you're hungry, and whisky when you're dry, all the girls you ever want, and heaven when you die!"

"*Salut*, Papa!" came back the chorus.

"*Salut*, Papa!" shrieked little Louis, raising his glass of ginger ale.

"*Salut, Monsieur!*" replied Louis, and he touched his glass against the glass of little Louis, and watched him as he emptied it down to the last drop, gurgled, beamed and puffed under the exertion.

"*Salut*, Grandpère!" screamed Anne, Thérèse's first-born, and she raised her glass to Louis. Slowly he bent toward her, took her hand gently, and bending some more, he kissed it with great seriousness, and with great seriousness, she accepted this as a pledge of the great secret they held in common. Some day, Louis was sure, both would find out what the secret was. Perhaps something about a royal straight flush in spades!

Then Cécile came in quietly, almost unnoticed in the brouhaha, her face drawn, yet radiant, beads of perspiration on her forehead, her long eyelashes drooping over her eyes. She looked at everyone, and then saw Emile. She covered her mouth with her hand but the sudden tears could not be hidden.

"I knew you would come!" she announced. She looked at him shyly.

"And now," he said, "I want a wet kiss. I'm not a priest yet!"

She ran to him and kissed him, and then looked at everyone, not knowing what to do next. The she picked up little Louis, sat in the little rocker, and began to rock him. She also began to sob gently. Louis went up to her and knelt near her.

"Tired, *ma belle?*"

"Pooped!"

"Is everything in good shape? The dress, the church?"

"Everything's ready, Papa. All I have to do is to take a bath, fix my hair, eat supper, sleep, get married and collapse!"

"Yes, *chérie!*"

She hugged little Louis with one hand and put the other under her chin thoughtfully.

"Papa, why should I feel so happy, and so sad too?"

"That's the way it is ordained," he said, "but then, there's medicine for that!"

He rose to his feet and Monique handed him a silver cup, dented, teeth-marked, and he reached for the whisky bottle and filled it to the brim. Just about two good shots, he figured.

"Now, drink this," he said, handing her the silver cup.

"It's her baby cup!" protested Tante Pauline.

"In whisky?" screamed Cécile.

"Yes," said Louis. "In Acadee, this means that you are now about to become a full-grown woman—God help us all!—and if you drink it without choking, or turning blue, the next generation will be healthy and strong!"

"More ceremony!" she said, laughing. She took the cup in her hands. "There's so much ritual when you get married."

"It has its place," said Hélène. "You'll find out."

Cécile sniffed the drink.

"Indian remedy?" she asked with a twinkle for her Papa.

"Not yet," he said, chuckling.

"Ceremony! Ceremony!" she said gaily. "When does the mumbo-jumbo stop and the magic begin?"

"Drink it slowly," advised Monique, shaking her head at all this.

"It's a shame!" said Tante Pauline. "She's just a baby. Never got to know about men all her life, and now whisky!"

"Yes," mimicked Félix, "and now she'll have to sleep with a man the rest of her days! Shameful!"

"Is it so bad?" pouted Noelle, his chubby wife.

"I recommend it!" announced Monique.

Now Cécile looked at everyone, and then at her Papa.

"Papa, I want to drink it all at one gulp. Like you do. From now on I want to touch all the bases. Tomorrow I won't be a baby any more!"

Then she put the cup to her lips, tilted her head backward, and drank the cup dry. Her eyes watered, her cheeks grew red. She did not cough, nor did she turn blue.

"*Miséricorde!*" she gasped. "It is strong!"

"Cécile," announced Emile, "you drank that just like Papa."

Louis gave her his hand, and she got up and he spun her around, and Laurent produced his mouth organ and began to play a lively tune, and Louis, drink in hand, began to jig a fast jig right then and there, while the others clapped hands, and the children ran from all parts of the house to see him do his stuff, and then he grabbed Marie and both jigged in fast time, while the others clapped hands, and both of them increased their tempo until they achieved an almost incredible rhythm before they came to a dramatic finish. Now Félix jumped up and did a crazy Charleston dance that had the children holding to their sides.

Cécile sat again in the rocker, hugging "Chou-Chou," and laughed at these antics, and once wiped her eyes. Then she saw that everyone was looking at her.

"Yes," said Louis, for everyone to hear, "she's as pretty as my Cécile was, the day I married her, same gray eyes, same confidence, and the same curves, you know where!"

Hélène tapped him on the shoulder.

"It's seven-thirty, Grandpère, and the children are hungry."

"Yes, Louis," said Monique, and Thérèse and Muriel and Noelle and Marie began to set the table in earnest. There were two tables, one in the *parloir* for the children, and the other, the large one in the kitchen, for the adults. Louis saw that everyone was in his place, and when Réné and Jean-Paul stopped whispering out loud, he walked to the spot where he would be between both tables, and bowed his head. Everybody else did the same, and he began.

"O Lord," he prayed, "bless the food we have here tonight. Lobster, I do believe, and everything that goes with it. And bless all my children who have come together again under my roof. And tonight, bless in a special way, Cécile, the last-born of my first bed. . . ."

"Amen!" cried out one lone boy's voice.

"Well, now, dammit," said Louis softly, "I'm not finished. . . ."

Marie and Noelle quickly wiped out the laughter from their faces and became deadly devout again.

"And, dear Lord," continued Louis, "bless her husband-to-be, Tom Whatever-his-name-is. . . ."

"Tom McLaughlin," said Cécile, helpfully.

"Oh yes," continued Louis. "The Irishman! Well, bless him, anyway, if you can remember his name, and watch out for him, and protect him . . ."

"Amen!" whispered Cécile.

"And, Lord," continued Louis, "keep this Irishman in good health, in pocket money, and in fighting shape . . ."

Laurent suddenly guffawed, and Maurice also let go. The children at the other table began to giggle freely.

"Papa!" gasped Cécile.

"And bless our happiness, O Lord," continued Louis, "and, while you're at it, bless our laughter also, which is a touch of heaven to come where all men of good will of whatever nations will laugh at the same jokes. . . . And, finally, O Lord, may our children, Irish and Canadian, who are marrying tomorrow have children as beautiful as we did. Amen!"

There was a loud chorus of "Amens!" and a roar of laughter.

"Shameful!" said Tante Pauline.

"Nah," said Emile. "God enjoys a good laugh too."

Everyone began to talk at the same time and to reach for hunks of lobster. Suddenly, Cécile was heard to speak up.

"And besides, Tom is a good, devout Catholic too!"

"For sure," agreed Muriel, "and I'm sure he's as good a husband as any French-Canadian anyone could find."

"As I always say," said Louis, "I have nothing against the Irish. They fought the good fight against the Henglish haristocrats. . . ."

"And still do!" added Laurent.

"But then," continued Louis, passing crimson-red lobster parts around the table, "what's wrong with an honest Canadien?"

"Nothing!" exclaimed Cécile. "I just happen to love an Irishman!"

And it had happened almost overnight. Cécile had had a lot of boy friends before him, but he had red hair and light blue eyes. . . . Also he was that rare specimen of Irishman whose parents' death had orphaned him in infancy among French-Canadian protectors. . . . An Irishman who spoke the Maine patois. . . . In the care of the Sisters of Charity until ten, then of Dominican Brothers, who taught him music, he'd never spoken a word of English, except during English classes.

A talented cornettist, who sang *Mother Machree* with a rolling French accent, he had left Groveton two years ago to join a jazz band. A month ago, he'd come to Groveton for a visit, and to greet some of his Dominican teachers, and had met Cécile at a school dance, and both had fallen violently in love. He was twenty-four, and committed to a job in New York City. And tomorrow, so would Cécile be as Mrs. Tom McLaughlin.

"Take Laurent here," continued Louis with a straight face and warming up to his subject, and to the lobster, "he has four healthy children, and Hélène, I suspect, right now has another one in the oven. . . ."

"Grandpère!" said Hélène severely, "the children will hear!"

"And now, take Maurice!" he continued, extricating a hunk of meat from a lobster claw, "and his Muriel! What can an Irishman, however honest and willing, do against that? Muriel has six, and Thérèse with her own two beauties, and more to come. . . ."

"I hope," said Thérèse and Muriel together.

"And Félix, with his three future champions of the world! Now," concluded Louis, as he tied an apron up to his neck, "what can an Irishman do here that Canadiens have not done, and better?"

"Plenty!" announced Cécile.

"How do you know, Cécile?" asked Laurent, his mouth full of lobster.

"I know what I know," said Cécile, reaching for a claw.

"Poor little girl," said Tante Pauline.

There was silence while each digested this recurring theme.

Louis stopped eating a minute, then put both elbows on the table and stared at everyone.

"That lobster will vanish in no time," he said softly, "and he's not here yet. . . ."

"Who?" asked Cécile.

"Tom McGillicuddy," said Louis.

"Tom McLaughlin!" asked Marie, shocked.

"Tom! Here, tonight?" gasped Cécile.

"Why not?" asked Louis calmly of everyone. "He's friendly enough."

"Because!" said Noelle, in a manner that accepted no argument.

"The night before the wedding?" asked Muriel.

"It's just not tradition!" announced Thérèse.

"It's bad luck, Papa," complained Cécile, "for the bride to see her man the night before. . . ."

"Pass me some more lobster," said Louis.

"Of course," said Hélène gently, "we hardly know Tom, and you're going away, and all that."

"But it's not done!" said Muriel.

"And you know why?" asked Louis. "I'll tell you why. It's a superstition that supports this tradition, and do you know who invented it? What kind of men?"

"What kind of men?" asked Cécile suspiciously.

"Married men! That's what. I think Canadiens should get rid of a few of their superstitions. . . ."

"Shameful, just plain shameful!" commented Tante Pauline.

"I agree with you, Papa," said Marie. "We are a superstitious people in an era of scientific facts!" Then she took a deep breath.

Emile looked up suddenly, then went back to his lobster.

"Now," continued Louis, licking bits of lobster out of his front teeth, "the tradition of a bachelor party the night before is a superstition, born of the pretext boys need to get together before a wedding to raise a little hell. . . ."

"But, Pa, you did the same thing yourself," said Félix.

"Well, then," he snapped, "do as I teach, not as I practice, and you'll all be better off. These bachelor parties . . ." He made a face of boredom. "You drink and tell dirty stories, and some I like myself, and you're supposed to do more than that, at least, you're supposed to give that impression. . . ."

"Now, Louis," said Monique calmly.

"Papa," said Cécile with a frown.

"Well, now, your Irishman should be at one of these parties right now, and the girls are supposed to ignore what goes on at these parties. Let me tell you: nothing much happens. The boys brag, the girls wonder, and worry, and tell themselves that men must act like fools once in a while. Nothing really happens, Cécile, let me tell you!"

"Oh, no?" said Laurent.

"Oh, yes!" said Félix.

"And tonight," continued Louis, "Tom McLaughlin would rather be here—I know some stories myself—told him a few yesterday—and since he has no family to spend this evening with—him being an orphan and all that, and no friends in Groveton since he's been away for so long. . . ."

"We've invited him here," said Monique.

There was a shocked silence.

"You have?" gasped Cécile.

"We have," stated Louis positively, "and if he's going to be my Irish son-in-law, I won't get to know him well enough ever, especially since you are going to live in New York. . . ."

"Papa," announced Emile, "you are so right. I'll go get him!"

"No need," said Louis. "He promised he would come."

"He did?" said Cécile happily.

"He did, but he had to go to confession. As you all know, Irishmen are great sinners. But he'll be here, so save some of that delicious lobster for the boy. . . ."

When he came in—his red hair contrasting with all the black hair around him—Louis introduced him formally to those of the family who had not yet met him. Hélène had spoken to him a few times, and now she came toward him, quietly smiling, and kissed him tenderly on the mouth. Without introduction, Noelle took her cue from Hélène and kissed him on the cheek.

"Oh, that red hair!" sighed Monique.

Cécile tried to get to Tom and to rescue him, but Thérèse and Marie and Muriel were next, and then the boys shook hands with him and "Chou-Chou" and Blanche kissed him and then Monique hugged him.

"Glad you came?" she asked, and Tom nodded shyly.

Suddenly there were women all around him, Monique, Hélène, Thérèse, Noelle, Marie, Muriel. . . . Hélène was mussing his red hair and Monique and Noelle had their arms around his waist. . . .

"Ah, Tom?" shouted Louis, "isn't this better than a bachelor party?"

"Much better, Monsieur Martel," he said softly, perspiration showing on his forehead, "and the girls are prettier!"

"Oh, he'll make out," said Hélène, and she kissed him, and then all the girls in turn kissed him again.

"It's not fair!" screamed Cécile. "Everybody's kissing him, and I can't even see him!"

"Break it up!" shouted Louis, roaring his laughter at the girls' maneuver, and Cécile got to Tom. Then Louis sat him down at the table next to him, and to Cécile who took a firm grip on his hand under the tablecloth.

"Pass your plate, Tom," said Louis, "that is, with your free hand."

Tante Pauline smiled shyly at Tom, served herself another potato, squeezed it, buttered it generously.

"Poor little Cécile," she announced.

"Now, now, Tante Pauline," said Laurent.

"I know what I know," she continued. "Nowadays, with the morals so slackened all around us, and so many people marrying outside their religion, and the dresses the girls wear these days, and right at Mass. . . ."

"These kids are doing all right," remarked Félix easily. "Don't you really think so, Tante Pauline?"

"Of course," said Tante Pauline.

"Then," snapped Louis, "have some more lobster."

"Anyway," said Cécile, turning soberly toward Tom, "we won't be like that."

"Poor little girl!" repeated Tante Pauline. "They all say that, and then the man sees another chick in another back yard, and he forgets all the decencies, and he wants this new chick. I ask you, why?"

"Perhaps," snapped Louis, "because she's a quiet chick!"

"He forgets," continued Tante Pauline, "the sacred vows he took right there in church, before God, but what happens? In time he abandons even this new chick. . . ."

"Still looking," snapped Louis, "for a quiet chick!"

Tante Pauline pouted a moment, the stopped talking.

"All I know," said Cécile, "is that if Tom McLaughlin won't stay on his own, with this particular chick, because he wants to, because he really prefers to be with me, and takes off, one fine day, with another chick. . . ."

"Then what?" exclaimed Tante Pauline, her hands turned heavenward in supplication.

"Then, the hell with him!" announced Cécile, and then joined in the laughter.

"Cécile!" said Emile, laughing. "Your language! There are grownups around!"

"I mean it!" she continued. "Sure, marriage is a sacrament, a solemn contract for life, one of the most beautiful of the Church, and all that . . ."

Louis put knife and fork loudly on the table and looked up.

"Good! Now we're about to have a bit of Catechism?"

"But marriage," continued Cécile, buttering a large slice of homemade bread, "is also a two-way deal. I'm going to give Tom all I have—no secrets, no reservations, no grudges, no little-girl stuff, no nagging . . . and plenty of loving!"

"Hear, hear!" said Louis.

"And I'm going to love him for the rest of my life, like Maman did with Papa, even with all his contrariness and cussedness!"

"Don't hear!" said Louis.

"That's our plan," said Cécile, enjoying a big sigh and biting into her buttered bread. "I don't know of any other tricks and I don't intend to invent any other better ones!"

"Bravo!" said Emile.

Marie turned to Tom.

"Still time to take off!"

He smiled toward everyone.

"Guess I'll stay," he said against the general chatter. "I've wanted to get married all my life, and to have my own home. . . ."

"Quiet!" thundered Louis. "Listen to an Irishman when he makes sense. Go on, Tom."

Tom swallowed against the sudden attention to his words.

"And to have my own home," he continued, "is the most important thing in my life. To me, marriage is like an insurance. An insurance for one another, between two people, and for their children. . . . Could I have some of that homemade bread, please?"

Tante Pauline was the first to pass it to him.

"Yes," said Emile, "it's an insurance for two special persons against the loneliness of oneness. . . ."

"That's what I mean," said Tom, buttering his bread.

"Aha, a sound Irishman," said Louis. "But then, with Cécile, you may need a horsewhip. Every woman should be whipped once a week. . . ."

Tom looked up, suddenly shocked, toward Louis.

"You mean it?" he asked. "I thought you believed in a blackboard. . . ."

"And this one, this Cécile, she's a thoroughbred, lot of temper and verve, and I know about horses."

"She's a temperamental filly, sometimes," Laurent assured Tom.

"Ask me, Tom, I know," added Félix.

Suddenly, Cécile broke into sobs.

"Well! I'm a horse now!"

She rushed from the table and ran to her room. Hélène looked at everyone, shrugged her shoulders, and went in to talk to her.

"Anything I said?" asked Tom, staring at his buttered bread.

"No," said Louis gently, "it's nothing. Nothing to worry about. We tease because we love. We tease because we hate to see her go. . . ."

"But we'll be back, I promise," said Tom.

"You will, but then. . ." remarked Maurice kindly.

"It won't be the same as tonight," mused Marie. "It will not be the same again—ever." She whimpered—just a bit.

"It is her last night home," said Monique. She dabbed at her eyes. "I feel as if she were my own little girl!"

"Poor little Cécile!" sobbed Tante Pauline. "Just a baby and getting married already! And going to live in New York!"

Once more Louis dropped his knife and fork on the table.

"If they're big enough, they're old enough," he barked. "And Pauline, don't weep for Cécile. She has no need for your tears. She's going to be very happy. We have taught her how it looks to be happy. I say that because I mean it. Let no one weep for Cécile. Anyone weeping tonight, and tomorrow, weeps for himself!"

And then there was quiet—for a short spell.

"Too bad Maman won't be here," said Thérèse suddenly, in a whimpering voice. She turned to Monique. "You understand what I mean?"

"Sure, *chérie!*" said Monique.

Suddenly Monique, Hélène, Muriel, Noelle and Marie were sobbing gently.

"Women! Women!" snarled Lois, suddenly staring into space.

"Maman is in heaven," asserted Emile forcefully, "and she rejoices with us."

"Yes," said Louis. "There was a woman for you. She wept only for joy and for nothing else. Excuse it Monique, I do not exclude you from this, but, by God, where in hell is the dessert?"

At the other table the children took up the question, and in the same words, and Louis tried to shush them with a wink and by passing a finger over his lips, but soon the house rang out with their shouts and now he laughed with them, as Monique, Muriel, Noelle, Thérèse and Marie served ice cream and cake, milk and tea, so that soon peace and quiet would return, and now it was nearly nine o'clock.

"Tomorrow, at this time," mused Louis, "just about at this time . . ."

And supper was over, and Louis, Laurent and Maurice lit their pipes, and Antoine lit a cigarette, and Emile lit a cigar. Félix did not smoke. The girls did the dishes, but Cécile sat in the bedroom, near the door, and waved at Tom: tonight, she would not do the dishes. Tonight she was formally excused, but tonight only, for this was her last night as *jeune fille*, and tomorrow she would be a woman, and would do dishes the rest of her life. . . .

Louis smoked and stared into space.

"To leave home," he observed, "is to die a little. . . ."

"Yes, Papa," agreed Emile, "and one never quite recovers from it. . . ."

Emile puffed on his cigar and his eyes wandered lazily toward the crucifix on the wall, on Maman's chime clock, on the blackboard that had contained all the names of the Martel family, and now that of the latest, Louis Joseph Michel Martel, age two-plus. He too would soon win his share of good and bad marks, and the bag of candy, and all that this meant, and the little things that were the good life, where laughter more often than tears would abide, if Papa could make it so. . . .

At nine-thirty the family council met. This was one night when the children could stay up until they no longer could hold themselves up and speak coherently. But most of them were already falling off, one by one, to an unwilling sleep in the arms of adults. Just as the meeting was about to begin, Cécile came into the kitchen, dry-eyed and sober.

"Forgive me," she announced. "I don't know why I acted so foolishly. After all, I guess I'm still a baby!"

No one paid too much attention to her.

Louis called the meeting to order by getting up from his chair, turning it around and resting his hands on the back of it. He smiled briskly toward everyone.

"I think," he started slowly, "we're agreed to do the usual thing for Cécile and Tom, provided you are all of my opinion."

Tom looked suddenly at Cécile. She put her fingers to her lips and smiled quietly at him.

"We wanted," said Hélène, "to buy all her linen and towels and a bedspread and some dishes, but we don't know where you're going to live, Cécile."

"We'll find an apartment in New York soon," said Tom.

"I was all set," said Maurice, "to get the kids a bedroom suite, but Muriel thought we should wait until you're set, if you agree to that?"

"Yes, Maurice," said Cécile, "let's wait."

"Until you get your apartment," added Muriel.

"We'll know soon," said Cécile happily.

"Very soon," added Tom.

"That's what I thought," said Louis. "We'll wait until you children are all set up, and so maybe we ought to make up a family dowry. . . ."

"That awful word," shuddered Marie. "As if women were bought and traded in an open slave market!"

"I don't care what you call it," said Louis. "Let's call it a family fund, if you're ticklish about it. And we'll all chip in. Anybody got a better idea?"

"Seems the best thing to do," said Emile.

"I vote that way too," said Maurice.

"And let Maman-Monique be in charge," suggested Thérèse.

"*Bon*," said Louis. "That sure was a short meeting."

Tom McLaughlin cleared his throat.

"Monsieur Martel," he said, "if I'm going to be in this family, I'd like to say that I've got two thousand dollars saved. . . ."

"And I've got eight hundred dollars," sang out Cécile.

Félix's jaw dropped.

"No wonder you never bought any candy at the corner store!"

"Saved it," sang out Cécile. "And you should do the same!"

"I don't give a damn," said Louis, "if you have a million. This money from us is not because you're poor or rich. This *is* tradition! And this one is good. Young people who get married need help, and I mean money, or land, or something! Soon they have children, if they work at it, and sometimes too soon for the cash on hand. Now, if we tell our young folks to behave . . . or get married . . ."

"Right," intoned Félix, and he punched his left hand into his right.

"That's right," added Emile, and everybody agreed.

Louis suddenly chuckled. He studied the married couples before him.

"Just a minute!" he interrupted himself. "Now don't any of you old married folks get too cocky! Remember that it's only by the grace of God that some of you managed to get under the wire!"

"Papa!" a few voices protested.

"Do you know what the bride is so smug about on her wedding day?" he asked suddenly.

"What?" asked Tante Pauline.

"She tells the world with her smile of victory: '*Bonguienne*, I made it!' So, let us be humble. . . . And so, if we tell the young folks to behave, or get married, it's only fair and square to give them as comfortable a start as we can. Cécile and Tom, the future belongs to you, but both of you belong to us! When you start a family, your own family has a stake in you. . . . You are our ambassadors in the years to come, after some of us have cashed in our chips. . . ."

"I thank you, Monsieur Martel. I understand," said Tom.

And so the family fund was pledged. Louis peeled off five crisp twenty dollar bills and put them into the pot. And while the money was being collected and put into the pot, Tom began to flush a deep red.

"Cécile," he whispered, "I can't help it, this is embarrassing!"

She squeezed his hand, but her eyes turned into steel.

"Cash," she said, "is always practical."

"Oh, yes," he agreed, "however. . ."

"And besides, some day someone else will be married, perhaps one of our own children, and it will be our turn to make up a family fund. . . ."

Tom gasped quietly, as if struck by a sudden thought.

"Children?"

"Sure, *chéri!* As Papa says, this is a happy, serious game, and it'll soon be time for us to play. Kiss me, *chéri!*"

"Before everybody?"

"Where else?"

"Before your father, right here?"

"Sure. Papa says that public kissing is better than war."

He kissed her, and everybody roared, even Tante Pauline.

Then Laurent reached for his harmonica and began to play *Vive la Canadienne!* And everybody raucously joined in the old song.

And then it was ten-thirty. And mothers began to prepare the children to leave, as well as their husbands. Everybody took a hand in carrying most of the children to the various cars, and now this left only Emile and Tom engaged in a private conversation in a corner, and Marie, Cécile and Louis. Monique was putting little Louis to bed. Suddenly, Emile looked at the clock.

"It's near eleven!" he announced.

"Yes," said Louis, "it won't be long now."

"I meant only," said Emile, "to warn those who are to receive Communion tomorrow morning not to break their fast after twelve o'clock."

"That's right, Emile!" Cécile gasped.

Tom rose.

"And maybe I should go to bed. Tomorrow I'll need all my wits about me."

He said *bonsoir* to all and went to the door of the kitchen and walked out, leaving the door open for Cécile to follow, as he and her other suitors had done before him. Tonight was the last time. She smiled gravely at everyone and followed him out.

"He's a nice fellow," said Emile, staring at the floor.

"Certainly is," agreed Marie.

"And I wish," said Louis, turning to Marie and winking at her, "that some time you'd take a trip out there yourself!"

"Oh, Papa," said Marie, ruffled, "I'll get married some day, but not just to get married."

"Fussy, Marie?" Emile asked.

"No," said she, plainly put out now, "I'm not. And then maybe I am! Most French-Canadian boys I know work in factories that open and close and throw their people out of work regularly like the tide at Old Orchard Beach. As a nurse I'll soon make more steady money than the majority of boys I know. It's unfair to say this, but it is the reality."

"It's better," remarked Louis casually, "to be poor together than to be rich alone."

"Another thing," continued Marie. "Some of these boys could do better if they left Groveton like Tom and took a chance somewhere else. But no! They are too timid to leave home, to explore the world, to snip off the home ties. . . . They're all nice boys—I could fall in love with any one of them—if I let myself go. But I don't want to. Period."

"Why?" asked Emile quickly.

"Because. There's a depression, Emile. You may not know it from living in your Grand Seminary. But when you become a priest, don't you forget it. A depression is a grave social sin, Emile, a mortal sin!"

"It is," said Louis slowly. "It is that."

Emile laughed.

"It's a new theology," he remarked casually. "Never heard of it."

". . . And when a girl marries," continued Marie, "a French-Canadian girl, anyway, she has children, Emile, one every two or three years, and that, my dear Emile, takes money. . . ."

Emile frowned and sat up in his chair.

"Come, come, Marie!" he snapped. "One can always practice rhythm! The Church approves!"

Now, Louis broke out into gentle laughter.

"You mean it?" he asked Emile.

"I do, most seriously."

"Well, let me tell you," said Louis, "about this rhythm. I know a carpenter—known him for years. He never could, and to this day cannot hold on to money. Good church man too.

And he's been practicing this rhythm for years. You see, Emile, this was his only chance to break even. . . ."

"Of course," agreed Emile earnestly.

"And, do you know what? He's got six running all over him, two crawling on the floor and one in the oven right now. Rhythm? He's got rhythm all over the place!"

Emile sat up suddenly, his mouth open.

"Another thing," continued Marie, "I work in a hospital. I know! It takes money, Emile, to have children. It takes money, Emile, not to come to have hatred in your heart for the children you can't take care of—or the City has to—while you're miserable over the child you may conceive at any time your husband gets a mind to. . ."

"Marie," Louis cut in firmly, "don't draw us any pictures."

"Forgive me, Papa," she said, "but I mean every word."

"I believe you," said he, gently now, "but the way you speak worries me a little bit."

"Well, don't taunt me, Papa, about getting married!"

He gave everyone an expression of hurt surprise.

"You did, Papa," said Emile. "We all did."

"Forgive me, then," said Louis, slowly. "Frankly, I don't want any one of you to leave this house, for as you leave, it gets roomier and emptier all the time . . ."

Marie got up and paraded around, dancing gingerly up and down in the kitchen.

"I shall remain," she announced lightly, "a spinster, a nurse devoted to the sick, I shall become famous, I shall be rich, and I shall be, all my life, a virgin. . . ."

"You will like hell!" thundered Louis, amidst laughter.

Monique returned from putting little Louis to bed. She yawned.

"Some day soon," she announced gaily, "we'll be celebrating Marie's wedding also. Meantime, it's getting late, and

Emile, you should go to bed, after all that traveling, and Marie, you look tired too. . . . Cécile? Well, I suppose you can stay up a little while longer, but you really shouldn't. . . ."

"Yes, Maman-Monique, because I am pooped. . . ."

And then there was only Louis, Marie, Cécile and Monique in the kitchen. It was nearly half-past eleven. Monique sighed.

"Louis," she said, "forgive me, but I too must get to bed."

She kissed him *bonsoir*, and turned toward Marie and Cécile.

"*Bonsoir*, Maman-Monique!" said Marie.

"*Bonsoir*, Maman-Monique!" said Cécile. She hugged her. "My Maman, number two!"

"Sleep well," said Monique, hugging her in turn, and then very seriously: "And don't forget what I told you!"

Cécile swallowed, and then nodded quickly with playful eyes.

Then the two girls decided to take their baths and they retired to their bedroom to undress, and Louis Martel was alone in the kitchen. It was very quiet and this was good. Tomorrow the house would throb and all he had to do now to prepare himself was to put a first-class shine on his shoes—his dancing shoes—and a brave face before the world, for to give his Cécile away. . . . So it was ordained that with one more going, he would soon be merely a Grandpère, fit only to spoil grandchildren. Well, by God, he swore, he would never, never, take up basket-weaving!

Then he heard the giggling and the splashing in the bathroom, as Marie and Cécile ran water into the tub, opened and closed faucets, opened and closed bottles, and splashed, and chattered very low, every now and then so low he couldn't hear, except an occasional eruption of nervous tittering. . . . It was the last time these two monopolized the place. . . . It had been a damn nuisance, so many women and only one bathroom, a damn, sweet nuisance. . . . Well, since it was only twenty to twelve, he decided to make himself a double shot of whisky in iced tea and to drink it quietly.

Could I have given them a better chance had I learned to read and write? Maybe I could have made things easier for them? Maybe, but then, Messieurs, by what golden footrule does a man measure his success or his failure?

"Louis?"

It was Monique, and the sound of her voice startled him. She wore a long nightgown and soft slippers.

"Yes, *chérie* . . . ?"

She sat in his lap and took a sip of his drink.

"Louis," she said, "you can be proud of your family."

He thought this over a moment.

"They are not repulsive, no."

"But, little Louis!" she exclaimed. "He will go to college, *non*?"

"Maybe . . ."

"Oh, but I want that as a promise!"

"Who knows? Maybe he is a lawyer-to-be, or a politician?" He paused. "Is that what the tea leaves say?"

"Or a doctor-discoverer! Maybe, like Pasteur, he will make great discoveries. . . . Maybe he will assault and beat cancer? Who knows?"

"Who knows?" asked Louis, "but in the meantime, let's keep him by our side. I'm partial to him."

"Yes, we had him late. Let's keep him long."

She kissed him and slowly went to bed.

He lit his pipe, checked the clock—it was ten to twelve—and finished his drink. Suddenly! He heard it, for the first time in years, he heard the tick-tock of the chime clock. For years he hadn't heard it, though he knew it tick-tocked away all the time, but now he heard it again with his ears. Tonight he could hear Time moving. . . .

Cécile is going, Time tick-tocked away, and of the first bed only Marie is left, and of the second, little Louis. . . . and the Time tick-tocked away. . . . Marry and multiply. . . . Tick-tock. . . . Work hard, drink hard, play hard, love hard, pray to the God you know is in Heaven, laugh once a day to stimulate your arteries, marry and multiply. . . . Tick-tock. . . . That's the real tempo, the true rhythm. . . . Tick-tock. . . . Time is what you spend, what you dispense so freely and then all you have left is Eternity. . . . Somebody is born, somebody dies, somebody marries. . . . That's immortality. . . . So it was everywhere, as it had been in Acadee, for Time, everywhere, had a way of committing Man, with Man's tacit acceptance, to a course beyond his will. . . .

Again he heard whispers in the bathroom. Cécile and Marie. He heard them move quickly to their bedroom. In the darkness he heard them whispering—they would not put on the lights for fear of awakening someone—and he wished he could hear what they said. He stiffened his head, and cocked it slowly to one side. Shamelessly he had always listened, like this, provided they did not know. . . .

Besides, Cécile was going tomorrow. . . . And it was almost twelve. . . . Soon now she would be a married woman, no longer the little girl who had raided, first the icebox, and later the refrigerator with him in search of an onion sandwich, a glass of milk, some cold clams. Now, thought Louis, who was the old man in the Ancient Books who had stopped the sun in its course? Joshua! It was a good trick if you could do it! For now, soon, the clock would strike twelve. . . .

"I'm starved," whispered Cécile, "just starved. Didn't eat right, all day!"

He heard this clearly and he got up and stood near the clock.

"I could eat a horse," whispered Marie, "with or without mustard. I'm literally agonizing from starvation!"

Louis opened the glass door to the chime clock.

"Oh, for an onion sandwich," sighed Cécile, "with cheese on a toasted bun!"

Louis inserted his big index finger near the clock mechanism and muffled the sound as it prepared to strike twelve. That night, for the first time, it was silenced. . . .

"Papa is in the kitchen," whispered Marie, "he'd see us!"

"We can't eat anyway," said Cécile. "It must be way after twelve!"

"I don't have my watch, but I know I'm starved!"

"Me too!"

Suddenly both appeared in the kitchen. Louis had a fresh drink before him and a blank expression on his face. The girls wore silk robes that extended down to their ankles and showed the lace of their nightgowns underneath and their bare feet. Their shiny black hair was grotesquely pinned up over their heads and their creamy complexion looked all the more glamorous for the lack of any rouge or lipstick, and he got a scent of warm, freshly bathed bodies that only babies have. Cécile came to him and sat on his lap and cuddled up to him. He put his arms around her.

"Want me to rub my whiskers on your cheeks? Give you real color for tomorrow?" he suggested.

"No, Papa. I just want to sit here a bit."

He pretended to rock her to sleep.

"My little girl! Huh?"

"Always, Papa. Always!" Then she gasped. "Marie! It's only a quarter to twelve!"

"*Tonnerre!*" she exclaimed. "Still time for an onion sandwich!"

"Papa," asked Cécile, jumping from his lap, "do you want anything?"

"Cheese on rye, with mustard, please," he said.

They made the sandwiches quickly, poured themselves each a glass of milk, and soon all were munching and staring in silence at the clock, and then once again, it was nearly twelve.

"*Bon*," said Louis. "Time for bed. Giddyup!" He stood up.

The girls finished their milk, and he put out his pipe. Cécile wiped her mouth, walked up to her Papa and stood, barefoot, near him, looking up and directly into his eyes.

"For everything, Papa, *merci!*"

"For nothing," he replied lightly.

"For everything!" she insisted, her head now on his chest. "For what I know you did for me, and for what I don't know!"

He kissed her on the forehead.

"For nothing at all, my little girl, for nothing at all."

"*Bonsoir*, Papa!" sang out Marie. She kissed her Papa on both cheeks.

"*Bonsoir*, Papa," whispered Cécile. She kissed him on both cheeks and for a long moment hugged him.

And they were gone. He sat down again and turned toward the crucifix on the kitchen wall.

Dear Lord, that little snack with my girls took about twenty minutes. . . . Sure, the Church specifies twelve o'clock, and no later, to eat and drink before Communion, but you and I understand. . . . And these rules change, like everything else, and I wasn't quite ready to give her up just yet, and I'm going to give her up only once, and now I'm ready to do it. . . . Lord, what's twenty minutes to you, when you possess Eternity? Remember too that in fifty years or so I've never missed Mass and in that time, in your Name, I've suffered many a boring sermon. . . . Against that, Lord, what's an onion sandwich after twelve?

"Papa!"

It was a small squeaky voice. It came from little Louis's room and it came again.

"Papa!" Paypee!"

"I'm coming," said Monique sleepily from her bedroom.

"I'll take it," said Louis.

He walked softly but swiftly to the small bedroom, reached for Louis in his bed—he was half awake, half asleep—and picked him up in his arms, carried him to the bathroom, stood him up on his own two feet, lowered his pajama pants and steered him to the toilet.

"Go, Louis, go!"

Louis did, his two strong little feet firmly planted on the bathroom floor, his firm shoulders arched for the test, and his eyes tightly closed. Suddenly he turned toward his Papa. Louis sidestepped just in the nick of time, like a batter before a low pitched ball.

"Papa, what do we do tomorrow?"

"Cécile's getting married."

"And after?"

"We'll have lots of company."

"And after?"

"We'll all be tired."

"You promised!" he shouted. "For sure!"

"A short walk," bargained Louis, putting a finger to his lips.

"A long, long walk!" insisted little Louis, as he pulled up his pants and pointed a finger at his Papa. "For sure!"

Louis picked him up and hugged him.

"Yes, Louis, for sure! I'll go for a walk with you, a long, long promenade, over the pink mountains of China and the blue rivers of the World, and we'll look for and find pearls and diamonds of many kinds and many colors for to wear at Sunday Mass and we'll skip along and hear the rat-tat-tat of the woodpecker and the joyful warbling of the purple finch, and as we walk, we shall sing, and sing, until we return once again to the land of youth, to Acadee. . . ."

"Is that far away, Papa?"

"Far, far away is Acadee, a land of plenty and of more-to-come, it is a long, long promenade to Acadee and the land of young men's dreams, where all prayers are answered in full in time, and there you meet again those you loved, and lost once, and there find again for good—if only you can wait. . . ."

"Ice cream cones too?"

"For sure! Together we'll see many things."

"Everything, Papa! Everything!"

He began to rock him in his arms.

"Yes, Louis, and no man should settle for less! You and I, my son, and every day of our lives like a double shot of whisky that leaves you gasping, gasping for more. . . ."

"More, Papa!"

He put his finger on both his eyes and closed them slowly.

"*Bonsoir*, little Louis," he murmured, "sleep well tonight, *bonguienne*, for tomorrow, and all the days after that are going to be whippersnappers!"

"For sure, Papa?"

"For damn sure, Louis, for damn sure!"

The old chime clock struck one—the first of the new day.

Gérard Robichaud, June 1953

In 1961 the author told the *Library Journal*: "I wanted to tell the story of a healthy, and lively family. In accents that I tried to make tender and light-hearted, I wished to speak of births, deaths and marriages, of love and customs that last, of a faith that endures, of superstitions that still cling, and also with humor to treat of ecclesiastical rigidity and institutional pompousness, the slow tempo of adolescent growth, the demands of the flesh, and the wisdom and follies of French-Canadian folkways."

–quoted in *The Mirror of Maine,* University of Maine Press and
The Baxter Society, Orono and Portland, Maine, 2000

ALSO BY GÉRARD ROBICHAUD

The Apple of His Eye (1965)

Pearl of Great Price (in progress)